CATALINA'S CARESS

SYLVIE F. SOMMERFIELD

ZEBRA BOOKS
KENSINGTON PUBLISHING CORP.

ZEBRA BOOKS

are published by

Kensington Publishing Corp.
475 Park Avenue South
New York, NY 10016

First printing: November, 1987

Printed in the United States of America

TOO WICKED TO RESIST

"Stop staring and let me go!" Catalina tried to sound authoritative. "Or is force not beyond you either?"

Marc's eyes sparked with anger, but his lips curved in a half-smile. He deliberately tightened his arms about her and his voice was suggestively smooth.

"Are you so sure it would be force . . . that you would not be more than willing?"

His loins pressed intimately against her, and despite her renewed rage she was aware of the hard masculinity of him.

She stiffened at the subtle humor in his voice.

"Tell me," he said with casual softness, "shall we put it to the test . . . or are you really afraid?"

The barb stung, for at this moment she was touched for the first time with a premonitional fear of something unknown.

And right she was to be afraid, for before she could find the breath to protest, his parted lips found hers in a kiss that stirred something volatile in them both, a kiss that flooded her senses until a raging desire consumed the last of her will and made her lose the reins of her self-control. . . .

Acknowledgment

I would like to take this opportunity to thank my dear friend and fellow writer Bobbi Smith. The fine research books in her personal library helped to make this book possible.

Prologue

1867

It was a breathlessly warm night, the kind of night the inhabitants of New Orleans knew well, one which even the breeze from the gulf did nothing to cool. The moon was high and lent a gray-white glow to the mist that made the waterfront buildings seem like apparitions rising from a vaporous emptiness.

The taverns that lined the docks were alive with music and raucous laughter, but very few hardy souls were on the streets. Those who were abroad often had motives that were less than honorable.

A carriage moved slowly through the narrow streets. Within sat a couple that would have raised the eyebrows of much of New Orleans society. The man was extremely large and solid looking. Even in the shadowed interior of the carriage he exuded strength. The woman, barely a foot shorter than his six foot one, carried only about half of her companion's nearly two-hundred-pound weight, yet she, too, seemed to be coolly controlled.

She had a small, somewhat wide, yet beautiful face with small features that made her dark almond-shaped eyes seem large and wondrous. She was slight and small boned, and her hair, long and perfectly straight, shone like ebony satin.

"So, Marc," she said softly, in a voice strangely inflected with an accent that bespoke her Oriental origins, "you have succeeded in the first part of your plan? What you did tonight was brutal. Have you no pity on the boy? What do you think this will do to the rest of his family?"

"Not enough, China." He spoke in a soft drawl, but she heard the steel blade in each word. "They could not suffer enough to make me change one step of my plan. What he got he deserved. Teach him not to be so damned arrogant and conceited. He was trying to cheat you, you know."

"Yes, I know . . . but he did not succeed. You took what you wanted. Can't it be enough for you?"

"You know the answer to that."

"Revenge is destructive," she said softly.

"Destruction is my intention."

"That is not what I meant."

"Don't play the Oriental mystic." His voice grew cold. "My plans were made long ago, and I don't intend to stop them. If you don't approve, you can always leave."

She seemed unperturbed by his words or by the harshness of his voice. China knew Marc Copeland much too well ever to be affected by his anger. With her, it was always short-lived.

She smiled, and in a moment his smile answered hers.

"Sorry," he said softly.

"I would not leave you, Marc."

"Whether I'm right or wrong?" He chuckled.

"I do not decide if you are right or wrong. You do what is in your heart."

He leaned forward and reached across the space between them, touching her cheek with the palm of his hand. "And you are so sure that I will not complete what is in my heart?"

"It could be that you will . . . but it could be that what is in your heart will one day change."

"I doubt that. You know why I do this. Don't you think I have a right to my anger?"

"Yes. You have a right to anger."

He laughed again and took her hand to draw her across the space separating them and onto the seat beside him. As she rested her head against the breadth of his chest, he curved his arm around her shoulder to hold her close.

"Ah, China, I am grateful for you. You're my looking glass in which I can study my conscience and all my dark thoughts, but you stay with me even when you think what I do is wrong. I have no other that would do the same."

They sat in companionable silence until the carriage stopped, then both disembarked to stand together on the dock and look at the boat securely tied up there.

"It is magnificent," China breathed.

"It most certainly is, but it's more beautiful inside than it is outside . . . and it belongs to me. It cost Joseph Carrington over two hundred thousand dollars . . . and it's mine. I'll bet by this time next week, when his son gets home, the old man will be livid."

"He is a powerful man. Sometimes, my dear Marc, I am afraid for you."

"Well don't be, China my girl." Marc laughed. "When this is over, I won't own just this boat—I'll own the whole damn Carrington line. I intend," he said softly, "to give the Carringtons a taste of their own medicine. Let's see how they handle it."

"Marc—"

"No more lectures, China. Come on board. It's time you saw where you're going to be operating. By the way, have you sent for all the girls you'll need?"

"I've sent for three. Paulette, Charlene, and of course—"

"Shawna," he finished.

"Yes. I also know of the other one that has been invited to share your stateroom."

"Nina?" Marc chuckled. "Now, China, how could I go cruising up and down this lonely old river without Nina to make the nights memorable."

"You have no . . . permanent ideas about Nina, do you?"

"Permanent." He scowled. "There's nothing permanent in my life except our friendship. The last thing in the world I need is a wife to spoil what the Carringtons left."

"One day you may be surprised. You may find a woman who does not give you what you want so easily . . . one who wants something as badly as you do and who is just as strong as you are."

"Look, China," he said softly but firmly, "there's no woman I want to marry. There's no woman I'd trust enough. We're friends . . . let's keep it that way."

They walked up the gangplank to the deck of the *Southern Belle,* one of them assured and making plans, the other frightened for the first time in years—not for herself, but for the tall handsome man who walked beside her.

Chapter 1

Catalina Carrington lay very still on her bed in the wee hours of the morning. She listened intently for the noise that had wakened her. She wasn't frightened, but not many things frightened Catalina, whose closest friends and family called her Cat because of her reckless nature and fun-loving, adventurous spirit that often brought her to the brink of disaster. At least often enough to irritate her father, who prayed a man who could handle her spirit would come along, and to upset her mother, who was just as certain there wasn't a man alive that could cope with Catalina.

The noise came again, and this time Catalina leapt quickly from her bed and ran to the large French doors that led to the balcony outside her bedroom. She had already identified the sound. Pebbles from the drive were being tossed gently against her window. It was an old signal first used by her and her brother Seth when they were still children.

Without putting on robe or slippers she threw open the French doors and stepped onto the balcony.

"Seth," she hissed. "What in heavens name are you doing? You're supposed to be going upriver on the *Southern Belle.*"

"Cat"—His voice came from below, and he sounded desperate—"I have to talk to you."

"Well, come into the house."

"No," he said sharply. "No, I can't talk to Father . . . not tonight . . . maybe not ever again. He'll never forgive me this time."

"Oh, Seth, not again," Catalina whispered to herself. "Come up the back stairs, I'll unlock the door."

"All right . . . hurry."

She did. Dashing across her room to stick her head into the hallway and look in both directions, she then hurried down the silent corridor to the back stairs, ran down the steps to the door, and slid the bolt open.

When she stood face to face with her brother, Catalina found it difficult to believe what she was seeing.

His clothes were rumpled, as if he had slept in them more than one night. This was unusual for the rather immaculate Seth.

His face was sweaty and flushed, his eyes puffy and red rimmed due to sleepless nights and to the misery that had kept him awake.

She put her arms about him, heard his muffled sob, and felt the trembling of his body as he hugged her.

"Come to my room, Seth . . . we can talk."

He followed her silently until she closed her bedroom door behind her and lit her lamp. Then she turned to him again.

Seth looked gaunt, his hands were making quick nervous movements. His skin was pale, his light brown hair disheveled. His blue eyes looked . . . almost frightened. He was tall, his height nearing six feet; although at this moment his shoulders were slumped.

"Seth, what is it? What's wrong? Why are you here and not upriver? Father will be furious."

"Father will be more than furious. I can't go upriver, Cat . . . I . . . I don't have the boat."

"What happened to it? Has there been an accident?

14

Are you all right?"

"Oh, Cat." Seth groaned. He dropped onto her bed, buried his face in his hands, and began to weep.

Catalina knelt before him. "Seth . . . Seth please don't. Talk to me. Tell me what's wrong. Maybe I can help."

Seth sighed raggedly and withdrew his hands. They were still shaking when he brushed the tears from his face.

"I've done a lot of stupid things, Cat. I've disappointed Father in a lot of ways. Last week was the first time I realized how much of a disappointment I've been to him . . . God, I can't stand what I've done. He trusted me . . . he trusted me."

"If you don't tell me what has happened I shall scream," Catalina said angrily. "How can I do anything to help you if I don't know what trouble you're in? Seth, dear God, don't tell me you've been gambling again? After that last terrible affair that nearly cost your life, how could you think of it?"

"Cat, Father gave me this chance—this last chance—to prove what I could do."

"I remember the argument quite well," she said grimly.

"He gave me the title of the *Southern Belle,* and told me, if in two years I could make enough profit to buy another boat, he would forget the past and let me be a full partner in the line with him."

"Seth for goodness sake I know all this."

"Cat"—he groaned hoarsely—"I've lost the title to the boat in a week-long gambling game."

Her face grew pale and for long moments brother and sister just looked at each other.

"You cannot condemn me more than I've condemned myself," Seth said miserably. "I was drinking and—"

15

"You are always drinking!" Catalina cried angrily. "How could you do such a thing?"

"Cat, don't—"

"Don't what? Be angry with you? I'm furious! I'm furious because I know you are not the foolish little boy you seem to be trying to convince your family and the world that you are. Why, Seth? Just tell me why?"

Seth couldn't, not because he didn't know the reason but because he loved Catalina more than any other person in the world. He would not lash out at her, revealing the frustration, the jealousy, and the deathly insecurity he always felt. Cat had always been his salvation in every situation, and he could not break the links of love that bound them together.

"I don't know why," he said sullenly, feeling intimidated by his sister as he had when he was two and she was six.

"You've got to know why! What are you going to say to Father? How could you possibly explain this?"

"I don't know that either. I only know I have to tell him and . . . I'm afraid of the consequences."

"Do we have any time at all, Seth? Maybe we could pay off whatever debts you owe and get the title back before Father knows. You could tell him after."

"Pay the debts with what?" he scoffed, miserable.

"I have some jewelry we could sell. The pearls Father gave me for my last birthday should bring a great deal of money."

Seth looked at her, an unfathomable expression on his face. He loved Catalina, but at that moment he hated her as well. Cat . . . always the stronger of the two. Cat . . . always quick and assured. And she was beautiful. Her thick, sable brown hair hung in a heavy braid down her back to her hips, and wisps of it framed her oval face which was dominated by large golden eyes that were as mercurial as her temperament. He could

16

have wept.

And Catalina gazed at him with the same depth of perception . . . and of love. Her face was strong boned, her nose classically straight, but her mouth was wide and sensual, inviting enough to draw any man's gaze.

Seth had always been very important in her life. At four she had been a willful yet lonely child, and with Seth's birth she had found someone to lavish her strength on, which she did, not realizing she might be making him weaker by doing so.

"I don't want you to sell your pearls, Cat."

"Then what will we do?"

"I will go to Copeland one more time and see if I can repair the damage. Maybe he will allow me—"

"Can a man as low as he must be prove to be a gentleman? I doubt it."

"I am going to see Travis."

"Travis Sherman! Why?"

"Because he's wealthy enough to help me. Why do you dislike him so much?"

"I don't dislike him. He's done nothing to me."

"Except propose half-a-dozen times."

"Well he can propose a million. I'll never marry him. In truth I don't think I will ever marry."

"Give poor Travis a break. He's in love with you."

"He's in love with Father's money too."

"I guess he thinks it and you would be a good combination . . . maybe that's so."

"Are you suggesting I trade myself for enough money to buy the *Southern Belle* back?"

"Cat!"

"I'm sorry, Seth. I didn't mean that. I guess I'm just so worried."

He rose from the bed, and Catalina watched him pace the floor. She felt a surge of almost violent anger at the man who, she knew, must have taken advantage of a foolish boy's stupidity to cheat him at cards, to rob him of more than a riverboat—to rob him of his future, his pride, and of any chance to redeem himself in his father's eyes.

"This man, the one you played cards with, what did you say his name was?"

"Copeland . . . Marc Copeland."

"Where is he now?"

"On board the *Southern Belle* I expect."

"Seth . . . are you going to talk to Father about this tomorrow?"

"Tomorrow," he repeated forlornly. "No. I'm going over to Rosepoint tonight. Maybe I can talk to Travis, get him to loan me the money, and be back to tomorrow night. That way Father need never know."

"Yes, Seth. You go to Rosepoint. I will be certain to be careful not to say a word to Father tomorrow, and I'll keep him from going into New Orleans before you get back."

"You won't tell them I was here tonight?"

"You know you can trust me, Seth."

"Sure, Cat . . . I know." He kissed her cheek and walked to the door.

"Be careful, Seth. Don't make any noise."

"Don't worry. Facing Father tonight would be little short of suicide."

He smiled, and she smiled in return, then watched him slip out the door and close it softly behind him.

"Oh, Seth," she whispered, "I wish you were right. But I think your salvation is Marc Copeland, and I think someone should do something about it."

Seth's mad dash from New Orleans to the Carrington mansion in Baton Rouge had taken him a day and a half of river travel and another day on horseback. He was more than exhausted, but the necessity to talk to Travis Sherman outweighed his physical needs.

The Sherman home was a two hours' ride from the Carrington's, and during this journey Seth Carrington faced himself.

Pampered by parents who knew there would be no chance for another heir to the Carrington fortune, he had also been overly protected by a sister whose will he could never bend. Always having been given anything he wanted, he had, as a young man, chosen the easy path, and had become a wastrel, a gambler, a heavy drinker, and a womanizer. Every time he saw disappointment in the eyes of those in his family, he sank deeper into self-pity.

He realized now that his father had given him one opportunity after another, yet he had failed. For the first time he placed the blame on himself.

As he covered mile after mile, his determination grew. He would find a way to redeem himself, not only in his own mind or in the minds of his parents. He needed to see respect and understanding in the gold-brown eyes of the one person he loved more than any other.

Seth rode up the gravel drive to the Sherman home just at dawn, unaware that Travis had gone to bed less than four hours before.

Travis Sherman was wealthy, beyond doubt. But the source of his prosperity was concealed, and he wanted no light shed on it. Nonetheless, he was strong enough, devious enough, and opportunistic enough to hold on to what he had and to grasp for more.

He grunted angrily when he was shaken awake.

"Mr. Travis, sir . . . Mr. Travis."

"What the hell are you waking me up so early for?" he demanded.

"There's a man here to see you, sir."

"A man . . . For God's sake tell him to go away and come back at a decent hour."

"It's Mr. Carrington, sir."

"Carrington." Travis sat up abruptly. "The elder or the younger?"

"The younger, sir. Mr. Seth Carrington. He appears to be rather . . . distraught, sir."

Travis smiled as he rose from his bed. "Go down and make him comfortable, Jeffers. See he gets a drink. I'll bet he needs one. So the little pup has finally come around for help. I had a feeling he'd need it one day."

Jeffers left, and Travis began to dress slowly. He would make Seth squirm awhile.

So you've finally come to me, Seth . . . my dear old friend. Well now, let's see if you're willing to pay the price I want for what I'm sure you need, he thought.

By the time Travis walked slowly down the steps and into the library Seth had been waiting for nearly a half-hour.

Travis smiled and extended his hand. He could read Seth's sleeplessness and his anxiety, but he studiously ignored them.

"Seth, my friend. What brings you to Rosepoint so early in the morning?"

"Travis . . . I've got to talk to you."

"Sit down. I'll order some breakfast. We can talk while we eat."

"I'm not hungry," Seth replied anxiously. "I need to talk to you—it's important."

"All right. I'll just order some coffee. You look as though you need some."

Seth controlled his impatience while Travis summoned a servant, requested coffee, and then returned to sit opposite him. Finally Travis leaned back in his chair, crossed his legs, and looked at Seth.

20

"Well, my friend, what do you want to talk to me about?"

"Look . . . Travis. I . . . I'm in a bit of trouble."

"Trouble? What kind of trouble?"

"I . . . ah . . . I need some help."

"Help? Trouble?" Travis laughed. "Good heavens, Seth, you haven't been dueling and gone and killed some important personage have you?"

Seth leaned forward to brace both elbows on his knees, his eyes intent. "This is no joke, Travis. No, I haven't killed anyone, and the person who will suffer the most from this is me if you don't consent to help me."

"Well, so far you haven't said one coherent word about the kind of trouble you're in."

"I need a great deal of money—fifty thousand dollars to be exact."

"Fifty thousand! Good God, you go in deep when you go, don't you? What's it for?"

"Gambling."

"Your family is wealthy. You can pay a little at a time if you show good faith."

"If that were possible, I wouldn't have come to you."

"Very well. Please explain all the details. This whole thing is not clear to me."

"All right. I'm sure once I tell you you'll know why I need the money now. My life and my future depend upon it."

Travis remained silent while Seth explained the whole sordid story, and his eyes were expressionless. So Seth was unaware of the satisfaction that surged through him. Travis couldn't have been happier over Seth's difficulty, for it offered him the key to something he had wanted for a long, long time . . . Catalina Carrington.

". . . So you see why I've got to get the *Belle* back before my father finds out. Once he knows, I'm finished. He will never trust me again."

"I understand your position, but your father has always taken care of any 'problems' you've had before. Why should this time be different? He is so wealthy that one boat can't matter that much."

"You don't understand, Travis," Seth said desperately. "It's not just the boat—it's me. I need to do something. I can't let my father find out I've lost the boat, and I don't have a whole lot of time to get it back. I've *got* to get it back!"

"Calm down, Seth. Let me think."

"Think," Seth said. "I've gone crazy from thinking . . . for hours, days. I don't have much hope unless you decide to help me. I would rather kill myself than go to my father and tell him the truth."

"Don't do anything stupid. You'd make a lot of people unhappy. What about Catalina?"

"I've told Cat. She's the only one I could hope would understand."

"She told you to come here?" Travis asked hopefully.

"No . . . not really. But I told her where I was going and she didn't try to stop me."

Travis stood up and paced the floor for several minutes; then he sat opposite Seth again.

"You said you only had a short time."

"Yes. I can't keep it from Father very long."

"All right. Now listen. I don't have that amount of money here, but I can go to New Orleans and get it. And I could be back in plenty of time for you to repay your debt. All you have to do is relax and stay here until I return."

"Then . . . then you'll help me?"

"I said I would, didn't I? You look exhausted, Seth. Go upstairs and get some sleep. I'll go on down to New

Orleans and get the funds you need. I should be back in a few days or so. That will allow you to settle this in good time. Tell me, who is the man who got your boat?"

"His name is Copeland—Marc Copeland."

"Be damned! Marc Copeland. You were stupid enough to gamble with him? What do you know about him?"

"Just that he came from a wealthy family that lost everything. He's a . . . a ne'er-do-well that's good at cards."

"Well, maybe he can be bought. It might take a little more than what you lost, but I'll bet he'll grab it. Stop worrying. I'll be on my way to New Orleans as soon as we've had breakfast and you're on your way to bed."

"I'm grateful, Travis. I can't tell you how grateful."

"Come on, let's eat. Then I'll be on my way and you can sleep."

As they ate, Travis assured Seth that his problem was over, and once Seth was safely asleep, he sent for his carriage.

He headed for Belle Haven, to make sure Catalina Carrington knew the price she would have to pay for her brother's peace of mind and the security of his inheritance.

More than pleased with himself, he thought back to the time three years ago when he had first seen Catalina Carrington. She had swept into a ballroom, beautiful beyond imagining with her ivory skin and sparkling eyes. He had heard her laugh, watched her vivacious play, and had fallen totally in love with her.

His love was not only unrequited, he was perpetually outside the circle of friends that surrounded her.

Yet he wanted her . . . God how he wanted her. He made a point of making friends with her brother. That drunken stupid child, he thought. Yet if Travis knew

23

nothing else about Catalina, he knew that she was loyal to her brother, and loved him enough to do anything she felt necessary to keep him safe.

I have the money and the strength, Travis reflected, to take care of any obstructions Marc Copeland might put before me. Aloud he said, "I guess it's time, Mr. Copeland, that somebody put a stop to what you're trying to do, and I'm the one who can."

Travis was six feet tall and his wide-shouldered frame was steely and muscular. Handsome to a point nearing beauty, his face was chiseled and firm like a classic statue's, straight and firm in line and strong of jaw. His eyes were blue and quickly intelligent, and his hair was thick and blond.

Upon viewing Belle Haven, a magnificent edifice, he again complimented himself on his good fortune. He could, one day, rid himself of the presence of Seth Carrington. Her parents would not live forever, and with Catalina in his possession, all the Carrington wealth would be his—the wealth and the beautiful Catalina. He had never felt such a satisfying surge of power.

He strode to the door and rapped forcefully. It was promptly answered by a young wide-eyed maid.

"Yes, sir?"

"I would like to see Catalina please," he said, but his smug control quickly changed to a frown at the maid's reply.

"Miss Catalina isn't here."

"Not here? Where is she then?"

"Miss Catalina . . . just isn't here, sir."

"But it is of the utmost importance that I see her. I . . . I have word from her brother."

"I'm sorry, sir. There's nothing else I can say. Miss Catalina . . . she just isn't here, and I just don't know where she is."

"I see," Travis said. As the servant closed the door, he walked slowly back to his carriage, deep in thought. He was about to get in when the driver spoke.

"Shall we go back to Rosepoint, sir?"

"No. We go to New Orleans. It seems Marc Copeland is the source of the problem, and I guess it's time I did something about him."

Chapter 2

The *Southern Belle* had been polished until she glowed.

She was a luxurious three-decker riverboat with carved embellishments that were ornately beautiful. Her main cabins were splendidly appointed with hand-carved wood furniture, crystal chandeliers, heavy carpeting, and large mirrors. The accommodations for her dining room included an expert chef, a complete staff, and exquisite china, shining silver, and sparkling cut glass. A novel feature of the *Belle* was her steam calliope that played popular tunes during the approach to a river town.

Marc Copeland walked the deck in the glow of the huge white moon that gleamed down on the water of the gulf. He stopped to strike a match and light the cigar he held between square white teeth. As its hazy smoke drifted up on the light breeze, he narrowed his deep green eyes against the sting of it and looked out over the water.

He bent to rest his elbows on the rail, and hunched his broad shoulders. His face revealed a conflicting nature: sensitive eyes shielded themselves under dark brows while a firm mouth clearly indicated strength. His bone structure was large, and his high cheekbones and a square solid jaw gave him the look of a vibrant Caesar.

He had waited patiently for several years, and now he was touched with a tingle of excitement. Something had to happen soon; he knew it. Enough time had passed, and the challenging guantlet with which he had struck the Carrington cheek demanded an answer.

He laughed softly to himself, but it was not a laugh of pleasure. It was expectant and maybe just a little tense. He knew the reaction was coming; he just didn't know when . . . or from whom.

He knew a great deal about the Carringtons, but the only one whose face he had seen was Seth. He had chosen Seth carefully, knowing he was the weakest link. Yet the names of all the Carringtons were familiar to him. They had been etched deeply in his mind as he'd stood beside his father's grave.

Pierce Garrison, the stone read, and beside him lay his wife who had died a year later. Emily Copeland Garrison. It had been her name he had chosen to use so the Carringtons wouldn't know until the last moment, when he had finally brought them to their knees, that he was Pierce Garrison's son.

Has it been eight years already? he thought. Eight years since my father put a gun to his head and ended his life.

He had wept bitter tears, until he could weep no more. Then his grief had been replaced by a cold determination to claim a life for a life—Joseph Carrington's for Pierce Garrison's. It had taken him a long time to put together the truth as to where guilt lay, and an even longer to win enough money to stake the game he intended to play with Seth Carrington. The game that would begin an even bigger game. The contest between him and Joseph Carrington.

27

Now it had begun, and he waited for the fly to walk into his spider's trap. He was more than surprised at the fly that approached that trap first.

He was caught in thought when he felt a touch on his arm and turned to find the cabin boy of the *Southern Belle* at his shoulder.

"What is it, Josh?"

"They's a lady at the gangplank, sir. She wants to come aboard and talk to you."

"A lady? What's her name?"

"She refused to give one, sir."

Marc's heart bounded. He wondered if he was about to be bribed, pleaded with, or seduced by a feminine envoy from the Carrington clan.

"Show her to my cabin, Josh. See if she wants anything, and tell her I'll be with her in a few minutes."

"Aye, sir," Josh said quickly. Then he disappeared.

Marc took a last puff on his cigar before flicking it into the water. Then he walked down the upper deck of the *Southern Belle* and knocked on a door. It was opened quickly, and Marc knew China had been waiting as impatiently as he.

"So," she said softly, "the big fish has nibbled on the bait."

"I don't think so."

"What?"

"It seems I have a lady visitor."

"Be careful, Marc. This may be some kind of trap."

"I don't think I need be afraid of one woman, China," he chided. "But I am interested. I wonder what kind of woman old Carrington would send."

"Just be very careful." She laughed. "You are still susceptible to . . . ah . . . a lady's charm."

"Well, if she's a tasty morsel, and I would think the old man would choose the best, I wouldn't mind enjoying any small benefits that are being thrown my way."

"Marc, you are the most incorrigible of men."

"I know." He chuckled. "And I love you too." He kissed her quickly and left.

He walked toward his quarters slowly. Let her wait, he thought maliciously. It might make her begin to wonder if her trip to the *Southern Belle* was futile.

Catalina paced about the cabin. She had waited nearly a half-hour. Now she was certain Marc Copeland was the inconsiderate and ignorant boor she had thought him.

She had come to beg if necessary, and she carried a magnificent double strand of perfectly matched pearls to offer the man if all else failed. She sat down, doing her best to control the fury that could preclude achieving her purpose. She couldn't afford to shout angrily at Copeland. The sound of approaching footsteps drew her to her feet again, and she turned toward the door, her hands clenched together in front of her to still their trembling.

When it opened and Marc stepped inside, they stood facing each other with only the width of the eight-foot cabin between them. Catalina's first impression was that Marc Copeland was the most flawlessly handsome man she had ever seen . . . and that he was also dangerously wicked.

Marc's reaction paralleled hers. He saw before him a woman of unusual beauty. But he was not about to forget that beauty often provided a shield behind which evil flourished.

He found himself swimming momentarily in gold amber pools—wide and deceivingly innocent eyes.

He closed the door behind him and leaned against it, folding his arms across his chest.

"So," he said softly, "at least the old gentleman has good taste in his ladies. You are a beauty, my love, but if you have been sent here to dissuade me from turning this boat into a gambling palace, you can go back and tell old Carrington that no matter how inviting a tumble in bed would be with you, it won't get him anywhere."

Catalina gasped, momentarily shocked by this obvious insult. Then she reacted in a flash of wild and brilliant rage.

In three or four long strides, she crossed the space between them and struck Marc as hard as her strength would allow.

"You are a deceitful, cheating, insulting beast of a man, and I loathe you. A woman of any sensibility would be insulted by your touch."

Marc's realization of who she might be was as abrupt as the slap had been, and he reacted like a coiled snake that has been trod upon. He whipped out both hands and grabbed her, slamming her against the length of his body. His arms pinning both hers to her sides, he crushed her close until she gasped from breathlessness and anger.

"Let me go!" she demanded.

In response, Marc favored her with an insinuating smile that spoke volumes about the position in which she found herself. There was not a hair's-breadth between their bodies and her face crimsoned at the feel of his lean hard frame against hers.

He spoke softly. "I do believe I'm being honored by the presence of the elusive Catalina Carrington. My, my," he taunted, "if I had known how delicious you were, I would have made every effort to meet you first instead of your brother. You would have been much more fun to . . . handle than he was. Although I have the feeling you would not have been as easy . . . or would you?"

Moments ago, Catalina had thought she could not be angrier, but now she literally shook with the murderous rage that filled her.

"You are foul scum who preys on the defenseless. If I had a gun, I would take great delight in shooting you."

Marc chuckled. "Anger becomes you. Your eyes look like storm clouds, and your mouth . . . soft . . . inviting," he murmured.

Catalina could only let out one muffled cry of protest before his mouth lowered to take hers.

She struggled valiantly, but his greater size made all her efforts ineffectual. He found her struggle just a little too exciting as she writhed against him, so as abruptly as he had grabbed her, he pushed her away from him.

She staggered back a step or two, her anger returning. Drawing herself erect, despite her ragged breathing she spoke coolly. "What do you want for the title to the *Southern Belle?*"

Marc chuckled. "I don't think you have enough money to buy it back. Maybe I should talk to your father instead."

He saw her face go pale and her hands clench into fists, and he knew he had struck a very vulnerable spot. It did not take him too long to put two and two together. He was pretty sure now that her father still didn't know the truth; she had come to see that he never did. He had another pawn on his chessboard . . . and he meant to use it.

Catalina reached into the small bag she carried and withdrew the pearls. Marc quickly realized that they were of uncommon beauty and probably worth a small fortune. He cocked an eyebrow and gazed at her in silence.

31

"I have enough," she said coldly. "This necklace alone is is worth more than what Seth lost. It was fifty thousand dollars, wasn't it?" She said the words with such scorn that Marc could feel her antagonism across the room.

"Your brother lost this boat," he reminded her calmly.

"I know that, but the sum of money was fifty thousand dollars."

"That," he said firmly, as if he were explaining the facts to a child, "was before he signed the title to me. Now, if you want it back, you'll have to pay the price of the boat . . . that is, if I remember well, a little over two hundred thousand."

Catalina's mouth opened in shock and her eyes widened at his words.

"You can't mean that! That's robbery!"

"That's the chance you take when you gamble," he declared calmly. "He lost, I won. If you want the boat . . . pay for it." He watched her hands tremble as she slowly put the pearls back into her bag.

"I take it you don't have that much?"

"Why can't you be reasonable?"

"But I am reasonable," he stated. "I have something you want; it has a price. If you can't pay it . . . well"— he grinned as he let his gaze rake over her body—"I suppose we could come to some kind of agreement— use some other terms."

It took a minute for his words to register, but when they did Catalina reached a new plane of fury.

"You are truly unbelievable. You are the lowest form of life. How dare you suggest that I . . . I . . ."

"You overestimate yourself," he said, his smile broadening. "I never suggested that you do anything. Besides"—he eyed her critically—"you're a trifle small. I imagine you wouldn't be exceptional in bed. Of course, you might change my mind. We could talk it over."

She was nearly choking on the combination of his insults and her desperation.

"I'll find you the money."

"Of course . . . you just need to speak to your father. He has an unlimited supply. After all, he's accumulated a lot of other people's."

Tears sprang to Catalina's eyes, which only succeeded in making her angrier. She refused to cry before this monstrously heartless swine.

"You want your boat back that badly?" he asked softly.

"Yes," she replied hopefully.

"I'm in a position to make you a bargain."

"A bargain?" she queried suspiciously.

"Do you want to listen?"

"Yes."

"Come aboard my ship. Share my cabin for three days as my mistress. After that, I'll return the signed deed to you."

He watched the murderous glow appear in her eyes, and knew if she had a pistol she would have shot him. But before she could put words to her rage, he stepped aside and opened the door.

"You have a week to think it over. If you're not here by then"—he shrugged—"I shall continue with my plans for *my* boat. Good night, Miss Carrington." He chuckled. "Sleep well."

Catalina lifted her chin defiantly. She still hoped that Travis would lend Seth the money he needed. If he did, she would laugh in Marc Copeland's face and tell him what she truly thought of him. She swept past him and was not amused to hear his soft chuckle.

Marc stood near the rail and watched her enter her carriage. He thought of how rewarding it would be to use and discard Catalina Carrington. It would make the taste of revenge even sweeter. In so doing, he would destroy the two things Joseph Carrington held dearest, his daughter and his son—and at the same time.

Marc was still deep in black thought when his attention was drawn to a carriage that had stopped at the foot of the gangplank.

He expected no visitors, but then he was almost always prepared for the unexpected. That sixth sense of his had protected him many times.

He recognized Travis Sherman at once, and wondered what was so important it brought him here so late at night. Then another thought occurred to him. How did Travis Sherman know he'd find him aboard the *Southern Belle?* If he didn't, just who was he planning on visiting? Which Carrington . . . and why? He didn't trust any of the Carringtons, and he most certainly didn't trust any of their friends either. He knew a great deal about Travis Sherman, and thought him a very appropriate friend for people like the Carringtons.

He met Travis at the head of the gangplank the moment Sherman stepped on the deck.

"Travis." He acknowledged the man's greeting with one word. "What are you doing down here?"

"Had some business in New Orleans and thought I'd drop by to share a little of your excellent brandy while I was here." Travis laughed.

Marc doubted that this was a casual visit, but he would wait until Travis got around to telling him why he had come. Travis's motives were always self-oriented. Marc was certain this man wanted something from him . . . and he was reasonably sure of what the something was. He began to wonder just how close

34

Travis Sherman and Catalina Carrington were.

They are two of a kind, he thought, and he decided that she had probably used Travis for reinforcement in case she failed to get what she wanted.

They went to Marc's quarters, where Travis accepted a glass of brandy.

"Always knew you were a smart one," he said, "but getting the *Southern Belle* from the Carringtons is quite a feat. I always thought the old man put a lot of store in her. He sure as hell paid a lot of money to have her built and outfitted like this."

"I'm sure you know exactly what he paid for it." Marc laughed.

"I do."

"And I'm sure you knew how I got it before you came here," Marc added quietly. "Just what do you think you can accomplish that she couldn't?"

"She?"

"Catalina Carrington."

"So she's been here already. I thought I'd be able to stop her from doing anything so foolish. Maybe," Travis said shrewdly, "she still doesn't have any idea that you hate the Carringtons so badly you can taste it."

"Nothing personal . . . just business," Marc replied.

"Business . . . you conduct business over a card table?"

"If it's necessary."

"Why was it necessary? You could have tried to buy the boat from the old man. You know, Marc, I've an idea there's a whole lot more behind all this than just a gambling debt."

Marc smiled and shrugged, but he had no intention of opening any doors to the past.

"I'd like to buy her from you," Travis stated quietly.

"What makes you think I want to sell her?"

"You can make a hell of a profit. I know you got her for a song."

"Well," Marc said amusedly, "there's profit . . . and then there's profit."

"What was the debt?"

"Fifty thousand."

"I'll give you a hundred—double your money."

"No."

"Just like that . . . no thought?"

"No thought, just no. I've no intention of selling her."

"A hundred and fifty."

"No."

"You're crazy."

"And you're anxious," Marc declared coolly. "What's in it for you, Travis, the hand of the 'Lady' Carrington? I don't think you'd part with a hundred and fifty thousand if you didn't stand to get something for it."

"Catalina is not the kind of woman you buy."

Marc chuckled derisively. "Every woman is the kind of woman you buy. They have different prices that's all. I have a hunch 'Lady' Carrington's price is high . . ."

"You've bought too many. You don't know the difference anymore."

"If your business is over," Marc said stonily, "I've got a lot to do tomorrow and I'd like to get some sleep."

Travis rose. "Marc, think over my offer. You're asking for a whole lot of trouble. Carrington won't sit still for this. I can save you a lot of grief."

Marc watched Travis through narrowed eyes as another piece of the puzzle fit into place.

"Your magnanimous offer almost overwhelms me. But I can handle my own troubles. Tell 'Lady' Carrington you didn't succeed."

"She didn't send me."

"Of course not . . . but tell her anyway."

"You can be a hard bastard, Marc."

"I've had a lot of good teachers."

"My offer still stands."

"Forget it. Oh, by the way, when you see 'Lady' Carrington again tell her my offer still stands."

"What offer? When did you talk to Cat?"

"Cat? Very appropriate name. Just tell her what I said, she'll know what I'm talking about. Tell her anytime she wants to discuss my offer she knows where to find me."

"You're a fool, Marc, a fool who's making a lot of enemies."

"At least I know my enemies. It's harder to know friends."

"Maybe you don't know all your enemies. You're careless enough to antagonize the Carringtons. They're more powerful than you know, and they happen to have a lot of friends."

"You among them?" Marc asked casually.

"Of course."

"I have a hunch you expect to do a little 'buying' of your own."

Travis's face flushed and his look revealed his hatred.

"I told you, Cat isn't the kind of woman you buy."

"And I told you, you're a dreamer. She has her price too . . . and I might just have what she's willing to bargain for."

"You do anything to hurt Cat," Travis warned coldly, "and you might find the Mississippi very deep and very cold."

"I'll keep that in mind."

"You do that."

Travis set his glass down and left, not closing the door too gently behind him. Marc gazed at the door meditatively. All the plans he had made over the past eight years were working with well-oiled precision . . . why, then, did he feel this aggravating twinge of regret. He knew what he wanted to do, and nothing was going to stop him. He would destroy Seth . . . then he would bring Catalina to her knees . . . and after that, he would kill Joseph Carrington.

Chapter 3

Catalina sat in the dark confines of her carriage, seething with an anger that made her tremble. Never had she been subjected to such blatant insults or to such an evil and malicious man.

He does not have one grain of honor in his entire body, she thought miserably. Yet she could still feel the heat of Copeland's gaze as it swept over her. It had set her skin afire, as if he had touched her in some sensual way, and remembering that sensation did not soothe her anger.

His soft taunting laugh when she'd passed him, that had been the *coup de grâce*. Did he really believe she would subject herself to him! Not even to save her own life would she do that.

As her anger became more controlled, her fear for her brother mounted. She knew this episode could quite possibly destroy the fragile relationship between him and her father. If that happened, the choice Seth might make caused her to know a moment of real terror.

She would have to think of some way . . . she would have to! But how? Marc Copeland held all the cards at the moment. Still, the game was not over yet, and Catalina was not one to give up easily. She would think of a way. She had to.

Catalina had slipped away from home in the middle of the night and had gone to Captain Lahey, the master of the *Silver Queen,* one of her father's fastest boats. She had traveled downriver, after sending a note informing her parents that a sudden emergency had called her to the sick bed of a very dear friend.

Once the boat had docked in New Orleans, she had gone to the home of her dowager aunt, Charlotte McNeil. Her aunt had seemed to believe her story, so she had waited until Charlotte had gone to bed and then had sent a surprised servant for her carriage.

It was now after midnight, and she entered the house as quietly as she possibly could. She tiptoed down the hall to the room she had been given, then breathed a sigh of relief when she closed the door behind her.

The gravity of her situation increased her anxiety. How could she sleep when she knew a man like Copeland held her brother's life in his hands? She paced the floor restlessly, annoyed by the fact that her thoughts kept returning to the arrogant and very suggestive smile on Marc Copeland's face.

Why, she wondered, did this man want to damage her brother and her and the rest of her family? Why? He had deliberately created this situation and she had to know what had set him on this path.

She worried about what had happened between Seth and Travis. Had Travis seen fit to lend Seth the money he needed to redeem himself? God, she thought, two hundred thousand dollars! It was a fortune.

She began to undress slowly, then sat before her dressing table to brush her hair. Her hand stopped in midstroke and she gazed into her reflection.

Her cheeks were pink, and the small red mark at one corner of her lips suddenly brought to mind the feel of Copeland's hard mouth against hers. Her body tensed at the memory of the strength in the arms that had held her, the feel of his body as it had pressed against hers. Then she slammed the brush down on the table, upset with her body's heated response. It was frightening.

She walked to her bed and slid beneath the covers, but after some time she reluctantly acknowledged that she was not going to find sleep very easily . . . if she could find it at all.

Travis walked up the steps to the McNeil home. It was a modest two-story dwelling built for Charlotte by her brother because Charlotte was independent. She refused to live with anyone or in someone else's house.

He knocked on the door, and it was opened by a slim Creole girl.

Travis had known where Catalina would go since Charlotte was her only relative in New Orleans, with the exception of several cousins she did not like.

"Good morning." He smiled and took off his hat. "Is Miss Carrington up yet?"

"Yassuh, she be up. She be havin' breakfast in her room."

"Would you tell her that Travis Sherman is here to see her please?"

"Yassuh . . . come in please."

She led him to a small parlor where he waited impatiently for several minutes before Catalina appeared in the doorway.

Try as she might, and though she knew that Travis might be Seth's only salvation, Catalina found it difficult to suppress her response to him when he rose and approached her. She didn't want to dislike this man; Seth needed him. And she didn't want to distrust him because of a feeling she could not even name.

"Mr. Sherman."

Travis stopped beside her. His smile was warm.

41

"Catalina, I've asked you many times to call me Travis."

"Travis." She smiled hesitantly.

"You know why I'm here."

"Yes, I do. Seth came to you?"

"He did. Seth and I have been friends for some time. Who else would he turn to for help?"

"And?" she questioned quietly.

"Do you doubt that I would want to help him?"

"Want . . . but can't?" she responded.

"No. Want and tried."

"I don't understand."

"Catalina, why did you go to see Marc Copeland last night?"

"How did you know that?"

"Because I was there right after you. I don't know what you said or did, but Copeland refused any offer I made. I tried to buy the *Southern Belle* back, for any price."

"And he refused to sell it."

"Yes. He refused. He also said something very strange."

Catalina moved away from Travis to sit on a straight-backed chair near the window. Travis watched, enthralled by her graceful movements and the way the light from the window glazed her skin.

"What did he say?" she asked softly.

"He said that I should remind you that his offer still stands. What did he offer you?"

Catalina stood frozen like an alabaster statue. Damn him, she thought, to have enough nerve to say such a thing. Did he truly believe she would stoop so low? Did he think that saying such a thing to Travis would frighten her into trying to keep him quiet by acceding to his wishes? Well, he had judged his victim wrong this time. There had to be a way out of this dilemma.

Travis watched her, wondering where her mind drifted.

"Catalina, there must be a way to best this scoundrel, and if you will allow me I will do whatever it takes to insure that he doesn't succeed in what he's attempting."

"There has to be a way to get the boat back before my father finds out. If not, Seth will be destroyed by this. Oh, that man is a monster!" she cried.

"If he won't sell it to me, then what do you suggest? Maybe Seth should go to your father and tell him the truth, just make a clean breast of it. Wouldn't your father understand? Surely with his wealth the money can't mean that much."

"You don't understand. Under any other circumstances that would be true, but . . ." She was hesitant to voice words that might damn her brother, but she went on, speaking with all the control she could muster. "For the past three years Seth has seemed to lose control of himself. It's . . . it's almost as if he is afraid. He has drunk and done . . . other things to the extent that Father is thinking of cutting him off."

These were not the worst words Travis could hear. With Seth gone, Catalina would be the heir to the Carrington fortune.

"Seth is . . . weak," she continued helplessly. "I am almost afraid of what he might do."

"And," Travis added, "you think of him as your responsibility?"

"He's my brother. Should I turn my back on him?"

"No. But this time there doesn't seem to be much else you can do."

"I must talk to him again."

"Him?"

"Marc Copeland."

"You are joking. You would go to him after he has refused you?"

43

"Don't you see, Travis, if I had the money he wanted, I could reach him and explain that this is all a terrible wrong, surely he would show some decency. Ultimately he would let me buy the *Belle* back."

This put an entirely new light on the situation. Travis was elated. Finally he had found some way to make Catalina indebted to him. First with money . . . and then with gratitude. He would be the one to be there when she needed him.

"All right, Cat," he said gently. He went to her, took her hand, and raised it to her lips. He kissed it softly. "I'll help you. Maybe together we can save this foolish brother of yours from himself."

At first Catalina blinked in surprise, then she smiled, her eyes warming with a gratitude that made Travis's pulse pound.

"I'm sorry I doubted you. You really are Seth's friend. I am grateful for your kindness and understanding. Seth and I will pay you back I promise."

"Don't worry about it. Let's just take care of this messy situation first. Then we can worry about paying me back. The money couldn't be put to better use."

"Thank you, Travis."

"When will you see him?"

"I'll go to the *Belle* tonight."

"Shall I come with you? He could be dangerous."

"No. I'm not afraid of him."

"All right."

"Travis, is Seth at your home?"

"Yes."

"Go and tell him we're doing our best. He must be worried to death. I'm afraid he will do something stupid."

"I can go to Baton Rouge and come back in a few days. Shall I bring Seth back with me?"

"Yes, bring him back. Maybe this has finally reached

44

him. We can finish it up, and he can start over."

"I'll get you the money this afternoon."

"Thank you."

He kissed her hand again, then turned to leave. Catalina watched him walk away. This was the only chance she had to keep her brother's mistake from becoming a tragedy, yet she couldn't fight the idea that she was making a mistake that might be hard to walk away from.

Travis did give Catalina a black carpetbag containing the money late that same afternoon, and she spent the balance of the day in her room, steeling her nerves for the night's confrontation.

Late that evening, thinking that Catalina was, at that very moment, with Marc Copeland, Travis sat in a darkened corner of a tavern with two unsavory characters.

"You know what he looks like?" Travis questioned.

"That we do, mate. We've seen the gent around for a while," one replied.

"You know where the *Belle* is berthed?"

"We know that too. What we wants to know is where the money is?" the second man growled.

Travis reached into his breast pocket and withdrew a thick envelope. He tossed it onto the table, and the man snatched it eagerly.

"I want him taken care of at your first opportunity," Travis declared quietly. "But make sure he's not on his boat. He'll have too much help there. I'd rather he just disappeared."

"Don't ya worry, we'll take care of him. He won't even know what happened."

"But remember to be careful. He's no fool, and don't think he'll be easy. If you strike and don't succeed, he'll

45

make you wish you'd never been born."

Both men nodded, smiled grim determined smiles, and then left the table. Travis finished his drink with satisfaction, and he soon left the tavern.

In good time, he thought, I will have access to what I have wanted for a long time, a place in the circle of the wealthy. I will move in the midst of the Carringtons and their friends. I will have Catalina . . . the boats . . . and everything I want.

There was much about Travis's past that no one knew. He had struggled against severe poverty, in a small town on the muddy banks of the Mississippi. The road to where he now stood had been a long and very difficult one.

He had used whatever means were necessary to travel it—brute force and deception and theft. Inside him burned twin fires: one for Catalina herself and the other for her wealth. He was determined to have both and he wasn't going to let her stupid brother or Marc Copeland stand between him and his goals. He would rid himself of any threat as he had before. He would simply eliminate it.

Travis left the tavern and walked to his carriage. He ordered the driver to head for the docks, and in a short while he was looking at the graceful beauty of the *Southern Belle* and wondering what was happening in the captain's quarters at that moment.

Seth was wretched. The longer he was inactive and frightened, the closer he began to look at himself and his wasted life.

He had enjoyed the wealth and prestige of his family without realizing he had a moral obligation to those who had given him so much. He realized now the effect his slide toward debauchery had had on his relationships with the people who loved him and consistently made excuses for him. He thought of Catalina and his misery worsened. Again he had let her take command and try to right his wrongs.

It had taken this final blow to scrape away Seth's veneer, to make him search for a strength he hadn't known he had.

After several hours of waiting and worrying Seth made a decision. First he was going to go to Catalina and tell her that this time he would be responsible for what he had done. Then he would tell his father the whole sordid truth and accept his punishment. After that, he would begin to build his life again. Maybe, he thought hopefully, in time his family would look at him with pride again. And maybe after a while he could begin to look upon himself without shame.

Seth sent for his horse and left Rosepoint, determined to talk to his family. But it was not to work out the way he had planned. When he reached Belle Haven, he found that Catalina was gone and his parents were not there either.

"Where are my father and mother, Thomas?" he asked the butler.

"They received an invitation, sir. They have gone upriver to St. Louis."

"And where is Cat?"

"She left for New Orleans, sir. It seems a friend of hers is quite ill and she has gone to help."

Seth groaned. "Her sick friend is getting sicker by the minute."

"I beg your pardon, sir?"

"Never mind, Thomas. Just pack some clothes for me."

"You're leaving again, sir?"

"Yes. I'm going to New Orleans. I have to find Cat. It's time she stopped playing nurse. She has one sick friend who has finally learned he can cure himself."

"Sir?" Thomas was truly puzzled by Seth's ramblings.

Seth laughed. "I'll explain some other time, Thomas. Right now I'm in a hurry."

He was already taking the steps two at a time. He entered his room, washed, and changed his clothes.

An hour later he threw a small satchel of clothes into the carriage and started toward New Orleans.

Marc and China were enjoying a quiet evening meal in her cabin. The strange relationship between them was only spoken of in whispers and never where either of them could hear. Yet they were well aware of the gossip, and it amused them to keep explanations to themselves.

Marc was relaxed and comfortable with China; that was so with no other human being. He trusted her completely, and she was the only person who knew the events that had led him to the path he now walked. She was quiet but frank when she spoke, very intelligent, and extremely competent at managing countless details. As Marc had said, China was a mirror, but a mirror that did not condemn or reveal flaws. She merely let Marc examine himself without deception.

He loved her in a way no other woman, and very few men, would understand. Their love had never been physical, yet neither questioned it. As for China her love for Marc was akin to worship. Indeed, she would have gladly sacrificed her life for him had the need ever arisen.

Yet in their talks they indulged in a freedom rare between a man and a woman. China was the only one who could ask questions—and get answers.

"She is very beautiful, this Carrington woman?"

"Yes, she is." Marc scowled. "Which means little or nothing. She's still a Carrington."

"Is that enough to condemn her?"

"The first thing she tried to do was buy me off. Right or wrong, those people think their money and position make then invincible. Don't you think it's time they learned that's not so?"

"You enjoyed making her plead?"

"That I did." He chuckled. "Too bad the game was over so quickly. I find myself wishing she would accept my bargain. Taming her first might prove rewarding."

"You might not laugh should you fall into your own trap. She might tame you instead."

"No chance of that, China. I have too long a memory. Her very name—Carrington—gives me nightmares. I would never trust her, and caring for someone like her would be a disaster. I don't intend to pay the price my father paid for trusting a Carrington. She's a beautiful temptress, but her heart would be solid stone like those of the rest of her family."

"Marc."

"What?"

"I know your hatred, but think of this one thing. Why would a woman as wicked as you paint her to be care so much for her brother that she would come to you and beg? That is not the thing a hard-hearted person would do. Maybe she does not have the soul of her father . . . maybe she loves this young brother."

Marc was annoyed when she expressed a thought that had already occurred to him in an unwelcome moment of weakness.

He rose. "I'm going out for some air and a smoke." He strode to the door, and when he opened it he turned to look at China again. "My plans aren't changing. Don't be deceived by your own gentle heart. She's wearing a beautiful mask, but scratch it and you'll still

49

find a Carrington. I intend to bring them all down. If getting her into my bed will be the faster way, then that's what I'll do. Don't feel sorry for her; she would probably spit on you."

He left quietly, and China watched the door for several seconds. The look in her eyes was remarkably close to pity.

Chapter 4

Marc paced the deck of the boat on which he still felt himself to be an intruder. The night was young, and the moon sat low on the horizon sending a path of light across the water.

Marc was deep in thought when a carriage stopped near the gangplank. He heard soft feminine laughter, and when the door opened, four women exited in a profusion of petticoats, slim legs, and bright smiles.

He smiled, knowing both he and the boat were facing a unique invasion. Slowly he walked to the head of the gangplank and watched the women begin to board.

The first to step on deck was Paulette Bordeau. She was a statuesque blond with wide blue eyes and a figure that could make any man forget his goal in life. She spoke with a thick French accent . . . until she was angry. Then she slipped into gutter language that would have shocked a deckhand.

"Paulette." Marc chuckled. "As beautiful as ever."

"Ah, Marc mon cher," Paulette laughed seductively as she kissed him with enthusiasm. "It is so good to see you again."

The woman directly behind Paulette was a flame-haired green-eyed beauty with a rich creamlike complexion. Charlene Gilbert lifted lush full lips to kiss Marc.

51

"Charlene my pet," Marc said, as he put both hands on her waist to pry her slim body from his. "I'm glad you came."

"For you, Marc," Charlene replied huskily, "I would go just about anywhere . . . anytime."

The third boarder to step on deck was a creature of delicate beauty. She seemed frozen somewhere between girlhood and womanhood. She was small boned and slender, with eyes of cloud gray and hair that was golden brown. Her innocent air reminded Marc of a lost child, though he knew the dreadful past that had created her.

"Hello, Shawna," he said gently.

"Hello, Marc . . . is China here?" Her voice was a soft whisper, as gentle as she was.

"She's here, Shawna." He faced the three, but was more aware of the fourth. "Why don't the three of you go to her stateroom? It's the last door at the end of the passage."

With a flurry they were gone, and he turned to look at the fourth woman who had just stepped on the deck. She was regarding him silently.

"Nina," Marc said softly.

"It's been a long time, Marc."

Her voice was deep and throaty, and probably the most sensual one he had ever heard. Despite her beauty and the dignity of her bearing, her sexuality was what you sensed the moment you laid eyes on her. It was a force that had a life of its own.

To women like her every man gravitates when he chooses to find the ultimate in love. In such a woman he seeks forbidden pleasures and the fulfillment of secret dreams. He sees her learning and teaching things that no "lady" should ever know.

"It's been too damned long."

"Shall I go on to see China?" She smiled, knowing

the answer, making it needless for him to say the words.

He laughed softly as he extended his hand to her, and when she slid hers into it, he drew her into his arms.

She was tall and luxuriously curved, and a low murmur of satisfaction escaped from Marc as she fit the length of her body to his. Thick lashes lowered over her dark brown eyes as his mouth blended with her parted lips.

"You can talk to China tomorrow," he said huskily. "I have other plans for tonight."

"I'm sure"—she laughed—"that your plans and mine are a great deal alike."

"It would certainly be a big disappointment to me if they weren't."

He slid an arm about her waist and they walked to his stateroom. Once inside it, words were unnecessary. Both knew what they wanted. He watched in silent admiration as she slowly undressed revealing lush charms he remembered well. Naked and unashamed she walked to him and began to help him remove his clothes. In moments, they were on his bunk, engrossed in sensual exchanges.

Their lovemaking had always been a source of deep pleasure to him. So, as he lay exhausted beside her, he couldn't understand the strange lack of completion he felt, as if something intangible were missing. He ignored it. There had been too much tension in his life. Nina would help him ease it while he carried out the balance of his plans . . . Damn, why did thinking of his plans conjure up a vision of a golden-eyed woman who had no place in his thoughts now?

Nina stretched luxuriously. Marc was always satisfying. She had enjoyed no other man as she enjoyed him. That his lean hard body could stir her to such rapturous pleasure often surprised her.

She rose and walked to Marc's wash stand, took his

brush from it. Slowly she began to work through the tangles in her hair before she again coiled it into glossy ebony ropes wound at the nape of her neck.

Marc watched with a great deal of pleasure, thinking that Nina had the most remarkable body he had ever seen. Their eyes met in the mirror, and both smiled.

"It's good to have you back, Nina. I really have missed you."

"Then why did you leave Natchez so suddenly? Only a note—'Sorry, Nina. I'll be in touch.'"

"It was . . . something I had no control over."

"Why"—she turned to look at him—"do I let you walk in and out of my life whenever you choose? You just come and go like a shadow."

He rose from the bed and went to her, bending to take hold of her arms and draw her up into his. They kissed slowly and very satisfactorily.

"Because love," he whispered, "we're good together, and"—he kissed her again—"you are a delicious creature who's the damnedest hellion in bed I've ever had. And"—he laughed—"you're as wild and untamable as I am. We both cherish our freedom, Nina; that's what keeps us together. No chains, no ties, and no promises."

"No promises." She wanted to say much more, to tell him that she had plans, that she intended to make their relationship much more permanent this time. But first she had to find some way to hold him . . . for good.

Marc walked away from her and began to dress, while Nina continued her toilette.

They were both half-dressed when the door swung open. Nina's eyes sparked in quick anger when she saw the woman framed in the doorway. Marc was so taken by surprise that he stood completely still, the shirt he was about to put on held in his hands.

"Well, Marc," Nina said coldly, "it appears you have company."

Marc's unbelieving gaze met Catalina's disdainful eyes. Of all the people in the world Catalina Carrington was the last person he had expected to see.

Catalina waited out the hours, her nerves stretched to the breaking point. The clock ticked away the minutes so slowly that she could hardly stand it.

She looked at the small black satchel that contained the money. Would he accept it from her when he had refused it from Travis? It was a slim chance, but it was the only one they had. If he refused there was very little more that could be done and Seth would be left to face . . .

She didn't want to think of it for deep inside she was afraid, afraid that her family would disintegrate before her eyes and that she would lose Seth. Hadn't she always been there for him? Well, she would be there now. She was certain Seth would do something foolish should Marc Copeland carry out his threat.

Catalina refused to give any thought to Travis. He had supplied the money, but he had no claim on her. Yet he brought Marc Copeland to her mind.

"What a despicable, hateful man he is," she muttered aloud. "But money seems to be important to him, and I suppose he enjoys seeing me beg. Whatever it takes to satisfy his demands, I'll just have to do."

She moved through the quiet dark house as she heard the clock chime midnight, making her way to the back door. From there she must cross the wide inner courtyard, exit through another wrought-iron gate, and follow the cobbled drive to the carriage house. She expected to find the small closed carriage already harnessed and prepared for her. She had used the last of her small coins to bribe the stable boy.

Upon opening the stable door she sighed with relief to find the equipage ready. An impatient stable boy was holding the bridle of the horse, and doing his best to keep it quiet.

She gave him the coins, and he opened the wide door so she could drive away, watching after the receding carriage.

"If Miz Charlotte finds out about this we's both gonna get skinned. I sure hope you don't run across no trouble, and get back before mornin' or we's gonna be in for it. Miz Charlotte don't take to bein' snookered . . . no sir, she don't take to it at all."

He continued to shake his head as he walked to a comfortable pile of hay on which a blanket was spread.

"She asked me to wait and open the doors for her, but she didn't say nothn' bout bein' comfortable while I waited."

He lay down on the blanket, and after a while its warmth took over and he drifted off to sleep.

Catalina drove through the dark deserted streets without mishap. When she reached the *Southern Belle,* she saw no sign of life aboard. She left the carriage and walked as quietly as possible to the gangplank, not expecting any problem with the crew abed. Nonetheles, she mounted the gangplank slowly.

Having been aboard the *Belle* more than once Catalina easily found her way to the captain's quarters. Seeing light beneath the door, she reasoned he must still be awake. She wanted to take advantage of the element of surprise, so she turned the knob and swung the door open. The scene that greeted her was the last one she had expected.

This was one of the few times when Marc had been caught totally off guard. He was stunned to find Catalina Carrington in his doorway, and piqued by the contemptuous amusement in her eyes.

He had a strong desire to throttle her—or kiss her—until she begged for release. What he did was smile coolly and continue dressing as if her presence meant little or nothing to him. It was Nina who bridled.

"Who is she?" she demanded, causing Marc's brows to furrow in annoyance.

"She's none of your business, Nina. Just someone I have a little . . . business with. We have to talk alone. Why don't you go down to China's stateroom and make sure the girls are settled?"

Nina's face was a study in ill-suppressed rage. She glared at Catalina as she gathered up the balance of her things. Then she went to Marc and kissed him slowly and leisurely. Finally, a half-smile on her lips, she walked to the door.

"Do hurry with your . . . business, Marc. It's been a long time, and we have a lot to talk about." Her throaty sensual voice made her meaning quite clear.

Catalina smiled through gritted teeth, and despite his amused grin, Marc could have thrown Nina overboard.

After Nina closed the door behind her, a heavy silence descended on the cabin. Marc chose not to try to break it. This was her game now and he wasn't going to help her one bit. He poured a glass of brandy and sipped from it while he watched her.

Catalina had to choose quickly just what kind of approach she was going to use. He is shrewd, she thought, and in that white shirt and dark pants he could be a pirate. She was well aware of the heady masculine aura about him. He was devastatingly sensual, and she was more than irritated by the fact that her senses responded despite her will. She had never been alone with a man she considered as dangerous as this one.

"Mr. Copeland . . ."

"Marc." He grinned. "Sounds friendlier."

"Mr. Copeland," she insisted coldly. "I've come to talk to you about the *Southern Belle.*"

Marc set his glass down and walked slowly toward her. Catalina held her ground, gazing at him defiantly. She would have given anything to be able to turn and run, but there was too much at stake. Valiantly, she suppressed the fear he aroused in her. She wasn't sure just what she was afraid of, and that angered her also. She could feel her cheeks grow warm under the intensity of his gaze, but she refused to budge an inch.

Marc's eyes were filled with alert awareness, but he, too, refused to move. His smile was openly challenging as he stood close enough to touch her.

When Catalina reached up to lower the hood of the cloak she wore, Marc's smile remained unchanged, but he grew tense. Her hair, deliberately left unbound, fell in a cascade over her shoulders and down her back. He was tempted to bury his hands in it, to inhale more of the subtle intoxicating fragrance that touched his senses.

Her features were creamy perfection, and his hands itched to trace the fine texture of her skin. He imposed a firm grip on himself and remained silent.

"I . . . I must talk to you."

He moved slowly around behind her, but she obstinately refused to turn and see what he was about. Scarcely breathing, she felt his presence close to her.

His hands came over her shoulders, and she shivered as he loosened her cloak and drew it from them.

"Make yourself comfortable," he said softly. "Would you like some brandy?"

"No!" she said quickly. The last thing she needed was something that would affect her senses even more.

God, he thought, does she have any idea how breathtaking she is? Then reason struck him: of course she knew. She had planned this carefully, and if he wasn't careful he would find himself wound around her little finger like some hot-blooded boy.

"I take it," he said with aggravating coolness and a soft laugh that pricked her ears, "that you have come to agree to my bargain?"

She spun about and rage she could barely control leapt into her eyes. Only by exerting the severest discipline did she respond to his words verbally rather than physically.

"I have come to discuss our situation," she said frigidly. The damnable beast, she thought. Does he honestly believe I will surrender to him? The battle is not over yet.

"Our situation?" he repeated. "I didn't know there was much about it to discuss. I have something you want . . . and you know the price of it. I thought you had done your thinking and had come to agree."

Offering neither a word of agreement nor of explanation, Catalina moved away from him. The combination of fear and anger were difficult to control. They put words on the tip of her tongue, words that would ruin all her plans if they were spoken.

She stood with her back to him because she could not trust herself.

"I have another offer for you. One you might find even more agreeable."

"More agreeable than three days—and nights—with

you?" he said with disbelieving humor. "I hardly think so. It would take a great deal to make a more tempting offer."

Catalina had set the small satchel just inside the door when she had entered the cabin. Now she turned back to look at him.

"You said the *Belle* was worth two hundred thousand."

"She is . . . in fact most likely more."

"There is two hundred thousand in that bag."

Marc cast a quick look at the bag, then another very irritated one at Catalina.

"And what simple-minded fool lets you wander the streets carrying something like that? You alone are enough to lure any scoundrel without that provocation."

"As a scroundrel I'm sure you would know." Catalina could not resist that one cut. Her reward was a wide white smile and a glimmer of mischief in his eyes.

"My lady, you do tempt me."

She refused to listen to the double entendre. "The pearls are there also. You should see at least sixty thousand on them. It is an immense profit."

"Very," he said gently. His eyes were warm as they roamed over her. "But then, much depends on what kind of profit I really want."

"You can hardly refuse such an offer! It's many times what Seth lost. Are you a fool?"

"Hardly. I am simply the owner of what you want. As such I've the right to set my own price."

"But you are unreasonable!" she cried.

"My dear Cat," he said seriously, "no man who looked at you would consider me unreasonable. I would be considered a fool if I passed up the chance to share your . . . charms. I have a great deal of money already, and possess one of the best boats on the river.

In fact"—he laughed softly—"I have just about everything I want."

"You could have the decency to listen to reason." Catalina was losing her control. "You have nothing to lose. With this money you could buy or build the best boat on the river."

"Undoubtedly."

"Then what is it you want?" she nearly shrieked.

His smile was an obvious answer, and anger nearly overcame her. She moved toward him, her hands curved into claws, fighting the urge to tear out his eyes and rip the arrogant smirk from his face.

"You are a damned pirate!" she cried.

He moved like lightning, snatching both wrists to force her arms behind her back. She was forced against a body whose reaction could be soon felt as his loins grew heated with her lush curves pressed so close.

His eyes burned into hers and for the first time she felt a trembling fear that left her knees weak and her body strangely devoid of the strength to resist. Her eyes grew wide as he lowered parted lips and moved them slowly, teasingly and warmly, across hers. His mouth was insistent as his tongue forced her lips apart and thrust to deeply taste the sweet caverns of her mouth.

Her world careened crazily and she fought just to regain her wayward senses. She was caught in the heat of a battle she did not have the experience to win. The kiss sent a heated stream of wild excitement through her, and the hard muscular length of him ignited her body despite her attempt to resist him.

Warmth seemed to seep into her every pore until her skin was aflame with it and she was lost in a searing scorching fire that twisted her will and melted it down into the slow simmer of passion.

With a surge born of desperation, she pushed herself from his arms. Both were raggedly gasping for breath.

"No!" she half-gasped half-moaned.

"I'll tell you now, Catalina Carrington. You take your money, you take your pearls. I will settle for nothing less than surrender. You still have five days. Make up your mind. If I sail five days from now without you, then consider the *Southern Belle* lost to you forever."

Catalina could think of nothing except getting away from the destructive emotion she had almost surrendered to. She almost ran to the door, snatched up the satchel and her cloak, and then she was gone, the door swinging closed behind her.

Marc looked at it, disbelief on his face. Despite all else he had wanted her as he had never wanted another woman, yet she was a mortal enemy he meant to destroy.

Chapter 5

On the ride back to her aunt's house Catalina was filled with such black rage that she was hardly aware of the distance.

She wakened the stable boy and gave him strict orders to care carefully for the horse. Then she went into the dark quiet house and silently made her way to her room.

Once inside it, she gave vent to her fury as she paced about like a caged lioness.

"He is an unmitigated scoundrel," she groaned half-aloud. She clasped her hands before her. "Whatever am I going to do? That man will ruin Seth . . . and our boat. Oh, God, I could kill him!"

Thoughts of murder and mayhem tumbled through her mind, creating a defiant shield between what she thought and what she felt.

She refused to remember that one wild moment of near surrender. It had meant nothing more to him than a point in whatever game he was playing.

Somewhere deep inside she felt there was much more to this than the problem between Seth and Marc. She had sensed a kind of vengeful violence even in his kiss. But why, she thought, why? What could she or Seth have done to him?

Whatever it was, however, that was the key to getting

back the *Southern Belle,* and she had a few short days in which to find the answers.

Reluctantly, even though she knew she could not sleep, she began to prepare for bed.

She was completely unprepared when her door opened and her aunt Charlotte entered the room.

"Aunt Charlotte! What are you doing here so late?"

"I've been waiting patiently for you to get home," Charlotte said crisply. "Now, my girl, you sit yourself down and tell me just what all this gallivanting around at unheard-of hours is all about."

"Now, Aunt Charlotte . . ." Catalina gave her a pacifying smile.

"Don't you patronize me, young lady." Charlotte chuckled. "I've been wise to your shenanigans since you were in diapers. Now suppose you just start at the beginning . . . and tell me the truth."

Catalina sighed, but sat down obediently. She had never succeeded in outfoxing her aunt, and she was sure she wasn't going to now. She began to explain as best she could, hardly noticing the glitter of amusement and understanding in her aunt's eyes.

Charlotte McNeil was an astoundingly vital woman despite her sixty years. Her body was still healthy and strong, and she walked erectly. Her skin, barely touched by time, still had a soft texture, and her hair, once a deep auburn, was white as snow but still thick and glowing. Yet it was the remarkable strength and understanding in her clear blue eyes that drew people to her like magnets.

The secrets of her past and the reason for her firm intent to remain unmarried had been held within her for forty years. Whatever these were, they had never defeated her. Now she saw through Catalina's words, recognized emotions Catalina would have preferred to keep to herself.

"You've told me a great deal, child. Now, suppose you tell me just why such a man would turn down the offer you made? He wants more than the *Belle* and money. What is it?"

Reluctantly and in subdued voice, Catalina told the truth.

"So," Charlotte said softly, "it's you he really wants."

"But I don't understand," Catalina protested. "I have never met him before. He has never seen me. Why would he do this?"

"Hmmm," Charlotte murmured. "It appears to me the gentleman has a secret of sorts."

"A secret. But what secret could he have that has anything to do with me?"

"That seems to be something we will have to find out You say he gave you a time limit."

"Five more days."

"Well"—Charlotte chuckled—"in five days a great deal can be accomplished. I would dearly love to get my hands on that scamp of a brother of yours. He might cast a little light on this puzzle."

"He's at Rosepoint."

"With that Travis Sherman." Charlotte looked closely at Catalina. "You haven't gone soft on that one have you?"

"No, Aunt Charlotte." Catalina laughed. "I haven't gone soft on anybody. It seems to me men mean a lot of trouble and grief."

"Some do and some don't. I think it's time we sought some sleep. I've some thinking to do and you look exhausted."

"I am."

"Well, climb into bed. We'll talk in the morning. Good night, Cat."

"Night."

Charlotte closed Catalina's door behind her. Then she stood in the hall for a moment. As she walked to her room, she laughed softly.

"I do believe I would like to meet this Marc Copeland," she muttered.

Seth had pushed himself to the extent his body would allow. It was the reason he'd arrived in New Orleans fully three-quarters of a day before he had expected to.

He knew Catalina well and even though they had other relatives in this city he was more than certain she would go to the place where she would feel the most comfortable, their Aunt Charlotte's.

When he arrived at Charlotte's home it was very late, and he was both tired and hungry. His persistent knocking was finally answered by the disgruntled housekeeper, who resented being wakened in the small hours of the morning.

"Mr. Carrington," she said reprovingly, "it is rather late, sir."

"I know, Mrs. Tucker, and I'm dreadfully sorry. I'm looking for my sister."

"Miss Carrington has gone to bed hours ago, sir . . . as most civilized people have."

Seth was amused by her pointed remark. "I suppose Aunt Charlotte has been in bed for hours too."

"Absolutely."

"Who is it, Mrs. Tucker?" Charlotte's voice came from the top of the steps. Both Mrs. Tucker and Seth looked up in surprise. Mrs. Tucker spoke first.

"It's young Mr. Carrington, Mrs. McNeil."

"Seth," Charlotte called. "Come up here, boy,

at once."

Seth smiled apologetically at Mrs. Tucker, moved past her, and took the steps two at a time.

"Aunt Charlotte, I want to talk to Cat."

"Not before you've done some explaining, young man. It seems you've created a problem or two lately. Come to my room."

"But I've got to talk to Cat. It's important."

"Not," Charlotte said firmly, "until we talk."

She walked toward her room without looking back, thoroughly expecting him to follow. He did.

Inside her room, Charlotte turned to face him as soon as he closed the door behind him. He read her face quite accurately.

"Just how much has Cat told you?" he asked.

"Probably as much as she knows, but I'm sure not as much as you know."

"Then tell me what's happened."

Charlotte motioned him to a seat near her on a small settee. She explained what had transpired between Cat and Marc Copeland. Seth was enraged, but he sat quietly until Charlotte finished.

"She need not worry any longer, Aunt Charlotte. I intend to straighten this all out."

"What are you going to do?"

Seth slowly but firmly told her all, watching his aunt's face as he did. "So you see Aunt Charlotte, Copeland will not be a threat to Cat again. He won't be able to do her any harm . . . or me. Sweet revenge, Aunt Charlotte. He can keep the *Belle*. One way or another I'll make it up to Father, but either way it's over."

"I would say, young man, that you have grown somewhat in the past days."

"I have. I hope to change everything."

67

"When will you go and see this gentleman?"

"In the morning. I want to talk to Cat first though. I'll feel better if she knows she has nothing to worry about."

"Good. Now I suggest you get some sleep. You do look terrible."

"I may look it"—Seth laughed—"but I've never felt better. Can I have the old room I used to sleep in when I visited you?"

"You may."

Seth rose, kissed Charlotte's cheek and left. For some time Charlotte sat in deep thought. She had a strange feeling that the Carrington family had not seen the last of Marc Copeland. She was almost certain there was some threat behind all that had happened and it was not going to go away so easily.

She would have given anything to look into Marc Copeland's eyes. She made a decision rapidly as she always did. Then, smiling, she rose and prepared for bed.

Catalina struggled up from a vague dream whose substance she had been struggling to grasp. A firm and insistent knocking on her door had aroused her.

As she sat up the door opened and a refreshed and smiling Seth stuck his head into the room.

"I've been waiting for hours for you to wake up. I'm too impatient to wait any longer."

"Come on in."

He stepped inside and, closing the door, came to sit on the edge of her bed.

"You look pleased with yourself." She laughed. "What are you up to?"

"Taking care of problems I should have seen to a

long, long time ago."

"What are you talking about?"

"I've made some decisions, Cat."

"Decisions?"

"I'm taking hold of my own life," he said gently. "I'm going to Father. I'll face the music and then tell Marc Copeland he can go to hell, that he can't do any harm to us. Maybe we'll lose the *Belle,* but we're going to be all right."

"Oh, Seth." Catalina reached out to him and he put his arms around her. They hugged each other and laughed, certain this was the end of the influence Marc Copeland had over them.

"Travis gave me the money. I shall take it back to him and thank him for at least trying to stand with me," Catalina declared in a pleased voice.

"Good idea, and I'll go with you. I must thank him too. That would have been some sacrifice," Seth replied.

"I know. We both owe him our gratitude."

"Cat?"

"What?"

"You went to see Copeland?"

"Yes."

"What did he say?"

"He was crude and obnoxious, and it would give me the greatest pleasure to see his face when you tell him all his trouble has been for nothing."

"Did . . . did you get the feeling this was something"—he shrugged—"more personal than just wanting the *Belle?*"

"Come to think of it, Seth, I've had that impression, but I can't see what it could be. I have never met him, have you?"

"Not before this incident but . . . It's just a feeling."

69

"Well, let's forget it. We'll see Travis this afternoon and return his money. Then tonight you can meet with Copeland and finish this affair."

"Good. Now let's go down and join Aunt Charlotte for breakfast. You know"—he laughed—"she'll want to know everything we've been saying to each other."

"And she'll find out too, so we may as well just tell her. She has a way of getting what she wants."

"She's a lovely old girl, and I appreciate how much she cares for us."

"Let's go tell her so." Cat threw back the covers and rose. "Now get out while I dress. I'll be down in a few minutes."

During breakfast Charlotte watched Seth and Catalina tease each other and laugh. When she inquired about their immediate plans, they told her they were both on the way to see Travis at his hotel.

"I want to return the money to him and thank him as soon as possible," Catalina said.

"Then, after I bring Cat back from there, I'll go on down to the *Belle,*" Seth added. "But I'll wait until we've had dinner."

"What will you do next?" Charlotte asked.

"Then comes the hardest part," Seth admitted.

"Your father?"

"My father. This is going to hurt, but it has to be done."

"Your father is not an ogre, Seth."

"You say that because he's never been mad at you."

Charlotte laughed. "He will get over his anger," she declared gently, "but he will never get over the renewal of his pride in you. You deserve it."

70

"Thank you, Aunt Charlotte. That means a lot to me."

"Well, let's send for the carriage," Catalina said. "I'd like to get this money returned."

It was a little over a half-hour's ride from Charlotte's home to Travis's hotel, and Travis was more than surprised to find both Catalina and Seth at his door. His surprise turned to well-camouflaged anger when he learned the reason for their visit. He hid his disappointment, however, when Seth handed him the satchel.

"You mean he refused all this money?"

"Yes," Catalina replied. "He did."

"He wanted more?"

"He said I didn't have enough money to buy the *Belle*. I guess it's really the boat he was after to begin with."

"What are you going to do now, Seth?" Travis questioned.

"After dinner tonight I intend to pay him a visit. It's time he was taught a little lesson. Then Cat and I are going home. My father expects me to meet him with the *Belle* in Memphis. I will go there and tell him what's happened. Whatever comes of that, the problem is finished. Cat and I just wanted to thank you."

"Yes, Travis," Catalina added. "I appreciate what you tried to do. Even though we didn't use the money, you provided it and I'm grateful."

"Cat," Travis said gently, "you know there is not much that you could ask of me that I would not try to provide. Might I join you for dinner tonight? I would like to provide the champagne for the celebration."

"I'm sure Aunt Charlotte would be pleased," Seth said, unaware that Catalina's silence indicated that she would have preferred to end the relationship between herself and Travis.

"Good. What time shall I be there?"

"About seven-thirty. Aunt Charlotte is prompt."

"And I will be."

Seth and Catalina returned to Charlotte's home only to find that Charlotte had been driven into town. She had left a message which said she had some business with her banker and that she would return later in the afternoon.

Seth went to his room to lie down for some much-needed rest and Catalina went to hers, assuring Seth she had the same intention. But she did not touch her bed. Instead she went to the window and looked toward the docks, wondering if she truly had seen the last of Marc Copeland . . . and why she still couldn't wipe the ghost of his touch away.

Charlotte sat across the desk from a man she considered one of her dearest friends. He was influential in New Orleans, possessing more wealth than anyone in the city.

Charles Dante was approaching sixty, yet he had the grace of a man who has lived a full and active life. He was tall and retained a touch of his youthful handsomeness. His hair was still dark brown, and the streaks of white in it gave him a touch of distinction as did the full mustache he wore. His eyes were hazel and they glittered now with pleasure.

"Charlotte my dear, I swear time is a man and he's in love with you as every man in New Orleans was. He has been good to you."

"Ah, you are still the silver-tongued Charles." Charlotte laughed.

"I speak only the truth, my dear. Tell me, Charlotte, to what do I owe this pleasure?"

"Must I want something to visit you?"

"Some years ago I would have questioned that since you so enjoyed creating gossip. But today"—he chuckled—"you want something."

"Well, you're right, Charles. I do."

"What is it?"

"You know everyone and everything of importance in New Orleans. Have you heard of a young man named Marc Copeland?"

"Copeland . . . Copeland. The name rings a bell."

"You know him?"

"I'm not sure . . . seems I heard . . . isn't he the one who . . . ah—" His eyes glowed. "I've heard rumors that the *Belle* has changed owners. Could it be the exchange was not to everyone's liking?"

"Hardly."

"Want to tell me about it?"

"No," Charlotte replied with a smile, "but I want you to find out about young Marc Copeland . . . all about Marc Copeland. No matter how trivial you think the information might be. I want to know everything."

"And I'll do this for you without a question?" He laughed enthusiastically. "Tell me, Charlotte, how do you keep that sweet face when you're such a diabolical schemer?"

"I admire you too, Charles." Charlotte joined him in laughter. "And I shall buy you the very best dinner in town when you have the information."

"That, my dear, is a bargain I shall look forward to."

"Good. Now I must get back. My niece and nephew will be having dinner with me tonight." She put her hand on Charles's arm and looked up at him. "I'm grateful for your help. I really am. One day, when this little affair is over to our satisfaction, I'll explain it to you. I promise."

"That's good enough for me, Charlotte."

She nodded, patted his arm, and left.

When Charlotte arrived home she checked on the preparations for dinner, then went to her room to change.

The meal, when it was served, was exceptional. The crystal seemed to shine more brightly, the china to be more beautiful, the candlelight to glow more softly. And pleasure filled the hearts of those at the table. It came as a welcome surprise to Catalina that Travis did not appear with the promised champagne. She did not know his reason and did not care. His absence pleased her.

After they had eaten and had enjoyed their brandies, Seth rose from his chair.

"Well, I think I'd best get down to the docks. I'm impatient to see Mr. Copeland's reaction when I tell him that the Carringtons can still spit on him and his shady dealings."

"I wish you'd let me go with you, Seth," Catalina said. "After all this negotiation was really between him and me."

"After the things he suggested to you, do you think I'd let him even be in the same room with you again? Forget it, Cat. He's a blackguard and I don't intend to let his influence touch you again."

The two women sat together and listened to the door close. Both were aware that at least two hours would pass before Seth would return.

Seth went to the stables. At any other time he would

have had a carriage made ready, but tonight speed was more important, so he saddled a horse and rode toward the docks.

It had been many months since Seth had ridden with such assurance. For the first time in years he felt his life was on the right path. The route he chose took him along the river for some distance before it was possible to skirt the edge of town nearest the docks. The dirt road was deserted, and he rode quickly, still allowing himself the pleasure of enjoying the balmy breeze and the beauty of the moonlit star-studded night.

He was relaxed and totally unprepared for the sudden attack. Two men leapt from the shadows and dragged him from his horse. He fought them wildly, but they had weapons. They struck swiftly and violently, and he felt the pain of several blows before unconsciousness claimed him.

They stood over him then, and one took a wicked-bladed knife from his belt. He knelt on one knee and was about to plunge it into Seth's back when a voice spoke from the shadows.

"Don't stab him. Just toss his body into the Mississippi. She'll take care of him."

Travis stepped from the shadows and stood nearby. He watched as they lifted Seth's inert body and, swinging it between them, tossed it into the swift current of the river.

"Now," Travis stated, "that's one barrier out of the way. Keep an eye on the *Belle*. When Copeland leaves, make sure he follows his friend. I don't want any bodies found. As far as anyone will know, he has just disappeared. Make it the same with Copeland."

"Don't worry," one man replied gruffly. "Nobody will ever find a sign of them. We do our work well."

Travis took a small pouch from his pocket and

watched the men's eyes glow avariciously as he tossed it to them. By the time they opened it and took out the money, Travis had silently faded into the night.

He was pleased with himself. He would soon have a clear path to Catalina . . . all the barriers would have been washed away in the muddy waters of the river.

Chapter 6

As the hall clock chimed midnight Catalina and Charlotte paced the parlor floor. Both knew it was long past the time when Seth should have returned.

Charlotte watched Catalina closely, somehow knowing her niece was coming to a decision, and afraid that she knew what the decision was. What she didn't know, at the moment, was how she was going to prevent her from pursuing such a course.

She watched Catalina, knowing she was seeing her own younger self, and she felt a keen camaraderie with her niece, even though she could not show it without encouraging Catalina to do something extremely dangerous.

"Do sit down," she said. "You have been pacing that floor for hours and you make me nervous."

"Aunt Charlotte, Seth should have been back."

"Seth is a young man. He has probably stopped to share a drink with friends now that he's cleared his mind."

"Really, Aunt Charlotte, you don't believe that any more than I do. Something has happened."

"What could possibly happen? He was only going to

speak to the man. For heaven's sake, Cat, is this Copeland foolish enough to do something to Seth when he must realize Seth would be expected to return?"

"Marc Copeland is completely without scruples. He would most certainly try something. Good God, he might—"

"Come, Cat. It would be idiocy for him to hurt Seth."

"He's shrewd, and he might just think that would solve his problem." Catalina began to walk toward the door.

"Where are you going?"

"To find out what happened," she called over her shoulder. She dashed up the stairs as Charlotte rose and came to the bottom of the steps. In her room Catalina grabbed up her reticule. Then she went to a drawer and jerked it open. She ruffled through piles of lacy lingerie until her hand came to what she sought—a small single-shot derringer. She slipped the small gun into her bag and then ran from the room.

When she reached the bottom of the steps, Charlotte grasped her arm.

"Cat, you cannot do this!"

"But I can, Aunt Charlotte."

"One woman alone! What do you expect to accomplish?"

"To find out what happened."

"It's too dangerous. I won't let you go." Charlotte gripped her arm firmly. For a moment the two women looked at each other. Then slowly and deliberately Catalina's free hand loosened Charlotte's fingers.

"Don't try to stop me, Aunt Charlotte. I must find out what happened. Most likely, if Seth is still there, we will come home together."

"And if he's not?"

"Then Mr. Copeland had best have some answers. Aunt Charlotte"—Catalina's voice softened—"don't try to fool me. If you were in my place, you would do the same. I'll be careful."

"Cat, please . . ." Charlotte began, but Catalina was already moving toward the door. In a moment, it closed behind her.

Less than twenty minutes later Catalina was slapping the reins against the horse's rump to urge it to pull the buggy more rapidly through the streets.

Marc drained the last of his drink and set the glass aside. He was annoyed. Annoyed with himself and with the unwelcome thoughts he had tried energetically to put out of his mind.

He had been certain there would be much more of a reaction from Joseph Carrington, had expected something explosive by now. He knew the story of his taking the *Belle* was no longer a secret. He had had alterations started and that would show all of New Orleans he fully intended to make the famous *Southern Belle* into a floating palace of gambling and other delights. That alone should be enough to bring the old man howling, he thought.

His confrontation with Catalina was one thorn that pricked him, but he was determined. After all, a need for revenge was all he had. It was a point of honor that he see justice done.

What irritated him the most, however, was his loss of pleasure in Nina. He had used business as an excuse and had promised her a special night tomorrow, then had gone to his own cabin to try and clear his mind.

Nina was less than happy about this, but she knew

well that Marc was not a man to push.

Now he removed his boots and jacket, and unbuttoned his shirt cuffs. As he slowly unbuttoned his shirt he allowed his mind to touch on the elusive Catalina again. His tongue explored his lips as he vividly remembered the taste of hers and the feel of her body against his.

Forcefully he pushed her from his mind. The luxury of enjoying her was more than he could afford. He wanted to seduce her, then discard her. He wanted to use her, to hurt her, to make her pay her share of the price. For one by one he would destroy the Carringtons.

He threw the shirt aside and removed the rest of his clothes. Then he extinguished the lamp and went to his bunk. It had been a very eventful day, nonetheless sleep seemed to, purposely, elude him. It was replaced by the misty apparition of a slim defiant woman.

It was past midnight and he was sure the next day promised to be more interesting. Surely repercussions would begin. He smiled as he turned over to try to sleep. Maybe she would come again to beg . . . and she might realize she was in a position where she would have to meet his demands.

This thought was pleasant enough to hold, and he did, until he relaxed and slowly felt sleep approach.

Catalina stopped her carriage some distance from the boat. She pulled her dark cloak about her and made her way through the dark shadows to the *Belle*.

The boat was dark, but she found her way slowly, making no noise.

She was amused that he had so much confidence in his power that he had not even posted a guard.

Such arrogance, she thought. He needs to be taught that others are clever too—clever enough to stop him.

She stood outside his door and reached for the handle. Gripping it, she turned it slowly . . . so slowly. When it clicked softly, she laughed to herself. He had made his first foolish misstep. Very carefully she opened the door, just enough to slip inside and close it behind her.

She had to stand immobile for a minute because her heart was pounding, her mouth was dry, and she was shaking. Slowly she regained control of herself, and her mind returned to her ultimate goal.

Her eyes began to become accustomed to the darkness, and she could vaguely see his form on the bed.

She moved very slowly, setting her feet down carefully to keep her movements soundless.

One step . . . another . . . another. She held her breath as she came close to the bunk. Slowly she removed the gun from her bag and bent forward to nudge him into wakefulness.

But before she could touch him a hard muscular arm came around her, pinning her arms to her body, and a large hand covered her mouth. She tried to scream and fight but both attempts were futile. She was most thoroughly caught against a body that felt as solid as granite. To make it worse she heard a soft amused chuckle and then a deep seductive voice spoke near her ear.

Marc had heard the first sound made when she had turned the handle of the door. He had immediately thought an assassin had been sent. He'd slipped from the bed, covered his pillows to make it look as though someone was still sleeping. Then he had moved behind a nearby chair to wait.

When the dark cloaked figure had entered, he would have struck, had not the scent of her perfume told him immediately who this shrouded intruder was.

He had moved close behind her and just as she'd bent over the bunk he'd caught her against him with one arm and covered her mouth with his hand.

"And I thought it was going to be a lonely and uneventful night. Welcome aboard. It's about time you came to your senses. This promises to be a very warm night."

She struggled and sputtered in anger, but, behind his hand, all that came out was a muffled sound of resistance.

"I'm going to let you go, but before I do, let me warn you. No screaming, unless, of course"—he chuckled—"you want all of New Orleans to know you are here with me. Are you listening?"

She nodded.

"No screaming?"

Again she shook her head, this time negatively. He released her mouth slowly, almost expecting her to scream, but she remained silent. Then he turned her around to face him.

It was impossible to see his face, but she was sure of one very startling thing, he was naked.

"I'm going to light a lamp," he warned. "Don't think you can make it to the door before me. I know the cabin, you don't."

"I . . . I won't . . . only . . ."

"Only what?"

"Put on your clothes."

She heard his soft laughter, and her face burned with

a combination of embarrassment and pure rage.

"You come into my bedroom in the middle of the night so I can only believe you have more delightful ideas about entertaining me. Why should I bother to dress?"

She heard him moving about and then the clink of the glass chimney of a lamp. She squeezed her eyes shut as light flooded the room. Again she heard his tormentingly evil laugh. Cracking her eyes open slightly, she found him with one hip braced on the edge of his desk, his foot swinging indolently back and forth. He had put on his breeches, but that was all. The taunting smile on his lips and the glitter of laughter in his eyes incensed her even more.

"Now, my dear lady, can I attribute this nocturnal visit as a desire on your part to share my very willing favors?"

"You are damned arrogant!" She snapped. He was completely unprepared when she raised her hand from the folds of the cape and the small derringer pointed at him. "I could easily shoot that smile from your face."

His eyes became wary, but the smile remained. He did not move and appeared to totally disregard the gun.

"It wounds me to think you didn't come to share the night with me. I thought our mutual attraction was what had drawn you here."

"Mutual attraction," she spat out furiously. "I find you a disreputable rogue and I'd die before I let you touch me!"

"Then might I ask," his voice dripped with casual amusement, "why you disrupted some very pleasant dreams?"

"Where is my brother? What have you done

with him?"

This was the last thing Marc expected. He had been prepared for threats or vindictive anger.

"Your brother? The last time I saw him was across a card table."

"You're lying!"

Marc stiffened and his smile faded. His eyes took on a cold glint and he stood erect, causing Catalina to step back a step or two.

"I'm not in the habit of allowing people to call me a liar. I have not seen your brother."

"He left my aunt's home with the sole intent of coming here. That was just after dinner. Are you trying to convince me he never arrived?"

"I don't recall trying to convince you of anything. You're the one who came here remember?"

He had moved closer to her as he'd spoken and she had been so caught by the dark scowl and the breathless effect he was having on her that she hadn't realized how close he was until his hand whipped out and struck the gun from her grasp, sending it rattling across the floor. She gave a startled cry and started after the weapon. But he caught her wrist, and the force of his grip as he pulled, combined with the forward motion of her body, slammed her against his hard frame.

He then gripped her other wrist and pulled her arms behind her back. She was effectively caught against him.

"Let go of me, you brute," she demanded.

"Sorry, my dear, but I've a strong inclination toward self-preservation. Besides"—he laughed—"I much prefer the position we're in now."

She writhed and struggled, glaring at him furiously, but succeeded only in exhausting herself and becoming breathless in the process.

Besides the glow in his eyes had changed in its intensity as her body began to create havoc with his. His gaze now seemed to smolder as it moved over her. To Catalina, it felt like a physical caress.

"Stop staring at me and let me go." She tried to put more authority into her voice but she knew the attempt was less than effective.

"Are you by chance frightened of me . . . or of yourself?"

She looked up into his eyes and saw a smiling warmth there. A multitude of strange and unwelcome emotions came over her, but, to her surprise, fear was not one of them.

"I'm certainly not fool enough to think I can fight you physically. I suppose"—she held his eyes with a stubborn gaze—"I am somewhat at your mercy. I can only hope you might have developed some sense of honor since we first met. Or is rape not beyond you?"

His eyes sparked with anger, but his lips curved in a half-smile. He deliberately tightened his arms about her, and his voice was suggestively smooth.

"Are you so sure it would be rape . . . that you would not be more than willing?"

His loins pressed intimately against her, and despite her renewed rage she was aware of the hard masculinity of him.

She stiffened at the subtle humor in his voice.

"Tell me," he said with casual softness, "shall we put it to the test . . . or are you really afraid?"

The barb stung, for at this moment she was touched for the first time with a premonitional fear of something unknown.

It was as if he did not hear the storm in her words,

only the uncertainty. His eyes were heated now with a real need she could not help but understand.

He stood towering above her, tall and bronzed, and for a long moment there was a silence in which Catalina could hear her own heart begin to pound. Beneath his touch she had felt herself begin to tremble.

Her lips were parted and her breathing was ragged, then her eyes half closed as he bent his head. His parted lips found hers in a kiss that stirred something volatile in both of them, forging them together; and time seemed to hover, motionless, in this moment preordained like the blending of sand and sea.

It was enough to sap their resistance, this strong intoxicating nectar. His mouth savored hers with a growing urgency that was echoed in her as her mouth opened and her tongue flicked against his teasing, taunting . . . accepting. The heat of his kiss flooded her senses until a raging desire consumed the last of her will and she lost the reins of her self-control.

The awakening pleasure deep within her was strong with the promise of fulfillment of the hunger that seemed to ravage her. Warm strong fingers expertly loosened and discarded clothing, and she watched with half-closed eyes as if she were not a participant but an onlooker. She was mesmerized by the glistening bronze of his body as he lifted her in his arms and carried her to his bed.

All her resistance and strength were sapped as he enclosed her in a strong embrace and his open mouth took hers again. She found herself molding to his frame and moaning softly under the expert touch of gentle hands. She forgot all her darkest intentions as his lips brushed her hair, her cheek, and then nipped lightly at her ear. She closed her eyes as his searing lips traced her throat and shoulders.

86

Slowly, tenderly, he leisurely aroused her, stroking her breasts and then her belly. She was filled with a warm tingling excitement.

The kisses, begun gently, turned savage and fierce as their mouths slanted across each other in mutual impatience. His lips, hot and wet, seared her breasts, and his teeth lightly nibbled the soft flesh of her belly.

She gasped, panting, breathless and pliable beneath his caresses as time seemed to hover on the brink of eternity.

Marc was unaware yet that all his grim intentions were floundering like sandy rock beneath the raging waves of an angry sea.

He had tried to hold his passion in control, wanting to use it to batter her pride when it was over, to reduce her will to ashes, but he was caught in his own trap. His body was afire as it had never been and he was sinking in the scented beauty of her.

His eyes were aflame as he lowered his weight upon her, parting her thighs, and, the sound of her rapturous sigh echoing in his ears, pressed himself deep within her.

An indescribably beautiful expanding bloom of joyous pleasure sent a splintering feeling pulsing through her. She arched against him with a fierce passion that matched his, and a wild ecstasy surged through them fusing them. They moved together as one, the thunderous beats of their hearts blending in a drumming tempo. Both had lost touch with reality, and their world careened crazily beneath rhythmic strokes. With fierce naked abandon they possessed each other, spiraling up to breathless heights and then tumbling into the oblivion of completion.

For a long moment they clung to each other as if

caught in a deep trance, neither wanting to break the spell, knowing already what lay beyond it. But the sweet taste of passion turned bitter in both as reality intruded mercilessly.

Catalina was struck by disbelief and dismay. His words had been true. There was no way she could say rape when she knew how willingly she had succumbed to his touch. She closed her eyes and wept at her body's betrayal.

Marc looked upon himself condemningly as well. He could not let the soft touch of the woman in his arms destroy all his well-laid plans. His every sense urged him to take and hold this fragile offering of something rare and valuable while his mind resisted these leanings. He had planned too long, hated too long, to let go so easily.

In a moment, that caused him more struggle and frustration than he could ever admit to her, he donned his armor of self-defense and the eyes he raised to hers were filled with all the assurance and self-control he could manage. He smiled, a knowledgeable I-told-you-so smile that struck her like a physical blow.

She gasped and closed her eyes, turning her head away as if she could deny the reality of what had happened. But her body would not deny the feel of his hard body.

"Let me go," she whispered raggedly.

"Running away again?" he chided. "Why not just face the truth of what you want?"

She choked on the anger slowly boiling to the surface. It filled her like a brilliant and painful explosion.

"If this is a sample"—he laughed—"in a few weeks I might just be willing to turn the *Belle* back over to your brother."

"Damn you! I didn't come here to sell myself to you. I came to find Seth!"

"You needn't cling to that story anymore." He chuckled. "It was a good excuse to come, but we both know this was the real reason. Now that we're done with the excuses and the preliminaries"—his voice lowered and his eyes gleamed suggestively—"we can concentrate on the pleasures we've only just tasted."

"You are a vile-minded person!" she shrieked, and doubling her fists, she pushed against his chest. "I would like to leave," she grated as coldly as she could manage, considering her body was forming arguments she refused to acknowledge.

"Why leave so soon?" he questioned, a touch of teasing humor in his voice. "It's a long and beautiful night and I have something . . . you want. Who knows"—he shrugged—"maybe one night would be enough to get what you want."

"You know where my brother is?" she cried triumphantly.

"No. I told you I don't, but I still have the *Belle*."

Now it was her chance to turn the tables and bring to an end any hold he had on Seth or on her.

"You have the *Belle* . . . and you may keep her. Neither Seth nor I will give you any hold over us. Keep the boat and know that you have failed in whatever it was you tried to do."

He was taken by surprise upon seeing her assured hold over herself and the glow of satisfaction in her eyes. He had misjudged her strength. But it was a mistake he would never make again.

In a quicksilver move she escaped his hold and leapt from the bunk snatching at her clothes. She dressed in haste, refusing to acknowledge his presence as if he were no longer of any account. Then she flung her cloak about her and nearly ran from the cabin, slamming the door behind her.

Marc rose from the bunk and walked to a corner to retrieve the derringer. He picked it up and looked at it. Then he smiled and tossed it into his desk drawer.

"We're not finished yet Catalina Carrington. Oh no . . . we're not finished yet."

Chapter 7

Catalina pulled her cloak about her. Her body shook with the effort it took to control her fury and the strange inexplicable pulse that beat through her body like a resounding hammer.

She could not explain to herself the deception of her body. How had she let him reach a place she had shared with no man before. She bit her lip and closed her eyes letting the tears she had held in for so long score her cheeks with hot rivulets.

Damn him! Damn him! How could she have let this happen? And why could she not force the memory of those moments from her mind, erase the feel of his touch when he had possessed her . . . first with gentleness, then with wild sensuous pleasure.

As she stepped out of the carriage she pulled the hood of her cloak over her head. She wanted no one to see the tangled profusion of her hair. She had tried to compose herself as best she could, angrily wiping the tears from her face. The last thing she needed now was the multitude of questions she knew she would face from her aunt. Charlotte would be more than difficult to fool. It would be best, Catalina decided, to get to her room before her aunt knew she was home.

She gave orders that the carriage and horse were to be cared for as silently as possible. Then, taking the back steps, she breathed a sigh of relief when she had safely climbed the dark stairway and closed her bedroom door behind her.

She poured some cool water from the pitcher into the bowl on her wash stand. Then she stripped off her clothes and vigorously washed her face and her body as if she could wash away Marc Copeland's touch.

But the tingling warmth of his caresses remained on her flesh and in her mind. She put on her nightgown and robe, then brushed her hair free of tangles.

She knew she wouldn't be able to sleep. She gazed at her bed for several moments, then decided against making the attempt. Instead she made her way down the stairs to the empty kitchen, hoping a cup of steaming tea would calm her nerves.

She had just put the kettle on when her aunt's voice came from the doorway.

"Well, it's about time you're back. I've been waiting for hours. Did you find Seth?"

"Mr. Copeland said Seth never arrived there."

"You believed him?"

"He was lying through his teeth."

"Did it take you this long to learn Seth wasn't there?"

"I tried to . . . talk Mr. Copeland into telling me the truth. It was useless. He is an unmitigated scoundrel. Oh, Aunt Charlotte, I'm so frightened for Seth. What do you think could have happened?"

"Maybe we are jumping to conclusions. Could the man have been telling the truth? Seth might have changed his plans when he left here."

"I told Mr. Copeland that we no longer cared whether he had stolen the *Belle* or not. That neither Seth nor I intended to let him use it to bully us into anything."

"I imagine he was not too impressed with that."

"He was . . . upset," Catalina answered thoughtfully.

Charlotte had not failed to note Catalina's condition. Her niece was tense and upset, and the look in her eyes was one Charlotte had never seen in them before.

Catalina paced about like a caged tigress, twisting her hands together and trying unsuccessfully to control emotions she had not tasted before. Charlotte listened, allowing her to talk some of her tension away. Then she urged her to drink her tea and try to get some sleep. But she herself was already making a plan of her own, a plan whose first step entailed seeing and talking to Marc Copeland.

Charlotte tiptoed into Catalina's room just after eight in the morning to make certain that Catalina still slept. She had no intention of waking her. Charlotte's plans did not include Catalina.

Her carriage awaited her, and when she sat back in it, she contemplated what she would say to this rogue who had so disrupted Catalina's life.

Marc had just toweled himself dry and was putting on his pants when Charlotte's presence was announced.

"A Madame Charlotte McNeil, sir."

"Charlotte McNeil," Marc said. "Do I know her, Tom?"

"She's related to the man who once owned this boat," he replied.

Marc lifted his white shirt from the bed and shrugged into it. As he buttoned it he smiled at the young man who had delivered the message.

"I'm curious about what she might want. Either she'll be shouting for my head for last night's delightful crime or the young lady has kept her silence and this is a social visit. Bring the lady to me and then ask China to join me." China's opinion of all new acquaintances was very important to Marc.

"Aye, sir."

In a few minutes Charlotte appeared in the doorway. She was a woman who commanded respect no matter where she was, and Marc could feel the magnetism of her presence when she stepped through the door.

He rose from his chair and walked to her side.

"Good morning, Mrs. McNeil. To what do I owe the pleasure of this early morning visit?"

Charlotte eyed Marc speculatively, a half-smile on her lips and a sparkle of amusement in her eyes. She had been touched by a faint wisp of memory, yet she could not grasp it. He seemed familiar, and she wondered if she could have seen such a dashingly handsome young man and forgotten him. It was very unlikely for since the age of sixteen Charlotte had had an eye for handsome young men . . . and she never forgot them as they never forgot her.

"It is Miss McNeil, Mr. Copeland . . . by choice not by chance."

"Miss McNeil. Have we met before?"

"I don't believe we have."

"Then I don't understand why you want to speak to me."

"I am Catalina Carrington's aunt," Charlotte said, watching his face closely. She saw recognition leap into his eyes, and despite his effort at control Charlotte saw much much more.

"Ah," Marc said softly, "the lovely Catalina. And how is my lady now?" Marc would have loved to know just how much Charlotte knew about last night. Had Catalina run to her aunt in tears to accuse him?

"I don't believe"—Charlotte chuckled—"that Cata-

94

lina is in any way your lady, Mr. Copeland. In fact, I do believe she is most upset with you. Why did you not tell her last night where her brother had gone?"

"Because I didn't know. I told her that, but I think the lady chose not to believe me. Won't you come in and sit down? I was about to have breakfast. Would you like something?"

"Some tea please."

"Of course." Marc went to the door and snapped out an order. Then he returned to sit opposite Charlotte. But before he could speak again the door opened and China entered.

If Charlotte was surprised by her presence, only a slight widening of her eyes betrayed it. She found China exceedingly beautiful, but she wondered about the nature of her connection to Marc Copeland.

"China"—Charlotte could hear the gentleness in Marc's voice—"come and have breakfast with us. My guest is Miss Charlotte McNeil. She"—he said calmly—"is the aunt of Catalina Carrington."

"Good morning, Miss McNeil," China said softly.

"Good morning," Charlotte answered.

China sat close to Charlotte, who could smell the delicate scent of her perfume.

"Now, Miss McNeil," Marc said, "I doubt if you came here to share breakfast. You have something to say to me?"

"You are quite certain we have not met, Mr. Copeland? Your face is so very familiar."

Did she see one moment of shock, one spark of fear in his eyes for that breathless second?

"No . . . as far as I know," Marc responded honestly, "we have never met."

"Oh, well," Charlotte said briskly, "I will remember. My memory is quite good. Maybe I knew someone who looked like you. Though"—she laughed softly—

"there are not many men as handsome."

"Thank you." Marc chuckled. If Charlotte were not one of the enemy he had a feeling they might have become friends.

"Mr. Copeland . . ."

"Marc." Marc grinned.

"Marc," Charlotte repeated. "I will come to the point. I have only two questions. What has become of my nephew Seth? And what happened between you and my niece last night?"

"What has she told you?" Marc questioned carefully.

"Nothing, which is why I suspect a great deal happened."

"It's of no importance whether you or she believe me or not. But her brother was not on this boat last night, and I have not seen him since the card game in which I won the boat."

"And last night?" Charlotte asked quietly.

"As your niece said," Marc replied, "nothing happened. She wanted her brother, he was not here . . . she left."

"That easily?"

"That easily."

Charlotte laughed softly and Marc chuckled.

"Obviously you do not know my niece very well."

"No. Actually last night was only the third time our paths crossed."

"I see."

"What do you see?"

"That my niece might be correct about you."

"Oh, in what way?"

"That you are a very unscrupulous young man. Tell me, Marc Copeland . . . is that your real name . . . and what is it you want from my family?"

Marc shrugged. "That," he said softly, "is not between you and me but between me and Catalina."

Charlotte rose, her smile intact and her voice unruffled and cool.

"We shall see what you are about, Mr. Copeland. We shall see." She swept from the room with the regal bearing of an empress.

When the door closed behind her, Marc whistled softly. "That is a formidable lady. It's like having an audience with the queen of England. I had a feeling she was looking right through me."

"I agree," China said. "Marc, I wonder why she expected to find her nephew here. Have you really not seen him?"

"Not since the game. I don't understand that either."

"And the girl?" China said softly.

"She was here."

"Last night?" China questioned. She was at first surprised, then amused that she was witnessing the first time in their relationship that Marc refused to meet her eyes.

"Yes, last night. She tried to shoot me."

"I heard nothing."

"The gun was never fired." He reached into a drawer in a small table nearby, took out the gun, and placed it on the table.

"So she just changed her mind about shooting you?"

"No," Marc said reluctantly. "I changed it for her."

"I see," China spoke very softly.

"No you don't, China." He shook his head negatively. "And don't go jumping to any conclusions. She tried to kill me, I took the gun from her . . . and sent her on her way. It changes nothing . . . nothing at all."

"I see."

"China, quit saying I see like you're looking into a crystal ball."

China laughed. But her astute gaze had read much more in Marc than he wanted to reveal.

"What do you plan now?"

"To go on with the work on the boat. I want her ready as soon as possible. It's time we slapped the Carringtons on the other cheek."

"All right."

"And," Marc said quietly, "send a few men out to scout around the city. I've got a strong suspicion we'd better find out just what did happen to Seth Carrington. If he's not with his family and he's not here, then I'd like to know just where the hell he is."

"You worried about him for his sister's sake?"

"No. I told you China, they're all going to pay their own price so I don't want him slipping through my fingers." He added quickly, "Don't say I see."

"I'll go and tell the men to start a discreet search," she responded.

"Good girl."

"When do you want the boat to be ready to leave?"

"By late tonight. If Seth Carrington is in the city find him, but I want everything else on the move."

"By the time the sun sets we'll be leaving," China declared. "Is there anything else?"

"No."

"Marc?"

"What?"

"I ran across Nina and Charlene chatting together in a very friendly manner on my way here."

"So?"

"For a man who thinks he understands women so well you don't see anything odd about two women who dislike and distrust each other as much as those two suddenly becoming so friendly?"

"I don't see what their friendship, or the lack of it, has to do with anything."

"You've put Nina out of your bed?" she asked quickly.

"For Christ's sake, China! What do my sleeping

arrangements have to do with this?" His anger was rising. "Aren't you nosing just a little too deep?"

"Marc, Nina can be dangerous, and Charlene even more so. Charlene is ambitious, and as for Nina . . . a spurned woman can be more than dangerous. Nina doesn't know all the facts, but she's clever and not beyond seeking revenge. She's in love with you, Marc. Be careful."

"I'll keep your warning in mind." Marc smiled. "China, you worry about me like a mother hen with only one chick. I'm a grown man. I can take care of myself."

"You are so set on one goal sometimes you do not see all that you should. I have only suggested you keep an eye on Nina. If she is no longer welcome in your bed, why do you not rid yourself of her?"

Marc made a soft sound of irritation. "China, Nina is not your problem. Suppose we get busy with more important things."

China nodded, bowed slightly from the waist, and turned to leave.

"China," Marc said softly. She turned back to look at him and he added, "I'll keep your words in mind, and thanks for worrying about me."

China smiled, then left, and Marc slowly sat down in his chair.

He hadn't thought of Nina for days. Maybe he should listen to China, he thought, but he needed someone now, someone to help him erase the soft scent and the warm lips of the elusive Catalina Carrington.

One way or another he would wipe Catalina from his senses, he would drown his thoughts of her in the arms of other women. No matter what his senses told him he knew that for him Catalina Carrington was the most dangerous woman of all.

* * *

Charlotte made several stops on her way to her planned visit with Charles Dante, stops to see remarkable people who would not, in the minds of her society friends, be persons the illustrious Charlotte McNeil would know.

All these stops were made for the same purpose. Slowly she spread a web across the city, created a network to find out who Marc Copeland really was. For in the back of her mind she was sure she had seen or known him. Ordinarily blessed with a good memory, she was annoyed that she could not put his face and a name together.

It was well after one in the afternoon when she again called on Charles, who welcomed her with warm enthusiasm.

"Charlotte my dear, two visits in just days. Could I hope that you have developed a fondness for my company?"

"I have always been fond of you, you scoundrel." Charlotte laughed.

"Then have dinner with me tonight."

"I might consider doing that if you can provide me with my answers."

"It's too soon for me to have found out anything. This Marc Copeland seems to have something to hide. His past just vanishes. He's a very elusive character."

"I thought he might be."

"Have you had lunch yet, Charlotte?"

"No, I haven't."

"Then share my lonely lunch with me."

"I'd be delighted."

Charlotte accompanied Charles to one of New Orleans most elegant restaurants, where they were greeted graciously. Seeing two such eminent citizens together sent a ripple of excitement through the other luncheon guests.

After they were seated and Charlotte had endured all she could stand of the nearly overwhelming maître d', they ordered and exchanged superficial conversation until the food was brought and they felt they enjoyed some semblance of privacy.

"Now, Charles, suppose you tell me what you have found so far."

"I told you, Charlotte, most of the people I have looking into his background have not yet brought me any information. The others have learned little more than what we already know."

"Which is?"

"He has a signed deed to the *Belle*. He has deposited a great deal of money in the bank, and he plans to turn the *Belle* into one of the most elaborate gambling casinos on the river. He has even acquired all the . . . ah . . . luxuries any man could ever expect to find."

"The word is *whores,* Charles . . . *whores.* And you mean he's hired a few beautiful and well-accomplished whores to ply their trade aboard the *Belle,*" Charlotte said in well-controlled rage. "The *Belle,* one of the most beautiful and well-known boats on the river!"

"Well at least you're blunt." Charles smiled. He was never surprised at what he heard from Charlotte's mouth. She is the only lady, he thought, in high New Orleans society who bluntly calls a whore a whore.

"He has a purpose, Charles. I know it, I can feel it. He is unscrupulous, and I've a feeling his purpose is directed at one goal. I want to know what that goal is before any more harm befalls my family."

"Maybe, Charlotte," Charles said gently, "if you were to trust me more and tell me all that has happened, I might be able to get some answers sooner. Don't you think it's time you laid all your cards on the table?"

Charlotte held his eyes with an intense look, and Charles had the very uncomfortable feeling she was reading his soul. But he knew if he did not return her steady gaze he would never get another word of explanation from her.

"All right," she said quietly. "I'll tell you all I know for certain . . . and what I suspect."

Charles breathed a sigh of relief. It seemed she had allowed him to take a step closer to her.

In a dignified and quiet voice Charlotte explained all that had occurred. Charles did not interrupt until she was completely finished.

"Charlotte, I want you to know I am honored by your confidence. No word of what you have said to me shall pass my lips. I will do everything, move every mountain, to find out just who this man is and what devious plot he has in mind. In the meantime I would like you to get Catalina to stay as far away from him as she can."

"One does not tell Cat what she can or cannot do. She rises to a challenge like a gladiator. I'm afraid my words of warning will only serve to make her angrier."

"She can be angry so long as she stays out of his reach until we can find some answers and some proof."

"She went to see him last night."

"How foolish!"

"I couldn't stop her. I have no idea what time she came home. I fell asleep on the settee in front of the fireplace and she must have thought I was in bed. After a while I woke and heard her in the kitchen. We shared a few confidences over a cup of tea, but I know no more about her visit to Marc Copeland last night than I knew yesterday. She was still asleep when I left this morning."

"Find out what happened if you can, but for God's sake keep her at home. I have a feeling this man doesn't possess a sense of honor."

"I will most certainly do my best, Charles."

"Good. Now that that is settled, where would you like to have dinner tonight, and what time should I call for you?"

The balance of their lunch was relaxed and filled with laughter. When Charles waved goodbye and watched her carriage roll away he was more than pleased.

Charlotte arrived home only to find that Catalina had gone out to have lunch with Travis. She waited patiently, but Catalina did not return before it was time for Charlotte to dress for her dinner engagement with Charles.

Oh, well. She is with Travis now, so Marc Copeland is not involved, Charlotte thought. I shall speak with her when I return.

She went to join Charles, not knowing that it would be a very long time before she saw Catalina again and that their lives would have changed drastically before she did.

Chapter 8

Travis sat across the table from Catalina in a small but excellent restaurant. He had had to coax her into lunching with him because she had been caught up in worry over Seth's sudden disappearance and even over her aunt's absence.

"It will do you good to get out of this house for an hour or two, Cat."

"But Aunt Charlotte—"

"Is probably having a good lunch with a friend."

"All right," she agreed.

Now, as they sat opposite each other, questions bubbled from Catalina. It seemed that she felt if she could voice her worries, she could find answers to them.

"Where could he have gone, Travis? He left our house with one destination in mind. I can't believe that he never got there."

"Most likely he did, and Marc Copeland is lying to you for some reason."

"But why? Why?"

"I don't know. I have some men out searching the city. If he's in it, we'll find him."

"God, Travis, he might be hurt somewhere. He might need us desperately."

"Cat, don't get so upset. I'll find him for you."

He reached across the table and took her trembling hand in his.

"There's a lot of other news I have to tell you."

"What?" she said. Her brow furrowed as if she knew what he was going to say was something she didn't want to hear.

"It's about Marc Copeland and the *Belle*."

"What more can he do? The boat is his."

"He's turned it into a gambler's heaven and plans to go up and down the river with it. He has made a point of not changing her name. That means he's deliberately making her a scandal to strike out at the Carringtons."

"He is an atrocious man. If my father hears of this he will be shamed. It will make any redemption for Seth impossible."

"I want you to consider something, Cat."

"What?"

"It might be dangerous and I wouldn't blame you if you refused."

"What is it? I'll do whatever is necessary."

"He's taking the *Belle* out late tonight."

"We can't stop him."

"No . . . but I think we should be passengers on her when she leaves."

"That's impossible!"

"Think about this, Cat. If Seth is nowhere in the city, he might just be aboard the *Belle*."

"Why?"

"So he could be gotten away from here and disposed of in a safer place. Or Copeland might be wanting more from the Carringtons and Seth might be his hold on your family."

"What else could he want?"

"Ransom," Travis said bluntly. "Your father might be angry, but what would he—or you or your aunt—pay to get Seth back?"

"Anything," she whispered, her eyes widening with the realization.

"I think it would be clever on our part—and it would spoil any plans he might have—if we were passengers on the *Belle* when it left."

"He would never let us aboard."

"I will have someone else book our staterooms. We will arrive at the last minute. Outside of admitting his reasons he can't stop us."

"I . . . I don't know," she began hesitantly.

"Think of it, Cat. We will watch carefully. If Seth is aboard, we will find him."

"I would like to talk to Aunt Charlotte."

"She is a cautious woman, and the trip would be hard for her. If she talks you out of it, your brother might be lost."

Travis was the only one who knew Seth was not on the *Belle,* but he wanted Catalina away from New Orleans and the protection of her aunt. He wanted her where he could seduce her with gentle carefulness. Her hatred of Marc Copeland would certainly preclude that man from coming to her rescue, and he would easily be able to convince Copeland that Catalina was his willing mistress. That should fan the embers of distrust between those two.

"Maybe you're right. Aunt Charlotte would never let me go alone. But I must find out if Seth is there . . . if he's alive. When does the boat leave?"

"Late tonight." Travis could hardly keep the elation from his voice. Catalina was walking into his well-laid trap. By this time next week, having used every ounce of leverage he had, he would have Catalina in his bed. After that, she would be forced to marry him. Society would brand her, and her life would be a disaster if she refused. The Carrington line was as good as his.

"Travis, please take me home. I must think."

106

"Do that, Cat, but remember your brother's life is at stake. If you decide to go, just pack a few things and come to me. In the meantime I'll have two staterooms purchased in case you decide to go."

The carriage ride back to her aunt's home was a troubled one, for Catalina was totally immersed in the fact that if she didn't grasp this opportunity, Seth might pay for her lack of courage with his life. She thought bitterly of Marc Copeland and his cold way of taking everything he wanted despite what hurt he caused anyone else. Maybe, if she did go, she might find some way to strike back at him.

Travis dropped Catalina off at her aunt's home, but he was certain he would see her soon. He had known her too long not to realize that if she had an opportunity to help her brother she would take it. He then went directly to the *Belle*. His request to talk to Copeland brought quick action, and he was taken to Marc's quarters.

Hiding his curiosity well, Marc sat back in his chair, displaying an attitude of disinterested nonchalance. He knew quite well what Travis was. He just couldn't figure out a legitimate reason for Travis's wanting to talk to him.

"Sit down, Travis. Would you like a drink?"

"No, thank you. What I would really like is to discuss something . . . ah . . . personal with you."

"Personal?" Marc questioned. He couldn't pin down the feeling he had, but he was suspicious.

"Yes. You're taking the *Belle* upriver tonight?"

"I am. I wasn't aware that too many people knew about that yet."

"Well, I would like to ask about the possibility of securing passage upriver for two."

"Passage can be arranged, but the *Belle* is not really a passenger boat."

"I know. That's why I wanted to book the trip on her. I want it to be discreet."

"Discreet," Marc echoed. Then he smiled. Obviously Travis had a mistress with whom he wanted to share time, but he wanted very few people to know that. Most likely a lady with a good reputation she didn't want to tarnish. "All right. What do you require?"

"Two rooms."

"Two?"

"Yes." Travis smiled. "With an adjoining door between of course."

"Of course." Marc chuckled. "One is for you, I presume?"

"It is."

"And what name will I put down for the other?"

"Catalina Carrington," Travis said softly, watching Marc's eyes for any sign of what he thought.

There was none, but only because Marc made an almost superhuman effort to control the rage that went through him. He had no right to be angry, but that made no difference in him. He suppressed a distinct urge to pound the pleased smile on Travis's face to a bloody pulp.

He should have known. Catalina Carrington was as much like her father as her brother was. He had been a fool to harbor thoughts of her that were almost romantic. She was a Carrington. They were all alike. He had come close to making a mistake, but he'd be damned careful not to trust her pretty face and enticing body again. Whatever happened now, Catalina Carrington would get what she so justly deserved.

"Two rooms, adjoining doors," Marc confirmed in a casual voice that disappointed Travis.

"If you want to be even more discreet, I will post them in the books under assumed names." He grinned knowingly at Travis. "No one need ever know you shared a . . . trip with Miss Carrington."

"Ah, a wise idea, a very wise idea."

"When will you board?"

"What time do you leave?"

"Just after midnight."

"We'll be here a few minutes before."

"I'll make sure your boarding is unobserved."

"I won't forget this, and Cat will be grateful too. I'm sure she'll find a way to tell you."

Marc smiled. "Maybe," he added softly, "I can find some way for Miss Carrington to express her gratitude."

Travis nodded and left Marc's quarters. By the time the door had closed behind him Marc's smile had faded.

"So Catalina Carrington wants to play, does she? Well"—his chuckle was less than humorous—"maybe I had best join the game."

Catalina wanted to tell Charlotte what had occurred, but the time was rapidly slipping away and her aunt had not returned. When it grew too late for her to put off the choice any longer, she hurriedly threw some clothes into a satchel and took her cloak from the closet.

She then sent a shocked servant for her carriage. As it careened through the damp night streets, Catalina smothered all her misgivings in the hope that this hasty journey would lead to her brother's rescue.

Travis waited in his room at the hotel, his feet propped up and a glass of brandy in his hand. Assurance kept a smile on his face, but he watched the clock as it ticked away the time.

She would be here, he knew it as surely as he knew the sun would rise. He was so certain of it that he had already packed some clothes and set his satchel near the door.

Eleven-thirty. But his confidence remained unshaken. A satisfied smile twitched his lips when he heard a slight rap on his door. He went to it and opened it.

"I kept my carriage below," Catalina said quickly. "We must hurry. It is still aways to the docks and time is growing short."

"Good. Let's go."

He picked up his satchel, and they rapidly left the hotel and entered her carriage.

Marc stood alone on the deck of the *Belle*. From the depths of the shadows he watched the carriage roll to a halt. Travis climbed out, then turned to help the heavily cloaked and hooded Catalina descend.

Marc clenched his teeth to keep from cursing, and the muscle in his jaw twitched. With almost silent steps he moved toward the top of the gangplank just in time to take Catalina's hand as she stepped onto the deck. It was jerked from his almost at once.

The cloak covered her from head to foot, and its hood was pulled forward until her face could not be seen.

But without seeing her Marc knew her by the heady scent of her perfume. He trembled momentarily at feeling her cool hand in his.

"Welcome aboard, Lady Carrington," he said softly, and heard the muffled sound of her indrawn breath.

"You have the lady's stateroom ready?" Travis said in a firm commanding voice.

Marc clenched his hand into a fist and held himself in

110

restraint, but his urge to strike Travis was difficult to control. Catalina had not said a word, but she watched the confrontation.

"It's ready . . . and yours is ready as well. You might hurry a bit now, we're ready to cast off."

Travis passed Marc and started below, but as Catalina began to move by him he reached out to grip her arm.

"This was a very foolish move, Lady Carrington." She jerked her arm from his grip, but did not move past him. Then she spoke softly.

"Does it trouble you that I'm aboard?"

"Trouble me." He chuckled. "I will welcome you aboard as warmly as I did the last time you paid me a visit."

She gasped in shock at this whispered attack and at the arrogant way he had reminded her of the last time she had confronted him on the *Belle*.

"You are a filthy scoundrel," she spat out.

"Why must you always put the blame on me, dear lady?" he taunted. "Each time it's you who come to me, not I to you."

"I am a passenger to you and a passenger only. If you try one trick I shall kill you."

"I do not think it's my trickery you have to worry about," he retorted. "I have a feeling you're two of a kind and your little rendezvous is just typical of the way the Carringtons do as they choose. Well, my lady, have your fun. I wouldn't intrude on it if you begged me."

She swept past him, barely controlling the urge to commit murder, and Marc watched her fade into the darkness with Travis beside her.

Why had she chosen to book passage on his boat when their mutual dislike and distrust of each other was so strong? Something beyond a tryst with a lover had brought her here. He knew Travis too well to believe the adjoining door would be any barrier. But he took a firm hold on himself, though he was aware of the unwelcome feeling that she would need some kind of protection.

This situation could only be a help when he decided on the final blow that would crush the Carringtons. Catalina would be stripped of her pride when word spread of her involvement with Travis and of their romantic little assignation on this boat. The tryst was a tool for her destruction, he thought angrily, and she had willingly given it to him.

He went to his own quarters and poured himself a liberal drink of whiskey.

After a while, he felt the slow movement of the boat and knew he had started a journey that would, at the very least, prove interesting. At best it would prove to be a satisfactory link in his plans. He was pleased, wasn't he? But the bottle, as the night wore on, grew emptier and emptier.

Catalina and Travis walked down the hall to their staterooms. If she noticed that they were side by side, she did not remark upon it.

"I imagine they will be departing at any moment," Travis said. "I suggest you get some sleep. Tomorrow will be difficult. He is clever and dangerous. One slip and he will know why we are here. Then, any chance of finding your brother will be lost."

"I am tired," Catalina responded. What she refused to acknowledge, even to herself, was that her very nerves were strumming a song she had no intention of listening to. She was here for a purpose and she meant to carry it out. Once she found her brother and ruined whatever plan Marc had, she would see what other steps might be taken to bring the man to some kind of justice.

"I'm grateful for what you have done for me, Travis. I could never have gotten on this boat alone."

"You would not have been safe if you had. Remember, Cat, the Carrington fortune lies in your brother's hands and yours. If Copeland ever gets total control over both of you, I hate to think of what he might do. And don't forget, I'm right here—right next to you should you need me."

"I'll remember, Travis . . . and thank you again."

"Good night, Cat," he said gently.

"Good night."

He stood too close and she suddenly became uncomfortable. Had she bitten off more than she could handle? She was on her own with two men she could not trust. She opened her door and stepped inside quickly, closing it and sliding the bolt home almost in one motion.

After setting her satchel on the bed, Catalina turned to look about the room while she removed her cloak. It was then her hands stilled for she had seen the door that adjoined her stateroom and Travis's.

The bolt was unlocked. Did he expect her to leave it so? Would he test the door, and if it was open, would he think he was welcome?

She almost ran across the room and slid the bolt into a locked position.

Travis stood on the other side of the door and he heard the bolt slide. He smiled to himself and began to remove his clothes. Tonight he would have most excellent dreams.

"In time, my dear Cat, in time you will find that bolt will not be enough to keep this door closed between us," he said softly.

Within moments, Catalina lay in her bed listening to the swish of the water beneath the boat as they moved

113

slowly upriver. For the first time in her life she was frightened, but she refused to let it weaken her resolve.

Had Travis deliberately taken rooms with an adjoining door because he believed she would open it and welcome him? If so, he would be more than disappointed.

She wished for the small derringer her brother had given her, only to be assailed with the memory of where it was and how it had gotten there.

Time and the river both flowed on at a slow steady pace. Yet Catalina was restless, and despite her efforts she couldn't sleep.

She rose and put on her robe and went to the window. Her stateroom being dark, she could see the moonlit river clearly. Beyond it was the darker line of trees. She felt confined and very much alone. Her fears for Seth were predominant, bringing visions of him hurt or worse . . . dead. What did Marc Copeland know of Seth's disappearance? she wondered. How far did his guilt in this situation extend? She would like to tear the truth from him. His denial had to be a lie. Who else would have harmed Seth? Only Marc had the answer, and she had to find a way to get behind the shield of arrogant assurance he wore. She had to find it. The danger of her own situation made her shiver, for she could not deny one truth. Marc Copeland had awakened feelings in her that were very hard to control, but she would have more strength next time. Next time she wouldn't let him close enough to penetrate her will . . . next time . . . next time.

Her thoughts were so tangled that the light rap on her door was repeated before she heard it. She turned from the window, her lips pressed firmly together. If this was Travis, she would make it completely clear that this was not the trip he had bargained on.

When she opened the door she was completely stunned to see Marc Copeland leaning against the frame, a smile on his face, and an unopened bottle of brandy in his hand.

Marc fought sleeplessness as long as he could. Then he rose from the tangled sheets and poured himself another drink. He had drunk a great deal before he had retired, and his mind was still filled with the torturous thought he had battled most of the night . . . Catalina in the arms of Travis.

He cursed himself for the effect he was allowing her to have on him. What did he care if she slept with every man aboard? So much the better. Why then couldn't he wipe the taste of her lips from his? Why did his body still feel the touch of hers? Damn it, he had to exorcise her from his mind and there was only one way. He had to find out if she and Travis were together, had to seek an answer to plaguing memories, had to wash them away once and for all.

He grabbed up a full bottle of brandy and made his way toward Catalina's stateroom. Outside the door he stood for a moment in silence. Then, angered by his own uncertainty, he rapped and rapped again. Was she asleep? Worse, was she not in the cabin at all? Then the door opened and Catalina stood before him.

He drew in his breath at the picture she made framed in the doorway. Wearing a blue nightgown and a robe of filmy lace, she was breathtaking. He smiled, totally ignoring the spark of anger in her eyes.

"It's rather late to be checking on your passengers, isn't it?" she asked coldly.

"Not checking." He grinned evilly. "I just thought you and your companion might need a stimulating nightcap." He held the bottle of brandy up and watched her anger burst into pure rage. But her anger defeated her purpose, for without thinking she flung the door wide and waved him past her.

"There is no one in this cabin but me. Now if you will take your filthy mind and leave, I would like to go back to bed."

But she had made the mistake of letting him move past her. She realized it as soon as he reached out and pushed the door shut, leaving them vague ghostlike figures in the moonlit cabin.

"I didn't invite you in," Catalina snarled. "Leave!" She reached for the door handle, but a large hand closed about her wrist in a merciless grip. It was then that she realized that Marc, although he was not drunk, was most certainly not sober enough to be pushed. She became still, her mind whirling and seeking a way to get him out. He was entirely too quiet as they stood there, his hold keeping her immobile.

"Marc, let go of me." Catalina's voice was controlled, but instead of releasing her, he drew her closer. Now they stood within inches of each other, so close that the scent of her perfume teased his senses. She could feel the warmth of his body and the heat of it flowed from his hand to hers. She felt as if she were being filled with vibrant warmth, yet she remained silent.

Marc moved slightly and she could hear the bottle of brandy being put down. Then he put a hand on her shoulder, his fingers lightly touching her throat. He could feel the rapid beat of her pulse through their tips.

"Your heart is pounding," he whispered. He reached to take her other hand and place it against his chest. "Like mine."

She felt the drumming of his heart as his other hand skimmed the soft flesh of her throat so lightly it was

116

barely touching her. Yet her skin seemed seared by it. She sucked in her breath and caught her lips between her teeth to stifle the sudden impulse to call out his name.

Gently the tips of his fingers brushed along her collarbone, then down her arm, to again capture a trembling hand in his. He lifted it and brushed his lips against her wrist, his tongue tasting the sweetness of her skin.

She wanted to say please. She wanted to beg him to stop, but no words would pass her half-parted lips. Still he made no sound. His tongue licked lightly across her moist palm. Then he caught her fingers, nipping lightly at them with his teeth, caressing them with his tongue.

She could feel a tightening deep in her, and a moist heat arose between her thighs. She damned him and damned herself . . . but still neither spoke.

Her hand was still pressed against his chest, feeling his heart beat wildly, and he placed her other hand beside it as he slowly loosened the tie of her robe. Then he drew her hands down and slid his fingers beneath the robe, to slip it from her shoulders.

She let out a soft half-whispered moan as his fingers drew the straps of her gown off her shoulders, then let it slowly drift down her body, in a sigh of silk, to puddle at her feet.

For a few minutes they stood immobile, not touching, just breathing in the scent of each other. Marc didn't speak because he couldn't. Every sense he had was totally involved in accepting her—knowing the touch, taste and scent of her. He felt as if he were afire and her flesh was cool—so invitingly cool.

He touched her tenderly, spanning her waist with his hands, then letting them slide about her body. He could feel her shiver as he lightly brushed her spine.

One bit of pressure, one show of force, would have

enabled Catalina to extricate herself from the tenuous thread that held them together. But he used her own senses against her. He bent his head to touch his lips to her shoulder, sending a shiver through her that made her knees weak. With the slightest of movements he stood behind her, and his arms came about her, one hand cupping a breast, and the other sliding lightly down her belly to stroke and caress her moist pulsing heat until she felt she might truly collapse. She was beyond thought, beyond all but feeling.

His face was buried in the scented silk of her hair and his hands were savoring the sweet feel of her. Marc was as lost as she.

All thought of tomorrow had vanished, and all thought of the past . . . What happened next was explosive. There was a hard rapping on the door and a masculine voice came through it.

"Mr. Copeland, sir! Mr. Copeland."

Catalina leapt from him as though she had suddenly been dropped to earth from the heights. Marc cursed and turned Catalina to face him. But the magic had been totally destroyed.

"Cat . . ."

"Mr. Copeland," the insistent voice repeated.

"Get out! Get out!" Catalina sobbed roughly as she fought against his hold. She broke from him to snatch up her gown and then put as much distance between them as the room would permit.

"Cat, I hadn't meant for this to happen. I don't want to leave you like this."

"Don't worry about me," she said scathingly. "I'll be much better when you're gone . . . and I'll be much safer."

"From me or from yourself?"

"Just get out, Marc," she said softly. "Get out."

He knew she was on the verge of violent behavior

118

and beyond being reached by any words he might say to convince her that he regretted the way it had happened. He opened the door and left. For a long moment the dark stateroom was totally silent. Then there was a soft muffled sob as Catalina threw herself across the bed and buried her face in her pillow. She could not cry. She could only muffle her gasps of disbelief. She had almost succumbed to his touch.

"I hate you! God how I hate you," she whispered. But she was not sure whether her words were directed at Marc Copeland or at herself.

Outside the door the young man stepped back, startled by the look on Marc's face.

"What do you want?"

"Uh . . . sir . . . there's a problem below and I went to your cabin to get you. When you wasn't there, I went to Miss China."

"And China sent you here?" Marc said in a cold disbelieving voice.

"Yes, sir. She said you might be here."

Marc's rigid anger was slowly cooling. He couldn't blame the young sailor for his interference. But China . . . At the moment he could strangle her, yet he knew he would say nothing to her. Her interference might just have been a warning, but he'd be damned if he'd give her the satisfaction of laughing or of asking questions that he couldn't answer.

Charles reached out a hand to help Charlotte down from the carriage. The night had been exceptionally pleasant, but of course he had always enjoyed Charlotte's company. He walked to the door with her and was more than surprised when she invited him in.

"Come and have a last glass of brandy, Charles. If Cat is awake I would like you to talk with her. Maybe

119

you can discern what her plans might be. A warning from you about how dangerous Marc Copeland and Travis Sherman could be, might change her plans."

"I would be more than pleased." Charles smiled.

Once inside, Charlotte led the way to the study where a fire still burned low in the fireplace. Not wanting to waken the servants she poured Charles's brandy herself.

"Do sit down. I will go up and see if Cat's awake," she said.

Charles sat before the fire, thinking how warm and comfortable this house seemed in comparison to his empty one. But Charlotte had always had a way of brightening a room. He knew the touches of beauty in this house were not due to the objects but to her.

Charlotte climbed the stairs slowly, her mind dwelling on her annoying inability to place an authentic name to Marc Copeland's face. But she was determined to keep Catalina from playing into his hands. Eventually the name would come to her.

At Catalina's door she knocked . . . waited . . . knocked again. Sure that Catalina must be sound asleep she then opened the door and stepped into the dark room.

In as familiar a room as this she needed no light to find her way to the bed. She reached out a hand to gently waken Catalina—and found the bed empty.

For a moment shock held her immobile, then she moved swiftly across the room to light the lamp. Its bright glow confirmed her worst thoughts. The bed had not been slept in, and the white rectangular envelope that lay against the pillow brought a soft sound of dismay from Charlotte.

She tore the envelope open and read rapidly. Then she rushed to the door and hurried down the stairs.

Charles saw the alarm on her face the moment she entered the room. He quickly rose to his feet.

"Charlotte?"

"She's gone!"

"Gone . . . where?"

Charlotte didn't want to waste words. She handed him the letter and he read it rapidly.

"Charlotte, get your cloak," he said firmly. "My carriage is still outside. If we hurry we may be able to intercept her before the *Belle* has a chance to leave."

"Oh, that foolish and impatient child!" Charlotte said angrily. "To have been so blinded by her fears as to board that boat without anyone to depend on should she run into trouble."

"But she's gone with Travis Sherman. Surely if she has done that she must feel she can trust him."

"Charles," Charlotte said coldly, "if she were not so blinded by Marc Copeland, she could see that Travis Sherman is a man with his own purposes. She stands between two very dangerous men."

"Then let us hurry."

Despite the fact that the carriage rattled through the New Orleans streets at an alarming rate of speed, they arrived at the dock just in time to see the lights of the *Southern Belle* recede into the distance.

Chapter 9

Seth struggled against the thick heavy blackness that seemed to be choking off his air by settling on his chest. He gasped, groaned, and tried to surface to consciousness. His eyes did flutter half-open, but he could perceive only blurred faces that seemed to waver in and out of focus.

He heard voices but they seemed to be hollow, like echoes coming through a long tunnel. Rivulets of pain channeled through his entire body, and to make bad matters worse, his extremities felt weighted. He gurgled some sounds he meant to be words, and when he did, someone came to bend over him.

He concentrated hard, and when he did, a face wavered into view. He could see a young freckled-faced boy, but he could not hear what he was saying. Funny, he thought. It's funny when you see someone's lips moving and no sound comes. He tried to laugh, but it came out a bubbling soundless gurgle.

Seth lay on a plank bed padded by two ragged blankets, and he was covered by two more that were just as worn.

The young face that had bent to listen to his jumbled effort to talk furrowed in a scowl of worry.

"He's mumblin' sumthin', Grandpa, but I can't understand what he's sayin'. Do you really think he's goin' to be all right? He sure looked near dead to me when we dragged him outta the water."

"Now, Jake, don't go gettin' upset. I told you he's goin' to be fine. He just needs some more time. He was banged up pretty bad, and I've a hunch he didn't just jump into the old Miss on purpose."

"He hasn't been able to eat for three days, Grandpa. Will he die?"

"You just keep shovin' my tonic down him, Jake, and I can guarantee you, he'll be coming around. Give him lots of water too, and some soup if he'll swallow it."

"'Pears to me he's had enough water." Jake laughed. "And that tonic of yours sure smells like whiskey to me."

"Don't get smart, mite." Benjamin Barde laughed. "Or I might just have to swat your rump for you."

Jake laughed softly, but obediently went to a small cupboard and removed a small squat brown bottle with a cork in it. Picking up a small cup from a nearby table, the lad poured an inch or two of liquid into it, then set the bottle aside and went to Seth's side.

Seth's head was lifted gently, and the cup was placed to his lips. When the liquid passed through them he sputtered, coughed, then groaned something unintelligible.

It was several hours later when Seth opened his eyes again. This time, although his vision was fuzzy, the details of his environment swam into view, and he was aware first that the room he was in seemed to be rocking back and forth. After quite some time he realized that he was on a boat.

With this thought, the memory of what had happened surfaced. He had regained consciousness only to find himself arching through the air while the muddy waters of the Mississippi were coming up to meet him.

He had felt the water close over him, and when the tremendous current tore at his body, for the first time in his life he had known real fear. He sensed that he was about to die; then the drive for self-preservation won out and he began to fight. But he had lost blood and strength, and slowly the river began to win.

His last thoughts were almost calm. He thought that Cat would never have to battle for him again . . . and that he loved her.

The boat had been on its way to the gulf for fish when Jake had spotted Seth and called out to the old man.

"There's someone in the water."

"Where?"

"Over there. See him? He just went under again . . . there! There! Look!"

The boat was maneuvered to Seth's side, and he was laboriously dragged on board, more dead than alive.

That had been three days ago. Three days of fever and a battle to stay alive.

Now Seth looked about him. He knew one thing immediately, whoever owned this particular boat had little or no money. To say the least it was rough, but another thing was clear. It was immaculately clean. Even the air in the small cramped cabin smelled clean.

Seth tried to rise, but his weakness made it impossible. He lay back against the pillow just as the door opened and an old man walked in.

"Well, boy, I see you finally woke up."

"Where . . ." Seth began, but his voice grated like a frog's. He tried to clear it, and the words finally came out harsh and ragged. "Where am I?"

"On my boat."

Seth tried to laugh, but even that was difficult. "I had

124

a feeling I was on a boat. Where is the boat?"

"On the ol' Miss." The old man chuckled. "Boy, don't you know where you was when you decided to take a midnight swim?"

"I know where I was, I'd like to know where I am. Besides I didn't take a 'swim' as you so politely put it. I was tossed in."

"Figures," the old man said, as he sat in a chair opposite Seth's bed. "You're lucky. The ol' Miss don't always spit up what's been tossed into her. Sometimes she just swallows it and nobody ever knows."

"I'm trying to remember how I got here."

"Jake spotted you."

"Jake . . . Oh, the boy who was helping you. I thought I saw a lad awhile ago. I'd like to thank him too."

The old man chuckled softly and folded his hands across the breadth of his stomach. Seth examined him. What he'd thought was fat had once been muscle over a very large frame. The man's brown eyes glowed with amusement, and though his face was seamed with years, he gave off an aura of vital health. His unkempt hair, white and long, was tied back in a queue.

"Yessir, Jake is the one responsible for draggin' you out of death's grip. Jake's quick and smart and kinda softhearted."

"Jake your son?"

"Nope. My grandchild. My boy's youngster."

"Then your son's here too?"

"My son's dead. There's only Jake and me."

"Well, I'd really like to thank Jake."

"Jake'll be comin' in a short while to look in on you. Been sorta anxious about your well-being. Probably be bringin' you some supper. You hungry?"

Seth laughed. "I feel like I haven't eaten for a month."

"Well, there's stew cookin' on deck. Jake'll be bringin' some."

"Good. I'd like to thank him properly. I owe him my life."

Again the old man chuckled and Seth felt a touch of annoyance, but he owed these people much too much to be annoyed at anything they might say or do. Before he could speak again, however, the door opened and a small figure came in, carrying a bowl he hoped fervently was food for him.

Seth knew immediately that this was the same youngster whose face had wavered in and out of his consciousness. He was small and the clothes he wore were overly large. Probably they had never been his. His face was half-shadowed by a large floppy-brimmed hat, but Seth could see the fine line of his jaw. Obviously, the lad was quite young for his chin seemed almost delicate, but he couldn't see enough of the boy's face to tell his age. The hands that held the bowl of food were fine boned and slender.

"Grandpa?"

"He's awake and doin' fine, Jake. Kind of anxious for that food though. 'Pears he's a mite hungry."

The boy's smile was quick and sunny, and his movement to Seth's side was rapid.

"I've brought you some stew. Can you set up?"

"I'll try." Seth chuckled. "But I feel about as weak as a day-old puppy."

Jake and the old man helped Seth to a sitting position, bracing his back against the wall. Then the bowl of steaming stew was placed in his lap.

Seth felt, at that moment, that he had never tasted anything better in the finest restaurants in New Orleans.

While he ate he tried to see beneath the wide brim of the floppy hat Jake wore, but all he could catch in the glow of the single candle was mellow light reflected in wide, intelligent green eyes. Maybe, he thought, I can do something later to benefit the boy for saving my life. It looked to him like just about anything he could offer would benefit Jake in some way, even if he only got him some new clothes that fit.

"Now"—Seth spoke, though his mouth was filled with food—"can one of you please tell me where we are?"

"Well . . . from the way we been runnin'," Benjamin said thoughtfully, "I'd say we was about halfway to the gulf."

"That far from New Orleans! How long was I unconscious?"

"Little over three days, but it was more from fever than anythin'."

"Lord I didn't know I'd been out that long or that we were that far away. What's your name?"

"Benjamin Barde," the old man replied.

While he and Benjamin had been talking, Seth had noticed that young Jake's eyes had never left him. They were unreadable, but they seemed to absorb everything about him. He wondered if Jake had ever associated with other people.

"Jake," Benjamin said as he rose from his chair, "you'n I'll sleep on deck. Let's let this boy get some real sleep. Come mornin', he'll feel like gettin' out of bed. That'll be a better time to talk than now."

Jake rose obediently but silently, and when the old man moved to the door Seth was surprised to see that he kept himself between Jake and him. Seth found it a protective gesture.

After they left, Seth was surprised to find that he truly was exhausted. He rolled onto his side and fell asleep almost immediately.

On the deck of the boat, Benjamin and Jake spread

out blankets and then lay near each other.

For several minutes it was silent except for the echo of night sounds from the shore and the lapping waves against the boat, now anchored for the night.

"Grandpa?"

The old man sighed as if he had known the questions that were coming.

"What?"

"He seems like a nice man. I'm glad we didn't let him drown."

"That's yet to be seen. You nor I don't know what kind of man he is. But them as throwed him in the river must not have thought him too nice."

"Even wet and dirty, his clothes were grand," Jake said wistfully.

"Can't judge a man that way either, Jake. Mind what I tell you and stay away from him 'til we find out a little more."

There was another prolonged silence before Jake sighed deeply, then turned away from the old man and drifted off to sleep.

Benjamin lay awake for a long time wondering if he had fished a lot of trouble out of the river . . . and if it wouldn't have been safer for Jake if he had been able to let the thrashing man slide beneath the water and out of their lives.

The next morning Seth did waken feeling a lot better. He sat up on the edge of his bed and tested his strength by slowly moving his limbs. Then he stood with very little effort. The slight dizziness he experienced passed swiftly.

He looked at himself and chuckled. His clothes were torn and dirty, and he felt as if he were a street urchin or a river rat. But, he cautioned himself, I am alive. That thought took away the discomfort of wearing dirty clothes.

The door opened and Benjamin came in. He smiled when he saw Seth on his feet.

"Ah, it looks like your feelin' better."

"I am. Much better."

"Very good . . . very good. But don't push yourself more than you should. You're young and the young retrieve their strength easily, but not always as easily as their conceit believes."

Seth laughed, but his legs did feel a little wobbly so he sat on the edge of the bed.

"Where's Jake?"

"Castin' off our lines, gettin' us afloat again."

Before Seth could say more there was a loud thump on deck, then a cry of anger followed by a voice that was obviously Jake's, obviously mad, and just as obviously using language that would make an old sailor blush. Seth's grin froze on his face, and Benjamin contained his laughter with a supreme effort.

"Jake has a rather bad temper," Benjamin said, his sober expression drawing a disbelieving look from Seth.

"That boy should have his mouth washed out with soap for talking like that. It's . . . it's revolting."

"Well," Benjamin said innocently, "not having a mother and livin' on the river has made it kind of hard raisin' Jake."

"Maybe someone else should try taking him in hand. Good heavens, sir, what kind of a man will he grow into if he reacts like that?"

As if to punctuate those words, Jake's voice came to them.

"You damn bilge rat, get your ass up and shove that line off before I have you tossed overboard. And you, you whore's son, I'll rip your . . ."

Seth gasped in shock as the words continued to filter through. It was beyond his belief that a boy as young as Jake could have acquired a vocabulary so full of the vulgar words he was hearing.

He clenched his teeth. "My God, Ben. You have to do something about that."

"I'm afraid I can't."

"Then I shall," Seth said determinedly.

"You're welcome to try."

Seth climbed the four steps from the cabin to the deck.

Jake stood with his back to Seth, legs spread and hands on hips. His language would have curled Seth's Aunt Charlotte's hair. Benjamin smiled as he appeared alongside him, for he did not expect Seth's next move.

Seth took three steps toward Jake and, raising his foot, caught him on the seat of the pants, lifting him several inches from the floor and sending him sprawling among the coiled ropes.

There was a shriek of absolute fury, a muffled sound of poorly smothered laughter, and then Seth's determinedly scowling face went through some rapid and astounding changes, registering anger, shock, and finally wide-eyed amazement.

The hat Jake had worn had flown in the opposite direction, and now Seth stood looking into the angriest green eyes he had ever seen. But they were surrounded by a mass of the most beautiful red-gold hair. Jake was a girl.

"You filthy spawn of a fatherless whore! You bastard! What the hell do you think you're doin'?"

Seth backed up a step, shaking his head negatively and searching for words that would calm Jake and that would put a stop to the convulsive laughter of the two crewmen.

"Jake!" Seth gasped. "Jake?" As if he had to repeat

130

the name, hoping a miracle of sorts would happen and he wouldn't be seeing what was before him.

Jake was rubbing her backside while she continued to advance toward a still-awed Seth.

"What did you kick me for?" Jake screeched. "I help pull you out of the river and nurse you like a pink-assed baby and you kick me!"

"I didn't mean . . . I mean I thought . . . Good God I didn't know you were a . . . a girl," Seth gurgled helplessly.

The laughter about them increased, provoked by Seth's obvious loss of equilibrium, and to Seth it looked as if Jake was now bent on murder.

Benjamin stepped between them, however. He had contained his laughter, but had decided it was time to bring the situation under some control. Besides, knowing Jake and her temper, he was quite sure Seth was going to need a little protection.

He had learned something about Seth the moment the man had backed away from Jake. Seth had obviously been trained to respect women. Of course, Benjamin thought with amusement, only the kind of women found in polite society. He was reasonably sure Seth had never run across a girl quite like Jake.

"Now, Jake girl, take it easy. Your mouth was runnin' again. The man thought you were a boy and was a little upset at your language."

"Upset! He kicked me! No river rat is going to kick me and live to tell about it!"

With a movement a little faster than Seth could follow, a silver-bladed knife appeared in Jake's hand.

If Seth had been shocked at finding Jake was a girl, he was totally stunned by the realization that she meant to use the weapon.

Now he was becoming irritated by the laughter of the two-man crew and by the fact that he was beginning to

131

look ridiculous.

With a firm hand he pushed Benjamin aside and stepped around him to come within inches of the knife's blade.

"This situation is out of control," he began. "I apologize for the kick. If I'd known you were a girl I would never have done it. But I won't say you didn't deserve something for that foul nasty mouth of yours. It's been a shock. I don't think I've ever heard a . . . lady talk like you do. And your temper is as vile as your mouth. I shouldn't have kicked you, I should have dumped you overboard and held you under until you learn how to talk."

"How I talk is none of your damn business. What kind of gratitude do I get for pullin' your scurvy half-dead body out of the river? You kick me!"

"I said I was sorry for God's sake!" Seth cried. He was losing his own temper now. "What do you want me to do, jump overboard and finish the job?"

"I oughta cut your damn balls off and throw you overboard!"

Seth choked and his face reddened. This was monstrous! Worse, he could hear Benjamin's amused chuckle coming from behind him. He couldn't understand a grandfather raising a girl to act like this. He also knew he couldn't back down or the laugh would really be on him.

"Your language is like a gutter snipe's!" he said angrily.

"Ungrateful bastard!" she retorted tauntingly.

"Don't you ever take a bath?" Seth shouted. "I can smell you from here, like a river rat!"

"Ahhh," Jake screeched, "you filthy pig!"

She lunged at him with the blade and in the height of her anger Seth was pretty sure she fully intended to murder him. He stepped aside and caught her wrist with one hand while his other arm encircled her waist, lifting her from the deck. In two strides he was at the rail, and amid Jake's shrieks of fury and the hilarity of the crew he calmly tossed her over.

She came up sputtering, eyes wide with shock. The knife had slipped from her grasp and was lost somewhere on the muddy river bottom. Jake wanted to cry, but she would never allow such a . . . a girl-like thing to happen. The words he had shouted at her had struck a chord no one else had ever touched.

She allowed herself to be hauled back on the deck, but this time her grandfather kept an arm about her waist.

"That's enough, boy!" he said to a still-angry Seth. "And you, Jake, get below and dry off."

Jake was shivering and Seth saw, or imagined he saw, a look of almost fragile vulnerability in her eyes. Regret for what he had done was instant . . . but too late. Jake let out a muffled sound, then ran from her grandfather's side and disappeared below.

"I'm sorry, sir," Seth said. "This got out of hand somehow. It's no way to show my gratitude for her having saved my life. I'd better go and apologize to her."

"I'd leave her be for a while if I were you, boy. Jake has always been able to handle herself from the time she was knee high. I think this is the first time she's ever been backed down."

"But she saved my life," Seth protested. "I at least owe her an apology."

"There's time for that when she gets over this."

"God, I feel like an ungrateful cad."

"Don't fret, boy," Benjamin warned. "You haven't

seen the end of Jake yet. She ain't one to let someone get the upper hand and keep it. I'd be on guard if I were you."

"I . . . I don't mean to be presumptuous, sir, but Jake . . . I mean . . . well she's a girl."

"Sure is. I know she's a little rough around the edges."

"A little rough!" Seth laughed.

But Benjamin's eyes had gone cold. "Don't be judgin'. Jake has had a rough time. I know I haven't raised her as a girl should be raised, but havin' to be here, on the river, it was best she got tough and learned to defend herself. What chance do you think a pretty girl would have growin' up on a fishin' trawler on the New Orleans docks? I had to teach her the best defense I could. But she's a good girl. You've only seen the bad side of her."

"I don't think I care to see it again."

"I'll have a talk with her."

"How old is she?"

"Let me see," Benjamin said thoughtfully, "gettin' nigh on to seventeen."

"Seventeen! She's a woman! Good God, you just stood there and let me throw her overboard!" Seth said miserably. "I really have to talk to her and tell her I'm sorry."

"Don't be sorry too soon. Jake has a way of diggin' at a man's temper. I have a feelin' you two will be shoutin' at each other again before long."

"No, sir," Seth vowed firmly. "No sir, I'm not going to let this kind of thing happen again. I'll be kind and gentle and that will change her."

Benjamin's eyes glowed with mischievous humor. He chuckled. "You do that boy and Jake'll walk all over you."

"I hardly think so." Seth laughed with a confidence

Benjamin knew from experience would soon disappear. "I find it hard to call her Jake now. What's her real name?"

"Jacqueline . . . Jacqueline Barde."

"Then I'll call her Jacqueline," Seth decided.

"You do that, boy," Benjamin said, a smile twitching his lips. "You just do that."

Chapter 10

More than half the day passed with Jake remaining in seclusion in the small curtain-covered cubicle set aside for her. Seth often went in and out of the cabin, anxious to apologize or at least talk to her and try to establish some neutral ground, but in this he was unsuccessful. He couldn't rip away the curtain and force her to confront him, for that would only make a bad situation worse.

He could hear her moving about and he even suspected that the smaller sounds he heard might be tears.

He tossed words about in his mind. Words that might help to make Jake—Jacqueline—understand that he really was grateful to her for saving his life, and that what had happened between them was an unfortunate mistake on his part. Then he thought of what had occurred and groaned again at the realization that he had actually kicked a young woman. Of course someone should have warned him. How was he to know a vile-mouthed creature that looked like a dirty-faced urchin from the docks was a girl.

"God," he whispered aloud, "what a revolting situation."

He thought about his sister, Cat, and superimposed her image over this girl's. The comparison was beyond belief, but it also gave him an idea.

The first step in bringing this idea to fruition would be a long informative talk with Jake. However, after his fifth trip into the cabin, Seth was forced to the conclusion that Ja— Jacqueline was not about to make another appearance that day. He walked out on deck and went to sit beside her grandfather who was meticulously mending a large net.

"Benjamin?"

"What?"

"Can I ask you a personal question?"

"Sure, boy."

"What happened to Ja— Jacqueline's mother?"

"Didn't take to bein' married to a fisherman. Oh, it was all right for a while, long as he could take her playin' and dancin'. But then she got caught with Jake. Wasn't in her plans, havin' a baby. Tied her down, but it didn't tie her down for long. By the time Jake could walk, so did her Ma."

"She just left her?" Seth said in disbelief.

"You might say she even left her before she was born. 'Twas always her pa who cared for her. Tried his best, but there was a lot of things about raisin' a little girl neither of us knew."

"And her pa . . . her father?"

"We hit a big storm comin' off the gulf one night. Got swept overboard. We never even found his body. I just had to come home and tell Jake her pa wouldn't be comin' back."

"How old was she then?"

"'Bout twelve or so."

"Twelve. What an awful blow to take just at the time when you need a family the most."

"Yes. Come to think of it," Benjamin said thoughtfully, "it was right after that she started insistin' we call her Jake. It was like . . . well, she couldn't stand bein'

137

who and what she was and decided to be someone else."

"She can't go on the rest of her life being Jake," Seth declared quietly.

"Look Seth," Benjamin replied, "this here boat is all me and Jake has. It's livin' hand-to-mouth, but it's livin'. She isn't on the street like some girls her age. I've kept her from that."

"I'm sure you did the best you could do for her. But Ben, she's a girl. She needs . . . things"—Seth shrugged as he searched for appropriate words—"things only a woman could give her."

"What things?"

"Well, I don't know," Seth said helplessly. "She needs to know about . . . what she should be, how she should walk and dress and talk. She needs to know she's a woman. Ben you don't want her living on the docks the rest of her life do you?"

"Long as I'm alive she won't. This boat is her home, and I think she's happy here."

"Are you sure?" Seth said quietly.

"What does that mean?"

"It means"—Seth hoped he would be able to understand without getting angry—"you're afraid."

"Afraid of what?"

"Of Jacqueline finding out there's a whole world she's never known about."

Benjamin's face froze and he bent close to Seth. "You're so clever," he said quietly. "Well let me tell you somethin'. I don't know what you've got in mind for Jake. But remember you come from another world. Oh, I can tell by everything you say and every move you make. So imagine what will happen when you open the door to your world—let her have a real good look— and then she has to come back and live in this one. You going to help her or hurt her worse than she has been?"

Benjamin rose and walked away, and Seth remained

still, looking at his intentions. In many ways Benjamin was right, but he still felt there was a way to help Jacqueline. He had to think about it for a day or so. In the meantime he wanted to make peace with her . . . and he found that wasn't going to be too easy.

They met at the table when they sat down for the evening meal. She had shoved her hair under the flop-brim hat again, and he was well aware of a pair of green eyes as cold as ice.

"Jacqueline I—"

"My name is Jake," she replied frigidly.

"Your name is not Jake," he said easily.

"Butt out of my business, bilge rat," she gritted out, her teeth clenched and her chin jutting out belligerently. "I don't need you nosing around in my life."

"I'm not nosing around in your life. I just want to talk something over with you."

"Well, I don't want to talk with you anymore, so heist your ass outta my cabin and go find some little doll on the docks that wants to hop in bed with you because I don't. Besides"—she grinned evilly—"you probably ain't too good anyway."

She was purposely goading him and Seth was sure it was due to a growing need in her for self-defense. But he felt he could play her little game as well as she could.

He laughed. "Go to bed with you! You skinny foul-mouthed excuse for a woman. I wouldn't go to bed with you if you were the last female in the world. Besides, if I did, I'd probably catch a good dose of your meanness and start frothing at the mouth."

Her face went from white to continually increasing shades of red. By the time it had reached a very interesting shade of magenta she exploded.

"You overgrown whoreson! You damn son of a bitch. Get your filthy self out of here! Get off this boat or don't sleep at night, for if you do, I'll cut your bloody throat!" She wanted a battle, she needed a battle.

He rose slowly, smiled, and spoke gently. "You're so stupid just looking at your ugly half-boy's half-girl's face makes me sick." He walked out and closed the door behind him, hoping he had struck the chord he wanted and hoping he had started her thought processes spinning, not to mention the feminine side of her nature.

Benjamin watched Seth and Jake circle each other the next day, always at arm's length. Yet he had a feeling Seth was waiting for something.

In such close quarters it was difficult to talk to anyone privately, so Benjamin waited for Jacqueline to go to bed. When he was sure the others were asleep on deck he went to Jacqueline's small cubicle. He had expected to find her asleep, but the moonlight showed her lying with her hands folded behind her head, her eyes wide and thoughtful.

"Jake?" he whispered.

"Grandpa." There was surprise in her voice. "What are you doing up? Are you all right? You're not sick or somethin'?"

There was a fear in her voice Benjamin had never heard before, but he understood it. She had had so many blows in her life that she couldn't bear another . . . and Seth had shaken her confidence.

"I just want to talk to you."

"About what?"

Benjamin sat beside her on the narrow cot and took one of her hands in his. He didn't speak for a while because he was searching for the right words to say.

"Jake . . . are you happy here?"

"Grandpa, what's wrong?"

"I just asked you a question, Jake."

"I been here always, Grandpa, and you never asked me that before. It's that . . . I shoulda let him drown."

"You couldn't do that. Besides he has nothing to do with my question."

"Course I'm happy. Why shouldn't I be? I have everythin' I need here. You, the boat, everythin'. What else is there to have but this? I'm happy."

She had said what he had already known. If he kept her where she was now her life would be the same. Never changing, never growing. She would never know what kind of a woman she was or what kind of future she might have.

Now he had to find out exactly what Seth had in mind, and how far the man could be trusted.

"Okay, Jake. Okay. Give your old grandpa a kiss and get some sleep."

She threw her arms about his neck and he held her close, wondering what the future would be for her . . . and for him.

When he left, Jake lay still on her hard, board bed. She had slept in this bed almost from the time she could remember. Sleep had always come easily. Now she found it a very elusive thing.

She had never been battered by such confusing thoughts before. Her life had been simple. No responsibilities, no worries, and no rules. Now some slick-talking mystery man was doing his best to spoil everything. The things he had said to her spun in her mind, making her fight valiantly against something she did not understand . . . and did not want to understand. She was safe here, away from the world that was a huge black void in which she could not walk. Still, questions poked holes in her resistance . . .

Besides, she thought miserably, I am not ugly!

* * *

141

Before Benjamin rose in the early morning, Seth came to him and asked if he had any books on the boat.

"Only my Bible boy."

"Would you mind if I read a bit?"

Benjamin was both surprised and suspicious, but he handed him the worn Bible anyway.

Seth curled up in a corner of the desk, opened the Bible, and waited patiently for Jake to get up.

When she did come on deck, he studiously ignored her and seemed to be deeply engrossed in reading. An accomplishment she had never achieved. He knew, although she kept her distance and moved about her work, that she kept an eye on him, so he pretended to be more and more deeply involved in reading.

He was counting on one feminine trait he hoped to arouse—curiosity.

He wanted to smile in satisfaction when he saw her working her way closer to him. Finally she was a shadow that fell across the book, and he looked up, pretending surprise.

"Oh . . . Jacqueline. Am I in your way?"

"My name is Jake," she said defiantly, but she still dropped down on her knees near him. "What are you doin'?"

"What does it look like, or don't you approve of what I'm reading? You've probably read it already anyway," he said coolly, and went back to his book, totally ignoring her.

It was a good five minutes before she spoke again. "That's Grandpa's Bible."

"I know. He loaned it to me. You don't mind, do you?" Seth asked as an afterthought. "You weren't using it, were you? If you were . . ." He didn't finish the sentence, only closed the book and handed it to her.

She gave an inarticulate sound that might have been construed in any way. But her eyes looked like two blazing emeralds and her cheeks were crimson.

She struck the book from his hand, sending it skittering across the deck. "Who needs to read a damn book anyway?" She sneered; then she walked away. But Seth smiled. He'd touched a vulnerable spot. Jake was too intelligent not to want to reach for the unknown, but she was afraid to do so.

Benjamin had listened to Seth's story and to his request to be returned to New Orleans. As he watched Jake being torn apart, he decided that the quicker he got Seth home and off his boat, the better it would be for all of them.

He motioned to Seth, who came immediately to his side.

"You want to talk to me, Ben?"

"Yes. I thought I'd tell you that I gave orders to my boys. We're turnin' back upriver. We'll get you home a day or two before you thought."

Seth was quiet for a moment; then he spoke firmly. "Getting rid of me is not going to get rid of the problem you've got."

"I don't have a problem."

"You don't? What would you call Jacqueline's future—something to play with?"

"What the hell is it you want, boy?"

"I don't want anything." Seth looked at Benjamin levelly, trying to make him feel his honest intent. "Jacqueline and you, you saved my life. That's worth a lot to me. I'd like to repay the debt somehow. The only way I can think of doing it now is to give her a future. Would you or Jacqueline take money as a reward?"

"No. We don't expect to make money from doin' our Christian duty."

"Well then, I have a debt on my shoulders that my honor and my pride says I must repay. Can you see another way?"

"Suppose you just forget it."

"I've a supposition for you. Suppose you tell me what you would do if I saved your life. Would you let me tell you to forget it? Besides, I think Jacqueline is a very intelligent young girl. Once you peel off that façade of hers, I think you'll find a girl who's trying to get out. I just happen to think she deserves the chance. Of course"—Seth smiled as he turned to walk away— "it's your decision."

Benjamin watched his retreating figure, wanting to do battle with his words, but unable to fight the reasoning behind them. His eye caught Jake working with one of the men to untangle some nets. She laughed, and he saw the beauty that could be hers under different circumstances. He also saw the ragged and patched men's clothes that hid her completely, and the old hat she wore to cover her mass of beautiful hair. With a sinking heart he knew Seth was right. He didn't know yet what Seth's plans were, but he intended to find out.

For the balance of the day, Jake avoided Seth to the extent the limitations of the boat would allow, but Benjamin, who knew her better than any other, was aware that she was watching him. And he knew that she was frightened. He even knew of what.

That night, when the boat rocked gently in the shallows, and everyone slept, Benjamin went on deck.

He sat beside Seth, not surprised to find him awake.

"Beautiful night," Seth said after a few minutes.

"Most times it is on the river. Guess that's why I gave my life to her. She's a beautiful lady."

"It's been a good life for you, Ben?"

"Yes . . . for me. But maybe you're right. I been givin' it some thought."

"What's really troubling you, Ben?"

"Troublin' me?"

144

"You didn't come out here to tell me it's a beautiful night."

"No, I came out to ask you some questions."

"About what?"

"About what you got in mind for Jake."

"I'll tell you what I was thinking would be best for her. I have an aunt . . . Charlotte. She's about the grandest lady I know, well-traveled, rich, and intelligent. And I have a sister, Catalina. She's beautiful. Aunt Charlotte and Catalina would be more than grateful for what you've done for me, and they'd be delighted to take Jacqueline under their wings and give her all the advantages she deserves. Ben, Cat could be almost a sister to her. She could teach her how to laugh and have fun, how to dress pretty. Maybe"—he laughed—"she'd be the belle of New Orleans with all the men at her feet. And Aunt Charlotte, well, she could do for her what she's done for Cat, sort of keep her level and teach her how to be a lady. No one is as honorable or respectable or capable a lady as Aunt Charlotte. Ben, she could have a new life."

"And you, boy," Ben said softly. "What is it you plan to teach her?"

Seth turned to look at Ben. At first he was surprised; then he smiled. "I'll tell you what I'd like to teach her, Benjamin," he said quietly. "I'd like to teach her what it's like to have a brother, a sister, an aunt—a whole family who'd like to love her if she'll give us half a chance."

"She'll fight it, boy."

"From the past two days I'd say I agree. But I'll fight too. Maybe she'll be so busy being mad at me, she'll make it easier on Aunt Charlotte and Cat." Seth grinned.

"I'd want to see her."

"Ben!" Seth grew impatient. "I'm not trying to cut

145

her away. You're her grandfather for God's sake. You can't lose touch with her. I just sort of want to . . . borrow her." He laughed. "Sort of polish her up. I wouldn't ever try to separate you, Ben. She loves you."

"I can't find anythin' wrong with it," Benjamin said, as if he were puzzled by that fact.

"That's because there isn't anything wrong to find."

"You're a damn stubborn man."

"Who's run up against a girl who's about twice as stubborn."

They both chuckled over the truth of that. "Seth . . . she's scared," Benjamin said quietly.

"I know."

"Her world's been destroyed so often. She's gonna take this hard, if she takes it at all."

"I know that too."

"I don't know what to do about it," Benjamin admitted. "I can't just tell her I'm cuttin' her loose. I couldn't stand the hurt in her eyes. I've seen it too often."

"It'll be another two days before we reach New Orleans you said?"

"Little better than two days."

"For these two days why don't you let me try to handle it. If I fail, then we'll tell her together and just let her scream out her anger until she's exhausted enough to weaken . . . then we can carry her off."

"Well, you give it a go, boy. Damn if I believe you'll get her to go. But it looks like you're stubborn enough to try."

"Thanks, Ben."

"Don't thank me too soon. Far as I can see you just got yourself into one hell of a fight. Me, I'm safe, I'm just the referee."

"Well, we'll see what happens in two days. I've a few

146

tricks up my sleeve too."

"Good night, boy." Benjamin rose and went below to his own bed. Surprisingly, he felt relaxed and comfortable, and went to sleep almost at once.

It wasn't quite as easy for Seth, who spent a long night pondering just how he was going to reach an independent, angry, and frightened girl.

The next day would offer generous proof that Benjamin was right in his warnings and Seth was right in his misgivings: it started with a fight.

Jake took quick revenge when she found Seth, who had not slept until the wee hours of the morning. She looked at him for a moment, and a half-smile touched her lips, bringing a glow to her eyes. He was curled with his face toward the rail, and the curve of his buttocks beneath the blanket was too great a temptation for her to resist.

She swung her foot with enough force to bring him awake with a yelp of surprise. He came scrambling to his feet, angrier than he had ever been in his life, then turned to glare into green eyes filled with satisfied laughter.

"What the hell do you think you're doing?"

"Breakfast is ready, bilge rat." Her smile broadened. "We eat early and we work around here."

"What kind of a way is that to wake someone up?"

She shrugged nonchalantly, but he could read the satisfaction in her eyes. "One good kick deserves another," she declared flippantly. Before he could answer, she went below.

He followed and sat opposite her at the table, trying to control the urge to strangle her or to slap the smug look from her face. He finished his food, and as they all stood to get about their work, he reached across the table and grabbed Jake by the front of her shirt, half dragging her across the table.

"The next time you call me a bilge rat, you little brat, I am going to turn you across my knee, strip down your breeches, and smack some sense into the only end of you that seems to understand anything."

Her eyes widened, and he saw the first drop of respect he'd noticed in them. Then he let her go and walked out.

Benjamin stood by silently, but he had to contain his laughter. For the first time he thought that Seth might just succeed in what he planned to do.

Jake worked in belligerent silence, but she was thinking. Seth knew it, and it was what he wanted. He intended to give her a lot more to think about. He started when they were all seated on the deck eating a hasty lunch. As if he had totally forgotten that Jake was a girl, he brought up the subject of girls he had met and parties he'd attended.

He was, ostensibly, talking to Benjamin and the other two men, but he knew quite well Jake was listening intently. He spoke of beauty, the kind she had never tasted. He spoke of music and fine silk dresses, of elaborate tables set with crystal, china, and real silver. He spoke of dancing and laughing, and then he began to tell them about his family, dwelling on Aunt Charlotte and Cat.

The meal was over much quicker than Jake wanted it to be, for Seth's words were like rain falling on drought-touched earth. She sat at the table after the others had gone about their business and only Seth remained, hoping she could at least ask a question or two.

"Is it really true?" she whispered. "You're lyin' aren't you? Nobody lives in a house like you say. Nobody eats like that." She stood up and he thought he saw the glint of tears in her eyes. "You're a damn old liar!" she cried. "A damn old liar! I wish I'd let you drown!"

Seth didn't know whether to laugh or cry. He had reached her, only he'd hurt her too. He just hoped he would have the chance to do something to ease her hurt. Time was running out on him.

He made a decision. Tonight he was going to try to talk with her. That was going to be a battle he really had no taste for.

He laughed to himself. Would any of his old friends believe what he was involved in? He wondered just how many of them were out looking for him . . . and he wondered if Cat had had any luck in buying back the *Belle* or in telling Marc Copeland to go to hell.

Anyway he'd see Cat soon, tell her he was all right and they would be fine.

Another thought, not quite as pleasant, intruded upon him—one he had been too involved to think about until now. Someone had tried to kill him in a most unpleasant way. Marc Copeland? Why would Marc Copeland want to kill him? But then, why would anyone want to kill him? It was certain he was going to move heaven and hell to find out when he got home. Remembering the beating and the heartless way he had been thrown into the river to drown, Seth knew a furious need to avenge himself.

Then he turned his thoughts to Jake and Cat, setting his anger aside but quite prepared to make locating his attackers a priority when he reached home.

With help from friends, he would search every tavern and disreputable place until he found the men who had attempted to kill him. Then, one way or the other, he would find a way to get from them the name of whoever was behind this. No one was going to attempt to kill him without his finding some way to get revenge.

Seth thought of the change in himself, and he

149

wondered if the old Seth would have cared enough to try to rescue Jake from the situation she was in. He didn't know for certain, but he wanted to do it now and that was all that mattered. With new resolve, he got to his feet. It was time to renew his campaign. He was going to bring Jake—Jacqueline, he had to remember that—home to his family if he had to resort to kidnapping her.

Chapter 11

Jacqueline Barde knew Seth wanted something from her, no, expected something from her, but she didn't know what it was and that frightened her more than anything else ever had. Because, she thought, I am supposed to know what it is.

For this reason she felt helplessly deficient in some way. She wanted to strike out at Seth. She wanted to wipe away the look in his eyes that told her she was lost. As her insecurity grew so did her almost violent resentment of Seth who seemed to be the source of her sleepless nights and miserable days.

It was fate that turned the tide—fate, a small storm, and a slippery deck. Gray clouds had begun to gather on the horizon by the time they sat down to supper. It was a meal enclosed in ice, for Jake was silent and cold as a glacier. The two crewmen ate quickly and left because of the chill atmosphere, but Seth refused to be the first to leave the table, knowing Jake would then think she was having the effect she wanted. As for Jake, she was determined to remain seated until Seth left.

Benjamin was totally engrossed in this amusing and unbelievable situation. Mentally he began to gauge how long it would be before they were at each other's throats.

Knowing Seth's goals he was more than interested in

how he was going to go about handling Jake in this mood—or any mood for that matter. He was surprised at the method Seth used.

"Jake?" He used the masculine name she had chosen because he realized there were more important things at stake.

He knew he had taken the right first step when he saw her gloating satisfied look. She thought he had finally given up on trying to thrust another name at her.

"What?" she answered, suspicious as well as satisfied.

"I'm really sorry about what happened—about the Bible. I had no way of knowing you couldn't read."

Jake cast an accusing eye at her grandfather, but she remained still, her pride gathered about her like a shield.

"I don't care. I don't need to read," she said sullenly.

"But, if you'd call a truce I'd teach you to read. As smart as you are, it wouldn't take long."

Seth knew there would never be enough time to teach her before they arrived in New Orleans, but he wanted to catch her interest, stir her desire to learn so his next offer wouldn't alarm her.

"I don't want you to teach me anythin'! I don't need you!" She rose to her feet. "Why do you keep on pokin' into my life?"

"Because," he said calmly, "you need someone to poke into it. What kind of life do you have? The life of a dock rat. One of these days you'll be an old lady. What are you going to do then, Jake . . . or have you ever thought about it? In fact have you ever thought about the rest of your life at all?"

A low rumble of thunder penetrated the cabin which dimmed as clouds shadowed the sun. Seth watched Jake's face, and it was hard to remain cool and detached when he saw the panic she was trying desperately to control light her eyes.

She started to speak when a louder crack of thunder sounded, and the boat suddenly lifted as if a large hand gripped and shook it.

The argument was forgotten as all three dashed for the door. Benjamin, who had been closest, reached it first. He yanked it open to be met by a sheet of rain.

The boat was heaving about in the waves caused by one of the sudden squalls that struck without warning in the gulf. It shifted drastically at the moment Benjamin stepped out onto the deck.

Momentarily unbalanced by the sudden change in his footing, Benjamin skidded on the wet deck, fell, and struck his head.

As he lay in a crumpled heap, Jake gave a cry of dismay, then rushed to his side and knelt by him. Seth was right behind her, and when she looked up into his face he was shaken by the mingling of rain and tears on her face. Jake was suddenly a terrified child, watching what she thought was her stability, her hold on life, slipping away.

"Grandpa."

It was a groan of sheerest misery, and Seth's heart was torn by it. Despite the face the girl turned to the world, within she was vulnerable.

Seth ordered the crewmen to carry Benjamin below, and Jake followed close on their heels, clinging to her grandfather.

Below Benjamin was laid gently on his bunk, and Seth firmly took over his care. He bathed the wound on the old man's head before examining it closely. It was a gaping one, but Seth felt it was not fatal.

Jake watched, fascinated, as Seth rummaged through drawers and cupboards until he found thread and needle. She did not turn away when he proceeded to sew the cut closed and then bandage it carefully.

Paying no attention to Jake he covered Benjamin with all the blankets he could find. Having done so, he left Benjamin with Jake and went back on deck.

For over four hours he and the two hands fought the elements and battled to keep the boat float. Only when the storm slowly began to die and the thunder was only an echo in the distance did he return to Benjamin who lay, only half-conscious, with a very silent Jake holding his hand.

Her eyes followed Seth's moves as he made some hot tea, then again went through the cupboards until he found a bottle of whiskey. He filled the cup, half with tea and half with whiskey, and returned to Benjamin's side. Lifting the old man's head gently, he forced some of the liquid between his lips.

Benjamin coughed and then choked on the first sip, but he drank the balance. By the time Seth returned Benjamin's head to the pillow, the injured man's pale cheeks were already beginning to flush with color and his eyes had begun to lose their vague disoriented look.

"You took a nasty fall, Ben," Seth cautioned. "Try to lie still. I've done some very ornate stitchery on your head. You'll appreciate it"—Seth laughed—"but not for a while. I think you'll have one grand headache for a couple of days."

"The boat . . . the storm . . ." Benjamin began.

"The boat is fine and the storm is nearly over."

"Thanks boy . . . thanks," Benjamin said weakly.

Seth smiled and patted his hand, well aware that Jake had not taken her eyes from him, nor had she uttered a word since Benjamin had fallen. Without looking at her, he rose to leave. It was her turn to act. He had made all the overtures he could. The balance of Jake's life rested in her own hands now. He firmly closed the door behind him.

* * *

Hours passed without any sign of Jake, but Seth remained on deck. Around midnight he told the two hands to try to get some sleep, and then he just sat on deck, enjoying the amazing serenity of the waters after such a tremendous upheaval. The sky was like black velvet, and it was studded with the piercing brilliance of millions of stars.

He sighed deeply. He was tired, but in a strange way exhilarated. He had stood his ground against fear and the elements of nature, and come out a winner. That made him feel as though he had conquered more than just the sea—he now was in command of his own self.

He barely heard the cabin door open, and was not aware of Jake's presence until she stood only a few feet from him.

She was still, but he refused to speak first. He remained silent and waited.

She moved closer when she realized he knew she was there, and dropped to her knees beside him.

"Seth?" she said softly.

"Is your grandpa sleeping all right?"

"Yes . . . he's sleepin' . . . he's fine."

"You ought to be in bed yourself. You must be tired."

He was prepared for immediate rebellion; what he got was a long moment of absolute silence. He could almost feel the struggle within her.

"Seth . . . I . . . I'd like to learn to read. I'd like you to teach me . . . if you still want to."

His heart leapt, but with an effort he remained still. He didn't want any sudden move on his part to change her shift in attitude.

Finally he spoke softly. "I'd be more than pleased to help you, Jake . . . more than pleased."

"I want to thank you." It was almost a whisper.

"For what?"

"For what you did for grandpa."

"I didn't do anything any other man wouldn't have done. It's the way people are supposed to care for each other. Jake, tomorrow ... when we start to learn together ... there's something I want to talk to you about. Something important. Will you listen to me?"

She was thoughtful for so long that he began to worry. She was still doing battle with herself.

"Yes," came the muffled and slightly reluctant reply.

"Good. Now why don't you get some sleep. Your grandpa should stay in bed tomorrow so that leaves everything to you and me. You're tired now, and we'll handle tomorrow when it gets here."

She left as soundlessly as she had come. Seth knew it was not going to be easy; they had taken only one tentative step. But at least it was in the right direction. They might still battle each other, but that would be secondary to the battle they would fight together for her future—a battle, he felt for the first time, she might just win.

Charlotte paced the floor nervously. Several hours had passed since Charles had sent her a message which stated that he wanted to see her.

They had returned from the docks together, stunned into silence by their failure to catch Catalina in time to stop her. Charlotte had been prepared to follow on the first boat she could find, but late as it was, none was leaving.

Charles, despite his anxiety, had been forced to laugh when Charlotte had become belligerently angry and had tried to buy a boat on the spot.

"Charlotte, it's late!" he had protested.

"What does the time have to do with it?" she had replied. "I will give the captain my letter of credit ... for whatever price he chooses. I want to follow that boat. Cat has no idea of the danger she is in."

"And neither do we. Charlotte, I have a much better idea."

"And what is that?"

"That we go home, and tomorrow I will find out not only what we have to know about Marc Copeland, but what his destination might be. We may be able to make more progress that way than by flying off like this. Cat is among many people. I don't believe anything serious can happen to her before we find a way to get to her."

Charlotte eyed him shrewdly, realizing he placed a different meaning on the word serious than she did. However, she reluctantly returned home with him, and when he left he cautioned her to relax and be patient. But patience was not Charlotte's strongest point.

Now, two days later, what little patience she did have was slipping from her. Awaiting Charles's arrival further drained her of it. She clenched her hands. Charlotte hated to wait.

When Charles was shown in, he smiled despite Charlotte's frown of displeasure.

"Two days, Charles. Good heavens, God created the entire world in seven!"

"I never claimed to be anywhere near Godlike," Charles stated. "And I think even He would have had a great deal of trouble finding out about a man who is as determined as this one to keep his past a secret."

"'Keep his past a secret,'" she repeated. "And for just what purpose?"

"His motive is something I cannot discover. What I have found out is his real name."

"Real name? Then he is not Marc Copeland?"

"Oh, he's Marc Copeland all right. If that's as far as you want to go."

"Charles, for heaven's sake," Charlotte said in

exasperation, "will you please tell me what you have found out?"

"His name is Marc Copeland Garrison. The Copeland is his mother's maiden name. Obviously he assumed it for the purpose of deception."

"Marc Copeland Garrison," Charlotte said thoughtfully. She narrowed her eyes as if she were searching through misty memories. Then her eyes brightened. "Copeland! Garrison . . . By any chance could he be a relative of Pierce Garrison?"

"His son. Did you know Pierce?"

"I knew him a long time ago. The family came from Natchez did they not?"

"Yes. It seems Marc's father . . . well he ran into some financial difficulties. As of yet I don't know what they were, but they must have been quite serious. He took his own life."

Charlotte's face grew pale. "He committed suicide?" she said in a disbelieving tone of voice.

"That seems to shock you more than it should. Don't you believe it?"

"Pierce Garrison was not the kind of man to take his own life," she declared firmly.

"Maybe not the Pierce Garrison you knew," he replied gently. "Years make a lot of changes in people and things. Maybe they changed him, Charlotte. Maybe he couldn't face these reverses."

"You could be right, Charles," Charlotte said, but she did not believe Pierce Garrison had taken his own life. She had known Pierce Garrison much better than she had admitted. "What else have you found out?"

"Well, Pierce Garrison lost nearly all of his fortune, but his son took what was left and built it up again."

"Shady dealings?"

"No, impeccable ones, for eight years. Then he liquidated everything—for an unbelievable sum of

158

money—and invested a great deal of that in Carrington Shipping."

This took Charlotte completely by surprise. "I don't understand this at all."

"I would say, taking a very rough guess, that Marc Copeland Garrison has something against the Carringtons."

"But why for heaven's sake? As far as I know we have never met him."

"You have never met him, Charlotte. That does not mean Joseph hasn't. As far as I can tell, Joseph and Pierce Garrison did a great deal of business together in Natchez."

"Then why would he want to take the *Belle* from Seth the way he did? To keep her running would surely have brought him more profit?"

"I don't have all the answers, Charlotte. I need more time to get them. There seems to be a lot of dark corners to this situation."

"Then," Charlotte said firmly, "let us shed some light on them. How long do you think it will take to find out what we need to know?"

"Another day or two . . . perhaps three at the most."

"Three days." Charlotte did not look favorably on the delay. "Three days and Cat is on that boat with a man whose motives we suspect."

"Marc Garrison," Charles stated quietly.

"And another man whose motives I don't trust."

"Travis Sherman. But Charlotte I think you are underestimating Catalina. After all she is not alone on a desert island with these two men."

"I suppose you are right. But as soon as you get word—as soon as you get the information we need—I want to go after Cat. She may need our help."

"We'll go after her. Surely, Charlotte, since Travis must be aware that you know who Cat is with, he will see that she doesn't have any difficulties."

"He'll protect her . . . from everything but himself."

"And," Charles said softly, "Garrison will protect her from everyone but himself."

They exchanged hopeful looks. "Then," Charlotte said, "let us hope Cat is as clever as we think she is, and is capable of playing the dangerous game of keeping two such men from succeeding in their devious plans."

"Yes, let us hope so. Cat is clever. She'll hold her own, I believe. Maybe even beat them both at their own game."

"I shall pack some clothes, Charles, and be ready to leave here in three days. In the meantime, please find out whatever you can. We will need all the ammunition we can get to be able to fight this man."

"Don't worry, Charlotte. We'll be well armed when we go after them. Well armed, indeed. I shall be back as soon as I can. Good night now, and please try to get some sleep."

"I will. Good night."

Charlotte walked to the door with Charles, and closed it behind him, sliding the bolt into place. She stood with one hand still on the bolt for some time. Then she turned and walked up the steps to her bedroom.

There, she lit a lamp, then carried it to the large chest that sat beneath a window. She knelt in front of the chest and set the lamp on the floor beside her before lifting the lid. The chest was filled with neatly folded clothes, but she reached under them and removed a small wooden casket twelve inches long, eight inches wide, and about ten inches deep.

She sat on the floor, resting her back against the chest and set the box on her lap. When she slowly opened the lid, soft tinkling music filled the silence

160

about her.

She listened to the familiar melody until the music stopped. Then she took from the box a small oval frame that contained the picture of a very handsome man. He was smiling. The picture had lain atop a packet of letters tied with a narrow pink ribbon.

She set these aside, exposing what had lain beneath in the bottom of the casket: a narrow gold ring, a thin silver chain with a tiny cross, an ivory lace fan, and some flowers that were fragile and dry. She took each item from the box carefully, reliving the poignant memories attached to it. Then, slowly, she replaced the mementos.

Taking the packet of letters in hand, Charlotte untied the ribbon, letting it flutter unheeded to the floor. She opened a letter and read it. Then she read the others, one by one.

The tears that touched her cheeks were allowed to fall and drop into her lap like autumn leaves.

When she had read all the letters she sat for some moments in contemplative silence. Then she folded each letter and replaced it in its envelope. Tying the ribbon about them again, she placed the packet upon the other mementos.

She looked at the picture for what she knew would be the last time.

"Oh, Pierce . . . no. I will never believe that you took your own life, never. You were strong, and if you had a son you would not have left him like that. No. I don't believe it."

Charlotte sighed as she put the picture away and closed the casket. Then she placed the box in the chest and drew down the lid.

She rose slowly and returned the lamp to the table by her bed so that she might prepare to retire. But she knew that when she slid beneath the covers and extinguished the lamp, it would be difficult to sleep this night.

Three days passed before Charles sent word that he would book passage for himself and Charlotte on the next boat to Natchez, and that he would pay her a visit later in the afternoon to talk with her. In the meantime she was to prepare to leave.

She waited with as much patience as she could, but was more than relieved when she heard the carriage roll up the drive.

She greeted him with a warm smile of welcome, and very quick questions.

"You've found out more, Charles?"

"Confirmation. Business dealings. There were a great many between Joseph and Pierce Garrison. It seems the Carringtons could have bankrupted Pierce at any time."

"But they wouldn't have!" she said, aghast. "Joseph wouldn't have done such a thing to a man he considered a friend."

"Well," Charles said gently, "maybe his son didn't know—or didn't believe—that."

"My God, do you know what you're saying?"

"I think so."

"Then it's very possible that Cat is in much more danger than I thought. What more do you know?"

"Very little else, Charlotte. Isn't that enough?"

"When do we leave?"

"About midnight tonight. Are you ready?"

"Yes."

"Well, we have some time so I think I will have a drink before we get started on this journey."

"I believe, Charles, that I wouldn't mind having

something with you. And you must have something to eat. Sit down and make yourself comfortable. I'll ask cook to make up some sandwiches."

Charles relaxed and within a few minutes Charlotte returned with a tray of sandwiches. She set the tray on the table beside him. Then she poured two glasses of wine.

She had just sat down and picked up a sandwich when they heard the front door open and close. Turning in her chair, Charlotte was astounded when Seth appeared in the doorway. She was even more surprised to see a bedraggled urchin standing beside him. It took her several minutes to realize the urchin was actually a girl.

Charlotte rose slowly from her chair, total disbelief written on her face.

"Well, Aunt Charlotte, aren't you going to welcome me back?" Seth asked. "Now don't tell me you and Cat didn't miss me."

By this time Charlotte had found her voice.

"Seth Carrington, where in damnation have you been for over a week, and what is this creature with you? You had best have some very good explanation, young man. You've cost me a year of my life!"

Charlotte's fierce explosion and her formidable appearance were enough to make Jake step back and gasp softly. This was the lovely and charming aunt Seth wanted her to stay with. Jake was having serious doubts about a decision she hadn't been sure of in the first place.

Seth laughed, which eased Jake's apprehension only a little. "Aunt Charlotte, if you'll control your temper for a minute and quit scaring Jake to death, I'll tell you what happened."

Charlotte had taken in Jake's wide innocent eyes, and she chuckled. "Jake," she said just a little more gently. "A very inappropriate name for a young lady, isn't it, Seth?"

"Her name is Jacqueline Barde, and if it were not for her and her grandfather I wouldn't be here today."

"Come here, Jake."

These words were spoken firmly by Charlotte, and Jake was surprised that she never even thought of defying her. Instead, she approached the older woman as a bird might approach a hungry cat.

Charlotte reached out to cup Jake's chin in her hand and she raised her head. They studied each other for several wary minutes; then Charlotte smiled. "Hello, Jake," she said gently.

A tremulous smile came to Jake's lips, a hesitant smile that touched her eyes. She was unable to define the strange emotion, the feeling of homecoming, that touched her.

"Are you hungry?"

"We're ravenous," Seth answered at once.

"Then join us and share these sandwiches. When you've appeased your hunger, we've a story to tell each other."

Charlotte allowed them time to eat; then she sat back in her chair.

"All right, Seth my boy, let's hear your story. And then I've one to tell you. I think we have just enough time before the boat leaves to solve some problems."

Chapter 12

Catalina brushed her hair until it glowed in the soft lamplight, then she coiled it at the nape of her neck drawing it back from her face. The severe hair style made her wide eyes seem even wider and drew attention to her lush lips.

She had laid out the gown that she had chosen to wear when she dined with Travis. Now she took it from the bed and slipped it over her head.

Shawna, who had been sent by China to help Catalina dress and to gather any information she could, rose to help fasten the buttons.

"The gown is very beautiful," she said. "It makes your skin look so soft and your eyes so gold."

"Thank you . . . Shawna, isn't it?"

"Yes."

"You are a friend of Mr. Copeland's?" Catalina asked as nonchalantly as she could.

"Oh, yes. Marc is a very good friend of mine and of Nina and Charlene and Paulette. But mostly he and China are . . . well . . . really close friends."

"I see." Catalina was enraged. The man had an absolute harem at his beck and call.

"You all live on this boat?"

"Yes," Shawna said brightly. "We live here and we work here."

165

Catalina nearly choked on her outrage. It was obvious that Shawna was not the brightest person she had ever met, and she was now certain that Marc chose women who would be totally dependent upon him. But curiosity and anger at Marc brought the next question to her lips before she could stop it. "What do you do here?"

Having asked it, she could have bit her tongue. She wondered if Shawna would be hurt by the question. But Shawna gave her such an innocent smile that Catalina was forced to realize the truth: Shawna was a little girl in a woman's body. Somewhere, somehow, nature had stopped her mind from growing although it had molded her body to perfection. A new anger swept over Catalina. What kind of man would take advantage of her.

"Oh, I deal the cards for the men who like to gamble, and I serve drinks. Sometimes I play the piano and sing. I like that . . . to play music and sing. Marc says I have a pretty voice."

"I'll bet he does," Catalina declared grimly.

"There," Shawna said, as she stepped back to look at Catalina again. "You really are so beautiful."

"Thank you, Shawna. Have you ever thought of leaving here and finding a nice home to live in, with friends or family? Do you have a family?"

Shawna's face blanched and tears sprang to her magnificent, yet innocent, eyes. Her lips quivered.

"No," she gasped. "I . . . I don't want to leave China. Marc says I don't have to—I don't have to. He says I don't ever have to go back there. I don't have to! I don't have to!"

Catalina was totally shocked, for she realized that Shawna was terrified. She was again filled with disgust. Marc Copeland was obviously taking advantage of Shawna's fear to keep her where he wanted her—under

166

his command.

She had to change the subject before Shawna succumbed to the strange fear that held her.

"China," she said gently. "China is your friend?"

"Oh, yes." Shawna's face brightened at once, as if she had shut one door and opened another.

"I haven't met China yet. She lives on the boat also?"

"Yes. She lives with Marc."

The words were said with such total trust that Catalina was nearly struck speechless. "I see," she said grimly.

She decided that Marc Copeland was a total scoundrel. What could she put past him after what she had heard? A wave of horror washed over her as she thought about what such a man might have done with Seth.

Seth had gotten in Marc's way and she was now certain that Marc had done something about it. She just wondered what. She had to find out, and she knew there were two people who might have that information—Marc and the elusive China.

"I thank you for helping me dress, Shawna," Catalina said gently. "It was considerate since I left home so quickly I had no opportunity to bring a maid."

"You're welcome. It was a pleasure to help. You're nice. I like you. Sometimes Nina and Charlene and Paulette can be mean. Oh, I don't mean real mean . . . but they're not like you."

Catalina's heart went out to Shawna, who seemed to be caught in a terrible life, and fury at Marc settled in her breast like a live coal.

"Catalina?"

"Yes?"

"Are you Mr. Sherman's mistress?"

The question was asked so casually that Catalina, at first, could only stare at Shawna in disbelief. Then she

167

realized in Shawna's childlike mind a man and woman who traveled together and were not married must be in such a situation.

"No, Shawna, I am not. Can you see that the door between us is securely bolted? I have no intention of unbolting it. Mr. Sherman is just a friend who is trying to help me find . . . something I recently lost."

"Oh . . ."

"What made you think I was . . . that our situation was involved?"

"He is very handsome."

"H'm, yes, he is."

"But not as handsome as Marc." Shawna giggled softly.

"Handsome only describes the exterior, Shawna. It is the man within that counts. I think Marc Copeland lacks what it takes to be truly handsome. He is a cold and calculating opportunist who does not hesitate to take what pleases him."

"Why do you feel like that? Marc is a good man."

"You are being deceived. Shawna, will you tell me something?"

"Yes, if I can."

"Is there another young gentleman aboard anywhere? I mean . . . maybe he is ill or something and your friends are watching over him."

"I do not think so. But I can ask China."

"No. Don't do that. It's all right. I was only curious. Please don't bother. I'll ask Marc myself."

Catalina had no intention of doing that, but she had thought it possible Shawna might tell her where Seth was without Marc and China knowing. Catalina was more than curious about the woman called China. She thought China was the madam for Marc's hoard of prostitutes and she envisioned her as a hard cold woman who used people as freely as Marc did.

168

Before either woman could speak again, there was a light rap on her door.

"Catalina?" Travis called from the hallway.

"I'll be with you in a moment," Catalina replied. She didn't want to invite him in and give the impression that he could come and go as he chose. The adjoining door still irritated her.

"Thank you again, Shawna. I believe it's time for dinner. Would you care to eat with us?"

"No, I will eat in China and Marc's rooms."

China and Marc. Of course. Was she his mistress too? The man must be an insatiable satyr. God, how she detested him. Whatever blow she could strike at him, she would carry out without hesitation.

Catalina opened the door and stepped out into the hall with Shawna behind her. Since she was draping a lace shawl over her shoulders, she missed Travis's lascivious glance. But Shawna didn't. Her smile faded, and she shivered slightly. She hoped Catalina knew what this man was like.

By the time Catalina looked up, the heated look in Travis's eyes had been replaced by a cool and friendly glance.

"You look lovely as usual, Cat," he said. "The dining room is exquisite, and I hear the chef is excellent. We can look forward to a very pleasant evening."

If he hoped the evening would end in Catalina's bed, he kept his thoughts in control. What Catalina didn't know was that he had laid a plan for their evening hours ago.

After asking several pertinent but subtle questions of the crew, he had found the man he wanted, a man who would do anything for a price, no questions asked. He had returned to his stateroom and sent for the man, who appeared after a lengthy wait.

The crewman was short, rather squat and shapeless.

His dark eyes were shielded by hooded lids that gave him a reptilian look, and his teeth were broken and yellowed. He had been hired by Marc's captain due to a last-minute need for a roustabout, but the captain had already decided to replace him at the first opportnity for this was not the type of man Marc liked to have on his crew.

Travis was appalled by the scent of the man's obviously unwashed body. But no matter, he was a tool Travis needed.

"What's your name?" Travis said in a commanding voice that cowed the roustabout.

"Best, sir. Willie Best."

"Well, Willie, I have a little job for you."

"Aye, sir." Willie's eyes followed Travis's hand as it went to his pocket and brought forth several gold coins. He licked his lips in anticipation.

Travis was assured that he had found the right man. He had seen the glow of avarice before. "It seems I need a door to be opened for me and a little . . . work to be done on someone. Can you do this?"

Willie knew exactly what Travis wanted, entrance to someone else's stateroom. He had no qualms about breaking in if he were paid enough for it.

"I can gets into any room on this boat any time I wants ta."

"Good." Travis smiled. "I want this little job done while the lady and I are at dinner."

"Sure." Willie's eyes narrowed. "What'cha payin' fer this little bit o' work?"

Travis let the gold coins clink from one hand to the other. Their glitter held Willie spellbound.

"They're all yours. I'll see you on deck when I finish my dinner. If you tell me this little job is done, I'll give you these." Again he let the tinkle of coins fill the air.

But Willie fashioned himself too shrewd for this

ploy. Besides he had been fooled too many times. "Give me half of 'em now and half later, and I'll do what ya want. If not, ya can just do the job yourself."

Travis laughed to himself, but he kept his amusement camouflaged. Without another word he counted out half the coins and put them into Willie's dirty hand.

"Now, Willie, here's what I want you to do."

Marc sat across the table from China. It was covered by an immaculate white tablecloth, on which fine china settings were placed, and crystal that reflected the light from the chandeliers. He had just looked toward the dining-room doorway for the tenth time, and China was worried. This woman had had more of an effect on Marc than he would admit. That was evident for each time he looked at the door his eyes registered disappointment.

China's greatest value to Marc was her ability to keep her face from revealing any judgment of him. He also relied on her to give him answers he needed before he voiced certain questions.

"She has not entertained him in her stateroom," China said quietly.

Marc's eyes flickered back to her, filled with questions.

"Shawna spent much of the afternoon with her. She likes her."

Marc laughed softly. "Shawna likes everyone."

"Marc, Shawna is like a child. Sometimes children see clearer than grown people whose viewpoints have become jaded by emotions and occurrences."

"This time she's wrong, China. Catalina Carrington is deceitful and spoiled—a little rich girl who is as unscrupulous as her father. She just hides behind a pretty face."

171

"You find her attractive?" China said, but as she watched Marc's face she found her answer. She knew without turning around that Catalina had entered the room and that her appearance was having a devastating effect on Marc.

Then, as if suddenly remembering that China was watching him, Marc's face froze into an unreadable mask. But it was too late. China knew quite well the turbulence in Marc had been stirred to new heights by Catalina's appearance. She also sensed that this woman was more at his mercy than she realized.

China began to wonder if she should not have a private conversation with Catalina, at least enough of a conversation to find out about her relationship with Marc. He had, so far, refused to share that information.

She still felt as she had at the beginning, that the truth was something Marc didn't know. It seemed to be just out of his reach, and she didn't want to see him hurt anymore, nor did she want to see Catalina suffer for something she'd had no part in.

As Catalina and Travis stood framed in the doorway, Marc suddenly felt he would not be able to take his next breath. She exuded a sense of delicate beauty that reached out with unseen tendrils to coil about his nerves and draw them taut as bowstrings.

Her hair, drawn back severely, left her face open to his hungry gaze, and he could actually feel the silk of her skin on the tips of his fingers. He imagined that he was touching her features, perfect and finely boned, as he looked into eyes touched to gold-amber flame by the glow of the chandeliers. Her cheeks bloomed with delicate color, and the soft curves of her lips would entice the most controlled of men into wanting to taste their tantalizing softness. She was smiling a half-smile that intrigued him. He wondered what she was thinking.

Her gown was cut simply, but its crimson velvet material enhanced her exposed shoulders and drew his eyes to the soft curves of breasts which seemed to swell from the lace trim of the low décolletage. The bright velvet gown made her sable hair seem even darker, yet it reflected the glow of the light and made him remember well the thick satiny feel of her tresses in his hands.

Marc totally ignored Travis until China's soft voice came to him from what seemed a long distance away.

"He is quite handsome, this Travis Sherman. They make a very attractive couple."

Travis was indeed striking, but China felt the coldness within him. A much better judge of the baseness in some men than Marc would ever be, she trusted her instincts. Travis Sherman was a man to be watched carefully.

China was aware also of the current that seemed to draw Catalina's eyes to Marc. She noted her sudden intake of breath and the unconscious parting of her lips as if she had whispered his name. Obviously she had not, for Travis did not react as China knew he would if Marc's name had been on Catalina's lips.

Catalina had stepped into the room, feeling that she was capable of handling anything that might occur. She let her gaze roam across the large elaborate dining salon. It was familiar to her, for her father had often taken her to see the *Belle* being built.

It was a long salon, designed to rival the most beautiful ballroom in New Orleans. The chandeliers were aglitter with reflected light, and the tables were set to accommodate those with the finest taste and the most demanding palates.

Catalina felt pride and satisfaction in what her father had built, and then her eyes met Marc's. She silently groaned and tried to tear her eyes away, but they refused to obey. Instead, they seemed to absorb him.

He was recklessly handsome, his firm, almost sensuous mouth flexed and the intensity of him reminiscent of a cat or a wolf—of strength ready to explode. Despite the black dinner jacket and the froth of white lace at his throat and cuffs, his body was that of a well-tuned animal with long and supple muscles, sinews that flexed and stretched and rippled.

Marc rose slowly and began to move toward them, the sureness of his stride setting Catalina's nerves on edge. Despite her determination to hate him, she had to admire his sensual grace.

"Good evening, Mr. Sherman . . . Miss Carrington," he said, and the velvet in his voice inflamed her. It was accompanied by a knowledgeable smile, and she watched him as his eyes raked over her in blatant admiration. "How lovely you look tonight, Miss Carrington. You grace my salon. Would you care to join us?"

Catalina was about to refuse when she saw the woman at Marc's table. China. The idea of meeting Marc Copeland's mistress was intriguing. She did not question her curiosity or fear she would be unwelcome.

"Catalina?" Travis questioned, hoping she would decline. His plans did not include spending any part of the evening with Marc Copeland. But his hopes were dashed as Catalina responded in a voice as cool and smooth as Marc's.

"We would be delighted, Mr. Copeland."

Marc stood aside and bowed slightly to let her pass him. Then he stepped between Catalina and an angered Travis to follow her to the table from which a narrow-eyed China watched them approach.

Catalina meant to be cool and aloof in the presence of Marc's mistress, but as she drew near her, she was aware that she had never seen anyone of such delicate and electrifying beauty. She wanted to dislike the woman, but in honesty she could well understand how Marc could be intrigued.

"China," Marc said with aggravating sweetness, "this is Catalina Carrington and her . . . friend, Travis Sherman."

Catalina smiled through gritted teeth. If she had had a knife she would have plunged it, to the hilt, into his breast because of the casual way he had implied that she and Travis were more than friends.

"Good evening, Miss Carrington . . . Mr. Sherman." China smiled pleasantly. "Please sit down. I have ordered wine."

Marc held Catalina's chair and "accidentally" let his hand brush her shoulder after she sat down.

Emotions raged through her, emotions so turbulent that she was afraid someone would read them on her face. His touch, like fire, had sent fingers of flame through her.

But he moved away, to all eyes heedless of her response. In truth, his matched hers and he was silently cursing himself for letting her affect him so.

The wine came and the four were silent as it was poured. Then Marc raised his glass to offer a toast, and his eyes glittered with dangerous humor as he spoke.

"To all kinds of friendships," he said. "Productive . . . and unproductive."

Catalina stared at him over the rim of her glass, longing to sneer at him, to strike him. It was his smug, self-satisfied expression that riled her. Her thoughts were venomous, but her smile dripped sweetness. She did not intend to allow him to see that any barb he'd used had annoyed her in any way.

She raised her glass to touch his with a soft clink; then she drank half the glass in one quick swallow. On her empty stomach, the wine was potent and a challenging glow appeared in her eyes.

They spent a bit more time with China and Marc; then Travis suggested they return to their table for dinner and Catalina quickly agreed. She was somewhat disturbed because China had not been the kind of woman she'd thought her. Instead, China was quiet, polite, and Catalina was well aware that her dark eyes missed nothing. This was something Catalina would have to consider.

After Travis and Catalina had ordered, Catalina positioned herself so she could look across several tables at Marc. He seemed to be enjoying his dinner with China, for he bent close to her to talk and they laughed often. Distracted, Catalina did not notice how often Travis filled her wine glass.

"Have you asked any questions of the crew?" she asked him. "Or any of the passengers? Has there been any sign of Seth?"

"I've hardly had time to do that, Cat, but I will."

"I've talked to one of his . . . lady friends," she responded. "Of course she denied any knowledge of Seth. Oh, Travis, someone on this boat must have seen something, even if he—or she—doesn't realize it."

"Cat, for God's sake. I have said I will talk to every member of the crew of this boat. If there are any answers to be found here, we'll find them. Now, let's relax and enjoy our dinner."

"I'm sorry, Travis, I'm just so . . ." She shrugged and reached for her wine glass again, to calm her nerves. All of her tension was not, to her deeper distress, due to worry over Seth. Some was caused by the pair who sat together so intimately on the other side of the salon.

Travis smiled as he emptied their second bottle of wine and ordered a third. He watched Catalina's eyes glimmer from the effect of the wine, and he began to think of the pleasure awaiting him.

Willie moved down the semidark hall very slowly, prepared to get away quickly should anyone question him. But that was unlikely for most of the passengers were having dinner. He finally stopped before the door he wanted and knelt before it.

He took a thin piece of metal from his pocket. It was four inches long and had a small hook on the end.

Slipping it between the door and the doorjamb he manipulated it for several seconds, until he heard a soft click. He smiled to himself and stood. Then he reached for the handle, turned it, and the door swung open.

Willie glanced up and down the hall. Then he stepped into the room and closed the door behind him.

Chapter 13

"The dinner was exquisite." Catalina laughed. "And I have most certainly had too much wine. I'm slightly inebriated. I would really like to go to my stateroom, Travis."

"One more glass before we . . . sleep."

"No, no really, I don't think I should have any more."

She rose, and Travis had no choice but to stand. Catalina wavered for a moment. Then, with Travis's hand on her elbow, she walked from the dining room.

As Marc watched a scowl drew his brows together. His mouth was a firm line of ill-concealed anger. She was laughing, going with the man to share his bed for the night. He wanted to put his hands around her slender throat and squeeze until she begged . . . until she spoke the truth . . . until she . . . He turned to face China again, not wanting to see them leave.

"I wonder," China said thoughtfully.

"Wonder what?"

"If things truly are the way they appear."

"Don't doubt it, China."

"Then why did she deny she's his mistress?"

"What?"

"I said, why did she tell Shawna that she is not his mistress. Surely it is obvious to all, and she must know that he booked passage in adjoining rooms. Yet she denies it. For the short time she was at our table I sensed—"

"China, I'm in no mood for female intuition. Stop trying to see things that aren't there because you don't approve of what I'm doing."

"Marc . . . what are your plans for her?"

He smiled at her over the rim of his glass. "Let the lovers enjoy tonight. Before they can do so again I intend to rid the *Belle* of one Travis Sherman. After that"—he chuckled—"we shall see how we can add to the illustrious Catalina Carrington's reputation."

He tossed off the last of his drink and then rose before China could offer anymore arguments. He was already in more difficulty than he cared to admit.

"I'm going up on deck for a smoke before I go to bed. Good night."

"Marc . . ."

"Good night, China." He reached down to touch her cheek. "Stop worrying about me, and for God's sake, China, she doesn't deserve one minute of your thoughts. She just isn't worth it. Eventually you're going to see the truth. In the meantime, just be there. All right?"

China put her hand over Marc's and her eyes glowed with affection. "As you were always there. I'm sorry, Marc. I just don't want you to make a mistake that will hurt you. You have been hurt enough."

"Good night," he said again. Then, ignoring her pleading look, he turned and left the room.

China watched Marc's broad shoulders until he was gone. Within moments of his departure, she rose and returned to her cabin.

Marc climbed the steps to the top deck. As he did he took a long thin cigar from his breast pocket. He placed it between his teeth, then paused to strike a match against the rail. Turning his back to the breeze, he lit the cigar and then tossed the match overboard. There were no other people about so he walked to the stern of the boat, folded his arms on the rail, and watched the huge paddle wheel slowly churn the water into white froth.

The night was warm, and the moon, full and golden, seemed to be resting on the water. It sent a path of light across the river, dappling it with mellow gold.

No matter how hard he fought her, how deliberately, Catalina slipped within the barriers and touched him. The scent of her perfume spun webs of remembrance, and he could almost taste the soft moistness of her lips. Again he held her cool sensuous body in his arms, tangled his hands in the thick sable shadows of her hair.

White smoke curled past his narrowed eyes as he fought his inability to blot out the vision that leapt into his mind—Catalina writhing in passion in the arms of Travis Sherman.

Catalina closed the door of her stateroom and slid the bolt locking it. The room was lit only by the lamp in the far corner. Its light touched the bed with a mellow glow, but left the balance of the room in degrees of shadow.

She moved slowly, laughing softly at her own inability to make her body obey her commands. Awkwardly, she worked the buttons of her dress, then let it drop to the floor, deciding she could pick it up in the morning. Loosening her many petticoats, she let them follow the gown. In her silk and lace shift Catalina's lush charms were evident. She went to the small table where her brush and comb lay, and sat on a low bench. As she removed the pins from her hair it fell about her in a tangled mass. She brushed it only from habit, and only for a few minutes, for she already felt the effects of the wine. Catalina promised herself not to be so foolish again. She had come to find out about her brother, not to make herself so incapacitated she was unable to find out anything.

She set the brush down wearily, and, her eyes heavy, she walked to the bed. She didn't even bother to change into her night gown, which would have covered much more of her than the scant piece of silk and lace she wore, but slid beneath the covers. In a few seconds she had drifted into a half-awake, half-asleep state.

Her mind, freed to wonder, drifted to Marc. In this state her emotions took over and she delved into memories. Memories of the touch of his hand, of the hard strength of his body, of . . . She drifted deeper and deeper into places her conscious mind would never go. She lost touch with reality, and was completely unaware that the door between her room and Travis's had slowly swung open.

Travis crossed the room soundlessly and stood beside the bed, gazing down at Catalina. He sucked in his breath at the exotic effect of her vulnerability and her beauty. His hands shook with the urgent need to touch her, and his loins tightened with desire.

Her hair was spread across the white pillow, and her lashes lay thick and dark against the soft flush of her cheeks. Her breath came slowly and deeply through half-parted lips . . . lush moist lips that he could resist no longer.

Removing his robe, he eased into the bed beside her, and gently put his arm about her, drawing her close to him. The shock of her warm curves excited him almost more than he could bear.

Caught in a dream, Catalina reacted to the hard arm about her, melting against the dream of Marc and the reality of Travis.

In the soft mist of her dream, Catalina felt his hands caress her gently and her lips parted in response to the soft pressure of his. But something was wrong. Some small alarm sounded in her mind, and slowly, as the pressure of the body against hers became more heated, more demanding, she struggled up from the depths of wine-drugged sleep.

Her eyes fluttered open and she looked up at the dark form above her. It was a moment before she realized that she was responding wantonly to Travis Sherman's passionate embrace.

He knew she was awake now, but he was certain she was as caught up in passion as he was.

"Travis!" she gasped, when his mouth released hers.

"Shh, sweet," he whispered, as his hands began to caress her. "Relax, Cat. It will be wonderful for us both. Relax . . . let me love you. Let me teach you what passion means."

"No . . . Travis . . . don't." She struggled to be free, but the weight of his body pressed her against the mattress. Sliding her hands between them, she tried to exert enough force to separate them.

But Travis had more than twice her weight and he'd tossed one leg across her lower body, so she was quite effectively pinned beneath him.

"Don't fight me, Cat," he said huskily, as he continued to kiss her cheek and throat. "You'll enjoy it, I promise. You want it as much as I do. I can tell your passion is as hot as mine. You're so sweet . . . so soft."

His mouth searched for hers again, but Catalina was rapidly regaining her self-control.

"Travis! How dare you," she cried. "Get out of here . . . get off of me!" Her voice rose.

Travis was so certain that she was as involved in sensual pleasure as he and would be unable to resist him, he stopped only for a moment. Then his arrogant self-assurance took over, blotting out both his common sense and his sense of self-preservation. He had taken into account only his desire and his strength, not Catalina's angry determination.

"Cat, there's no need to pretend with me," he assured her confidently. "What is wrong with us enjoying whatever pleasure we can find in each other? No one will know. You are a warm, seductive woman. Let's take our pleasure to the fullest. Don't fight what I know you want as much as I do."

Catalina's fury was rising. Like a tidal wave, it swept through her, bringing a new strength to her body. She began to battle, closing her fists to strike and kicking out furiously with her legs as she bucked her body beneath his.

"Let me go! Who gave you the right to come in here, you sneaking rake? Let me go!"

Travis was beginning to get the idea that Catalina was unwilling, but it made no difference to him. He was wild with desire, and he meant to have her.

"Little fool, be quiet. What will people think if you draw attention to us? The door between our staterooms is open. No one will believe you to be anything other than a temperamental mistress. You're frightened now, Cat, but after I prove to you how wonderful your surrender will be, you will learn to enjoy our coming together."

What he'd said about the bolted door caught Catalina's attention.

"How did you? . . . I bolted that door!"

He smiled, still holding her firmly. "There are ways, Cat. I knew once I had convinced you of what we had to share, the bolt would no longer matter."

"Get out of my bed! Get out of this room, or I shall see you dead for this. You have no right to be here. You are not welcome, no matter what your overblown conceit may tell you." Catalina spoke through clenched teeth. "If you aren't out of here in five minutes I will scream until every soul on this boat is awakened."

"Cat, be sensible." He laughed. "You will blacken your own name. Besides, I could feel your response so why fight it."

"You egotistical, arrogant, deceitful ape, let go of me!"

A few minutes more of struggle proved to Catalina that Travis had absolutely no intention of doing that, and he seemed certain she really wouldn't scream. Her mind began to race, and Travis smiled, believing Catalina had struggled only for modesty's sake and now intended to surrender.

She could feel his body relax as hers did, and she wanted him to do just that. She let her body grow soft and controlled her anger so that he could read only what he chose to in her eyes.

"Travis, please," she said softly. "Your leg is so heavy."

He shifted his leg so that it was no longer across her, and a sense of triumph lit his eyes. But only for a moment.

Catalina knew she would be lost if she lingered too long over deciding what to do. She mentally calculated the distance between her and the door, figuring the few seconds it would take to slide the bolt and get it open. She wasn't sure where she could run, being clothed in nearly nothing, but she could afford to wait no longer. This was the only opportunity she had.

Travis lay on his side facing her, and she rolled slightly to face him. As his gloating smile revealed his thoughts, she struck swiftly and with every ounce of strength she possessed. Bringing her knee up in a full thrust, she caught him in his well-aroused groin. At the same time she pushed against his chest to roll herself away from him.

She heard his gurgling muffled cry of sheer anguish, but she had no time to waste. She rolled away and fell to the floor beside the bed, then scrambled to her feet and ran for the door. Behind her there were muffled curses and movement, and she knew despite the pain he was in pursuit.

Fear brought a soft moan from her as she slammed against the door and fumbled for the bolt.

To her it seemed to move very slowly, and she could almost feel his gripping hands. Then the bolt was shot, and she tore the door open with a relieved sob. Blindly she dashed into the shadowed passageway, only to collide with a rocklike form that grasped her trembling body.

She looked up through angry tears, and to her dismay into the shocked green eyes of Marc Copeland.

Marc had been furious over not being able to exorcise Catalina from his mind. With grim determination, he had tossed away the stub of his cigar and had started below, quite prepared to immerse himself in two things—a bottle of whiskey and the charms of Nina Brent. The two would help him blot out the unwelcome thoughts he could not seem to control.

He walked slowly until he came to the corridor that took him past Catalina's stateroom, battling his thoughts. He refused to think about what she might be doing. He would not allow himself to believe that the door between her stateroom and Travis's had been opened.

He was just a foot or two from her door when it was suddenly thrown open, and too quickly for him to realize what was happening, he found his arms full of a very nearly naked Catalina.

She gave a soft choking gasp, and for a heart-stopping moment she clung to him.

"Damn," he muttered in surprise. He looked at the door, still hanging open, expected to see someone or something in hot pursuit. But there was no sign of anyone.

Catalina finally achieved some semblance of control over her trembling body and shattered nerves. She looked up into Marc's eyes and saw total shock in them.

"What the hell's going on?" he asked. But he didn't loosen his hold on her, for he enjoyed the feel of her softness in his arms and the way she clung to him.

"You! Of all people, you," Catalina groaned.

He frowned deeply. "I was just passing by. You"—he grinned evilly now—"are the undressed lady who has just thrown herself into my arms. Oh, I'm willing all right." He chuckled. "I'd just like a little notice and better circumstances. Don't you think this passageway is a bit public?"

She leapt back from him as if she had been burnt. He regretted her leaving his arms, but he certainly enjoyed the picture she presented.

Her hair fell about her in wild profusion, nearly to her waist. What little she wore revealed more than it concealed, and he was more than just aware of her; his body was responding to every curve and valley of her slim form. The peaks of her breasts were clearly visible through the sheer fabric of her shift, as was the dark valley between her thighs.

She was breathing harshly, as if, he thought with a stab of aggravating jealousy, she had just been involved in a very passionate and intimate moment.

Catalina thought of the unbolted door and of what he must be thinking. Giving no more thought to her undressed state, she drew herself erect, her fury magnificent.

186

"I want another stateroom, now!"

"How about mine?" He laughed.

"Oh, you men are all alike. You are governed by what's between your legs. You have no honor or pride when it comes to your baser appetites."

"Just a minute." His smile faded. "If I'm not mistaken you attacked me, and besides"—his eyes raked her body—"I don't think you're in any position to be talking about my baser appetites. It looks like you've been appeasing a few appetites of your own."

"I've very nearly been raped," she almost shouted. "Or is that such a usual happening on your boat that one is supposed to overlook it."

"Raped!" he said, in shock. Then he reached past her and pushed the door open. There was no sign of anyone. "By whom?"

She gasped and turned to step back into the room, treating a very appreciative Marc to trim legs and buttocks as she did.

Travis was clever; he had stepped back into his room. Knowing he had to do something to make it appear that he was an innocent participant in this affair, and not caring if he damaged Catalina's reputation, he waited until he heard Marc's voice, then slipped into his robe, opened the door, and leaned against the frame. The smile on his face was very suggestive.

"Come on, Cat, just because we've had a little lover's spat doesn't mean you have to run for the captain. We can kiss and make up and it will all be over."

Catalina let out a half-shocked gurgle and then a shriek of surprise and anger.

"Don't you dare lead him to believe I planned this! You tell the truth!"

"Now really, Cat." Travis chuckled. "I do believe your unbolted door and your bed are truth enough."

187

The tangled sheets on her bed gave mute evidence that someone had been moving about wildly on it.

Marc's gaze went to her side of the door and took in the fact that it was unbolted. Her eyes followed his.

"I didn't unbolt that door!"

"Who did?" Marc asked, disbelieving amusement in his voice. "He couldn't have done it from his side."

Catalina didn't have the answer, and suddenly she no longer cared. Her distrust and hatred of both men had brought her to the brink of frustrated tears—tears she had no intention of shedding before either of them.

She knew she would have to be on her guard from this moment on. She almost ran to her chest, withdrew a robe and slipped into it. Then she turned to Marc.

"I want another stateroom and I want it now—this minute," she demanded coldly.

"You're sure of that?" Marc retorted, the glitter of something unnameable in the depths of his eyes.

"Yes . . . quite sure. My things can be moved in the morning, but I want another stateroom now."

"All right," Marc said softly, "I'll see that you get another room. While I make the arrangements, go down to room twelve, here's the key. China will join you there. You can stay with her."

"I don't—"

"Go right now," Marc said coldly, "or you can just stay here and play games for the rest of the night with your lover."

Catalina fairly tore the key from Marc's hand. Then, unable to articulate one word that would have been acceptable in polite society, she glared at him and passed him, making sure she did not come close enough to touch him.

Marc was left alone with Travis, and for a moment Travis contemplated Marc's almost unreadable face. Then he chuckled softly.

"The other room will only be temporary. Cat just became angry at something I said. She'll be back here before the night is over."

His assurance grated on Marc's nerves, as did Marc's own doubts about Catalina and the unbolted door. He tried to be civil, but his dislike of Travis made it difficult.

"I wouldn't push it tonight if I were you. Give the . . . ah . . . lady a chance to cool off a bit."

"You needn't worry." Travis smiled. "Cat and I are very old friends. She'll get over this soon. She always does."

"You've had these altercations before?"

"Quite often."

"Well, I don't think you'll have to worry about her tonight. She's safe."

"You said number twelve?"

"Yes, but I wouldn't try going there tonight." Marc flashed a white and innocent smile. "China has a gun and she's a deadly shot at close range."

Travis remained silent, but his decision to rid himself of Marc Copeland grew. It pleased him to know that he had the means to keep Catalina and Marc apart. No matter how Catalina felt about him now, she hated Marc even more.

As Marc moved away, he sensed that Travis's eyes were burning into his back. Once he was out of Travis's sight he moved quickly. The room he went to was number thirteen.

There he found China preparing for bed. She was surprised at his knock.

"Marc?"

"China my love, I'd like you to do me a very big favor."

"Of course."

"Spend the balance of the trip in Shawna's cabin. I

189

need this one."

China seldom questioned Marc's decisions, so she gathered a few things. When she left, Marc went to the door of number twelve. He smiled to himself as he lifted his hand to knock.

Catalina Carrington had played right into his hands. He now had her where he wanted her. What she didn't know was that she was firmly entrenched in his quarters. And he meant to keep her there until he exacted the payment from her he'd been thinking of for a long time.

He knocked firmly on the door.

Chapter 14

Catalina slammed the door so hard that it swung back open and she had the satisfaction of slamming it again. She had often been angry, but she'd never felt such all-consuming fury before.

Travis's deceit plus Marc's arrogant attitude, his amusement-tinged disbelief, were too much for her. She paced back and forth like a caged lioness, her body still quivering with rage. What she didn't realize was that her anger was really directed at Marc. Suddenly she stopped pacing and breathed deeply to regain control of herself. It was then she realized the stateroom looked occupied. It took only a few glances around to figure out whose cabin this was. It was Marc Copeland's.

He thinks I've jumped from the frying pan into the fire, but he has a few surprises coming, she thought.

She had not expected Travis's move, but now she was ready to take care of herself.

The rap on the door made her jump, but she regained her equilibrium, and a glow appeared in her eyes as she jerked the door open to find Marc leaning indolently against the frame, his thumbs hooked in his belt and a lazy grin on his face.

"I just came to see if you were all right, and to make sure that you have observed that there are no other

191

doors to this room." He laughed, softly and teasingly. "Anybody invited to this room will have to come through this door."

Catalina clenched her teeth. "I did not unbolt that door, and no one—no one," she repeated firmly, "is welcome in my stateroom."

"You know this is my cabin?"

"I surmised that."

He shrugged. "You don't mind if I come in, just to gather a few things. It will only take a minute."

"Is there no other cabin empty?"

"No. Of course you could go back to your own cabin. I'm sure your . . . ah . . . friend would welcome you with open arms."

"I don't want to put you to any trouble. I'd be glad to . . . if you'll see that the door between those two staterooms is nailed shut."

"Hardly. I don't ever damage what belongs to me, especially something as beautiful as the *Belle.*"

Being reminded that the *Belle* now belonged to him stirred Catalina to anger again, but she forcefully reminded herself that she was here for a purpose. The thought entered her head that she might find some trace of Seth if she waged a less obvious battle. To Marc's surprise she stood aside and motioned for him to enter.

As he walked in, she turned from the door, fully intending to leave it open. It was bad enough that she wore so little. If any of her family or friends were to see her in this compromising position, they would be scandalized. But Marc, as she passed him, reached back to swing the door shut. It closed with a sharp click causing her to spin about.

The taunting glow in his eyes killed the angry words on her lips. She would be damned if she'd let him think for one minute that the situation was out of her control.

He went to a cupboard and removed some clothes,

then to a small chest from which he took personal material. Putting all these things on the bed, he knelt to slide a satchel out from under it.

He started to pack the satchel, aware that Catalina's eyes had never left him. He laughed to himself, for despite her bravado he could sense both her anger and her fear. She was prepared to dash to the door at the first wrong move from him. Closing the satchel, he placed it on the floor and turned again to face her.

She watched the amusement in his eyes change to a blatant perusal of her, and she flushed as she folded her arms defensively before her.

"Would you like me to go back and get some of your things?"

"No!" she didn't want him pawing through her personal belongings. "Can they not be packed and brought here tomorrow? Maybe Shawna would help me. She is very kind."

The unreadable look in Marc's eyes took Catalina by surprise.

"You trust Shawna?"

"Of course. She's . . ."

"Innocent," Marc supplied softly.

"Yes . . . innocent," Catalina said, as if it surprised her.

"She is that," he added thoughtfully. "A little too innocent to be corrupted. I'll send someone, most likely China, to get your things."

"Are you suggesting that I . . ." She sucked in her breath, her temper aroused by his suggestion that he did not consider associating with her positive for one of his playthings.

"I'm not suggesting anything." He sounded amused. "Just being protective of Shawna. She means a lot to me."

"Yes," Catalina said scornfully. "I can imagine she

193

does. And I can imagine why you don't want her to be exposed to any outside influence. She might just realize there's a world out there that's got more to offer than you do."

"Don't talk about what you could never understand. I'll send someone to gather your things. They'll be brought to you in the morning."

"Thank you," she said, her words dripping acid.

"Tell me"—Marc leaned casually against the bedpost and folded his arms across his chest—"are you really sure you want all your things moved? I understood that you and your friend were taking this trip together."

"In this case," she replied coldly, "together does not mean in the same room."

"Or in the same bed," he added.

"As I told you, Mr. Copeland," she said with antagonizing patience, "only people of your caliber, and Travis's, think with their loins. I prefer to choose very carefully the person with whom I would share intimacy. You can rest assured that neither you or Travis would find me receptive."

"Well then, if this little tête-à-tête isn't just fun and games for you and your friend, just what are you doing on the *Belle?* I'm more than sure there were several other boats you could have taken."

"None as beautiful as the *Belle.*" She didn't want his thoughts moving in this direction. It wouldn't take him long to put two and two together. She realized she was in a difficult position. She had to let him believe what he suspected about her and Travis was the truth, not that she was on his trail. Unable to say the words that would brand her as Travis's mistress she decided to let him think what he wanted, though she knew what that was. She turned away from the intensity of his gaze. It was too knowing, and its effect was unwelcome.

Marc was mildly confused, but he still believed that Catalina and Travis were lovers, and he knew it would give him a great deal of pleasure to spoil their plans. He had plans of his own for her, and Travis had no part in them. What had happened that night had worked into his plans so well he could hardly believe it. Still some sixth sense sent a warning through him. He was well aware that Catalina could be treacherous; all the Carringtons were treacherous.

Despite this, and to his immense surprise, he found he was reluctant to leave her. He did not question the fact that he now had an opportunity to begin to wreak his vengeance. Who could stop him if he chose to take her? For a moment his eyes glittered, and Catalina would have tasted real fear had she turned to look at him then.

But he controlled his body and his mind by exerting his will. Not this way, he cautioned himself. He didn't want her to be able to say he had forced her. No, he wanted her will to bend. He wanted her pride in the dirt. He wanted her to be completely at his mercy so that when he threw her away he could tell her the reason, could watch her break. Only then would his vengeance against her be complete.

His silence forced her to turn and look at him again. That silence filled the room as they looked at each other.

The thought that leapt into his mind shocked him. What if he had met her at another time, under different circumstances? If that were . . . But it wasn't.

She stood before him and her reserve only served to make him realize he had to regain his control before he let her beauty and seeming vulnerability break through his guard.

"No, there are not many boats as beautiful as the *Belle*. I'm going to enjoy owning her, and I expect she'll

195

make me a great deal of money."

"How can you think of using a boat as beautiful as the *Belle* for a floating bordello?" she asked.

"Bordello." He chuckled. "I'm afraid you are confusing my intentions with your own. Why else would you and your friend choose the *Belle?* Obviously you put truth to rumors and believe the delights you choose to indulge in are the same others seek."

Being openly called a whore was just about the last insult Catalina could bear for that night.

"How dare you!" she grated.

"Dare? How dare I do what?" His smile made her feel the distinct urge to kill.

"You are a most nefarious man, Mr. Copeland." She tried to control her voice because her anger was nearly out of control. "If there were another stateroom I could have, I would be out of your quarters immediately, but I am forced to use it for the night. Surely under these circumstances I can do so without the discomfort of your arrogance and your evil thoughts. If you please, just leave me alone. I would like to sleep."

He unfolded his arms and crossed the few feet that separated them, watching a wary fear leap into her eyes. Yet he took little pleasure in this for memories touched him. He stifled his desire to see another look in her eyes.

"It's my pleasure to have rescued a damsel in distress," he said wickedly. "Of course if you should need to be rescued from anything during the night you need only call out. Oh, I forgot to tell you"—his smile left her little doubt that she should be afraid of him—"I'm right next door. This was my room and the one next door is China's. You will call if you need anything . . . anything at all."

"Damn you, get out of here. I wouldn't call you if I were dying."

His satisfied chuckle was soft in the air as he bowed slightly, took up the satchel, and then walked to the door. As he pulled it open, he turned to her.

"Good night, kitten," he said softly. "Sleep well."

When he closed the door after him, she raced across the room and slid the bolt home. Then she returned to sit on the edge of the bed, all thoughts of sleep gone.

She had not been so severely shaken in a long time. She had made many mistakes, but she had always been sure that she could face whatever might arise. Travis had taken her unprepared, but she had felt less fear when he had her trapped on the bed than she had felt when Marc Copeland had stood close to her and their eyes had met. He was the kind of danger she had not planned on, a danger that seemed to sense her every weakness.

She forced her mind from Marc and tried to form some kind of plan. She stood between Travis and Marc—two unscrupulous men. But at least she knew them. She expected no more help from Travis unless she was willing to pay for it.

If she only had some clothes, something dark to wear. Then she could slip out and search for the hold of the boat, or any other place where Seth might be.

She bit her lip as she looked at Marc's cupboard. He had not taken all his clothes. Slowly she got up from the bed and began to rummage through his things, tossing them onto the bed as she did.

She rifled his drawers until she found a pair of scissors in his desk. Then she set about shortening the length of what she maliciously hoped as his best pair of pants. They came just to her ankles when she put them on and the waist was many sizes too big. This she solved by using a strip of cloth as a sash. She put on an oversize shirt and tied it at her waist. Only then did she think of her hair. She could never be mistaken for a boy

197

with such wayward curls. Again she returned to the cupboard and searched until she found a seaman's cap. She stuffed her hair beneath the thick wool hat and pulled it down low over her brow and her ears. Since his large boots would not fit her feet, she decided to go barefoot as many of the crew did.

She didn't glance in the mirror, knowing how terrible she must look. But she found comfort in the thought that her disguise would help her find Seth, whether he was aboard or not.

The only places she would be unable to search were the staterooms occupied by Marc and his lady friends, but if necessary she would become friendly with each and every one of them. If Seth was aboard she would find him.

She blew out the lamp and the room was bathed in darkness. Then she went to the door, slid the bolt open as silently as possible, and stuck her head out to look up and down the passageway. There was no sign of anyone.

Not too many people knew the *Belle* as well as Catalina did. She was familiar with every nook and cranny in the hold where someone could be hidden.

Silently she hurried to the stairs leading down into the dark caverns of the boat. Then she gingerly began to climb down into the darkness.

As Marc left Catalina he was struck by the thought that he should have stayed with her. He had no idea why except for the fact that he didn't trust her.

As he started to go into China's stateroom another thought tingled through him. He smiled to himself, but he didn't enter her cabin. Instead, he walked down the long passageway to the heavy door that led to the deck. Once he'd gone through it, he crossed to the opposite side of the boat, went through a door that closely resembled the first, walked down another passageway, and then knocked on a stateroom door.

Charlene was surprised to see him, but she smiled invitingly.

"Marc," she said in a velvet voice filled with seductive suggestion, "what a surprise."

"Charlene my sweet, I'd like to ask you to do me a very great favor for which I will reward you with anything you name."

"Anything?" She chuckled.

"Anything."

"It must be difficult."

"No, but you can probably handle it better than anyone I know."

"Come in and tell me exactly what you want."

Marc entered her cabin and closed the door after him. It opened again a half-hour later when both Marc and Charlene stepped out into the passageway.

He slid an arm about her waist and they walked down the hall together. A great deal of money and a few subtle promises had made Charlene agree to spend the night with Travis Sherman . . . and to make sure that Catalina knew she had done so.

Travis was mentally preparing an apology for Catalina. His plans had been upset, but that did not stop him from creating new ones.

He would have Catalina as a wife if he had to tie her to the bed to seduce her. Then, for the protection of the Carrington name, she would marry him. Nothing was going to stand between him and the Carrington fortune. He would make abject apologies, throw himself on her mercy, tell her he had drunk too much and that when he had found the door open, he had thought it was an invitation.

He could blame Marc Copeland for the door's having been open, tell Catalina that Copeland was the only person on the boat who would have a key to her room. He would separate Copeland from her so that she would be left defenseless.

She would believe what he said about Marc, for to her it would sound logical. After all, Marc was her enemy, wasn't he?

Satisfied that he had concocted a good story and that Catalina's hatred of Marc would work against her, he decided he would have her back in the stateroom next to his soon. And this time he would be much more careful.

He would make sure Catalina was unable to fight him. He'd see that she had more champagne and maybe one of the small white pills he carried in a little vial for just such an emergency. Yes, he thought, the next time will be different.

The knock on his door startled him, and when he opened it, he was even more surprised.

Charlene smiled seductively. "Hello."

"Hello," Travis said with growing interest.

"I saw you at dinner tonight."

"Oh?"

"Yes. It took me a while to find out that the lady was not your wife."

"You took the time to do that?"

"Yes. I thought you might be alone and interested in a little company."

Travis smiled. Passion, thwarted by Catalina, still simmered within him, and this woman was lushly beautiful, openly seductive.

"Come in, come in. I was feeling a little lonely."

"Well, you need feel lonely no longer."

Charlene entered the stateroom, and Travis closed

and bolted the door behind her.

At the far end of the passageway, Marc chuckled as he moved out of the shadows, satisfied that Charlene would take good care of Travis and that Catalina would be one of the first to find that out tomorrow.

Marc returned to China's stateroom. He did not hear any movement in the next cabin and there had been no light beneath its door, so he felt certain Catalina must be asleep.

He started to undress, removing his jacket and shirt. Then he went to a small table and poured himself a drink.

He was uneasy, and he didn't know why . . . Of course, I know why, he thought, angry at himself. She was close, within reach, and he wanted her. He damned his own desire, but he could not deny it. He wanted her.

He finished the first drink and poured another, amused by the fact that he was so aware of himself. He intended to get drunk so that he could go to sleep and forget that she was in the palm of his hand. When he took her, it would not be with passion, but with a cold and brutal determination to subjugate her—to break her.

Expertly, he denied the emotions that bubbled inside him, refusing to let them surface. He was in control and he damned well didn't intend to lose that control this time.

Like a spider waiting for a fly to cease struggling, he had patience. He had been patient for years, he could be patient now. He tossed off his second drink and poured another.

Catalina slowly moved about in the confines of the boat. There were two types of riverboats, the Eastern and the Western built. The *Belle* was an Eastern model with a low-pressure engine, a deep hull, and the fine lines necessary for speed.

It had been created for speed, and it had enclosed upper-deck cabins for the comfort of passengers. Landing without a dock was facilitated by giving the stem of the boat a long rake, or an angle. This made it possible for a boat to strike the mud and sand of the sloping riverbank, and thereby be close enough to shore to lower a gangplank.

The areas below the main deck, those in which Catalina had begun to search, were shadowy. The presence of mice and spiders, and of things her imagination created, made her move slowly and gingerly. Her anger at Marc Copeland increased at every step.

She had just come to a small narrow compartment and bent her head to look inside. It was empty, but as she withdrew her head an arm encircled her waist and a huge hamlike hand covered her mouth and nose closing off her breath.

She struggled and fought for air, but the man who held her was immense. Slowly stars began to sparkle before her eyes. Then her fighting ceased and unconsciousness claimed her.

As soon as she sagged in his arms, the man removed his hand. He caught her up in his arms as if she were a ragdoll and tossed her over his shoulder. Then, moving as if his burden were nothing, he started toward the upper deck and the captain's cabin.

When he got to Marc's quarters, he knocked but received no answer. He knocked again and again. Finally he shook his head, surprised that his usually alert captain didn't answer.

He moved to the next cabin, feeling that China would know where Marc was. He knocked.

Marc struggled up from a euphoric half-sleep,

muttering a curse at this intrusion. He went to the door and pulled it open, and his eyes widened as he looked at the huge black man carrying an unidentifiable person.

"Jacob, what have you got there?"

"Stowaway, suh. Found him crawlin' round below. Thought yo might want to see him. Cain't be mo' dan a boy of twelve or so, suh. Yo might be able to knock some sense into him."

"Dump him on my bed, Jacob." Marc sighed. "I'll see what needs to be done."

Jacob crossed the room and dumped Catalina unceremoniously on Marc's bed.

"You're keeping a good eye, Jacob. Thanks for bringing him up. The hold is no place for a boy to sleep."

"Yassuh." Jacob chuckled. "Bet that chile was scared to death."

"I'll take care of it," Marc repeated. He closed the door after Jacob left and then walked back to the bed.

"Seems there's a conspiracy to keep me from sleeping tonight," he muttered. He stopped by the bed and his eyes widened in shock as he looked down into the unconscious face of Catalina Carrington.

Chapter 15

Catalina sucked in her breath sharply. She then gasped, coughed, and opened her eyes. She didn't know where she was until a soft aggravating chuckle from somewhere nearby made her close her eyes again and groan half-aloud. Marc Copeland.

He had been waiting patiently for Catalina to waken. Now she turned her head to glare at him.

He drew a straight-backed chair to the bed, straddled it, and rested his folded arms on the back.

His eyes were alight with such fiendish amusement that Catalina made soft inarticulate sounds that closely resembled words no lady would have spoken.

"Welcome back," Marc said, laughter in his voice. "Did you find what it was you were looking for? You gave Jacob a real scare."

"I gave him a scare!" She turned away from his penetrating gaze. "He tried to kill me!"

Marc laughed outright. "My dear Catalina, if Jacob had wanted to kill you, he could have crushed you between his hands like a walnut. Why were you prowling around my boat anyway?"

His eyes raked over her body, and from the glimpse she got out of the corners of her eyes, his look was one of fascinated wonder.

"I do believe those clothes used to belong to me. This

is a puzzle that intrigues me. What were you up to?"

"Where am I?" Catalina asked, unwilling to answer his questions.

"In my bed of course," he said, mischief dancing in his eyes. "You seem to be determined that I shan't get any sleep tonight. Not that I mind"—his voice lowered seductively—"if you insist that whatever bed is mine is also yours, I don't mind sharing."

Catalina sat up abruptly and swung her legs over the edge of the bed. She held his eyes defiantly, revealing not one ounce of regret or embarrassment over her capture. He had to admire the fire in her look.

"You may have your bed all to yourself," she said as she stood.

He didn't rise, but rested his chin on his folded arms and smiled. "Those were a pair of my very best breeches."

"Good," she replied with satisfaction. "Now if you'll excuse me I'm leaving."

He let her walk halfway across the cabin before he spoke again.

"I'm afraid you'll need a key." As she spun about, he dangled a key from outstretched fingers. "Only before I give it to you I must tell you that it annoys me very much when someone takes something that belongs to me without having asked my permission. So," he said calmly and quietly, "before you go I'd like my clothes back."

"You're insane! Give me that key." She reached for it only to find it whisked into his pocket. His eyes met hers, challenging her.

"I will," he stated. "When you return what belongs to me."

She had only the thin piece of sheer silk and lace beneath Marc's clothes, and the thought of what he was demanding raised her anger to a level that promised impending disaster.

Their eyes met and held, and both knew the other would not retreat. The moments ticked by. Then Catalina's pride won out over her stubbornness. She was not going to give an inch to this monster. She wanted that key, and she meant to have it.

Marc watched her make the decision, again admiring her self-control.

Slowly she unbuttoned the shirt and shrugged it from her shoulders, letting it fall at her feet. Her hands fumbled for a moment at the tie about her waist before the knot came undone and the cut-off breeches slid to the floor. She tugged off the hat and threw it at him, letting her hair spill about her. Then she bent and scooped up the clothes and flung them at him.

Marc was caught between conflicting emotions. He had to admire both her pride and stubbornness as well as the extraordinary picture she made. He was slowly coming to realize that breaking Catalina was not going to be as easy as he had thought. Another woman would have been in tears by now, begging to be let go, defending her honor as any proper lady should. But Catalina was not any other woman.

He rose from the chair slowly and deliberately and walked to her, hoping to intimidate her. He was rewarded, when he was close enough, by the barrier of her outstretched palm and a glow of defiance in her eyes.

"The key please," she said coldly.

"I don't know," he replied in a quiet suggestive voice. "Maybe I've changed my mind and you won't be needing the key."

Instead of fear he watched scorn appear in her eyes as a derisive smile tugged at her lips.

"Of course. Should I have expected anything less? You are not a man to be trusted to keep his word. Like

206

a rat you will scurry for any hole as long as it leads to what you want."

Marc felt the fire of anger. She had him. To keep her, he would have to use force, and that was repugnant to him. He reached out and took hold of her shoulders. The softness of her flesh made him tingle with warm excitement. He drew her to him. She did not acquiesce, nor did she resist. It would be a battle of wills. His mouth took hers.

Neither would bend as the brilliant flame of desire burst around them. Reluctantly he released her lips and their eyes met.

It took all Catalina's will to contain her desire to melt into his arms and to keep the look of derision on her face, for he read her eyes, looking for one sign of weakness.

"The key please," she said. "Or are you going to resort to rape? I assure you I will fight until you are forced to kill me before I let you succeed."

He almost flung her from him. He was not aware that every nerve in her body was quivering and that if he kissed her again, held her close again, she just might not have the resistance to fight him any longer.

She smiled the last arrogant smile she could muster, telling him that she was Catalina Carrington and she was not about to allow him to drag her into the dirt willingly. Then with slow deliberation, while her eyes rebelliously held his, she held out her hand for the key.

He was more surprised at himself than at her when he dropped the key into her outstretched palm. It was the end of a battle, not the winning of the war he'd promised himself.

Catalina smiled, turned from him, and gave him a good view of her as she walked to the door. That view would linger in his restless dreams during the long, unrewarding, and uncomfortable night.

The door clicked softly behind her, and Marc laughed. "We will see, 'Lady' Carrington, if one skirmish proves anything. We have a long way to go you and I—a long way."

Catalina was shaking so hard that she had to lean against the door for a minute until her trembling legs gave her the strength to walk to her own stateroom. Once inside, she made sure she locked it carefully. She had had enough of mysteriously locked and unlocked doors for one night.

The release of tension left her cold and weary. She crawled beneath the blankets and drew them about her. Closing her eyes, she sought sleep, keeping at bay the pulsing needs of her body—the warmth of strong arms and the taste of heady kisses.

If tears stung her eyes at her untenable position, she ignored them. She knew more battles would follow. She sensed much more in Marc Copeland now, more than a seducer of women. Women he could have anytime he chose. No, there was more than that to him, and she was going to find out what it was. She was almost certain now that Seth was not aboard the *Belle,* and she wondered what kind of game Travis and Marc were playing. She didn't know the rules, but she intended to learn them and then prove to both of them that she could play the game better than they did. There was only going to be one winner, and it would be her.

Marc remained thoughtful for several minutes. He could not quite believe that he had let her walk away from him like that. The kiss had very nearly brought him to his knees. It was still having an effect on him for that matter. Willfully bringing his body under control took some effort, for it urged him to complete what her touch had begun.

He changed his clothes and walked to the cabin China and Shawna were sharing. A sleepy-eyed Shawna answered the door, but her face brightened the moment she saw Marc.

Despite his ill-assorted feelings, Marc's eyes softened and his smile was warm and very gentle.

"Shawna, is China still awake?"

"Yes, Marc. We were only talking and getting ready for bed. Do you want to come in?"

She stood aside, her wide eyes looking at him worshipfully. She was always sensitive to Marc's moods and adapted herself to them. In Shawna's mind Marc was the parents she had never known, the brother she had never had, the friend who had taken her from hell and given her a life, a life she would gladly give for him if he should ask.

He nodded and entered, to find China curled in a chair with several cushions on the floor at her feet. Shawna had obviously been sitting on them. Next to Marc, China was all that Shawna had. To most eyes their relationship would have seemed strange.

"Marc," China said softly. If she was surprised, she did not show it. She rose from the chair and stood before him, and Shawna went to her side. Their attitudes summed up their experience with Marc. They reflected love and compassion offered and returned.

"China, I'm afraid I have to ask you to do me another little favor. This seems to be my night for that."

Her lips parted slightly in a half-smile. "Of course, Marc, what is it you desire?"

At first he hesitated, then he shrugged and explained the situation between Travis and Catalina. He left out his own confrontation with Catalina, and just requested that in the morning they go to Catalina's cabin, remove all her personal effects, and take them to his quarters.

209

China expressed no curiosity, but Marc could feel it and he was annoyed. He had no inclination to explain to China something that she might disapprove of.

Shawna's limited comprehension could only follow one path. The Marc she knew and loved had never, in the nearly five years she had known him, given any woman a permanent place in his cabin or his life. Obviously if this woman had been accepted in this way, she must hold a place in Marc's heart. If she did, then the doors to Shawna's heart were open to her as well. Marc should have thought of this, for in Shawna an open heart meant she could say anything she chose.

"Shawna and I will move her things first thing in the morning," China told Marc. "What happened between her and her friend? I thought they were"—she shrugged—"comfortable."

Marc laughed softly and tried to explain the situation he had run into. "It seems the lady has a temper, and in this case something he said or did set her off. She was even mad enough to make it look as though he had tried to force himself on her. She said she didn't let him into her room, didn't unbolt the door."

"Marc—"

"Now come on, China. How else could he have gotten in there? I myself saw that the door had not been forced. She unbolted it, all right; and if the man hadn't been foolish enough to make her angry he might have shared quite a night. The lady is remarkably beautiful."

"It makes no sense that she would decide to unbolt the door, change her mind, then try to convince you she didn't unbolt it when the evidence is right before you. Don't you question this?"

"I'm not interested. Right now she's where I want her to be. Tomorrow I'll make plans to rid myself of her friend. Then"—his eyes went to Shawna—"we'll see what happens."

"Don't worry, we'll take care of her clothes," Shawna said. "I'll see they're well taken care of and nothing gets damaged."

"Somebody should have been caring for mine tonight," Marc muttered in an amused voice.

"What?" Shawna questioned.

"Nothing," Marc answered quickly. "I'm grateful Shawna, my sweet. Remind me to buy you a new gown in Natchez." His gaze returned to China whose eyes had never left him. "Thank you, China. I'm going to get some sleep. See you in the morning."

"Good night," they both said as Marc left.

He returned to his cabin and to a bed that seemed cold and empty because Catalina was only a few steps away.

China listened to Shawna's chatter, but her mind remained fixed on the puzzle of who could have unbolted that door besides the one and only occupant of the stateroom.

"Shawna dear, I think it's best we both get some sleep. In the morning I want you to practice some of your songs. Marc intends to entertain some very wealthy and important people in Natchez, and he wants you to sing for them."

Shawna agreed, and it took very little time for the uncomplicated young woman to find sleep.

But China lay awake quite some time. Unanswerable puzzles bothered her. She finally came up with the conclusion that if Catalina hadn't wanted the door open, it was Travis who had. But how had he managed to accomplish it? I will look into it tomorrow, she decided.

The next morning Catalina was awakened very early

by a soft insistent wrapping on her door. She rose and put on the robe, the only piece of clothing she had, and walked to the door.

She was surprised and more than pleased to find a smiling Shawna standing in the passage and holding an armful of dresses she quickly recognized as her own.

"Shawna, how considerate of you. I was worried about how I was going to skip half-dressed from this cabin to get my clothes."

"Marc came last night and told us to bring all your things to you today," Shawna replied, as Catalina stepped aside and motioned her in. "China says she will come soon and help us move the rest. She has something to do right now."

Shawna placed the pile of dresses on the bed. "I thought I was going to trip in the hall and spill them all over the floor. You have some very pretty dresses."

"Thank you," Catalina said.

"Marc says he'll buy me a new dress in Natchez after I sing for some of his guests."

Catalina held back the sharp retort on her lips because she knew the words would be lost on Shawna. She wanted to tell this young woman that Marc was using her for his own ends, and deep inside she wondered what else was expected of Shawna. Did Marc use her as easily for his friends' pleasure as he did for his own?

Shawna turned to leave.

"Shawna, stay and talk to me for a while. You've been so kind I thought I might ask you to help me dress again. This dress," she said as she lifted one from her bed, "has at least a hundred buttons down the back."

Shawna's white smile appeared like a brilliant rising sun. "I'd love to."

Catalina engaged Shawna in random conversation while she washed her face and cleaned her teeth. Then she slipped into a dress with wide green and white stripes. Its sleeves were long and fitted, and the bodice molded itself snugly to her curves. It gave her a cool, tall, and very slender look. Shawna went behind her to fasten the buttons.

"Do you sing for all of Marc's friends?"

"Only very special ones."

"I see," Catalina said gently. "Do you go out with them?"

"No. Usually they stay on board the boat. If they're really important, Marc says we should be nice to them."

Catalina was outraged. Now, more than ever, she was determined to find the answers to her questions and to rescue this innocent from the clutches of a man as conscienceless as Marc Copeland. She would take Shawna with her when she left, give her a good life and put her beyond the reach of men like Marc and his friends who used Shawna for "entertainment." Her heart went out to Shawna and all her protective instincts surfaced.

Catalina sat on a small bench and began to brush her hair. Then she coiled it into a chignon at the nape of her neck. The wisp of curls that framed her face lent her an air of cool sophistication.

"I'd really like you to visit my home in Baton Rouge some day, Shawna. You'd like it and we could have fun together. We could shop, and I could introduce you to all my friends. I . . ." She stopped in midsentence as she saw Shawna's face blanch. When Shawna's eyes filled with the same terror she had seen before, it became obvious to Catalina that Marc had Shawna terrified of even thinking of leaving him.

"I . . . I don't want to go to Baton Rouge. I want to stay here with Marc." Shawna began to regain control. "I guess if Marc would come to visit I would come, but

213

I want to stay with Marc and China."

Having finished with her hair, Catalina walked to Shawna. She smiled as comfortingly as possible, and her eyes were gentle. "I'd like to be your friend while I'm aboard the *Belle* anyway. Sort of like a sister."

"Oh, that would be fun."

The door swung open silently, but the two young women did not notice China for some time.

China had gone to Catalina's old stateroom with Shawna and had helped her gather Catalina's things together. Then she had given Shawna some of Catalina's dresses and had told her to take them to Catalina.

After Shawna had gone, China studied the door between the two rooms. It was evident that no one on the other side could have slid the bolt. It had to be opened from this side.

This was the obvious thing Marc had seen and had taken at face value, but China had long since gained the knowledge that what seemed obvious was not always the truth. She studied the hall door for a while, then walked to it, opened it, and knelt on the floor to examine the lock.

The scratches in the outline of the keyhole confirmed her suspicions. Someone had tampered with the lock to gain entry.

She rose and went out into the passageway, pulling the door shut. She went first to the captain, then began to question the crew one by one. She did not speak of the deed. She only asked if one of the customers on the boat had been circulating through the crew asking questions. It did not take her long to come up with two names, those of Travis Sherman and the man he had questioned the longest, Willie Best.

She returned to Shawna's cabin after sending for Willie Best and telling him to come to it, that she had a little job for him to do. Then she locked Shawna's door, slid the key into the pocket of her dress, and waited in the passageway for Willie.

In a short while he scuttled toward her. There was no doubt in Willie's mind as to the kind of power China wielded on this boat. One word from her and the arm of Marc Copeland would descend on whoever was foolhardy enough to have caused her a problem.

"You sent for me, Miss China?"

"Yes, Willie. I have a little problem."

"Ya needs my help, Miss China, I kin do just 'bout anything."

China was reasonably sure that the "anything" included mayhem and murder, but she smiled.

"I'm afraid I've locked Shawna's door and have lost the key. Do you suppose there is any way you can get it open for me? I'd be very grateful and I'm sure Marc would reward you . . . with just what you deserve," she added with tongue-in-cheek humor.

"Do ya want me ta break it down?" he asked warily.

"Well, I'd hate to damage the door if I don't have to. If there's any other way . . ."

Seeing a reward before his eyes, Willie nodded. He swelled at the idea of displaying his prowess to this woman.

"I kin git it open for ya."

"I'd be grateful, Willie." China smiled.

Willie knelt before the door and took a strange hooklike instrument from his pocket. China watched while he fumbled with the gadget, making the same small scratches around the keyhole. She was more than sure now that this explained what had happened to Catalina's door.

Willie grunted in satisfaction, stood at the sound of

215

the final click, and swung the door open.

"There ya be, Miss China. There ain't no door what can hold Willie Best."

"Come in for a moment will you, Willie? I'd like to discuss another little job with you."

Willie was puffed up with blustering satisfaction. He would prove valuable to this beautiful woman, and when she finally realized the number of things he could do, she might become more to him . . . maybe even . . .

He walked past China without noticing her look of aversion. Inside, he turned to look at her as she shut the door and faced him.

"You are quite good with locks, Willie," she said softly.

"Yep, the best," he gloated.

"You've done this before?"

"Sure have."

"And," China added quietly, her smile fading and her eyes narrowing, "you've done a little job on this boat within the past twenty-four hours, for a passenger. Have you not, Willie?"

His gloating face hardened and his smile faded as he realized the trap he had walked into. His mind spun, looking for a way out, wondering just how much she knew . . . and how she had found out.

"I don't know what yer talkin' about," he protested.

"Please, Willie, don't waste my time by lying to me. I would be forced to let Marc find out the truth—the hard way."

He gulped and his face whitened. He knew Marc could get him to talk. With his cowardly nature, he made the decision quickly.

"It was Travis Sherman. He had me open a door for him, but honest to God, Miss China, I thought it was his door. I wouldn't have opened anybody else's for him." He continued to babble on as the look in China's

216

eyes grew colder and colder. "Honest to God, Miss China, I thought it was his room."

He was sweating now, and his hands shook as China smiled.

"Why, Willie," she said gently, "when did I say it wasn't Mr. Sherman's door?"

Trapped again, Willie sagged into morose silence.

"Now, Willie, I think it's time you tell me what you really did . . . and just how much Mr. Sherman paid you to do it."

Chapter 16

China warned Willie against repeating one word of what he had told her, and he was more than relieved to agree to this. Travis and Marc were the last two people he wanted to have any trouble with.

"Willie, it would be best if you left the boat as soon as possible. I will see that you receive some money for your information."

Willie nodded and shuffled closer to the door. All he wanted at that moment was to get as far away from all the people on this boat as he could, and as soon as possible. He didn't know what kind of games they were playing with each other, but he wanted out of the whole thing.

"We'll be in Natchez day after tomorrow. If you come to me when we're ready to dock, I'll make sure you have some money. Willie," she added, in a voice that told him she meant business, "if I find you've contacted Mr. Sherman between now and then, I shall make very sure your life, or what you have left of it, will be worth very little. Do you understand me?"

"Yes, ma'am. I understand."

"Good," China said. Her smile chilled Willie's last attempt at bravado, and when she opened the door, he stepped back so he would not have to pass too close to her as he left.

China closed the door, satisfied with what she had learned, but a small nagging thought told her that she should have rid the world of Willie before he could do more harm. She was sure, in a strange fleeting way, that they had not seen the last of him. Discarding that thought, she returned to Catalina's stateroom, where she gathered up the balance of her things.

Then she made her way to Marc's cabin, and found Catalina sitting on the bed next to Shawna, talking.

The door had swung open soundlessly, and she stood quietly watching them for several minutes without drawing their attention. She used that time to critically regard Catalina. Shawna was smiling at whatever Catalina was saying, and Catalina bent toward her, resting a hand over hers in an almost sisterly gesture.

She is exquisitely beautiful, China thought. She could see why Marc was so drawn to her that he was becoming confused about his motives. For this, China was grateful; she still felt Marc's course was leading him down a destructive path on which he might be hurt worse than anyone else.

Shawna caught China's presence out of the corner of her eye, and rose to her feet while Catalina turned to see who had come in.

China was well aware of the wary distrust that leapt into Catalina's eyes, and she noted that it was accompanied by another look. If China had to guess she would have labeled it jealousy. This thought brought a smile to China's lips, for jealousy could well be the predecessor to stronger emotions.

China moved across the room to stand near the two women.

"Good morning," she said, bowing slightly toward Catalina.

"Good morning," Catalina answered. "Thank you for bringing my things."

"You are quite welcome. I am sorry for the difficulty that forced you to vacate your room."

Catalina's cheeks flushed. She wondered if China's words held a double entendre and she was curious how much this woman knew about the situation.

"Shawna has been gracious enough to help me dress."

"Excellent," China replied. "If you would care to join us, Shawna and I would be delighted to have breakfast with you . . . unless you have other plans?"

"No," Catalina said quickly. "I would like to talk to you."

China was more than certain this was true, but she, too, wanted to talk to Catalina. And she wanted to listen to her, to decide for herself about this woman who had stirred more emotions in Marc than any other.

They made their way to the elaborate dining room and were served a breakfast so extensive that Catalina wondered if this was China's habitual fare. She was quite aware that China was assessing her every word and every movement, but she wasn't quite sure what China was looking for. Was she seeking information for Marc . . . or for herself? Was Catalina a threat to China? Was China jealous of her? Impossible. Marc and China were . . . The thought, once it had insinuated itself into her mind, jolted her with an emotion she could not put a name to.

By the time they had finished eating, China's curiosity seemed to be satisfied, and Catalina decided to take a walk on the main deck. She refused to admit, even to herself, that she had been looking about the boat for any sign of Marc.

As she walked through the dining room, she absorbed the beauty of it. The ultimate in steamboat Gothic splendor had been achieved in the main cabin or grand salon of the *Belle*. Its décor befitted its function as the center of life on the steamboat. Decorated in the most ornamental manner, the ceiling was supported by rows of ornate columns, their connecting arches carved in lacelike patterns. In the stern of the cabin, which was reserved for ladies, a huge mirror created an illusion, seeming to double the salon's length.

The windows, of stained glass, created a colorful interplay of sunlight on the rich Brussels carpeting and on the fine furnishings. In the evening it was illuminated by crystal chandeliers.

On the *Belle* an intermediate deck, above the main deck at the stern, was provided for those wishing to enjoy the view, the breeze, or a stroll. Catalina knew of it and chose to go there. She wanted to be alone, to think, and she did not want to cross Travis's path yet. The anger in her was too virulent. Losing her temper where Marc Copeland might be around to find some amusement in it would be embarrassing.

She stepped out on the deck and lifted her face to the soft breeze with pleasure. As a child she had always enjoyed finding places where she could retreat from everyone and enjoy the river. She planned to do that now as she walked toward the rail, but as she leaned both arms on it, closed her eyes, and inhaled deeply, she heard a soft taunting voice.

"Very beautiful. I kind of thought you might come out here."

She spun about, completely unprepared to see him leaning against the wall, arms folded across his chest and a half-smile on his lips.

"I'm sorry," she said frigidly. "I didn't mean to intrude on your privacy." She headed toward the door, but he stepped between her and it in one lithe move.

"Don't go," he said. "The view is not my personal

possession. Besides, I'd rather look at you."

The look in his eyes was more of a challenge than anything else, and Catalina refused to be awed by it.

She turned from him and returned to the rail. In a moment he was beside her, one elbow resting on it, his eyes filled with deep appreciation for her intoxicating beauty.

The breeze brushed fine wisps of sable brown hair across her cheeks, and the morning sun made her seem aglow . . . vital, alive, and very disturbing.

"It seems your friend sleeps late in the morning."

"He is not my friend."

"Aren't you the least bit curious about him?"

"Not really. Why Travis chooses to remain in bed is not my affair and I don't choose to make it so."

"Is that jealousy I hear?" Marc laughed. "I hope it's not the violent kind. Charlene is a woman of beauty, but sadly lacking in temperament. She's apt to become angry when interrupted."

Prepared for a display of anger and distress because Travis had chosen a lover so quickly after she had left him, Marc was surprised when she gave him a cold and disdainful look.

"Really, Mr. Copeland. If you can discuss only the amorous antics of that disgusting man I would prefer to be alone. Why don't you go below and seek out one of your 'ladies.' Then you and Travis would both enjoy your trip more."

He was surprised by her lack of anger at Travis, but he kept his reaction from registering on his face.

"Catalina."

"Yes?"

"Look at me."

She turned her head toward him, and her eyes sparked icy shards that could have bloodied him.

"What made you book passage on my boat?"

"The boat is mine."

"Was yours," he corrected gently.

"If you were any kind of gentleman you would return what you have stolen."

"Wrong again," he declared calmly. "Gambling losses are considered perfectly legal gains, and I have the signed papers to prove my ownership."

Catalina now turned fully toward him, studying his face.

"Where is my brother?" she said suddenly, and then in a controlled voice, "Whatever you've done with him at least tell me. I have to know. Where is Seth?"

"So," he said softly, "that's why you're aboard?"

"Where is he?"

"Your friend, Travis, was he—"

"I said he is no longer my friend. I want an answer."

"Then I'll give you one. You asked me that question once before and I told you I had not seen him since I won the boat. I repeat"—he held her eyes and spoke levelly and with conviction—"I have not seen your foolish brother since we gambled together."

"Gambled," she scoffed. "Hardly a gamble for you. I've a feeling my brother was like a child when gambling against you."

Marc didn't want to tell her how right she was. For the first time he felt a tug of conscience for having taken advantage of an unskilled gambler in order to ruin him. He tried his best to deny this.

"If a man gambles he must expect to lose as easily as he might win. In this case I was the winner."

"I want to know . . . I have to know," she said, coming as close to pleading as her pride would allow. "Where is my brother? Is he alive?" Her voice suddenly broke.

She watched his smile fade, his eyes grow warm and intense. "Catalina, no matter what you think of me I am not a man who commits murder. I won the boat from your brother, but I have not seen him since and I have not raised a hand to injure him. I do not know where he is, but he has not been aboard the *Belle*."

Despite her worry, her anger, and her distrust of most males, she found it difficult to admit that she actually believed him. Flooded by a surge of relief, she sagged momentarily, grabbing the rail. When Marc reached out and took her hand to steady her, she made an inarticulate sound, half-protest and half-sob. But the hand that held hers was strong and firm.

He drew her close to him and slid his arm about her waist, but she pressed her hands flat against his chest, preventing him from drawing her close as he wanted to.

If Catalina had been unprepared for the shock of accepting his words, Marc was just as unprepared for his unexplainable need to make her understand that Seth had come to no physical harm at his hands.

His plan to destroy the Carrington family had started out well. He'd meant to drive them to their own destruction, but now he felt that his control had been slipping since that first night he had held Catalina in his arms.

The early morning sun lit her amber eyes and gold flecks danced in them as she gazed hopefully up at him. She needed to believe, but it was not to be that simple. Something unsaid, untouched, lay between them. There was a current below the surface of all that he said, and it was treacherous. It would pull her under and perhaps drown her in emotions she couldn't control.

Marc reached blindly for the blankness of his desire for vengeance to prevent succumbing to her charms. This was not part of his plans and he did not intend to fall victim to Catalina's charms.

With effort, he regained his equilibrium and the

224

warmth in his eyes was replaced by a wary scorn. Searching for her brother. He laughed to himself. What a feeble excuse for a rendezvous with a lover.

He even began to wonder if the battle he had witnessed between Travis and Catalina had been planned to deceive him somehow. He had to force himself to remember who and what she was . . . and that having her here was only a first step.

"Rest assured your brother is most likely back in New Orleans enjoying himself, maybe even wondering where you are."

Nothing he said rang true to Catalina, but his intoxicating nearness was playing havoc with her body, with memories she couldn't stifle. They had suddenly come alive.

"Tell me when you saw Seth last. What did he say? What did he do? Did he give you any idea where he might go?" she said, as she moved from the circle of his arm.

He sensed her uncertainty, and it pleased him . . . another step.

"You want to talk about your brother and nothing else?" He smiled as he asked the question, but his eyes were laughing at her obvious insecurity.

"Damn it!" she snapped. "Why can't you just answer a question?"

"I will . . . in my own time."

"What is that supposed to mean?"

"It means I'd find myself more of a conversationalist over a nice meal for two served with champagne . . . in my—oops—your cabin."

"I doubt that," she replied.

He shrugged and turned to walk away.

"Wait a minute, where are you going?"

"I've some business to tend to."

"You could at least be enough of a gentleman to

225

help me."

His smile was quick. "That's the second time you've accused me of not being a gentleman. You're free with your accusations, but you get offended if I suggest that you might not be the lady you claim to be. That gives me the idea you're a little girl hiding behind a woman's skirts. I've things to do," he said, his voice quiet but firm. "Let me know if you ever decide to grow up. As for me, I think you'll be afraid the rest of your life."

Her need to learn what he knew about Seth and her anger at his accusation that she wasn't yet a woman silenced the small voice that tried to warn her.

"If I am afraid of anything, it is most certainly not you."

"Dinner then?" he questioned, his raised eyebrow telling her of his amusement.

"Yes."

"In my . . . your cabin?"

"Yes."

"Eight?"

"That's fine."

"Good. I'll make the arrangements. We have a great deal to talk about. . . . I'll bring the champagne."

"If you plan on getting me too intoxicated to know what I'm doing you can forget it. One glass of champagne is my limit."

"Too bad." He chuckled. "But then, a lot of things are just as intoxicating as champagne. Maybe, if I make an effort, we might run across one or two."

"Conversation is all I want from you, Marc Copeland. Just conversation. If you have any other ideas I suggest you go find one of your little . . . toys to play with. I don't play your kinds of games."

His eyes were brilliant emeralds, alive with a knowing laughter that set her teeth on edge.

"Too bad. Maybe you don't know what you're

missing. Ah well," he added softly, "maybe we can find some games you are willing to play. I suspect"—his voice was charged with a current she didn't understand—"your kind of woman knows more games than this brain of mine could imagine. Until tonight." He smiled again as he gave her a half-salute and walked away leaving her so angry she was inarticulate. In her fury she turned her back on his retreating figure and gripped the rail. It was quite some time before her anger lessened and she again saw the beauty about her.

Marc stepped inside just in time to see Travis walk into the dining salon. Travis's eyes were scanning the room, and Marc was sure he was looking for Catalina.

Knowing the state she'd been in when he had just left her, his malicious humor came to the fore, and with an expressionless face he walked over to meet Travis.

"Marc," Travis said when he was close enough, "have you seen Catalina?"

Still believing that Catalina had given Travis access to her room, Marc was again struck by a streak of perverse humor. "I've just been with her," he said. "I believe the lady is still on deck. Maybe she is thinking about your small misunderstanding last night and would like to make amends. She seemed in fine spirits. In fact she was asking if anyone had seen you."

Not wanting Marc to suspect the truth, Travis continued to damn her. "Good. I . . . ah . . . know her temper can be controlled with a strong hand. Cat and I have had these minor problems before, but a few gentle words and some . . . friendly persuasion, and she is more than willing to be receptive."

Suddenly Marc had the urge to put his hands around Travis's throat and squeeze the life out of him. The darkening in his green eyes and the tightening of his jaw, combined with the rigidity of his features, revealed his urge to commit violence.

227

"Well," Marc said in a controlled voice, "she's on deck."

He moved away before he gave vent to the jealous rage that had taken him off guard, filled with shock and disgust with himself for the hatred he felt toward Travis. He had no right to be jealous when his motives concerning Catalina were less than honorable.

Travis watched him walk away, a puzzled frown on his face. Unless there was something between Marc and Catalina, he saw no reason for the man's sudden shift in attitude. Could something have transpired the night before when he had been busy with Charlene? No. He had made sure Catalina's distrust and dislike of Marc had been well fed. He decided it was just his imagination, and proceeded to the deck to make peace with Catalina. He had rehearsed his glib apologies, and was quite certain Catalina would be gullible enough to swallow them.

He opened the door and stepped out, his attention drawn immediately to Catalina, who stood with her back to him. As his eyes absorbed her, his desire to possess and tame this sable-haired beauty increased. He could imagine her in his bed, warm and willing, bending to his will. The thought was delicious and he savored it for a minute; then he walked toward her.

He was less than two feet away when Catalina, drawn from her reverie, sensed his presence. She spun around thinking Marc had returned to taunt her. Her eyes were aglow with a look Travis had never seen before, a look Catalina would have denied had someone confronted her with it. In them was excitement and virulent passion temporarily leashed. Travis made the mistake of thinking that look was for him.

Assuming that she had changed her mind about his advance the previous night, he smiled and reached for her.

228

The crack of her hand against his cheek startled them both. The print of her fingers stood out clearly on his flesh.

"How dare you?" she grated. "How could you even approach me. Such arrogant unmitigated nerve."

"Cat, at least let me explain. This is all a most dastardly misunderstanding planned by Marc Copeland."

"I don't believe you." Her voice was so firm and hard that he was unaware of the renewed doubts that assailed her.

"I've just learned the truth about what happened last night. Can I at least explain? You damn me when it isn't my fault. I only made the mistake of falling for his treacherous scheme myself."

"Explain," Catalina said shortly.

"He set this up . . . arranged it. He is the one who had your door opened. I received a note that was, so I thought, from you. The whole thing seemed an open invitation—and I took it. A woman who is as beautiful as you should understand that I could hardly contain my excitement. I thought . . . well, in my passion for you I thought you were . . . enticing me to your bed. I can't be held to be totally at fault, Cat, and I hope you can understand and forgive me."

Chapter 17

"I would prefer to forget the entire situation ever happened. We are aboard a boat and I know space is limited, but I want to keep as much distance between us as possible."

"Cat, I've been your friend too long for you to be so unforgiving of this one mistake. Please let me make amends. Accept my abject apology. I swear to you no such thing will ever happen again."

Catalina was weakening. He knew it and pushed his slight advantage.

"I've been asking a great many questions of the crew and the roustabouts."

Her curiosity was piqued, and he whet her interest more.

"It seems Seth was aboard this boat the night he disappeared."

"Travis!"

"If you'll give me time I'll find out the entire truth, whatever it is."

"Marc Copeland told me he hadn't seen Seth since the night he won the boat."

"The man is clever, devious, and quite a liar. He wanted to split us up so he set me up for the incident that occurred last night. I'm ashamed that my pride made me say things I shouldn't have. Please, Cat . . .

please forgive me. Don't throw away the only friend you have on this boat."

"Let's just let it lie, Travis. I'd rather not speak of it anymore."

"Good. Will you have dinner with me tonight?"

"I . . . I can't. I'm eating in my room."

"Of course," Travis said sympathetically. "This has been an uncomfortable trip for you so far, and you must want to rest."

"Yes, I really need to rest," she replied, uncomfortable with the lie.

"We will be in Natchez day after tomorrow, and I shall take you to the finest restaurant. By then I should have some answers for you."

"I will enjoy that, but I will enjoy the answers even more. Travis, maybe I should speak to the crew and—"

"No, Catalina, that is no job for a woman. I'll do it," he said with a condescending attitude that set Catalina's teeth on edge. "Now why don't you just enjoy the rest of the day and I'll talk to these people. A few well-placed coins will make them talk to anyone about anything. Now be a good girl and stay out of trouble, or Marc and his slant-eyed mistress will realize what you are up to."

Remembering her short association with China, Catalina was profoundly irritated by his ugly reference to the woman. Whatever Travis might think, Catalina knew that China was an extremely beautiful woman.

Suppressing a sudden urge to lash out in defense of China, she decided she would rid herself of his presence.

"I appreciate your help, Travis. I shall rest much easier tonight knowing you are moving among the crew and asking the questions I need answered, and we shall have dinner in Natchez. In the meantime, if you don't mind, I'd like to be alone for a while . . . to think."

231

"Of course, my dear." He took her hand in his and bent to kiss her cheek. "Enjoy your quiet dinner in your cabin. Should I send someone to check on you later, to see that you're all right?"

"No, please Travis. I believe I'll be fine tonight. I'll retire early, and we can spend some time together tomorrow."

"Then, if you'll excuse me, I shall begin asking questions."

"Good."

He smiled and left her, and she turned back to the rail, not wanting to look in his direction again.

As she gazed over the water, Catalina let herself savor the pleasure of the boat's slow journey upriver. Then her gaze began to roam the length of the craft.

Her attention was quickly caught by a figure. He sat against a bale of cotton that must have weighed three hundred pounds, and he looked as if he could have lifted it himself.

Catalina thought she had never seen a man so large, and that thought was followed by the memory of the huge hand and the strong arm that had caught her in the hold the previous night. She left the rail, and slowly, so as not to arouse suspicion about where she was going, she went inside, down the steps and out the door to the main deck. Then she walked in Jacob's direction.

He half lay on the wood deck, his back against the cotton bale and his long legs stretched before him. He wore only a ragged shirt and a pair of pants. He was barefoot, and his hamlike hands rested across his flat abdomen.

She stood near him, debating his size should he stand. Then she remembered what Marc had said, and it brought a soft laugh to her lips. She had scared Jacob—that thought, when she looked at him, was

232

utterly ridiculous. Her laughter bubbled aloud. It brought Jacob awake, then to his feet when he saw who was standing near him.

He seemed to unfold his length, and Catalina's eyes grew wider and wider as he finally towered above her. What she didn't realize was that Jacob was frightened. Frightened of her soft delicate beauty.

"Ma'am?" he questioned.

"Your name is Jacob?"

"Yas, ma'am. How be yo kno's me, missy?"

She smiled a comforting smile. "It seems I caused you a bit of a problem last night, Jacob, and I've come to apologize."

"Missy, ah doan know what yo'all be talkin' 'bout. I hain' nebber seen yo'all befo."

"You remember grabbing a stowaway last night, Jacob?"

"Yassum, a young boy. I takes 'im to Mista Marc."

"Well I'm afraid the young boy . . . was a young girl."

She watched his eyes widen in shock and his huge hands grip into fists.

"No, ma'am. Ah wouldn't do no such thing."

"It was me, Jacob. I stole some clothes so I could roam about the boat."

"Oh, ma'am, yo'all shouldn't tease me like that."

"But it was, Jacob." Catalina proceeded to describe what she was wearing. "I deserved what I got and I've come to tell you so."

"You hain't lyin' to me?"

"No, Jacob. Can I sit and talk with you for a minute?"

Her request so took Jacob by surprise that he stood speechless. Such a thing had never happened to him before.

"Jacob?"

"Yassum." He moved aside so she could sit on the cotton bale. Her skirts spread wide about her, she lowered herself onto it, while Jacob stood in stricken awe, looking down at her.

"Jacob." She laughed softly. "Sitting down and talking to you when you're standing is somewhat like talking to a mountain."

"Yassum," he muttered, and refolded his huge body until he sat cross-legged on the deck before her.

"Wha' fo' yo'all wan' to talk to me, missy?"

"How long have you been on the *Belle?*"

"Mista Marc, he done brought me from da *Princess* when he cum on board."

"The *Princess* was his boat too?"

"Yassum."

"Do you remember the night he won the *Belle?*"

"Yassum . . . dey waz playin' on de *Princess.*"

"Jacob, do you remember the people in the game? The one who lost the *Belle?*"

"Yassum."

"Did you know him?"

"No, ah din' know none of dem."

"But you remember what they looked like?"

"Yassum." He was puzzled now. "Wha' fo' yo want to know what dey look like?"

"I'd like to know if the young man, the one who lost the *Belle,* came aboard her the night we left."

"Dat same boy? De one dat lost . . . no, missy, he ain' been 'bout heah. Ah sees everyone comes 'board de boat. Dat boy, he ain' never come back heah."

"Jacob . . . you knew Marc a long time ago?"

"Yassum, ah knows him since he was a boy, when his pappy—"

"Jacob!" The voice was firm and commanding; both Catalina and Jacob turned to see Marc standing before them.

Jacob was quick to find his feet, and even though he towered over Marc, his attitude and his warm smile spoke of a profound respect.

"Yassah." Jacob grinned.

"You have work to do, Jacob?" Marc said in a gentler voice. He smiled so Jacob would not be worried. He knew his anger was one thing Jacob found very difficult to cope with. But Jacob was alert enough to realize he'd been saying something Marc disapproved of.

"Yassah." He grinned amiably at Catalina and ambled off, promising himself to steer clear of Catalina Carrington and her questions.

Marc smiled, an aggravating, knowledgeable smile. "You weren't berating Jacob for the unconventional way he 'discovered' your presence on the boat, were you?"

"On the contrary," Catalina replied coolly. "I was simply telling him I understood his protective attitude toward you. As far as I can see it's something that is frequently used. Jacob deserves a commendation, either for being the most devoted of employees or a friend who has been sadly abused."

Catalina swept past Marc with a disdainful look and returned to the dining room, passing through it to return to the cabin that had once belonged to Marc.

Marc chuckled. Catalina was certainly unpredictable, and intriguing. As he watched her disappear, he realized how intensely he'd been wishing away the day. The evening was going to prove to be an interesting challenge, to say the least.

When Marc returned to his cabin he sent for China, who appeared within minutes. She came in without knocking and closed the door silently. Marc was seated on the edge of the bed, and she stood for several minutes before she realized he was so lost in thought he

235

hadn't even heard her enter.

She remained silent, watching his face, knowing almost intuitively that he was caught up in an emotion he couldn't understand, and didn't want to understand. China wondered if there was a way she could remove the blinders from Marc's eyes long enough to make him see that he was falling in love with Catalina.

She wished she had a few more answers to the questions that plagued her. Although she wasn't sure that the situation with Marc's father and the Carringtons had been what Marc believed, she still had too many loose ends that couldn't be tied. Nonetheless, she had as many outlets for information as Marc did, and she hoped to secure answers soon enough to keep him from making what she now felt was a grave mistake. She had become certain when she had met Catalina.

"Marc?"

His eyes jerked in her direction almost as if he were surprised to find her before him. The swift lack of recognition passed, and he smiled and rose to his feet.

"China, I'm going to need a little help from you and Charlene."

"Help?" She laughed. "What are you up to now, Marc?"

He chuckled. "We get to Natchez tomorrow night. By that time I hope to put into motion a plan that will rid the *Belle* of one Travis Sherman."

This was not a proposition to which she was averse. The sooner Travis Sherman was taken out of the picture, the sooner Marc and Catalina would find their way to each other. Their close proximity on the *Belle* would make them unable to resist what she felt was growing between them.

Time, she thought. Time and their close proximity will be enough.

236

"What is it you want me to do?"

He looked at her quizzically. "No arguments, no questions?"

"I am not overly fond of Mr. Sherman, nor, I think, is Catalina. I'm sure after the little fiasco of the bolted door she doesn't trust him very far."

"The bolted door," he repeated. "You sound as if you still believe her."

"I'm afraid I do."

"China, how could you possibly believe a story like that? How could you explain it in any other way than that she unbolted that door for the purpose of indulging in a little romantic interlude."

"I can explain it in two words." She laughed.

"Two words?"

"Willie Best."

"What?"

"He is a roustabout that works on this boat."

"A roustabout." Marc was truly puzzled now. "What does he have to do with that bolted door?"

"He, my dear suspicious friend"—she reached out to pat his cheek in a teasing way—"is how the door got unbolted."

"China, would you kindly tell me just what the hell you are talking about?"

"I'd be delighted . . . no, more than delighted. It seems one Travis Sherman paid Willie to get into Catalina's room and unbolt the door." China added in a soft voice, "You made a very big mistake."

Marc was silent, in fact he couldn't seem to find the words to reply for several minutes, for no matter how much doubt he felt, he knew China would not say what she could not back up.

Finally he grated roughly, "Mistake . . . China, tell me the whole story."

Slowly, elucidating each word firmly, China told Marc what she had found out and how she had verified it.

"I intended to make sure Willie left the boat in Natchez, to spend the gold Travis gave him."

"And just when did you intend to tell me about this?" He scowled.

She looked at him innocently. "Why, Marc, why should I? You really didn't care that she was innocent of this, did you? She played right into your hands, and it worked out just the way you wanted. Guilty or not. She might as well take the blame for this as for everything else. After all," China added softly, "if she's her father's daughter, she must be guilty of something . . . mustn't she?"

Marc held her eyes for a minute; then he laughed again. "Won't work, China. So maybe he managed the lock. That doesn't really change a thing."

"You mean you don't even owe her an apology?"

"Apology? What the hell for? Because she didn't have time to open the door herself? Because he thought of it first? Come on, China."

China sighed and shook her head. "You are most certainly a very stubborn man. I do hope the gods are smiling on your impossible single-goal mind."

Anyone else would have wilted before the frigid ill-controlled anger in Marc's eyes. But China had no fear of him, and her love for him drove her to try to make him forget the path he was on and to turn his hatred to love, for she was more than sure Catalina was one way to the truth—the truth that would free Marc from this quest he should never have begun.

"Don't worry about your gods, China. I can take care of myself and any little tricks they might play on me. For now I'd like to concentrate on how we're going to get Travis off the boat."

238

"You have thought of a way?"

"I think so."

"What do you have in mind?"

"For a while I considered having Jacob just . . . take care of it."

"Kill him?" she asked in surprise.

"I don't want anybody's blood on my hands. Besides, Jacob couldn't kill a bug."

"Then there has to be another way."

"I guess a woman would be the most effective ploy."

"I'll talk to Charlene, but won't Catalina wonder where he's gone?"

"By that time we'll be on the river again."

"He won't leave this boat without talking to her."

"He will if he thinks she's tricking me. That's where you and Charlene come in."

"How, Marc?"

"I think you'd better sit down, China. By the time I join the lady for dinner I want this plan clear so there will be no slip-ups."

China sank down onto a chair, quite willing to hear any plan that would take the barrier of Travis Sherman from between Marc and Catalina.

Wanting to stay away from Marc and Travis, Catalina made her way back to her cabin. Annoyed that she would be forced by circumstances to remain inside when the day was beautiful, she began to search the stateroom for something to occupy her time. What she found taught her more about Marc than she wanted to know.

The cabin was not large, but when she looked about she realized it was the habitat of a creature who enjoyed his comforts. The carpet beneath her feet was thick and comfortable, and the walls had been painted a pearl gray white. Two of them were lined with shelves that contained books. Upon examination she found that his taste in reading ranged from poetry to navigation.

The bed was not large, and she kept her eyes from it, knowing full well it was clean and comfortable. She remembered too well when she had shared it. The memory only increased her aggravation and her sense of imprisonment.

Unable to cope with quarters that seemed to grow smaller and smaller, she finally left the cabin, determined to walk in the sunshine despite anything or anybody.

Again she walked the deck, and this time she was not disturbed. Then she stood at the rail and watched the Mississippi roll beneath the boat. She thought of the trips she'd made with her parents up and down the *meck-e-se-be,* as the Algonquins had named it, and of how she had loved the always different, always amazing, and always beautiful views.

The Mississippi was a grand river. She could feel the power of it beneath her feet. Graceful trees dipped their branches into the swiftly flowing water and small lazy towns, like miniatures, were set against the small rolling hills that extended from the banks.

If Travis and Marc hadn't been aboard she would have taken great pleasure in this trip. But they were both present—and both dangerous. She could not afford to trust anyone but herself.

The truth was something she had to learn. If Marc knew where Seth was she must persuade him to give her an answer. Yet she found that she had a tendency to believe Jacob. What nagged at her was that even if Seth had not come aboard Marc could know what had happened to him, might even have brought it upon him. That thought frightened her.

Catalina was so engrossed in her speculations that

she was totally unaware of China's presence until she spoke.

"It is beautiful," China said softly.

Catalina turned as she approached to stand beside her.

"Yes, very beautiful."

"You have taken this journey before?"

"Many times. With my parents, from the time I was a little girl. It's always different and always so beautiful."

Catalina's curiosity was piqued. China was close to Marc Copeland. She could not trust her either, yet something drew her to the woman. Some intuitive feeling told her that China's presence beside her was no accident.

"Marc has always found it so too."

"You have known Marc a long time?" Catalina did not turn to look at China, but felt her eyes on her. She had tried to speak as casually as she could.

"I have known Marc for many years." The reply was noncommittal.

When Catalina turned to face China, there was nothing to be read on China's face.

"Catalina," China said softly, "I think you will find here something you seek. I would only warn you not to judge what you hear or feel too quickly. I have watched you and have spoken with you, and now I warn you to think carefully. You have much to gain if you are as courageous as I believe you are."

"Are you telling me to trust no one?"

"Trust your heart. Trust what you feel is truth and not what you hear."

"China, I don't understand. Why can't you tell me—"

"I can tell you nothing. Just that you are in less danger than you think, and that if you have the courage I believe you possess, you will find something much

241

more valuable than you even dreamed of."

Before Catalina could speak again, China moved away, leaving her to ponder what had been said.

Catalina sighed and turned back to her thoughts, forgetting the river and the view. There were so many puzzles to find the answer to . . . and tonight she would begin the search. But she had a nagging suspicion that something intangible, shrouded in the mystery of Marc Copeland, was going to have more of an effect on her life than she had bargained on.

Chapter 18

Why do I care what I wear or what my hair looks like? Catalina demanded of herself as she dressed for the coming dinner with Marc. She violently denied that she wanted to look her best, yet she had chosen the prettiest dress she had brought. It was the color of wild violets, and ivory lace trimmed it where it bordered the enticingly soft flesh of her breasts. The décolletage bordered on the scandalous, yet she had a secret desire to shatter the cool amused reserve that always seemed part of him.

She had deliberately brushed her hair and let it fall about her in waves that glistened with deep flame. She would see if two couldn't play the game of cool detachment. As she laid down the brush a rap on the door drew her attention. She paused to gather her courage, then crossed the room.

She had expected to see Marc, but instead she found two young men with covered trays and a third with a small table.

They carried these items inside, and as if performing a feat of magic, they grinned in pleasure upon producing an immaculate table cloth and napkins. Next came fine china and crystal wine glasses, and the table was set for two. A silver candelabra was set upon it, to light the table with a mellow glow.

Having done this in a few minutes, the young men bowed their way from the room.

Catalina knew food and Marc would soon appear. It was the food that arrived first, and again she had to smile at the precision with which things were arranged. It seemed that Marc had set his people through the same paces many times. She wondered how many unsuspecting females had succumbed to his masterful touch.

To make the effect work to her advantage Catalina extinguished all the lamps and left the lighting of the cabin to the candelabra.

She stood on the periphery of the light, faced the door, and waited for the soft rap that came within a few minutes.

"Come in."

Marc anticipated many things when he swung the door open. All of them had crossed his mind on the way to the cabin. He would be met by a wronged woman, a distraught sister, or an arrogant and demanding Carrington. He was prepared for any one of them, but not for the vision that met his eyes.

He had expected cold resistance, defiance, anything but the half-smile on her lips and the entrancing vision she made. He stepped inside and closed the door behind him.

The candle glow burnished her skin to a mellow gold that was enhanced by the violet of her gown. He restrained himself from crossing the room, slipping his fingers into her hair, and kissing her into submission. Only the glint in her eyes told him he should feel like the proverbial fly in the spider web.

He smiled, like a warrior who knew the best defense could be offense.

"I should have forgotten about the food. You look delicious enough to make me lose all appetites . . .

except one."

He watched her force herself to keep from snarling an answer, and was amused to see her succeed.

"The food looks delicious," she replied. "May I pour you some wine?"

"Please."

She moved to the table, poured two glasses, and handed him one. Then she raised hers to touch it to his.

"Here's to truth," she said.

"Strange toast." He smiled, but he sipped the wine.

"You find truth strange . . . or difficult?"

"I find it hard to find."

Marc walked to the table and slid a chair out for her. She sat down, hoping that the subtle perfume she wore would weaken his reserve. She had no idea of how effective it really was.

He sat opposite her, lifted his napkin and placed it across his lap. He reached out and took her plate.

"Do you mind?"

"No, please."

He placed liberal helpings on her plate, and put it before her. Then he filled his own.

He ate with a healthy appetite, but Catalina's nerves were so taut she could only play with her food.

To keep her trembling hands occupied, she often reached for her wine glass, which he kept filled.

"You told me today," she said with a half-smile, as she again sipped the wine, "that you talked more comfortably with good food and wine. Now that you have satisfied yourself with both, tell me what you know of my brother."

"What I told you before was the truth. After your brother left the *Princess* I never spoke to or saw him again."

"Why did you do it, Marc?" she said softly.

"Do what?" he answered, but he knew what she was

245

talking about.

"Why did you deliberately take the *Belle* from Seth? What could he have done to you to make you do anything so calculated . . . so cruel?"

"*Cruel . . . calculated.* Words you use but don't really understand."

"There is so much about you I don't understand."

"Ah, I'm a simple man, Catalina." He laughed softly.

"*Simple.* That is not a word to describe you."

"What is the word that does?"

"I don't know. You're . . . mysterious. Yes, *mysterious* is the word. You have a lot of sides to you. What do I believe?"

"I've asked you to believe nothing."

She bent toward him, her eyes wide, searching his.

"But I need to believe something. I need to believe that you're telling me the truth, at least about one thing. Tell me about Seth. Please."

She said the last word softly. Marc reached across the table and traced her cheek lightly with his fingertips. Then he caught her chin and lifted it so their eyes held.

"Catalina, I have not harmed your brother. True, I took the boat from him. But he was alive and well the last time I saw him."

"But you must have known what you were doing when you gambled with him."

Marc stood up and walked to the small stand nearby. He was uncomfortable under her intense gaze. He picked up another full bottle of wine and returned to the table.

"Of course I knew what I was doing. I intended to take this boat from a man who wasn't strong enough to hold it."

"He was a boy."

"Stop it, Catalina! He was a man, though you might

246

see him as a boy. And what about you, pretty Catalina? If you don't have your way, is it because you're not woman enough to get it? Are you a little girl too?"

She fell into his trap neatly, her anger making her rise from her chair. Her eyes lit with rebellion, she walked to him, and he was suddenly ripped by a surge of desire.

"And what about me, Mr. Mystery Man? What about me, Marc? What is it you planned to take from me?"

"Why, Catalina," he said suggestively, "I've already had a small taste of what I want from you. A very small taste which has only whetted my appetite for more. The woman Catalina . . . is she here?" His voice was low and caressing.

"There is so much you are not saying. I feel—"

"What do you feel, pretty Catalina," he whispered. "What do you feel?" He put his hands about her waist and drew her closer. "What I feel? An excitement . . . the same kind of excitement that heats my blood."

She pressed her hands against his chest, but he could see the pulse at the base of her throat beat frantically. She wasn't able to keep him from pulling the length of her body close to his. The lean muscle of his thighs pressed intimately against her, and the arm about her felt hard and strong.

An inner voice shrieked a warning that his challenge was a trap, but his head had already lowered and his mouth was already claiming hers. He took possession of her lips in a way that almost frightened her. She was aware of a deep all-encompassing hunger that pulled at her, body and soul. It was almost as if she might disappear into him. The edges of her being softened and dissolved as he caressed the length of her body, reverence and intensity in his touch, as if he were a sculptor intent on molding them into one.

Somewhere in the back of her mind she could hear a small, despairing voice asking why she could not end this, why she could not overcome the feeling that she was drowning in his warmth.

Marc was immersed in a seething cauldron of desire that was rapidly melting the bones within him until he felt that he was flowing about her. This was all a part of his plan, wasn't it? To seduce her until he bent her will to his, until she was broken and dependent upon him. Wasn't having her willing and warm in his arms a part of his goal? Why then did he have to battle his guilt, to submerge it and drown it before it overcame him?

The world seemed to rock and sway about them as he let his mouth roam from her lips to her cheeks and throat. His hands were now deftly removing her clothes, scattering them randomly, uncaring of where they fell.

She was lifted, and her head fell back and her eyes closed. Her arms looped about his neck. Then she felt the softness of the bed beneath her and she looked up into the green eyes that burned into hers with the flame of passion.

His hands moved over her breasts and down the length of her body, exploring its curves and hollows. Her mouth still clinging to his, Catalina realized dimly that she had wanted him to make love to her from the minute he had walked into the room. But none of her memories of his touch, none of her imaginings, had ever been like this reality.

She felt his mouth on her breasts, lips, and his tongue teased her nipples until she groaned, a muted, strangely incoherent sound. At the same time his hands moved lower.

She was flushed and shaking from the recurrence of these same wild and thoughtless emotions . . .

A FREE ZEBRA
HISTORICAL
ROMANCE
WORTH

$3.95

BUSINESS REPLY MAIL

FIRST CLASS   PERMIT NO. 276   CLIFTON, NJ

POSTAGE WILL BE PAID BY ADDRESSEE

ZEBRA HOME SUBSCRIPTION SERVICE
P.O. Box 5214
120 Brighton Road
Clifton, New Jersey 07015

thoughtless! No. Like a flash of brilliant lightning she knew—she loved him. Despite everything, she was in love with him. And she wanted him to love her. Could she ever capture the mercurial Marc Copeland? She wanted to try.

He felt her surrender and slipped into the melting heat that emanated from her.

His fingers stroked gently . . . firmly . . . rapidly . . . until she forgot who she was and who he was and strained her body upward against him.

"Catalina," he half groaned, as with silken body and bold seeking hands she stirred to higher heat the fury of their passion.

His tongue traced patterns on her flesh, sending tingling shudders through her with its feathery touch. Lower and lower he moved, nipping gently at her flesh with his teeth until she wanted to scream. Gentle hands parted her thighs, and suddenly she felt the piercing heat of his seeking tongue and her hands caught at him, tangled into the thickness of his hair to urge him on. Suddenly he was above her and her body arched in shock as, with a deep thrust, he embedded himself in the depths of her.

As he began to move, inexorably and steadily, her body quivered with delight. Her breath came in short gasps and soft moans escaped her. Prisoners of unexplained enchantment, they moved together, her slim body arching to meet his driving thrusts and her hands moving over his body, digging into the muscles of his back, sliding down to his hard muscular hips to urge him to even deeper possession. Each was hungry for fulfillment, each aware of the other's needs. Giving and taking, they rose higher and higher until his mouth was all that silenced her cries of ecstasy as they soared to the pinnacle and beyond, clinging to each other.

The pale golden glow of the candelabra on the table some distance away put the area of the bed in partial shadow.

Marc gazed down on Catalina, caught by the magic the pale light wrought on her skin.

No woman had been able to hold him after their first mingling, but despite the completion he felt, he had an urge to embrace her, to keep alive the amazing emotions they had shared, to hold her captive in his arms for as long as possible.

He still refused to see that the moment would come when he would relinquish her willingly. He called what they had shared by the lesser name of passion, but Catalina was instinctively wiser. She knew this man would be the only one who would be able to reach the part of her that completed her being.

She recognized love for what it was, and in the same moment recognized his firm resistance to such an acknowledgement. As her thoughts tumbled into place she found that she believed what he had said about Seth. But she again began to wonder why he had deliberately taken the boat from Seth and why he had seduced her. Both acts were connected to some ultimate purpose, and she also knew only Marc could explain it.

Could she mold this passionate beginning into something deeper? Could she change the purpose that seemed to drive Marc to destroy her and Seth into an aim which would permit the construction of some more promising thing? She didn't know. She only knew she was going to try, for the alternative was to let Marc crush her heart and to walk away from the ashes of what could have been.

Marc was as entangled in disbelieving thoughts as Catalina. Permanent commitment to this woman, to any woman, was not part of his plan. He was angry that only part of his mind seemed to be listening. The rest was swirling in a confusion matched only by the violent sensual reaction of his body.

There was no room for love in his plans! Love! He thought in angry wonder. Now where the hell did that thought come from? She had a delightful body which could drive him to the pinnacle of passion, but that was not love and he damned well didn't intend to let this go any further than sensual completion.

He had accomplished what he wanted. He had heard her soft sounds of ecstatic surrender. He knew he could reach her again and again, until the walls of her resistance crumbled and she was totally at his mercy. Then and only then would he cast her aside and witness the total destruction of Catalina Carrington.

For now he would sink into the pleasure of her warm, soft, and delightfully rounded body. The night was young, and he intended to enjoy it to the fullest.

He paid no attention to his wounded craving for vengeance, which warned him that standards of battle had been raised and that the first skirmish had gone to the one intended to be the victim.

His hands gently stroked her body, savoring the petal softness of her skin and the way she trembled beneath his touch.

For Catalina there was no denial left. There was only the need to find the path that would lead to Marc's well-guarded heart. If that required total surrender, she would take that chance. Success would bring happiness; failure, the loss of all she was. Yet she instantly made her decision. The goal, if she could reach it, would be worth the battle.

His eyes sparkled in the half-light and she could read nothing in them but the pleasure they had shared.

Would she ever read more there?

She raised both hands to enclose his face between them.

"Who are you, Marc Copeland . . . what are you? You torment me in every way possible. You have said such terrible things to me, and yet I feel so alive in your arms." She whispered the words.

"Then why can't that be enough?" he replied as he kissed her cheeks, her eyes, and then let his lips brand her throat and shoulders with soft feather-touch kisses that made her shiver. "Why do you listen to all those questions that don't need to be answered?"

"Is that always enough for you, just the moment?"

"Why not?"

"Because when I look into your eyes I do not see a man who lives day by day and takes only what chance provides."

"Just what do you see?"

"A paradox . . . a puzzle."

He laughed softly as he nibbled gently at the curve of her shoulder, and his arms drew her to him again. "If I'm a puzzle you are the key," he answered more truthfully than either of them knew. "It's so simple, Catalina," he murmured as his mouth sought hers again, "so very simple."

She was caught again in the splendor of the white-hot flame that engulfed them as his mouth sought a response . . . and found it.

She moaned with pleasure as his hands moved over her body softly, light as a butterfly's touch. He proceeded at a studied pace to caress her, sending her emotions spiraling upward.

She became abandoned, but was not shocked by the wildness that overcame her. The sound of his soft laugh mingled with her purring sighs.

The night lengthened and the candles sputtered and

died . . . and Catalina slept in his arms.

In the small hours of the morning the gentle rocking of the boat and the brilliant white moonlight wakened Catalina. She lay very still, intensely aware of the form beside her. It was the first time she had ever wakened with someone sharing her bed, and she found the experience disconcerting.

She turned her head to look at Marc, to study his face. In repose, he seemed much younger. She studied him at her leisure, gazing at the firm straight mouth softened with sleep, the long thick lashes that lay on his bronzed cheek. Gently she placed her hand on the broad expanse of his chest, sliding her fingers in the mat of dark hair.

His body lay bare to her gaze. He was magnificent, like a sleek lion, muscular and superbly conditioned. His belly was flat and hard, his hips were narrow.

Something wild and tempestuous stirred deep within her. Slowly and very gently, she let her hand follow the length of his body to rest on his hip. Caught by the turmoil within her, she could not help but view his body with wonder.

She had never been so conscious of anything as she was of his latent strength. Memories of their love-making flooded her. As they tingled through her, she closed her eyes.

If she had had to choose a man to belong to, could she have chosen a better one? Yet he carried some deep dark secret, and a part of him blocked her out. She wanted more from him than to share this one night, but she knew her desires and his were worlds apart. She had no idea of what he expected to achieve by trying to force her body into total submission. He was aiming for some goal she could not see. But she had a goal of her own. She only wondered if she had the courage to seek it as devotedly as he pursued his.

He was playing a game with her, a game with rules she didn't know. But she began to create a game of her own. She had yet to devise the rules, but she would.

She would have a man she could share the rest of her life with . . . or a man who would use her and one day leave her to a fate she could hardly contemplate.

Entangled in thought, she had allowed her hand to venture farther and she found it hovering . . . wanting to touch . . .

She inhaled deeply and was about to withdraw her hand when his closed over it and forced it to its original destination.

Her eyes lifted to his in shock as she felt the heat in his loins surge.

"Don't stop now, sweet," he said softly. "So far it's been most exciting."

Her decision must be made. She could cringe before him and be his victim until he was finished with her, or she could reach for more than one night's passion. Her hand did not resist him, but became possessive as she pressed against him, her eyes glowing with acceptance.

His breath caught in his throat, his blood surged in his veins. Almost fearing that he was dreaming he reached to draw her head down to his. Her skin was warm and silky smooth and her intoxicating fragrance encircled him. His mouth eagerly took hers and their bodies strained together hungrily.

She found herself returning his fierce fevered kisses, and she clung to him, giving herself wholly to his passion. When she felt his manhood against her, gently searching, she moved to accept him.

He luxuriated in the intimate moment. Her kisses were full and inviting, flaming under his lips, as her tongue warred with his, penetrating his mouth with a heated desire that matched his.

Marc began to move, trying at first to be gentle, but the violence of their passion consumed them both in a thunderous storm.

Catalina's eyes widened as sensation after sensation rippled through her and they dissolved in mutual fire.

The utter completion they knew was something Marc had never experienced before. She had been a tigress, demanding and passionate.

As he held her and they regained their equilibrium, unwelcome thoughts filled his head.

She was where he wanted her to be, and she would be here for as long as he wanted her to be.

But a subtle nagging voice chuckled softly in his inner mind, saying that when the time came to rid himself of her it was going to prove difficult. . . .

Chapter 19

When Catalina opened her eyes the next morning she found Marc gone from the bed. She had no way of knowing that before he had left he had stood near the bed, watching her, a puzzled frown on his face.

Before dawn he had arisen, amused at himself. Why should it bother him if everyone on the boat knew she had spent the night with him, had welcomed him to her bed? That had been part of his plan. But—he shrugged—he could see to that in time.

Now Catalina rose and swung her legs over the edge of the bed. She had to organize all the thoughts that had become tangled in her mind during the night. She had to have a plan to follow. Marc was a very clever man, and he certainly was not set on any permanent involvement with her. To say the least, she admonished herself. He had asked her at their first meeting to be his mistress. That was proof enough of his opinion of her. His mistress . . . mistress. She pondered this for a few minutes; then a small smile played across her lips. It would be a dangerous game and if he ever found out her motives . . . She shuddered at the thought.

She sat on the edge of the bed and brushed her hair while she tried to mold her thoughts into something firmer than the fragile threads they were now.

"After all," she muttered, "it was his idea. He must

have some motive for this and for making Seth lose the boat. Somehow I've got to find it out."

A light rap on the door brought her from the depths of her thoughts.

"Yes?"

"Miss Carrington, Mr. Copeland would like to know if you would join him in the dining room for braekfast."

Catalina inhaled deeply and dredged up all the courage she had. "Would you please take Mr. Copeland a message?"

"Yes, ma'am."

"Tell him it is imperative that I speak to him first. Please ask him to come to my cabin just for a moment."

"Yes, ma'am," the weary voice replied, and she heard departing footsteps.

Her heart thudded painfully, and she was so nervous she could not sit still. She wanted her appearance to suit her proposal so she remained dressed only in a very revealing shift and let her hair fall about her.

She gripped her hands before her as visions leapt before her eyes. Her parents—worse yet, Aunt Charlotte. What in God's name would they think of her should her plan not work? What a gamble it was. If she failed she would pay first with Marc's laughter, then with her own shame for the rest of her life. For a moment her courage failed and she began to tremble. Just then the door swung open and Marc stood before her. His brows were drawn together, and if she hadn't known better, she would have thought he was worried. But she couldn't allow herself to think that. Not yet . . . but maybe someday.

"Catalina, what's wrong?"

Her act began when she smiled as seductively as she could and moved a few steps toward him.

"Why must something be wrong?" she said. "You left

257

so soon I hadn't time to talk to you."

"We can talk over breakfast."

"Not about the subject I have in mind."

Marc had been impatient when he had found her well, but his impatience died as he finally began to pay close attention to the warm look in her eyes and the even warmer look of her half-dressed body.

He stepped inside, closed the door behind him, and leaned indolently against it.

"You're a crafty little kitten, and I'd love to know what's going on behind those beautiful eyes. What's on your mind, Cat?"

She had never been so nervous or frightened in her life, but she controlled her face.

She could not see past the shuttered look in his eyes, but if she had, she might have been more than surprised.

He thought of her, warm and soft against him, and of the feel of her soft mouth parting beneath his. His eyes sought the throbbing pulse at the base of her throat, a most tempting spot. He wanted to press his mouth to it. Then he reminded himself that Catalina was a very dangerous creature.

"I want to discuss an offer you once made me."

"An offer?" He was puzzled.

"How terrible that after last night you don't remember," she whispered as she moved to sit on the edge of the bed.

It rushed to his mind, the casual offer he had made only to hurt her, to belittle her.

"I remember, my sweet," he said in a deep firm voice. She smiled, for the first point was hers.

Her eyes scanned him brazenly, and she noted the small flame that touched his eyes. She had seen the look before.

"I could repeat some of the words to you just in case

you might have forgotten. I believe you offered me the very unique position of being your mistress."

"I did that." He chuckled. "I think I remember your answer. I believe you told me I could go to hell."

"You've forgotten a woman's prerogative," she said softly, and was more than satisfied by the slight stiffening of his body and the visible effort it took to retain his smile.

"There was another part to the bargain."

"I'm going to have to watch this slipping memory of mine. Do me a favor and remind me again."

"If I'm not mistake the second part of the bargain was the *Belle.*"

"I see," he replied softly. Now he moved from the door and walked slowly toward her. He was certain she was up to something and that the *Belle* was only a small part of it. But what did she have to gain? An alarm in the back of his mind told him to be more careful, but the sensuous delights she seemed to be offering drew him like a magnet.

Catalina turned partially away from him as he drew close to her, the flame within his eyes brighter now. She licked her dry lips, but did not move.

He stopped beside her, and his hand reached up to gently push a lock of hair from her bare shoulders, then lingered to caress her flesh gently.

"So now you bargain with me?"

"Yes."

"Just what kind of bargain do you have in mind, Cat?"

"Why do you ask me? You made the first one, why can't we just stick to it. Surely you must have thought it fair at the beginning?"

"The beginning," he murmured. "At the beginning I wanted a mistress in return for a boat. If I'm not mistaken you were, to say the least, insulted. What has

259

made you change your mind?"

"I told you, you forgot . . ."

"I know," he interrupted with a small laugh, "a woman's prerogative."

She turned and looked up into his eyes, and he was shaken for the first time by the intensity of her gaze.

"So do we make a bargain, Marc," she said softly. "Are you willing to gamble again?"

"A boat . . . against all you have to offer? I can only come out the winner."

"Then you agree," she whispered, hoping he couldn't feel the way her body trembled.

"Yes, I agree. Tell me, do we have a time limit on this little . . . arrangement?"

"It will last until we get to Memphis," she answered. "Then I will go home and our agreement will be terminated."

"In that case"—his voice lowered and his arm slid about her, drawing her to him—"I think we ought to seal this bargain."

"As you wish," she murmured as she melted against him and her arms encircled his neck.

Any reservations Marc had were driven off by a searing kiss.

Catalina felt the strength of his arms about her, and prayed silently her gamble would work. If she failed, she would lose all to him.

China was seated at the breakfast table in her cabin. Shawna was with her. Both had preferred to eat away from the main dining room.

As usual China remained silent, merely answering Shawna's questions and listening to her rambling conversation with half an ear while she sorted out the situation that was unfolding on the *Belle*.

She had tried her best to tell Catalina something that she hardly understood herself. She had only known that her love for Marc had urged her to find a way to make him see that this vendetta of his was wrong, and that it could only hurt him.

What she had seen in Marc's eyes when he had looked at Catalina had told her the truth. Catalina had gotten past his urge for vengeance and had touched him deeply. China only wondered if Catalina would be wise enough, and woman enough, to see beyond Marc's façade to the man beneath. She was determined that for the balance of the trip she was going to do her best to be a friend to both Catalina and Marc, and to throw them together at every opportunity.

She had no way of knowing about the bargain that was at that very moment being made. . . .

The rap on the door took both Shawna and China by surprise. They were even more surprised when they heard Nina's irate voice from the hallway.

"Shawna! Open this damned door. I have to talk to you!"

China laughed softly and motioned toward the door. "Do go and open it, Shawna, before her shrieking wakens the entire boat. She can be such an obnoxious creature. I cannot believe that Marc still finds pleasure in her company."

"I'll let her in," Shawna said delicately. "But would you mind if I go on deck while you talk? I find her rather . . ."

"Obnoxious." China laughed. "No, I don't mind. I'd join you if I could."

"Shawna! I know you must be awake."

"Well, if we hadn't been, we would be by now," China said. "Go on, Shawna. Let her in."

Shawna opened the door, and found herself facing a half-dressed and angry Nina.

261

"Well, it's about time," Nina said as she pushed her way past Shawna. A calm China sipped her tea and looked up at Nina with a slight smile.

"Good morning," she said. "Would you like to join me? There is still plenty . . . since Shawna was not given the opportunity to finish her breakfast."

Shawna giggled softly, but when Nina turned blazing eyes on her, she quickly stepped out into the hall and pulled the door shut.

Nina turned back to China, who controlled her smile with some effort.

"Where is Marc?" she demanded.

"I am not his keeper," China said softly.

"You know every move he makes! And I'll just bet you can tell me whose bed he's been warming for the past few nights."

"You," China calmly declared, "are not his keeper either. In fact, Nina, I would try to be a little more discreet if I were you. Should you incur his anger this morning, you might find yourself ejected from the boat by the time we reach Natchez tomorrow."

"You really do know where he is and who he's with, don't you?"

"If I did, you would most certainly be the last person I would tell. Sit down and let me give you some very sound advice."

"I don't want to talk to you," Nina said through gritted teeth. "I want to know whose bed I'll find Marc in . . . Charlene's . . . Paulette's? I'll scratch out their eyes, the little sluts."

"Sit down Nina!" China's voice was sharp now. "And for heaven's sake be quiet!"

Nina sat down and for a moment her eyes narrowed thoughtfully, as if she had just realized something. "What are you doing here in Shawna's room?"

"I spent the night with her."

"Was she sick?"

"Of course not."

"Then why—"

"It's none of your business. What happens on this boat is Marc's business and Marc's business alone. Again, I would advise you to keep silent or you will find yourself back on the streets—without Marc or me to help you."

"China," Nina said in a pleading voice as she bent forward, "I . . . I just want to see him. He hasn't . . . I mean, I haven't seen him for almost two days."

"Marc brought you aboard this boat for a purpose. You were to find it out when we reach Memphis. But," China declared coldly as she rose to stand above Nina, "one more action like this and I shall see that you are dragged to the filthiest brothel in Natchez. Believe me, Nina"—China's voice was like the edge of a glittering blade—"I know many people who would be more than pleased to take you and keep you very silent."

There was no doubt in Nina's mind that China meant what she said, or that she had the power to carry out her threat.

China walked out of the room and closed the door with a soft click. But a smile formed on her lips as she walked down the passageway.

Nina sat for some time, but China's threat was not enough to suppress her desire to see Marc again. Her mind twisted and turned until she came up with the obvious answer: the room belonging to China had been given to someone else, and that someone had to mean a great deal to Marc. Anyone of little consequence would not have been able to displace China, nor would China have willingly moved for anyone she had not thought very important to Marc.

263

Raised in the streets of New Orleans Nina was not one to let someone take something she wanted from her. She rose slowly and, leaving the cabin, went to China's door. It was not locked, and it swung open easily under the touch of her hand.

But the stateroom was empty. This surprised her so that she remained immobile for some moments. That was opportune for her, for it permitted her to hear the voices in Marc's cabin.

She walked to the door and pressed her ear to it. There was no doubt the masculine voice was Marc's, but the woman's voice, soft and cultured, was not a voice that belonged to anyone she knew.

She turned the handle and swung the door open, and a dismayed squeak was all she could utter when she saw the woman in Marc's arms.

When Marc and Catalina swung about, Nina could see Catalina's half-dressed state.

"Nina," Marc demanded, "what the hell are you doing here?"

Catalina looked from Marc to Nina, realizing immediately the situation she was facing. But she had no intention of letting anyone stand between her and what she wanted, not even someone who had shared Marc's time before he'd met her.

Their mouths had blended and Marc had held her close. For a moment he thought of all the plans he had laid and of how easily Catalina had fallen in with them.

By the time they reached Natchez, there would be nothing left in Catalina's life but him and the *Belle,* and he would see that she had neither. But now he meant to enjoy all she offered, and he was thoroughly engrossed in doing just that when the door opened and he turned to look into Nina's enraged eyes.

Asking what she was doing there was an open invitation to Nina. She leaned against the frame of the door and her teeth gleamed in a feral smile.

"So this is the little bitch you've left my bed for," she snarled. "Really, Marc, your taste is disastrous . . . or were you drinking?"

Marc could feel Catalina's body grow stiff in his arms. China had warned him about Nina's possessive bent, but he had refused to listen. He promised himself to heed China's advice in the future. But now he had a jealous woman on his hands . . . and Catalina in his arms. He couldn't let the situation build any further or Catalina would be off the boat by the time he reached Natchez and all his well-laid plans would be for nothing.

He had no idea that leaving the boat didn't fit in with Catalina's own plans. She had found something in Marc's arms she had never hoped to find, and she wasn't about to give up without a battle.

Before Marc could put words to his growing anger, Catalina spoke in a voice dripping honey.

"I must ask you, Marc," she said softly, "to have all the locks on the *Belle* checked. They have caused no end of difficulty since I boarded. One never knows just"—she shrugged—"who might take a notion to wander into one's cabin uninvited."

Nina started toward Catalina, a murderous glow in her eyes, but before she could reach her, Marc put himself between the two.

He wanted to laugh for he'd just discovered his Cat had sharp claws. His Cat? . . . He would have to stop thinking like that.

He had no idea why Catalina had suddenly decided to do battle for him, but it most certainly wasn't

265

because she was his.

"I asked you what you were doing here, Nina. I expect an answer."

Nina looked at Marc, feigning innocent surprise. "I thought I was always welcome here . . . anytime."

"You'd better go back to your cabin, and get dressed," Marc replied, ignoring her words. "While you're at it, you might just pack your things. You'll be leaving the boat in Natchez."

"Leaving," Nina sputtered. "You can't just throw me off this boat. You're the one who sent for me in the first place. Why don't you throw that little tramp off and then we can pick up where we left off."

"I don't think so, Nina." Marc's voice was cold and his anger was apparent from the wicked flames that danced in his green eyes.

"You can't do this to me! I gave up a lot to come when you called. You owe me—" Nina saw her mistake at once. She had pushed Marc one step too far.

"You're right. I owe you. You'll be well paid for your time before you leave the *Belle*. And as for what you gave up for me, I don't think the brothel China rescued you from was so alluring. But I'll be more than pleased to pay your way back to it."

Nina swung her hand, but it was caught in a viselike grip before it found its destination.

"I suggest you leave now before I get any angrier. I've never struck a woman before but you're tempting me. You came here for profit, and profit is what you leave with. There have never been any promises between us. Now go back to your cabin and start to pack. I expect you off the boat in Natchez. China will see that you get what you bargained for."

"China!" Nina's rage-filled eyes fell on Catalina who had never felt such hatred before. It was like a physical blow. "And you . . . you'll pay for this. Do you think you'll keep him? He and his precious China will rid themselves of you as soon as they're finished with you."

Catalina felt a moment of sympathy for Nina. The realization that Marc could do just that made her very aware of the harsh reality of her gamble.

"Get going, Nina." Marc's voice lowered in a veiled threat.

Nina's eyes and Catalina's had met and held. "You'll pay for this—you'll pay," Nina half whispered. Then she left the cabin, leaving the door open.

There was a heavy silence as Marc walked over to close it. Then he turned to look at Catalina, but he couldn't tell what she was thinking. She watched him silently for a minute, but her mind was spinning.

It would be safer to run, to find a way to get off the boat at Natchez. Maybe she could locate Travis and travel back home with him by coach. At least she knew exactly what Travis wanted from her. She wasn't too sure about Marc.

"I'm sorry about that, Cat," Marc said quietly, and Catalina suddenly knew she didn't want to leave him. She had seen him sever his ties to his last mistress, and she knew she was in the most tenuous of positions . . . yet she didn't want to go.

He was watching her through narrowed eyes, expecting an explosion that didn't come. What did happen was what he had least expected. Catalina moved toward him, and in a moment her arms were about his neck and her body was pressed close to his.

Everything was too smooth . . . too easy. His self-protective instincts became alert.

"We have a bargain you and I," she said in a soft throaty voice. "We don't need to make any decisions about the future until we reach Memphis."

"A bargain," he agreed, "but why do I get the feeling I've leapt from the pan to the fire?"

"Why, Marc. Are you the one who's afraid of the fire now?" Her voice was like silk, but her challenge was all steel.

She was rewarded by a look that combined pleasure and puzzlement.

Chapter 20

Seth completed his story without being interrupted by Charlotte or Charles.

"... So, I've brought Jake—Jacqueline—here so you and Cat can help show her there's a much better world. By the way"—Seth smiled—"where is Cat, out at some local affair?"

Charles and Charlotte exchanged quick glances that were not lost on Seth. His smile faded.

"Where is she?"

"She's not here," Charles began.

"You mean she's not in the house."

"No," Charlotte said quietly. "She is not even in New Orleans."

"Aunt Charlotte, something's wrong. Suppose you tell me what's been going on since I've been gone."

"Much has happened and a great deal of it is not good," Charlotte replied. "But don't you think this child is tired and should be in bed?"

Seth turned to look at Jake, realizing that in his worry about Cat he had almost forgotten her.

Jake had tried to listen quietly to the conversation, but a full stomach and exhaustion had made her numb and heavy eyed.

"Jake, I'm sorry. I know you must be tired. Aunt Charlotte can take you up to your room so you can get some sleep."

"My . . . my room? All to myself?" Jake asked in disbelief. She had never had a private domain and she found this hard to believe.

"Your room—all to yourself," Seth replied with a gentleness that made Charlotte's eyes narrow as a soft smile touched her lips.

Charlotte rose and extended a hand to Jake. She was touched by the quickness with which a small trembling hand was put in hers and by the vulnerability she saw in Jake's eyes.

"Come, child," she said gently.

This first breath of such gentleness, this first touch of feminine kindness was almost too much for Jake, who had lived her entire life in the company of rough and careless men.

Charles and Seth watched the two leave the room; then Charles turned to Seth. "Before Charlotte gets back, why don't you tell me just how you ran across this wild little creature."

Seth laughed, but he quickly began his story.

When Charlotte stopped before a door and swung it open, Jake gasped in disbelief. She had never seen such a beautiful room in her life.

She walked slowly into it, tears stinging her eyes. Suddenly, she felt dirty and displaced, and she wasn't too sure she could handle her upsetting emotions.

But Charlotte, who had been studying her, felt a touch of pity. She kept it from showing, for she knew Jake just might be astute enough to perceive it. She was certain that Jake had enough pride to resent such a reaction.

"I'll have some water drawn so you can bathe, and I'll have one of my nightgowns brought so you can sleep comfortably."

Jake turned to Charlotte, tears that could be restrained no longer welling in her eyes.

"You are so kind. I . . . I can clean and cook," she began enthusiastically. "And maybe I can care for your clothes, I'm really a good worker. I'm strong and—"

"Child, child," Charlotte said, her eyes now growing suspiciously moist, "you are a guest in my house. I want you to enjoy your stay here. We can become friends. I will enjoy having a young woman to talk to."

"Friends?" Jake questioned, aghast. "I've never . . . I mean . . ."

"I know," Charlotte replied in a conspiratorial tone. "To tell you the truth, child, I don't recall having many real women friends either. But if you'd like we can share breakfast in the morning and get to know each other better, would you like that?"

"Oh, yes," Jake breathed out.

"Good. Now enjoy your bath, have a good sleep, and I'll see you in the morning. I'll send a maid to waken you and show you to the breakfast room. Good night, Jake. Sleep well."

"Good night . . . and thank you."

Charlotte patted Jake's cheek, then left, pulling the door closed behind her.

Alone, Jake turned in a slow circle in the center of the room, her eyes trying to absorb all of its comfort and beauty at one time. The bed was a large oak fourposter, a white ruffled spread covering what promised to be soft welcoming warmth. The thick carpet was soft beneath her feet, and she could inhale the clean scent of the room. The walls were papered in soft blue with small pink and white flowers, and to Jake's delight there was an ivory white mantel over the hearth upon which a fire briskly glowed.

Jake felt she could cry out in delight, but a light rap

announced a young maid who carried a soft white nightgown over her arm.

"Good evening, miss. I was to lay out this for you and to tell you your bath is ready." The young servant spoke as she crossed the room to place the nightgown on the bed.

Jake didn't want to appear foolish so she remained silent.

The maid turned from the bed and smiled again. "If you will come with me, miss, I'd be delighted to help you."

Jake followed her from that room to another, which astounded her even more than the first. Never having taken a bath in anything but a wooden tub filled with heated river water, she could not hold back a gasp of pure awe. They actually took baths in this huge white tub! Right inside the house! This was beyond her imagination, and she stored this knowledge so she might impart it to her grandfather at the first opportunity.

The tub was nearly full of steaming water on which there was a covering of thick white suds. She closed her eyes to again inhale the exquisite scent that emanated from the enticing tub.

"Shall I help you undress, miss?"

Ashamed, both of the outer clothes she wore and of her rough cotton undergarments, Jake could only shake her head negatively.

"Here is a robe, miss, and there are some warm towels. I shall return in an hour."

The maid left, drawing the door closed, and Jake went to the tub, almost tearing her clothes off as she did.

She sank into the water, thinking that she had never felt anything so wonderful in her life. The water had begun to chill before Jake rose reluctantly from it. The towels were soft, and she leisurely dried herself before donning the robe.

She wasn't too sure she should try to find her room herself. Maybe Seth's aunt would not want her to be wandering about in the halls.

Insecure and more than a little nervous, Jake sat on a small stool and waited for someone to come for her.

By the time the maid finally came, Jake, who had begun to think she was forgotten, sat huddled on the stool.

"Miss, I've turned the bed down."

Jake followed her like an obedient child, and was left alone again in the large bedroom.

She slipped out of the robe and took up the soft nightgown. It slid over her skin like satin and she closed her eyes, enjoying the sensuous feeling. Then she blew out the lamp and climbed into the bed.

The room was now lit only by the red glow of the dying fire, and Jake lay gazing at it, letting forbidden dreams have their way. She could enjoy them because she was alone and no one would ever know. Finally she slipped into a peaceful sleep.

Charlotte returned to the sitting room to find Charles and Seth in deep conversation. Seth had been telling Charles what had happened from the night he had left the house.

"And I never got to the *Belle* at all," he said.

"So he was telling the truth," Charlotte mused.

"Who?"

"Marc Garrison," she replied thoughtfully.

"Marc Garrison?"

"That's another story, Seth." Charles laughed.

"Well, tell it to me. I want to know just what Cat's involved in and why she's not here. Come on, Aunt

Charlotte, out with the truth, all of it."

"Yes, Seth. You deserve an explanation. If you had not come home when you did, both Charles and I would have been gone."

"Gone where?"

"After Cat, who is on board the *Belle* with both Marc Garrison and Travis Sherman."

"By herself!" Seth's alarm made it quite obvious he had very little faith in either man.

"By herself," Charlotte reluctantly responded. "The next boat for Natchez leaves tonight. Charles and I have accommodations."

"Aunt Charlotte, I know you want to go after her but I think Charles and I would be more effective, and"— he bent toward her, his gaze intent on hers—"Jake needs you desperately. I've made her a lot of promises, and I'd hate to disappoint her. She needs what only a woman can provide. She . . . well she's kind of helpless."

"I understand, Seth." Charlotte smiled. "I don't want to, but I'll stay behind. She's a sweet child, Seth, and I do believe we are going to become good friends."

"Aunt Charlotte, I would be most appreciative. You have no idea how difficult her life has been or how grateful I feel that she saved my life."

"I do have a slight idea how appreciative you might be," Charlotte said softly. "You go after Cat, and leave Jake in my hands. Cat needs you now."

"Thanks." Seth chuckled. "You can add this to all the other things I owe you. You will explain to Jake in the morning—tell her I'll be back as soon as I can?"

"I'll explain. And you might just start getting some clothes packed. Your boat will leave soon. Charles can see you to the dock."

Seth rose, bent swiftly to kiss Charlotte's cheek. "I love you, Aunt Charlotte. You're a grand lady. I couldn't have brought Jake to anyone better."

Charlotte was silent. The constriction in her throat forbade words, but Seth had expected none. He left the room and took the stairs two at a time to go to his room, removing his jacket as he went.

He changed his clothes and packed. Then he returned to the sitting room. Charles rose, and they said their goodbyes quickly, then left Charlotte standing in the open doorway and waving.

When they were out of sight, she stepped back inside and closed the door. Going up the stairs, she went to the room in which Jake slept. She opened the door quietly and crossed over to the bed.

As she stood looking down at Jake, a smile touched her lips. Relaxed in sleep, Jake had lost her defenses, and Charlotte could see beyond them now.

She was looking down at a girl who would develop into a beauty. Her skin, tanned by exposure to the sun, was smooth and flawless. Her body, slim and small, was nonetheless a soft womanly form. A mass of red-golden hair was spread across the pillow, and Charlotte knew that with proper care it would be extraordinarily beautiful. All in all, Charlotte quite approved of Jake, and she approved of Seth's interest in her as well. She had noted the change in Seth, and it had pleased her. For the first time in his life, Seth was thinking first of someone else.

"I think, little Jake," Charlotte said softly, "you are going to be the best thing that has happened to our Seth—yes, the very best. Sleep well, child. Tomorrow we will begin to let the butterfly out of her cocoon."

She left the room as quietly as she had come.

Jake opened her eyes at the same moment the door opened. She was momentarily disoriented, but when the young maid who had prepared her bath entered, Jake gathered her thoughts.

"Good morning, miss," the girl said brightly as she drew the drapes open to let in the morning sun. "Miss Charlotte is waiting breakfast for you. Did you sleep well?"

"Oh." Jake sat up, wide-eyed. The announcement that Charlotte was waiting for her shattered her composure. She searched wildly for her clothes.

"Miss Charlotte told me to bring you something of Miss Cat's to wear," the girl explained as she took a pile of clothes from a chair and brought them to the bed.

Jake just stared at the lovely dress. "Oh no, that's too beautiful! It must be one of her best dresses. She will be angry if I wear it."

"Oh no, miss." The maid laughed. "I assure you, it is one of her oldest. But even if it were her best, Miss Cat would be pleased to share it with you."

Jake was doubtful about this, but she rose from the bed, almost reluctant to remove the soft comfortable nightgown.

"If you'll dress, miss, I will brush your hair and pin it up for you. I've done Miss Cat's hair a lot, and quite nicely I'm proud to say."

Still full of doubts, Jake dressed slowly, savoring the touch of silk against her flesh. She had never felt pretty in her life until this moment.

She sat nervously on a small bench while her hair was brushed and pinned atop her head.

"Now, miss, why don't you come to the mirror and look at yourself. You're ever so pretty."

"Pretty? Me?"

"Oh yes, miss."

Jake walked across the room to a full-length mirror and stood in wide-eyed disbelief. She had changed so, she did not even recognize herself.

"Grandpa won't even know me," she whispered, and somehow this thought sent a shiver of fear through her. She was no longer her grandpa's Jake . . . but she didn't know who she was.

A sharp stab of loneliness and fear overcame her. At this moment she wanted only to be safe aboard her grandfather's boat, away from strangers who wanted to take away her past and leave her with a future she did not understand.

She was not yet prepared to let go of the Jake of yesterday. She tipped up her chin in a defiant lift and turned from the mirror.

"I don't like her. She isn't me. I want my old clothes," she said.

"Sorry, miss." The maid's smile faded. "I was told to dispose of them."

"Dis— What does that mean?" Jake demanded.

"It means . . . I was supposed to throw them away."

"Throw them away!" Jake almost shrieked. "You have no right to throw away what belongs to me! You go get them, do you hear me, you go get them!"

"But, miss, I can't do that."

"Well, you damn well better, or I'll carve my name on your soft little ass. Now you just get them, you hear me!"

The young maid was overcome by tears and shocked disbelief.

She backed away, for the blaze in Jake's eyes promised murder and mayhem.

"Oh . . . miss . . . I just can't . . . I . . ."

Jake stalked the maid as she backed toward the door. Her eyes were cold chips of green ice, and her smile was really a threatening grimace.

"I got me a big shiny knife, and if you don't find my clothes in just about five minutes I'm going to cut off pieces of you and leave them all over the house."

The maid, by this time totally terrified, was almost hysterical.

At that moment the door opened and Charlotte stood in the doorway.

"Jake!" Her frigid command brought a choked sob of relief from the maid and a muttered curse from Jake.

"Hell and damnation!" Jake exclaimed.

"You will calm yourself right this minute, and apologize to Sophie. She is a kind and sensitive girl, and she had only been trying to help you. Now apologize at once!"

"I want my clothes!"

"You are wearing your clothes. The rags you came in have been destroyed at my order. Now apologize."

"I will like hell!"

"You, my dear Jake, have a nasty habit of cursing. Use one more such word in my house and I shall promptly wash your mouth with soap. Do I make myself clear? You are my guest, and I suggest you begin to act like one. Develop enough manners to keep Seth from being ashamed he ever wanted to help you. Now apologize!"

Jake opened her mouth to shout a reply that would have made the devil blush, but the words never found her lips. At that moment her eyes met Charlotte's and Charlotte took a threatening step toward her.

Again Jake was meeting a challenge she had never faced before. Her wicked mouth, her more wicked knife, and the company of men who usually gave her her way had not prepared her for the menacing Charlotte.

"You are supposed to be a lady, and a lady would never hurt anyone unable to fight back. It is dishonorable and disgusting to do such a thing. That is your first lesson. Now you can remain the ugly little urchin or you can justify Seth's faith in you and apologize!"

Jake gulped. She looked from Charlotte's cold determined face to Sophie's distressed one.

"I . . . I apologize," she whispered.

"I didn't hear you," Charlotte declared.

"I apologize," Jake said firmly, her eyes burning and her cheeks pink.

"Very well. You may go, Sophie."

"Yes, ma'am," Sophie replied, still awed by Jake's ferocity.

When the door closed behind Sophie, Charlotte visibly relaxed. She smiled at Jake.

"You are a very intelligent, young lady. I'm pleased to see that you have enough good sense to learn to control what I assume is a very wicked temper. I hope I never see it again. Now"—Charlotte smiled pleasantly as if nothing had occurred—"suppose we have breakfast and that long talk you promised me. We are going to have a grand time today. I have planned a shopping trip to purchase all you will need, for when Seth returns, I plan on having a ball at which you can be introduced into society. I firmly believe you will eventually take New Orleans by storm."

"Miss Charlotte?"

"Yes?"

"I truly am sorry. I guess I was just . . . afraid."

"Do you think I do not know that, child," Charlotte said softly. She reached out to lift Jake's lowered head so their eyes could meet. "But you have something strong within you, Jake, so I will tell you something I hope you will understand and remember. Being a lady is much more than just wearing pretty clothes and going to parties. You will also have responsibilities, to yourself and to others. Can you demand respect unless you respect others? Can you expect to be loved if you give no love? And can you ask for honor and discipline unless you possess both?"

"Oh, I will never be a lady." Jake moaned softly. "Seth will be ashamed of me."

"You care so deeply about what Seth thinks about you?"

"I owe him so much. I don't want him to think I am nothing . . . someone he wishes he had never seen."

"Then, if making him proud of you is so important, why don't we begin again? Let us go down and have breakfast. Then we'll go shopping. During that time we will discuss your future and just what you want to do with it. Agreed?"

"Yes," Jake said softly. Her eyes glittered with tears, and she longed for something she couldn't name but Charlotte understood.

Without a word she drew Jake into her arms and rocked her gently, like a child. She was rewarded by clinging arms and the sound of quiet tears.

Chapter 21

Jake opened her eyes, wondering at the amazing warmth and comfort that surrounded her. She had never enjoyed such luxury, and she hated to leave the bed.

The door opened and Sophie entered. She drew back the drapes to let in the morning sun, then turned to the bed.

Jake giggled softly at the cautious way she approached her.

"M-miss?" she said carefully.

When Jake sat up abruptly, Sophie let out a startled squeak and stepped back.

"Oh, Sophie. I am truly sorry about all the things I said to you yesterday. I was just so frightened. I'd really like to be friends with you. I don't have a friend around here. You'd be my first."

Sophie smiled hesitantly and came a little closer to the bed.

"Miss Charlotte's waiting in the breakfast room, miss. She said you're to dress for shopping."

"I'll dress . . . as soon as you say you'll forgive me for being so mean."

"Oh, miss." Sophie giggled. "It's not up to me to be forgiving you."

Jake got out of bed, went over to a very startled

Sophie, and took one of her hands in both of hers.

"You're a person, Sophie, and I'm a person. I lived on the docks all my life. If I come in here and put on pretty clothes, does that make me any different, any better?"

"I don't know, miss."

"I don't want to be better, Sophie. I just want to be friends. Will you be my friend?"

Sophie realized now that Jake truly meant what she was saying. She smiled. "All right, miss, I'd be truly pleased."

"Thank you," Jake said softly. "Thank you."

"But I'll be skinned, miss, if you don't get down to breakfast. Miss Charlotte isn't one to be kept waiting."

"I wish—"

"What, miss?"

"That Seth wasn't gone. This is all so . . . big, so frightening."

"He'll be back before too long, and you'll have a grand time at parties and all."

Jake was silent, thinking that she was now alone to face the newness of her life. "Sophie?"

"Yes, miss," Sophie replied as she placed on the bed the bundle of clothes that Charlotte had ordered her to take from Catalina's room.

"You've been here some time?"

"Yes, miss."

"Can you tell me about this family?"

"You mean Mr. Seth, miss?" Sophie giggled softly.

"Don't get impertinent," Jake said arrogantly, trying to mimic what she felt was the proper tone for a lady to use under such circumstances.

"Sorry, miss," Sophie replied. She remained silent as she started to help Jake dress, too silent to suit Jake.

"Well?"

"Well what, miss?" Sophie said innocently.

"What about Seth?" Jake said impatiently, her cheeks pinkening.

"He's quite a nice gentleman, miss. Always been just a little bit wild, but Miss Charlotte says a young man's got to sew his wild oats while he's young. Mr. Seth, he's really a good-hearted lad. He's always been kind to all of us, and he surely loves Miss Charlotte and his sister, miss."

"His sister?"

"Yes, miss. Miss Catalina. She's a lovely creature and Mr. Seth has always felt her to be very special."

"I suppose," Jake said, her uncertainty surfacing, "she is a lady?"

"Oh, yes, miss . . . a lovely lady. All the gentlemen love her, and she's kind and generous and unselfish and—"

"My goodness," Jake said flippantly, "she's about perfect."

"Yes, miss." Sophie totally misconstrued Jake's words. "She's truly a lady."

When Sophie finished buttoning Jake's dress, Jake spun to face her.

"A lady, a lady. Well not everybody wants to be a puny lady. I'll bet she'd faint if she had to walk the docks for a day. Being a lady isn't so special."

"No, miss. I guess it isn't that important. But you see, Miss Cat, she's nice. I mean, she never says anything to hurt like some people do. I don't think it would matter where Miss Cat was or what she was doing. Even on the dirty docks, she'd still be a lady. That's what makes her special."

Jake felt ashamed for lashing out at Sophie when she knew it was her uncertainty and jealousy that had spoken.

"I'm sorry again, Sophie." She smiled. "I suppose I've a long way to go."

"Yes, miss. And you'd better get started cause Miss Charlotte isn't pleased when she's kept waiting."

Jake nodded and walked to the door. As she walked down the steps beside Sophie, she began to plan. One day Seth and his perfect sister Catalina would return. When they did, she would prove that she was every bit as much a lady as Cat.

As Charlotte watched Jake walk across the room toward her, she smiled.

Awkward and uncomfortable in the clothes, she nonetheless moved with an innate pride that Charlotte found captivating.

She was entrancing, half-child, half-woman, and Charlotte was more than certain Seth would be in for the surprise of his life—more of a surprise, she felt, than Jake herself was in for.

"Good morning, child."

"Good morning, Miss McNeil," Jake said.

"No . . . Aunt Charlotte. Call me Aunt Charlotte."

"Thank you. I . . . I wasn't sure just what would be proper. And Aunt Charlotte, please don't call me . . . child."

"All right." Charlotte laughed softly. "I shall call you Jake until you tell me to call you something else. Is that a bargain?"

"Yes. Thank you."

"Now, come and eat. The carriage is being brought around, and we will spend the day seeing just how pretty we can make you. The thought excites me. It's like dressing my own daughter. And tomorrow night we are going to the theater. I have plans for every hour—almost every minute. By the time Seth returns we shall have had a grand holiday."

Charlotte kept her word and they were always busy as the days turned into weeks. Caught up in this whirlwind of activity, Jake was much less conscious of

284

her metamorphosis than Charlotte was. The older woman was watching a small miracle unfold before her.

With her natural spontaneity and gaiety Jake was soon popular with a group of young people who helped educate her without knowing they were doing so. Within two weeks Jake had learned to laugh freely, to dance, to choose the best clothes, the best wines. She had even learned how to tease and flirt while giggling with young people of her own age.

At Charlotte's urging, she began to learn to read and to write and to think. For the unleashing of her mind, Jake was most grateful. She now saw all the things of beauty that she could enjoy and, under Charlotte's guidance, learn to appreciate it.

Seth stood at the stern rail and watched the paddlewheel churn the water.

His thoughts were torn between the situation Cat was in and the one in which he had left Jake.

He worried about how Jake would accustom herself to the abrupt change in her life.

It would be hard, but as much as he wanted to turn back and help her, he knew Cat needed him much more now.

He was involved in thought when Charles joined him at the rail.

"A penny for your thoughts." Charles smiled.

"There are too many of them. You'd owe me a banker's ransom."

"Can't be as bad as all that."

"It's just that I'd like to be in two places at once."

"Damn near impossible."

"I know. Charles, this Marc . . . Garrison, Copeland, or whatever the hell his name is."

"Marc Copeland Garrison," Charles supplied.

"Whatever. Tell me a bit about him."

"You mean his situation with women?" Charles asked astutely. Seth turned to him and nodded silently.

"He's got quite a reputation with the ladies. If he's made as many conquests as he's been given credit for, he must spend the majority of his time in bed. But I suppose one cannot put much stock in rumor."

"Where there's smoke there's fire."

"Well he travels about with a lovely Oriental creature called, of all things, China, and, from what I've been told, a bevy of other beauties. Whatever the truth is, the man never lacks feminine companionship."

"God," Seth murmured. "I wonder how Cat is faring."

"Cat is an enterprising young woman."

"But can she defend herself against this rake?"

"If she chooses to."

"What does that mean?"

"Garrison does not rape women; he seduces them."

"Cat is no fool."

"Of course not. But she's in a vulnerable position that will require wit."

"Between men like Travis and Marc," Seth said, "she's in a difficult position. Neither man can be trusted."

"Well, we can only follow her, Seth. Maybe they'll still be docked in Natchez when we arrive. It is a lovely city, and perhaps Cat will be intrigued enough to want to stay there for a few days."

"With any kind of luck we just might catch up with them there."

"Seth?"

"Yes."

"What will you do?"

"What do you mean?" Seth asked, though he knew

what Charles meant."

"Should you find them, and find . . ."

"That my sister has been dishonored?"

Charles nodded.

"I have brought a rather ornate box with me. It's in my stateroom. It contains my father's dueling pistols. I shall defend my family's honor in the only way left."

"You will challenge them both?"

"I shall."

"I don't know about Travis, he is not known for being honorable. But Marc Garrison, he will fight you and he is no novice with the dueling pistols."

"Whatever may happen, Charles, I have little choice in the matter."

"But you have."

"What choice?"

"Allow Catalina to make her own decisions. It could be that she has already done so and honor has nothing to do with it. She chose to go on this journey of her own free will. She began the game, and maybe she will choose to end it in her own way . . . without violence, without bloodshed—and without your help."

"What are you telling me, Charles?"

"I really don't know. I have found out a lot about Marc Garrison, but none of it has darkened his name. I just have a feeling that fate may have arranged something that has nothing to do with any of our plans."

"You sound like a mystic." Seth laughed.

"Maybe so. But I don't want to see either of you hurt."

"What do you suggest?"

"If you find them in Natchez, go to your sister first. Find out what is truth and what is rumor. Then abide by her will and save yourself a lot of grief, maybe even a tragedy."

"And if I don't find them in Natchez?"

"We will continue on until we do find them."

"Why do you feel Marc isn't guilty?" Seth asked quietly.

Charles looked at him, unable to put into words exactly what he felt. He had sought an answer, and had come up with a question instead.

"Seth, what makes you think he's not?"

Seth sighed. "I don't know. When he won the *Belle* from me, it was my foolishness and an honest game. I surely am more guilty than he is, because it is my fault that we are all in this position. Still, I have a feeling that there is much more to all this. I would like . . ."

"What Seth?"

"I would like to face him and ask him what his intentions were and are. I'd like to know if he meant to damage me, or to reach Cat. I'd like to have some answers."

"Well, let us pray we will find them in Natchez."

"Yes."

"Why don't you get some sleep, Seth? It's very late."

"No, you go below. I'll stay here and think for a while, if you don't mind."

"All right. Good night."

"Good night."

Charles went to his bed wishing he could have said something that would have eased Seth's mind, while Seth watched the waters of the great river pass behind the boat in a white froth of lace.

He thought of Cat and realized that Charles had been right. Cat had a right to decide the outcome of the situation. He would be prepared to do whatever was necessary, but he would speak to Cat first. Many questions needed to be asked, and he felt that she might have secured answers to them, to the why of Marc Garrison.

He thought of Jake, of leaving her, and decided that he would make it up to her as soon as he returned home. He began to think of all the fun things they could do, of the places they could go. Why, he thought, I can introduce her to all of my friends, and if Aunt Charlotte and Cat are successful in polishing Jake's rough edges, she might be able to find a good husband and have a good future.

He began to think back on their meeting and the many confrontations between them. The memories made him smile, and he was surprised to find that he already missed her vivid temper, her poignant little girl's innocence. To him she was a child, a sweet child that needed a helping hand.

What he had done brought on a feeling of pride, but it also brought the realization that he had rarely done anything for anyone else in his entire life.

Now he would make up for that by turning the proverbial sow's ear into an enticing silk purse. Jake would be grateful, so would Ben.

Jake leaned both arms against the window sill and stared out into the balmy star-studded night. She wondered where Seth was now and if he was thinking of her.

Then she took up the book she had taken from the shelf in the library that day. Charlotte had insisted that she read as often as possible, and she was allowed to choose books at her own discretion. She sat in a large chair, her feet curled beneath her, and absorbed the story of Juliet and Romeo.

Her mind was fertile ground, and the seeds of beauty and romance sprouted energetically.

She began to dream, to romanticize, and to envision herself as a lovely heroine—as Juliet or Guinevere or

Helen. It did not yet occur to her that each heroine was accompanied by a handsome hero—Romeo, Arthur, Paris—strangely enough, all in the image of Seth.

She contemplated the night and the new emotions that were beginning to stir in her. Charlotte had told her it could be months before Seth returned. She wondered if he would be pleased by the changes in her. Then she thought of her grandfather and felt a twinge of self-pity and of loneliness, longing for her familiar, simple life. It had been so much easier, so carefree; and a part of her still longed to return to it.

Seth was the only tie that bound her to her new life, and she wished he would return soon. How would she ever know she had succeeded in being what he wanted her to be if he did not assure her of her success?

Caught up in her dreams she did not hear the knock on her door, nor did she hear it open and close. She remained unaware of Charlotte's presence.

Charlotte stood quietly by, watching Jake, and a smile touched her lips for she remembered well a young girl's dreams.

"Jake," Charlotte said softly.

Jake turned to look at her, and Charlotte was again caught by her delicate beauty that was more evident each day.

"Can't you sleep?" Charlotte inquired.

"I'm restless for some reason," Jake admitted. "I just feel . . ." She shrugged, unable to put words to emotions she could not understand.

Charlotte sat on a chair near Jake. "There has been a tremendous amount of upheaval and change in your life lately. You cannot expect to be at ease yet. But do not worry about it, Jake. Things will become better as time goes on."

"Aunt Charlotte?"

"Yes?"

"Would it upset you if I went to visit my grandfather tomorrow? I just want to know that he's all right, and that—"

"And that he misses you as much as you miss him. No, I wouldn't mind. In fact, if I would be welcome I'd like to come along. I would like to meet the man who took on the responsibility of raising a little girl, one who turned out to be as sweet as you are."

Jake's eyes lit with pleasure. "I would be pleased if you would come. You will like my grandpa. He's kind and wonderful!"

"I'm sure he is. Shall we plan on going first thing in the morning?"

"Yes . . . please."

"Then I would suggest you try to get some sleep." Charlotte chuckled softly. "Sophie still finds it quite earthshaking to waken you when you have not had enough sleep."

Jake flushed, but she laughed. "I think I have made some of Sophie's days miserable. I'm sorry. I shall try to be less—"

"Verbal?" Charlotte asked. "Don't worry so, Jake. Sophie cares for you, as we all do."

"Do you think Seth will be pleased with me? I mean . . . I don't want him to be sorry he gave me this chance. I owe him so very much. I don't think I could bear to disappoint him."

"Jake, listen to me. You have done more for Seth than you know. But no matter how much you think you owe anybody, you owe yourself more. If you hadn't had the courage to change your life no one would have done it for you. So stop thinking of what you owe others. Can't you see that just watching you make a new life is reward enough?"

"No, Aunt Charlotte. I do owe Seth my life, and I would do anything in my power to repay him, anything." Jake added solemnly, "I would die for Seth . . . truly, I would die for him."

Charlotte's brow furrowed and she suddenly wanted to warn Jake not to romanticize her friendship with Seth. She feared that along with her first taste of real happiness Seth might also give Jake her first taste of real pain.

Chapter 22

At breakfast Catalina had been surprisingly warm with Marc. When she put her mind to it, she could be an entrancing creature and she had thrown herself into the game they were playing. They had met on the battlefield of passion, and had created their own rules for the war that was to be waged, neither knowing the other's ultimate goal.

Now, with breakfast over, Marc and Catalina were on deck. Catalina deliberately tucked her hand under his arm. The breeze carried the scent of her perfume to him, and her intoxicating nearness made him caution himself for he knew he was treading on very dangerous ground. He was in danger of losing sight of his goals due to the captivating charms of this woman beside him.

Catalina Carrington was where he wanted her to be, wasn't she? She would be at his mercy by the end of the journey, and he would then throw her to the scandalmongers and gossip carriers. She had fallen neatly into his trap. Why then did he feel like a tiger in a cage, pacing in confinement?

They stopped by the rail and turned to face each other. Marc braced one elbow on the boat's rail and leisurely admired the remarkable Catalina.

Her hair, loosely tied with a ribbon, was lifted by the

breeze and wisps of sable brown were blown across her cheeks. Her eyes sparkled with an alluring glow, and he was intrigued by his own inability to read them. Her skin was clear and healthy in the early morning sunlight, and he could almost taste the lush softness of her mouth as she half smiled at him.

"We will dock in Natchez tomorrow?" she asked.

"Thinking of going ashore?" he replied.

"Are you telling me I can't?"

"No. I am merely reminding you of our bargain. It does not include disappearing in Natchez."

"I do not make bargains I have no intention of keeping." She smiled, but the light in her eyes could have been lit by anger. "I had thought maybe you would escort me ashore, to see the city."

"Escort you ashore?" He grinned. "And what about your dear family friend, Travis Sherman?"

"The bargain was struck between you and me. It does not include Travis."

"That is the last straw. He will not be pleased with the arrangement."

"Why do you keep dwelling on Travis?" she demanded teasingly.

Marc shrugged. "I would hate to have to force the gentleman to understand our . . . situation."

"I doubt that you would hate it. I think it would give you a great deal of pleasure to tell Travis something like that. You are no gentleman, Marc Copeland, and I'm not so stupid as to believe you are going to act like one. You will most likely savor telling Travis, much as you would savor a gourmet meal."

Marc was forced to laugh, for the look in her eyes told him that she had read the meaning between his words.

"You are quite a challenge, Cat," he said softly as he reached out to catch one wayward curl and feel

294

its texture.

"But you have defeated the challenge, have you not? I am your mistress, I have agreed to your bargain. What more do you ask of me?" The question was asked so gently that he remained silent, still holding the soft strand of her hair between his fingers. He wondered why he again felt that she was as easy to hold as mercury and that he had done no more than scratch the surface of the elusive Catalina. She intrigued him. He could have almost any woman he chose, yet he hadn't been able to think of another one since he had tasted her.

He had to get a grip on himself before he fell into her silken trap and lost sight of his ultimate goal.

"I've only seen part of your bargain," he reminded her coolly. "The real challenge comes later, doesn't it? After all"—he grinned—"you still have to prove you're worth a boat like the *Belle*. Who knows"—he shrugged—"we might both find our contract unsatisfactory."

He watched anger leap into her golden brown eyes, saw her struggle to retain her composure, knew that she wanted to strike him. He smiled in satisfaction.

"My dear Marc," she said in a soft and very seductive voice, "we shall see who is unsatisfactory. Perhaps the one who will be unsatisfied will be me."

She turned to walk away while he digested the insult.

He walked up behind her and took hold of her shoulders, abruptly drawing her back against him, and he heard her gasp in surprise. He inhaled the delicate scent she wore, felt the silk of her hair against his cheek.

"Don't push me, Cat, or I'll begin to feel safer in our bargain if we go below and fulfill it now. You force me to believe I might be lacking, and I'd hate to feel so . . . insecure."

Catalina inhaled deeply, forcing control on her

body. She could feel the strength of his hands as he held her immobile with little effort. The length of his body pressed to hers stirred her memory and her senses.

For a moment she was stirred to find pleasure in his arms in the seclusion of his cabin. But she controlled that urge by reminding herself that he was an unscrupulous scoundrel who would use her and discard her. She wanted more from Marc Copeland than that.

She felt his arm slip around her waist, and he drew her against his side as he moved to her side.

The last thing Marc could tell Cat was that Natchez was where he made his home. Yet he wanted to take her to his house. The reason for this was something he forced from his thoughts.

She turned her head and found his intense, though somewhat brooding, gaze upon her. But as soon as their eyes met, he chuckled.

"I think I would like to taste those soft and very inviting lips," he murmured.

Apprehension traced its icy fingers along her spine, and she wondered if she really had the courage to win this battle. He was taunting her and she knew it, but she had only two choices. She could meet and defeat his challenge or run from him.

He grinned like a sadistic devil, and she forced her sweetest smile. His eyes widened in surprise, then narrowed as they raked over her and finally looked again into hers. The cold steel of his gaze burned into her until she could feel the heat of it stirring within her.

Her breath caught in her throat as he raised a hand, allowing his long fingers to slowly trace her collarbone, the line of her chin, and the curve of her neck.

"I said, my very willing mistress, that your lovely mouth looks much too inviting to resist. Do you hesitate, my sweet? Is the bargain done then? Is the

Belle still mine?"

His nearness stirred some strange, pleasurable spark that flickered along the ends of her nerves. But in her eyes he saw no fear, only calm deliberation, before she bent toward him. And the kiss she bestowed upon him, had he not exerted all of his control, would have burnt to ashes his well-conceived plans.

He masked his surprise and the desire that nestled like a white hot ball, in the pit of his loins.

"Not bad," he murmured. "Not bad at all."

She ignored his teasing and placed both of her elbows on the rail.

"Tell me of Natchez."

"Natchez. The lady whose father owns half of the boats on the river has never been to Natchez?"

She turned again to look at him, a flicker of surprise in her eyes at this mention of her father and his wealth. Was this why he was trying to break her will, to defeat her?

"My father," she said questioningly, "do you know him?"

Marc was instantly alert. He knew he had nearly made a costly mistake. "I know of him, as every river man does."

Her gaze returned to the river. "I have gone to Memphis with Father and we've passed Natchez often, but I've never stopped there."

"When we stop tomorrow I'll take you ashore for a few hours if you'd like. Natchez-under-the-hill is a rowdy and wild place, but I have friends who have a house on the hill. I'll show you the city; then we'll visit them. There's a beautiful view from the garden. You can see for miles and miles up and down the river."

"I'd like that."

He watched her like a hawk watching a choice prey, annoyed by the knowledge that he might enjoy their time ashore.

His sister still cared for the magnificent mansion on the bluffs overlooking the Mississippi, but a carefully worded note to her would take care of the problem. Now that the thought had entered his mind he couldn't rid himself of it. It would add some spice to the game.

His sister had been adamantly against what he was doing, but his anger had silenced anything she could say about it. And since she didn't know the full intent of his involvement, he was sure she would go along with the charade without too much trouble.

Marc was about to draw Catalina into his arms to indulge in the sweet torment of her lips when a frigid voice spoke from behind them.

"So, this is where you are, Cat. I have scoured the entire boat looking for you."

Travis's words were for Catalina, but his cold eyes were directed at Marc who smiled pleasantly but refused to remove his arms from about Catalina's waist.

Marc's eyes glittered with malicious pleasure at the thought that Travis might push him far enough to give him reason to taunt him with the truth. Whereas Catalina had no doubt that Marc saw the interruption as an opportunity to make their situation clear to Travis. She was certain he would take delight in pushing her to see how far her new sweetness and her pride would go before they broke.

"Good morning, Travis." Catalina did not look in Marc's direction in the hope that he would let the opportunity pass. "I had an early breakfast and decided to walk on deck, it's such a beautiful day."

"I'd like to talk to you . . . alone," Travis said, looking pointedly at Marc, whose smile remained as did the dangerous glow in his eyes.

Marc's hand tightened on Catalina's waist, and she

could feel his body tense. She bit her lips in desperation, seeking some way out of this dilemma, some way to avoid an open battle between Marc and Travis.

She was rescued by China's velvet voice, and could nearly have wept in relief.

"Marc?"

Travis turned to look at China, his annoyance clear. But before he could speak and make a bad situation worse, Catalina smiled. "China, join us. It's such a lovely day."

China could read distress in her eyes, and she could easily read the intent in Marc's.

"I would love to, but I am afraid I must speak to Marc alone, on an urgent business matter." She saw the relief on Catalina's face and the amusement on Marc's. He knew exactly what she was doing.

Marc left Catalina with Travis, and walked a short distance away with China. "All right, what do you have up your sleeve? Or am I right in believing you are so misguided as to believe you were coming to Cat's rescue?"

"Your performance for Travis Sherman's benefit was outrageous," China said with a smile.

"But effective." Marc chuckled.

"At least," China said wryly as she cast a quick look at Catalina and Travis who seemed to be having a disagreement. "Marc, your situation with Catalina is one thing, but I feel this man, this Travis Sherman, is not one to take blows in a very forgiving way. Marc, he's dangerous."

"And you're being the keeper of my health . . . and my conscience again, China my love." He grinned. "You don't need to worry about either of them."

"One of us should."

"I can't think of one good reason why."

"Marc—"

"China, I'll play this game out my way."

"I just don't believe she should be punished for something beyond her control. She is not the young woman I thought her to be. Shawna . . ."

Marc kept Catalina in view while China talked, and he realized that she had not been quite what he had expected either. She was . . . He shook the thoughts away as he watched Travis reach out and grasp Catalina's wrist, and his face grew fierce.

Catalina's eyes widened, more in anger than in fear, but Marc clenched his teeth, then started for them.

When Marc had stepped away with China, Travis had turned his attention to Catalina. He had attempted a pleasant smile, but had been thwarted by the look in Catalina's eyes. Did she know that her face had softened, that her eyes had taken on a sheen that had nothing to do with the bright sunlight, that her lips had parted slightly as if she were suddenly breathless?

"Cat," Travis said, attempting to keep his self-control.

"Yes, Travis," she replied, reluctantly drawing her eyes from Marc's broad-shouldered form.

"I asked how you felt this morning . . . since you retired so early last night."

"I'm fine, Travis, fine."

"Good. Then you won't forget we're having dinner together?"

Now her attention was fully on him, and she remembered promising to dine with him.

"Travis . . . I . . . if you would excuse me, just for tonight. I must see Marc. Travis, I'm sure he'll return the *Belle* to us. All I need do is—"

"Is tumble into his bed and sell yourself for this boat," he snapped.

"Travis!"

"Don't tell me he doesn't find you attractive, Cat. I can see the way he looks at you, like a ravenous wolf."

"I'm hardly a child, Travis, I can handle Marc Copeland."

"No, you're not a child, but you can't see how clever he is. He holds the *Belle* before you as a reward while he entices you into his bed."

The truth stung Cat, but it did not deter her. Awakening in her was the vibrant emotion of love, and she sensed that Marc was near to feeling it, too.

She wanted him to remember the exotic emotions they had shared, wanted him to discard his reasons for doing what he had done. She wanted him to see her as the woman he desired above all others. She needed to be with him.

"Travis, your concern is unnecessary. I shall do what I think is best, and I do not have to ask for your approval."

He reached out and gripped Catalina's wrist. His viselike hold drew a soft cry of pain from her. She tried to jerk her arm free, but it was held in a grip she could never hope to break. He drew her to him, well aware of the fire of rebellion that leapt into her eyes.

"Cat, I won't let you fall victim to that man. You can't possibly realize what you are getting yourself into. When we reach Natchez tomorrow, I will take you ashore and we will find a boat on which to return to New Orleans."

His demanding voice and his overpowering attitude spurred her temper, but before she could answer him a strong lean hand closed over Travis's wrist and an unconscious sound erupted from Travis's mouth. With an iron grip, Marc squeezed his wrist until Travis was certain the bones were shattered.

"I believe the lady came aboard of her own choice, and she can leave when *she* chooses. If you would care

301

to depart before we dock, I have men who are more than willing to send you off royally."

Travis jerked his arm free, fury burning in his eyes. But he remained silent before the threatening coldness in Marc's eyes, for he knew Marc wanted him to fight back.

"Cat boarded this boat with me," Travis said angrily, "and when we dock tomorrow in Natchez, we will return to New Orleans on another boat."

"Oh, really?" Amusement played at the corners of Marc's mouth. "Let's ask the lady if she chooses to leave. I believe you'll find she has other plans."

Catalina wanted to slap the arrogant self-assurance from Marc's face, but she was too aware of Travis's anger to do so.

"I am not leaving this boat until we get to Memphis," Catalina stated firmly, as she glared at first one and then the other. "I make my own choices about where I go and what I do, and I'd like to remind you both that I need no help in doing so."

China watched from a short distance as Travis fought for control. He refused to look in Marc's direction, but Catalina was aware of the look in Marc's eyes, of the relief in them he would have denied.

"I think this is a decision you are going to regret, Cat," Travis said stiffly, "but, as you say, it is your decision." He turned to Marc, his glance frigid. "How long will we be in Natchez?"

"We'll dock tomorrow, stay one night, and leave the next day."

Travis nodded, then returned his gaze to Catalina. He had control now. "Whether you believe it or not, Cat, you need protection, and I intend to be here in case you discover what a deceptive liar he is."

"Be very careful with your accusations, my friend," Marc said in a deceptively casual voice. "I'll consider

302

the circumstances once, but the next time you call me a liar, be prepared to defend yourself and to prove what you say."

Travis inhaled deeply. He wanted to attack Marc there and then, but his long-term plans were more important.

Without another word he turned and walked away.

China followed like a silent shadow. She was impatient for the boat to dock in Natchez. Among the assortment of unsavory characters that lived in Natchez-under-the-hill, China had many friends who could supply her with information. Her suspicion of Travis Sherman had grown, and she meant to get a few facts about him.

Catalina was still shaking with ill-controlled fury as she turned to face Marc.

"You didn't tell him."

"Did you want me to?" he asked innocently. "I thought you wanted to spare the delicate feelings of your . . . friend."

"Is that the only reason you said nothing to him?"

"Why, sweet." He chuckled. Then he bent to kiss her half parted lips leisurely. "What other possible reason could I have? Outside of the fact," he added in a wicked suggestive voice, "that I don't share such a lovely mistress as you with any man. Remember that, Cat," he added softly. "What's mine . . . I keep."

He had drawn her breathlessly close. "I am not yours," she said in a voice as controlled as his. "And you remember that, Mr. Copeland. I'm not yours."

She moved from his arms and walked away, pleased by the look she had seen in his eyes when he had realized she was not going to be so easily conquered.

Chapter 23

Marc and Catalina sat across the table from each other in the elaborate dining room of the *Belle*. They had shared a magnificent dinner, and were now sipping wine and covertly studying each other for signs of vulnerability.

The night was beginning here and both knew it. The terms of their bargain were to be fulfilled. Yet Catalina denied the tingle of excitement that warmed her blood, blaming it on the wine.

Could she change the course of Marc's life in one night? She didn't think so, but trying was the only way she had to reach him, the only way to open his mind to the amazing emotion that drew them to each other.

In a moment of panic she wondered if she was the only one who felt it. Had what she had read in his face and in his touch really been pretense?

In a moment of truth, she realized she was placing her future in jeopardy. Risking all, on the chance that she could reach past passion and touch his heart.

The game had no rules. If she won she would have everything she dreamed of. If she lost . . . The very core of her trembled at that thought, for she would have no future.

Marc had made no mention of the coming night. He had not teased or tormented her. In fact he was being unusually considerate and charming. It took her some time to realize that he was trying to make her transition into being his mistress as easy for her as he possibly could.

Marc watched the reflected light from the crystal chandeliers dance in Catalina's gold-brown eyes. He enjoyed the soft sound of her laugh when he said something amusing, and had kept her wine glass full all evening in the hope that wine would make the situation easier for her.

He found himself suddenly boyishly impatient, as if Catalina were a loved bride and this was their wedding night. He had to remind himself that Catalina Carrington wanted something from him and that she intended to use her body to get it.

He could not allow her moist red lips to continue to invade his senses. He had to keep in mind that he had to control emotions easily wasted on a woman who was at best a charming deception and at worst . . . He wasn't sure yet.

He touched the lip of her glass with the wine bottle as he poured more wine for her, purposely neglecting to fill his own glass. He wanted to be completely in control when Catalina came to him. He had been thinking about her surrender all day.

He knew by her flushed cheeks and the brilliance of her eyes that she was close to being inebriated. He lifted his glass and smiled.

"Shall we propose a toast?" he inquired.

She raised her glass to his.

"A toast to what?"

He shrugged. "To whatever might please you, my lady," he said softly.

"To the mystery of the future . . . and the hope of finding solutions."

They drank. Then he chuckled as he sat his glass

down. "Strange toast."

"Why strange?"

"What mysteries do you hope to find the solutions to?"

"Ah"—she laughed softly—"is not every woman preoccupied with the mystery of love?"

"Love?" His eyes glowed with a derisive look. "Love is a fantasy, my pet. A silk trap in which a woman snares a man who will then calmly lay aside his own dreams to crawl between the sheets with her. Love is for children. Smart adults know better."

He sat back in his chair and his eyes roamed thoughtfully over her. "But you do not strike me as a lady pining for love, for a man to take her away from the wickedness of the world."

"Oh, and how do I strike you, Marc?"

"As a lady who knows what she wants and sets out to get it, much like a man would."

"And that annoys you?"

"No, not really, I admire courage in a woman. I admire intelligence also. I do not admire foolish sentiments. They are usually a cloak for more dangerous ones."

"And love is a foolish sentiment," she said softly. "Have you never loved anyone?"

Again he laughed, deliberately misinterpreting her words. "I have made love to many, and I hope many more will pass my way."

"I did not ask if you had made love," she retorted. "I asked you if you have ever loved anyone. Tell me, Marc Copeland, has any woman ever loved you, or have they all been butterflies—flirting, loving, and flying away?"

"I prefer butterflies." His lips twitched in amusement. "Much less demanding."

"Then maybe you are afraid of demands. Could these women have found you lacking? I suppose it is

306

safer to remain with butterflies than to face a challenge that might prove more than you can handle."

As she watched, anger flickered in his eyes, though he retained his smile of tolerant amusement.

"I do not refuse challenges, and have never found one too difficult to handle yet."

"Pride often walks before a fall."

"I don't speak with misplaced pride, Cat," he declared in a hushed voice, "and I have no intention of falling. If you've any more on your mind than our bargain, put it aside."

"I was speaking hypothetically, Marc," she replied. "Surely"—she lowered her voice seductively—"you do not believe I would harbor thoughts of anything permanent between us. We made our bargain. The *Belle* is my goal. Once it is mine, seek out all the butterflies you choose. You will have my blessing."

She was not certain what effect she had had on him, for he remained in complete control. Still, his green eyes were unnaturally bright, and had she understood him better, she would have realized that he was both excited and challenged. These reactions, combined with the anger that had been stirred in him, put Catalina in a more vulnerable position than she knew.

He rose slowly and extended a hand toward her in utter silence, yet his eyes now spoke volumes. They sparked with a dangerous glow that made her quiver and suddenly become frightened.

"I understand you well, Cat, and I am most willing to pay your price. The only rub is that now it is time to prove the worth of our bargain."

She wanted to run, yet she wanted to throw herself into his arms and plead with him not to force her to keep a dishonorable bargain. She wanted this night to be a beginning for them both. But she could not tell him, for she knew such words would drive him from her. Her eyes reflected emotions she would have denied as she put a trembling hand in his.

He drew her up from her chair and tucked her arm in his. Then they walked out the dining-room door and onto the moon-bathed deck.

For a moment, as she walked beside him, she chastised herself. Marc Copeland would never surrender to the profound emotions she felt. She was a fool, but she loved him. And if there was the slimmest chance he would respond in kind, she would take it.

Marc was acutely aware of her. She excited his every sense, sang along his nerves like an electrical current, the force of which shook him. He had never felt for any woman what he was feeling, but he attributed that to the excitement which bound them.

He had never forced a woman to bend to his will, and that thought rankled a bit. He wondered, if the *Belle* did not exist, if his need for vengeance did not exist, could he bring Catalina Carrington to his bed. The question, once raised, was difficult to dispose of, and it shook some of his resolve.

They stopped by the boat's rail, and turned to face each other.

She was breathlessly beautiful, and Marc was again struck by the elusive thought that there was a great deal about Catalina that he did not understand, would never understand. The thought intrigued him. She spoke of mysteries, but she continued to be the greatest mystery of all.

He reached out and traced the line of her jaw, then let his fingers roam down the soft flesh of her throat to rest for a moment on her shoulder. He watched her eyes widen as he slid his hand to the back of her head and drew her to him.

She made no effort to fight him or to resist in any way. In fact he was momentarily surprised when her hands slid about his waist and she stepped into his arms as their lips met. His mouth took hers eagerly, as wisps of thought misted his mind until he craved only a deeper and more satisfying taste of her.

If he wondered why she hadn't resisted, his question was lost in the searing heat of his pleasure as her mouth, soft and moist, opened to his like a flower welcoming the heat of the morning sun.

Catalina not only returned his kiss with wild abandon, she clung to him with an intensity that amazed her as it did him. When his mouth reluctantly left hers, her breath was coming quickly and her heart pounded rhythmically. Her senses seemed to be filled with his presence.

Marc's breath caught in his throat, and he was not quite sure he would be able to take the next one.

His eyes swept her in a deep passion-filled caress. His world had seemed to lose its sense of balance.

"Marc . . . please give me just a little time. Wait here for a few minutes before you come to me."

She sounded like a frightened bride, and Marc, if his urge for revenge had been predominant, would have been rough and demanding. But he had forgotten all but the promise of the sweet intimate pleasure they would share.

He nodded and felt the void as she stepped from his arms and only the subtle scent of her perfume remained. He stood in silence, trying to keep his mind centered on the purpose he intended to accomplish on this night. But he failed miserably. He could only envision her preparing for him, her body pale gold in his bed.

It took all the self-control he had for him to remain still and allow the time to build into a half-hour. Finally, he could tolerate no more. He turned from the rail and strode purposefully toward his cabin.

When he reached the door, he was amazed, and laughed softly, at the fact that his hand actually trembled. He swung the door open and stepped in. Then he stopped and sharply drew in his breath, for a vision met his eyes. The room was lit only by the glow of a few candles, and their mellow haze enhanced the mood.

He swallowed as if something had interfered with his breathing, and his blood surged through him in a violent flood.

She lay on her side against the pillows, her sable brown hair spread about her. The gown she wore was a wisp of material that revealed much more than it would ever hope to conceal, and her breasts, pressed against the soft white material, were vaguely pink, their erect nipples suggesting a need to be free. One leg, revealed by a split in the gown, was creamy smooth and delightfully inviting. She smiled a Mona Lisa smile, and her eyes held a seductive promise as she extended an inviting hand to him.

As if he moved within a dream, Marc approached her and reached out to take her hand. As he bent over her, she slid her other hand into his hair to draw his head to hers.

Her intoxicating fragrance drew him to her as potently as the tingle of warm smooth skin, and he savored the feel of her. Then he stood to remove his clothes, his eyes sweeping over her as if to memorize every line, every curve.

Cheeks flushed, Catalina caught her lower lip between her teeth as vibrant excitement coursed through her when she viewed his muscular body in the glow of the mellow candlelight.

Again he stood for a moment, looking down at her. One day, in the future, he would recall that at this moment his resolve had begun to slip and for a fleeting moment he had envisioned Catalina as more than his mistress. Then he joined her on the bed and drew her warm body to his.

A soft whispered moan escaped her a second before his lips caught hers in a moving kiss that left her weak and clinging to him. As his mouth took hers eagerly, they strained together in a mutual hunger heightened by the feel of flesh on flesh and by exploring hands. The flame of desire intensified, surged through Catalina's veins until it consumed her. Yet his lips nibbled and played, parting hers and leaving her gasping with breathless and rapidly rising passion.

They were caught on the wings of a whirlwind that carried them to the dizzying heights. The reasons he had for retaining control deserted him in the face of the slim silken body, velvet smooth beneath his hands, that surrendered to a primitive, demanding need that matched his, touch for touch, passion for passion.

It was an eternity of exquisite torment as hands caressed, lips blended, and bodies merged. He was heated pride as he pressed himself to the depths of her and felt her enclose him, hold him. She moved urgently against him, arching her body to meet his driving thrusts. Gentleness was forgotten as they dissolved in the fire of desire.

Finally they lay in each other's arms, legs entwined silently, enjoying the luxury of mutual completion. Catalina felt as if she were floating in a heavy mist, held in iron-hard arms. She was content. She realized she had found such contentment nowhere else but in Marc's arms.

Yet she had been aware all along of a subtle undercurrent in Marc, a part of him that excluded her.

With all her heart she wished that there was some slender crack in the iron casing that enclosed his heart, a small fissure that she could find her way through.

She had so little time. They would be in Natchez for only one night. Then, in a few more nights, they would arrive in Memphis.

Would he return the *Belle* to her or just walk away from her as if the wild and beautiful magic they now shared was less than the perfection she knew it to be?

She would have derived a great deal of pleasure from knowing that despite all his efforts to retain control, Marc's mind was moving in the same general direction.

"What will we do while we are in Natchez, stay aboard the *Belle?*" she asked.

"No. There are a few people I want you to meet," he replied casually, knowing she was thinking the worst and allowing her to do so.

"You want me to meet . . . You mean you want to display your new conquest?" she said bitterly.

"One does not acquire a mistress like you every day, my pet." He chuckled. "Do you blame me for wanting to show you off a bit?"

He heard her soft intake of breath as she twisted to look up into his eyes, shock and disbelief on her face.

"You wouldn't dare," she groaned. "I won't be displayed like some . . . some . . ."

"It goes along with the bargain, love," he replied, and she could not mistake the taunting humor in his voice. "What good is it to have the loveliest mistress on the Mississippi if one cannot see envy in other men's eyes?"

"I won't do it! I won't!"

"All right, no argument," he agreed amiably. "We'll just forget the whole thing right now."

She knew he was deliberately pushing her to the limit to see how far she would go.

Did she have the courage to face his friends with only her pride as a shield? Did she have the daring and the wit to allow him to claim her while she was silently claiming him? Could she turn the game to her advantage, make him see that she was woman enough to belong at his side?

For a long moment her pride refused to allow her to think of such a thing. Then a subtle thought came to her. She could envision his surprise when his arrogance was tossed back in his face. The price was high, but the reward she had already tasted; and it would be heady wine if she could bring him to her side as . . . her husband.

To his surprise, she nestled close to him, laying her head against his chest and drawing one leg across his lower body while her fingers slowly threaded through the mat of hair on his chest.

"You are right again, Marc. A bargain is a bargain. I won't back down."

He raised himself on one elbow and looked into her eyes, knowing some devious thought was spinning in her mind. But her expression was wide-eyed and innocent—too innocent.

"You continue to surprise me, Cat."

"I." She laughed softly. "How can I surprise you? There is little you do not know about me now."

"I think," he said quietly, "that there is little that I do know about you."

"You make me sound so mysterious."

"Yes," he said thoughtfully, *"mysterious* is the word. You are a mystery, but one I intend to solve before we reach Memphis."

"Solving this mystery might prove more difficult than you think."

"Is that a threat, love?" He smiled and his eyes glittered with wicked humor. Then his arms slid about her and drew her to him as his mouth hovered close to hers. "If it is a threat, let me remind you that I don't frighten easily and difficult things usually prove to be intriguing and definitely challenging."

"You like challenges, don't you?"

"If they are as lovely as you, most certainly. What an entrancing creature you are when your eyes light up with anger like that," he teased, but his smile faded as his eyes lingered on her mouth.

Catalina could feel the heat of his gaze tingle through her, and she shivered suddenly as if she were cold.

"Yes," he whispered, as his mouth brushed lightly against hers, "you are deliciously exciting and if you're a threat, love, you are the most exciting threat I've known."

His arms tightened about her, and no protest on her part could have stopped the kiss that swept away her breath.

Her coldness turned to warmth and then to heat, which spread from the center of her being throughout her body, turning it into a cauldron of renewed desire.

The night was long and they were both lost to all but the pulsing pleasure that touched them both again and yet again . . . until the gray light of dawn touched the day and they slept in sated exhaustion and utter contentment.

Chapter 24

In its surging passage from Memphis to the gulf of Mexico, the Mississippi came to a high, sun-splashed hill. To the west, the green alluvial lowlands of Louisiana stretched mistily toward the horizon. To the east rose two hundred feet of red-brown bluff, crowned by vines of wild grape, magnificent magnolias, and the sweep of oak. Here, the river became a wide crescent of lakelike tranquility; then it turned to glide, silver and yellow, into the distance, away from Natchez.

Natchez! The name came from an Indian nation, an offshoot of the Aztecs. The fields about the city were whitening with cotton, for Natchez was the capital of the cotton empire. On the bluff and beyond, the planters lived a secure life, while on a table of muddy ground lay Natchez-under-the-hill—a violent place where anyone could get away with anything if he was strong enough.

As the *Belle* docked, Catalina and Marc stood at the rail. The sun was just above the horizon, but it was bright enough to reveal the colorful scene before them.

Marc was amused when Catalina's eyes glowed with excitement as she watched this tableau. In this moment he knew she had been pampered and protected all her life. He paid no heed to the fact that he felt a distinct urge to treat her in the same way. Natchez-under-the-

315

hill was the kind of place in which he had intended to desert Catalina Carrington. What good would the Carrington arrogance do her there?

But that would come later, when their bargain was finished and he was done with her, when her kiss no longer excited him and her body had lost the magic that made him desire her as he did even at this moment.

Watching her lips part in breathless excitement, seeing her cheeks pinken in the breeze and her golden eyes glow with an enthusiasm that was contagious, he was shaken by the fact that he wanted to crush her in his arms and hear her call to him in passion.

Damn! he thought. He had tired of most women after a few tussles on the sheets, but this one seemed to have a new magic each time he looked at her. Something about her made his limbs grow weak and his body heat with desire. Her sable hair was rich and luxuriant, and he had to restrain the urge to reach out and touch it. Her skin was flawless and blooming with color, and her features seemed perfect, fine boned.

He knew, if she turned to him, her eyes would be unfathomable as always, filled with some mystery he would have the renewed urge to explore. He was reasonably sure it would take quite a long time to tire of her lush charms.

Catalina, unaware of the intensity of his gaze, bubbled with pleasure as she watched the milling crowds.

The colorful sight before them, vibrant with life, would be a magnet to any onlooker who had not tasted the brutality beneath the façade. Knowing this, Marc moved closer to Catalina without even realizing he had done so. The current of her excitement drew him to her.

"I'm going to send a few messages, but I'd like to leave the boat in an hour or so. Can you be ready?"

316

"Oh, yes. Will we be spending the night in a hotel?"

Marc laughed outright. "A hotel! In Natchez-under-the-hill? My dear Cat, unless you intend to share your delightful charms with every man jack in Natchez we will make our way past this den of hell." He pointed to the cliffs above the city. "We'll be going up there as soon as a carriage can be brought for us. A closed one." He chuckled. "For I'd never be able to hold you on a ride through the city. I don't have enough guns to do it. You're a beauty and there is not much beauty in Natchez-under-the-hill."

Her lips parted as she gazed up at him in surprise.

"Believe me, Cat"—his voice gentled without his realizing it—"I'd kill to keep you right now, and that's what I'd have to do to keep you if you were to show that lovely face and that delicious little body to the degenerate scum in Natchez."

Her eyes sparkled, but she turned back to the bustle below her. She had heard, in his voice, things he would deny. Why would a man with a very temporary mistress protect her—vow to kill to protect her—if he had no feeling for her? It was a spark, and she fervently wished it could be induced to grow into a fire.

"It seems so . . . so small to have such a reputation," Catalina said.

"For the size of it, there is not a more profligate place in the world. It's a drinking place, a fighting place, and a killing place."

"How do you come to know Natchez so well?"

"As a rought and unruly boy, I spent a great deal of time here," Marc replied. He didn't want Catalina to know that the house in which he had been born and raised stood in magnificent splendor atop the bluff and its gleaming white columns could be seen in the distance.

The Garrison home was a serene place perched in the

317

clouds. When mist settled on the river, the house looked as if it were suspended in nothingness, riding a gray ocean. It was the first sight of upper Natchez that greeted visitors, and the last. The clean white pillars supported a hipped roof, and an immaculate captain's walk.

To the side and behind the house were smaller buildings, set amid the gardens and off the bordered paths that followed the curve of the hill.

At the bluff's edge, benches were placed so those visiting Garrison Hall might inspect the river and landscape below. And when one sat in the gardens beneath the trees, the tall pillars of the house seemed a challenge to time and man.

He couldn't tell her that as a boy and a young man he had been as wild and untamed as many others in Natchez, nor that his prowess in bed could be traced to the more elite local whores. And he was held momentarily silent as he realized he had a deep desire to share his life with her. It annoyed him.

He turned his gaze up to his home, and for a moment he was caught in a mixture of emotions, some violent, some poignantly beautiful. They tugged at his senses. He thought of the comfort of the place, of how it had been years ago. Then his mind drifted to the day he had set out on his present course.

He had gotten the house back, had returned to it with his sister and had then told her that she would have to remain there alone until he got some satisfaction for what had nearly destroyed them both. She had wept and pleaded with him to forget the past, to help her, to build a new life. He remembered. . . .

"One day we'll both marry, Marc. We'll have children and we'll rebuild. We'll make this house all that Mama and Papa wanted. We'll make it a memorial to them."

"A monument you mean," he had growled in bitter anger. "A monument is more like a tombstone. I can't let it go like that, Lorelei. I have to clear father's name, and clear my own before I can give it to any woman . . . or to sons."

"I don't want you hurt, Marc," she had whispered through her tears. "Worse yet, I don't want you to hurt someone else."

"I'll only hurt those that are guilty, only the guilty. . . ."

He was drawn back abruptly to the present.

". . . guilty of some of the things you were telling me about," Catalina was saying.

"What?"

"I said I hope you're not guilty . . ."

"Now or when I was a younger man?" he asked with a chuckle.

She laughed softly, and her eyes appraised him with a look that shook his already fragile control.

"I can see you as a devilish little boy, even as a wayward young man, but . . ."

"But what?"

"But I can't see you as a gambler, a rake, or . . ."

"And how do you see me, my little kitten?" he said gently, as he reached to brush aside stray strands of hair the wind had blown against her cheek.

"I don't know. It's as if I'm only seeing a part of you . . . as if I were looking out a window when it's raining. Everything is vague and uncertain . . . almost unreal."

"Well, this is real enough for both of us," he said softly as he bent to touch her mouth with his, so lightly his lips were like a whisper of wind.

"Go below and pack a few things—enough for a day or so—and please bring that beautiful green gown you wore the other night. We will be entertaining guests

319

later and I want them to get a good look at the most beautiful woman from New Orleans to Memphis."

"Marc, I—"

"Shh, love, I want you to meet another young woman who is very special to me. You two will get on famously. Now I have some messages to send."

"I'll stay here and watch a few more minutes; then I will go to my—your—cabin and pack."

He knew she was annoyed that he would deliberately flaunt her, but he couldn't seem to resist bringing Catalina and Lorelei face to face.

"Good girl. I'll come back to get you after the midday meal."

She nodded, hurt by his deliberate disregard of her emotions, and Marc left her stewing silently. He could not suppress a grin of satisfaction, and it became a broad smile when he saw Travis coming his way, distaste clearly written on his face.

"Good morning, Travis," Marc said pleasantly.

"The amenities are hardly appropriate," Travis growled. "Where is Catalina?"

"Catalina," Marc said innocently. "Why, I believe the last I saw her she was standing on deck watching the boat dock. Natchez seems to have quite an attraction for her."

"Well, we won't be staying here long. I know this hellhole. Cat is not going to disembark here. We'll stay on board until it's time to leave tomorrow night. I have plans for the two of us for this evening, and they do not include anyone else. Do I make myself clear?"

He moved away from Marc, who remained still for a moment watching him. Then Marc's eyes narrowed and his mouth twitched in a controlled smile. "We shall see, my friend, just how easy it will be to change your plans."

Marc went to China's cabin, where he found her

and Shawna.

"We're docking now," he said. "Can you get someone to carry some letters for me?"

"Jacob?"

"All right. Shawna, run and get him, will you?"

Shawna left immediately, and Marc dropped into a chair and propped his boots on a nearby table. He folded his hands behind his head and grinned amiably at China, who laughed softly in return.

"When you look like that I know you are very satisfied with yourself," she said. "I also know you've been up to something that is either illegal or immoral."

"China, you wound me," he replied, a hurt expression on his face. "You've a very suspicious nature."

"Hardly, I just know you. What are you up to now, Marc?"

"I'm going home for a day or so," he said quietly.

She looked at him levelly for a few minutes. "I take it you are not going home alone?"

"I'm taking Catalina with me."

"And Travis Sherman is just going to let you walk off this boat with her? I hardly think so."

"You have no faith, China my girl. Mr. Sherman is going to be busy—extremely busy. In fact, he is going to be so busy he just might not make it back before the *Belle* leaves. Yes . . . I think he's going to have a long eventful stay in Natchez."

Before China could speak again, Shawna opened the door and Jacob followed her into the room.

Marc swung his feet to the floor and reached inside the breast pocket of his jacket, withdrawing two sealed envelopes.

"Jacob, I want you to take these to Mrs. Thatcher."

"Yassuh," Jacob replied. He took the letters and stuffed them inside his shirt.

"You remember my sister well, Jacob. I don't want

them in anyone's hands but hers. She'll send a closed carriage and you will ride back with it."

"Yassuh."

"And, Jacob, I don't want you to talk to anyone. That slip with Miss Carrington was a mistake. Just remember what I told you about keeping the past a secret."

"Yassuh, I 'members. I makes one mistake wif da young miss, but I doan do it nebber again. I keeps ma mouf shut, yassuh, I keeps it shut from now on."

"Thanks, Jacob. Now get going. I want that carriage back soon."

Jacob left, and Marc turned back to Shawna and China. "I know you're putting Willie ashore and that Nina will be leaving the boat. And I don't want Travis to find his way back to the *Belle*."

"I'm quite sure Charlene will be glad to help you there." China smiled. "She is more than pleased with Mr. Sherman."

"Good. Give her a good price and tell her to make damn certain the *Belle* sails tomorrow night without him."

"Shawna," China said, "go and tell Charlene to come to my cabin in a half-hour."

When Shawna was gone, China turned again to Marc who knew she wanted to speak with him, alone.

"Your sister will not be pleased."

"She won't say anything," Marc replied. "She's always a lady, barring her tempers of course. She may not like it, but she won't do anything to harm me."

"Why are you doing this, Marc? You can accomplish your goal without taking her to your home. You could leave her in Natchez-under-the-hill. Surely"—China's voice softened—"she would pay dearly, in one night there, all the debts you imagine the Carringtons owe."

Marc looked momentarily into China's eyes, then

away. How could he tell her that the thought of leaving Catalina in Natchez-under-the-hill was repugnant to him? How could he tell her that he had a driving urge to show Catalina his home, to have her in his bed. To make love to her in a place he loved, in a place where he had spent happy hours. He couldn't, so he said nothing.

Travis stood in the shadowed doorway and watched Catalina for several minutes. She stood at the rail, in the brilliant sunshine, and her beauty was breathtaking.

He had seen Marc with her, had watched her laugh as she gazed up at him, and her gesture had revealed more to Travis than she could have imagined. He hated Marc now.

Travis walked through the door and across the deck. He was standing beside Catalina before she realized he was there.

"Cat?"

She spun about and for a moment her smile faded. Then she caught herself and smiled again. But she recovered too late, and Travis's hatred of Marc rose within him like a black flood. He forced a smile.

"It looks like a very promising day."

"Yes," she replied. "It's lovely."

"It's a shame we're pinned to this boat for almost two days. I hope to pass some of the time in your company."

"Travis, I . . . I'm going ashore."

"In Natchez-under-the-hill! Surely not. Surely someone has told you what a terrible place this is. It is no place for a lady."

"Well, it seems"—she turned from him to look again at the high bluff towering over them—"we are going to

323

visit friends of his—up there."

Travis looked up toward the bluff, his eyes registering an emotion Catalina would not have understood if she had noticed it. He was smugly confident. "So he'll take you to meet his friends."

"Yes, I believe so," Catalina replied coldly, wondering why she should be defending Marc. "In fact I believe there is to be a dinner of sorts tonight."

"Catalina, what is happening? When we boarded this boat we knew what kind of a man Marc Copeland was. We both had our suspicions." He reached to touch her arm. "What of your brother, Cat? Have you forgotten this man could be responsible for whatever might have happened to him? My God, do you believe the lies he's been telling you? Cat, I won't let you go with him."

Aware only of the dominant emotion guiding her, Catalina was not about to be pushed into anything.

"I'm not a child, Travis. I shall do what I please. I'll not be told where I can and cannot go."

"You are going to make a fool of yourself and you will disgrace the Carrington name. Can't you see that he wants to bring shame and dishonor to the Carringtons?"

"Travis, I . . ." Her temper was rising and she was about to lose it.

"Catalina?" It was a gentle speaking of her name, and relief swept through her as she turned to see Marc.

He stood in the doorway, one broad shoulder braced against the frame, his arms crossed. There was a smile on his face, and Catalina could only gaze silently at him, aware that he was devastatingly handsome and maddeningly arrogant.

"The carriage is here, Cat," he said softly. "I can see you've been . . . detained. I'll send someone back for your things."

"Stay here with me," Travis cautioned in a lowered

voice. "You cannot trust him."

"And she can trust you?" Marc laughed. "Why don't we let the lady make her own choices, as she seems prone to do? Cat?"

Catalina looked from Marc to Travis, then back to Marc. Travis's eyes begged her not to go. Marc's face was impregnable—it told her nothing and asked her nothing. His half-smile taunted her to keep her bargain or run.

If she stayed with Travis, she would never know whether Marc could learn to love her. She would never know whether she could have been victorious or not.

"I'm sorry, Travis," Catalina said quietly. Then she walked past Marc, unaware of the satisfied smile he gave Travis as he turned to follow her.

Chapter 25

Marc handed Catalina up into the carriage, then climbed in behind her; and they started through the streets of Natchez-under-the-hill. It was on low ground, and was often pervaded by yellow fever, whereas the town was higher up.

Catalina looked up through the small square windows of the carriage. Within a radius of a few miles she noted at least a hundred houses of masterly design. The people of Natchez knew the value of a raised house with the upper floor, the main one, set high to catch the pure air and to escape dampness, and they favored broad porches for the hot afternoons.

They soon left upper Natchez and rode along the bluff. As they approached Marc's house, Catalina's eyes widened at the almost breathtaking beauty of Garrison Hall.

She turned to look at Marc, and saw that he was lost in a different world as he gazed at the place. Was he wishing he had such a home? He was a riverboat gambler, but did he aspire to a different world, one more gracious and gentle than the one in which he existed?

After a few minutes Marc became aware of her scrutiny, and his protective mask reappeared.

"These friends of yours . . ." she began.

"What about them?"

"Have you . . . I mean . . . have you told them?"

He knew what she meant, but he refused to make it easy on her. He again caught himself searching for motives. Did he want to continue to push her to see how far she would go to stand by her word, or did he want to embarrass her? Or maybe he wanted to see if this puzzle fit any other part of his life.

He continued to gaze at her and watched, fascinated, as her cheeks flushed and he could see her eyes glitter with anger.

"Told them what?" he smiled.

"You know very well what I mean. Why do you pretend!"

"That you're my mistress? Well, I've told Mrs. Thatcher . . . Lorelei . . ."

Catalina's face went pale and she caught her lower lip between her teeth. Inhaling deeply, she sought control.

"Mrs. Thatcher?"

"She is the young lady who lives at Garrison Hall. Her name was Lorelei Garrison. Her husband, Rodger, is a very charming man. They're a lovely couple and they've been close . . . friends for a long time."

"You actually told her I . . ."

"Well, since you're going to share my bed, I'm sure she would have found out sooner or later."

"You are truly an unmitigated scoundrel!" Catalina snapped, aghast at the position he had forced her into.

"You needn't worry about Lorelei, she is a very discreet woman. She's smart enough to keep her thoughts to herself."

"Why must we spend the night here?" she cried. "Can we not return to the boat?"

"Why so shy, love?" He grinned. "I thought you might enjoy a little more comfort."

"Ohhh," she groaned through gritted teeth. "You talk about comfort and drag me to the home of people you have calmly told that we are . . . are sleeping together! How can you be so callous, so contemptible."

"Why, Cat, I didn't know you'd be so upset. If you want to call off our bargain we shall have separate rooms and your reputation will be saved."

She closed her eyes for a moment and her body swayed with the carriage. Why couldn't he see what he was doing? Why didn't she just deny the bargain and return to the boat? But she knew the answer. He might win this day, this contest, but she would win the war.

She opened her eyes and they met his deep penetrating green ones. She smiled. "No, I do not want to return to the boat. Let's go on to Garrison Hall and meet your friends."

If he was surprised, he said nothing, but she was aware of the furrowing of his brow and the narrowing of his eyes as he reached for the answer to Catalina Carrington.

Lorelei Garrison Thatcher had taken the envelope from Jacob's hand. She had known the huge man all her life.

"What's my brother up to now?" She smiled warmly at Jacob, who stood before her hat in hand. "Why didn't he come home?"

"Ah doan rightly know, Miz Thatcher. He jus' tol' me bring dis letter to you. Den I wuz to jus' wait fo' a carriage."

"A carriage. For Marc?" She laughed. "Don't tell me he's suddenly developed a fear of old Natchez-under-the-hill? He was never afraid to chase any petticoats down there."

"Ah . . . no, ma'am. De carriage hain't fo' Mister

Marc. It's fo' de young miss what cum on de boat wif him."

"Young miss!" Lorelei's eyes sparkled. "You mean he's bringing a young lady home? Good heavens, has somebody finally caught my elusive brother?"

"Miz Thatcher . . . yo bes' read de letter."

Lorelei looked at Jacob curiously. "Come in," she said, and she began to tear the envelope open while preceding Jacob into a small sitting room, where she sat down.

Within moments she was grateful that she was sitting.

The letter was four pages long, but before she reached the second page her eyes had widened and she was registering shock. It grew with every word she read. When she had finished the letter, she dropped her hands into her lap and gazed up in profound amazement.

But Lorelei had known her brother too long, had watched him commit more than one deed of mischief. She did not always believe what she heard . . . or saw.

Her eyes changed from amazement to shrewd curiosity.

"Jacob, do you know what's in this letter?"

"No, Miz Thatcher."

"This Miss Carrington, is she pretty?"

"Yessum, she be right pretty."

"So he's brought his vengeance here," she said thoughtfully. Then she added, almost to herself, "But I think there is more to it than that. He could have taken his revenge anywhere." She remained deep in thought for so long that Jacob began to shift in discomfort. "Well, we shall see what he's about," she said softly, "but I think my dear brother must have a problem . . . yes, and I think the problem has a pretty face. Go back with the carriage, Jacob. I shall send some notes to the

329

friends he wants to invite. This should prove more than interesting."

When Jacob had gone Lorelei went to her room and, seating herself at the desk, wrote several short notes. Then she rang for a maid and instructed her to have them delivered at once. That done, she sat near the window and watched for the arriving carriage.

She thought of the brother she loved so deeply and of the angry bitter days they had spent in the rooming house in Natchez-under-the-hill after their father's death.

She knew his bitterness had been forged by their disgrace due to what had happened, knew how his shame had hurt him. Now he wanted the daughter of the man he felt was guilty to taste that same shame. Lorelei had never been so sure of Carrington's guilt, yet Marc had refused to listen to her. He had seen her homeless, with ragged clothes, and very frightened, and he had battled his way back, facing all that could be thrown at him, yet shielding her.

Her husband had come to her when the tide of her fortune was at its lowest ebb. He had made her feel safe and secure, and she had loved and married him. Marc had asked them to live at Garrison Hall because he was away more than he was home, and he wanted the house to be cared for. Out of sympathy, Lorelei and Rodger had agreed.

Now he was bringing here the woman whose father, he felt, was responsible for their tragedy. But what was his real reason for doing this? If he wanted revenge, if he wanted to embarrass her, he could accomplish that anywhere. What did he want from this woman?

Lorelei's mind continued to struggle with these thoughts; then, suddenly, she became very still and a small smile tugged at her lips. Perhaps, Marc had run across a problem he could not deal with. Perhaps this woman had touched him in a way he had least expected and he wasn't sure of how to handle the situation.

"One bedroom prepared . . . his," she murmured. Slowly her smile turned to a soft laugh. She was eager to meet Catalina Carrington.

The carriage came to a halt and the door swung open. Marc stepped out, then raised a hand to help an awestruck Catalina descend. Catalina had been used to luxury, but this was the most beautiful edifice she had ever seen.

The servants, to their surprise, had been cautioned by Lorelei to remain silent and to welcome Marc and Catalina as visitors. Marc was amused to see the strain that caused for many were servants he'd rehired; they had worked for his family when he was a child.

When the pair stood in a large white-and-black tile entrance hall, Catalina slowly turned about to absorb her surroundings. A large spiral staircase curved up gracefully several feet from them, and she was about to remark on its beauty when a woman appeared at the top.

As she watched the woman descend, her heart was wrenched. She was lovely, and if she was another of Marc's mistresses, then Catalina's battle would be more difficult than she had ever expected.

She caught a glimpse of Marc as she turned her head and wished she hadn't.

His smile was warm, his eyes appreciative. Indeed, he seemed to have forgotten her as he walked to the bottom of the steps.

The woman's smile widened as she neared the foot of the steps and her descent quickened. Catalina heard her laugh softly as she extended both hands to Marc, who took them, then drew her into his arms.

He held her close, rocking her in his embrace, and though he did not speak, Catalina could sense his strong emotion. She studied the woman closely.

She was slightly taller than Catalina, and her deep auburn hair was gathered so that it cascaded from the crown of her head nearly to her waist. Pulled back severely from her forehead, it enhanced her wide amber eyes and flawless complexion. She had an excellent figure, softly curved breasts, and a slim waist. All in all she would be harsh competition for any woman.

"Lorelei, my sweet, you look marvelous," Marc said as, grasping her hands, he stepped back to look at her. She smiled up into his eyes warmly.

"I have missed you. What kind of deviltry have you been up to?"

Marc chuckled and drew her with him to Catalina's side.

"Lorelei, I want you to meet a very lovely lady who is going to be our guest tonight. This is Catalina Carrington. Cat, this is Lorelei Garrison Thatcher."

"How do you do, Miss Thatcher," Catalina replied, and Lorelei knew by her stiffly formal attitude that she was upset. But why? Unless . . .

Lorelei smiled warmly. "Mrs. Thatcher."

"Mrs. Thatcher," Catalina repeated, not sure that she should believe there was a Mr. Thatcher.

"Do come in and make yourself comfortable. I shall ring for something. What would you like—coffee, tea?"

"Brandy," Marc replied.

"Tea please," Catalina said.

Lorelei rang for a maid and ordered the tea. Then, while Catalina and Marc sat down, she went to a cabinet and removed a bottle of brandy and a glass.

She carried both to Marc and set them down on the table near him. "I am more than sure old habits will require more than one drink so help yourself."

Marc chuckled as he poured himself a liberal glass, but Catalina was dismayed to learn that the very beautiful Lorelei knew all of his habits.

"Where's Rodger?" Marc asked.

"Gone to New Orleans on business," Lorelei replied.

"I imagine you've been bored." He grinned.

"A little. I sent your messages, and we'll have a nice late buffet. I'm sure"—Lorelei smiled at Catalina—"Marc's friends will be delighted to meet you."

Lorelei meant what she said, but Catalina imagined innuendo in her voice and saw laughter and derision in both Lorelei's and Marc's eyes.

She lifted her chin stubbornly. If this woman wanted a battle she was going to get it.

"You have a lovely home, Mrs. Thatcher," she said, coolly polite.

"Oh, I'm afraid it actually doesn't belong to me."

"Really?"

"No, it is a family home. Left to my brother and I."

"Your brother?"

Marc's smile was frozen as he watched Lorelei's face. But her teasing smile was his reward.

"My brother travels quite a bit," she said.

"I see," Catalina replied.

The tea came, and while Lorelei poured it, Marc poured himself another glass of brandy which he raised in a silent toast to Lorelei.

She sipped her tea and, as unobtrusively as possible, studied Catalina. She is a beauty, Lorelei thought. She decided her brother's taste had developed since she had last seen him.

"Do you come from this territory, Catalina?" Lorelei asked.

Catalina's voice was controlled as she explained that her family was from Baton Rouge, but she had just come from New Orleans.

While she spoke Lorelei let her eyes drift to Marc who, though seemingly relaxed, was absorbed in Catalina, and it took her only a minute to realize that it wasn't what Catalina was saying, but Catalina herself who held him spellbound. She smiled, but had an urge to laugh. Marc had never looked at another woman in this absorbed way. She wondered if he had any idea how deeply he was attracted to this one.

Marc, after patiently listening to the polite conversation of the ladies, took another deep drink of brandy and rose to his feet.

Both women looked up at him in surprise, and he grinned amiably.

"I'm sure you two will have plenty of time tomorrow for chitchat. Right now I'm going to show Cat where she'll be staying. Then I'm going to give her a tour of the house."

Lorelei's eyes returned to Catalina. Her face was frozen in a rigid smile, but her cheeks were tinged with red and her eyes were smoldering.

Catalina would have voiced her objection, but Marc was too quick to allow it. He reached down and, taking her hand in his, drew her to her feet and very nearly into his arms. His eyes had already told her that he would gladly do just that.

Lorelei watched them walk across the room and head up the steps. Then she set her teacup aside and allowed a smile to spread across her face. Tonight and tomorrow were going to prove to be very interesting.

As soon as they were out of sight of Lorelei, Catalina tried to snatch her hand from Marc's but was unsuccessful.

"Don't be so upset, Cat." He chuckled. "We'll be gone from here in a day."

"It wasn't necessary to be so obvious."

He stopped before a door and drew her close to him, his eyes smoldering with an easily discernible intent. "I want to show you where we'll be later. In fact"—his voice lowered and he slid his arm about her waist—"I'm finding it very difficult to wait until later. You're a damned exciting creature, Cat, different from any other I've known. You're a puzzle I haven't solved yet . . . but I will."

"I should think you would be tired of me by now. Does not the illustrious Marc Copeland have women at his beck and call? Surely you can find someone exciting to take my place." She smiled, but her smile was really a taunting challenge.

"I probably could at that," he replied aggravatingly. "But a bird in hand is usually better than two in flight. Besides I'd hate to end our bargain and leave you without the *Belle* when you've worked so hard to get it back."

He reached out to swing the door open, then waited for her to walk away or enter.

As Catalina looked up at him, she knew what he was thinking. She stood on tiptoe, placing one hand against his chest for support, and kissed him fully and leisurely. Then she smiled up into eyes filled with surprise that was rapidly being overshadowed by a much more volatile emotion.

She walked into the room and heard him enter, then close the door. The room was large and square, with several windows that faced the east and the rising sun. She gazed about it for a long time until she realized what was giving her the strange tingling feeling. It was a masculine room. Could it belong to Marc? But that would mean he spent a great deal of time in this house. This thought led to a more potent one. If he was here so often, if he had a room that was so totally his it almost whispered his name, then was the attraction that drew him here an amber-eyed woman? Did she share this bed with him when he had not brought another to do so?

Marc sensed these thoughts as he looked at her mobile features, and he was suddenly and surprisingly elated to think that she was jealous.

"No, Cat," he said softly.

"No what?" she answered, but her eyes fled his green ones when she saw amusement glittering them.

"No, I've never shared this bed with Lorelei. In fact, I've never shared this bed with anyone."

Although she tried to keep from reacting to his answer, she was pleased. She didn't want to be with him in a bed he had shared with many others.

The night was promising. She had carried herself well in the face of his blatant exposure of her as his mistress. She had taunted and tantalized him into thinking of her here in his bed. Now she had to make him wish that she would be here to share it for a long time, and maybe to fill the balance of his life.

She went to him and moved against him, looping her arms around his neck. Her smile was soft and sensually inviting.

"I'm glad you haven't shared this bed with another woman. If memories are to be created, I don't want ghosts hovering nearby."

"Are memories being created?" he questioned softly.

"Much of that depends upon you. Shall we test the possibility?" Her voice died to a whisper as she drew his head down and his mouth met hers.

Chapter 26

Catalina gazed nervously in the full-length mirror, examining her reflection for the hundredth time in the past hour.

She was molding her resolve so she would have the courage to face the people Marc had invited to the small buffet supper. She had been amazed that they had responded to such a sudden invitation, but, of course, Marc was a man of unusual accomplishments.

She smiled to herself, remembering the surprise that had leapt into his eyes when she had kissed him earlier. He had then left her to see to the baggage she would need brought from the boat, and she had again drifted about the room, sensing his presence in it more and more. She wondered how it would be to spend the rest of her life in his home . . . wherever that might be.

Her reverie was interrupted by a light rap, and when the door opened, Lorelei came in. Her smile widened when she saw Catalina and she walked to her.

"My dear, you do look beautiful. Our guests have arrived, and Marc has sent me to get you. He seems slightly impatient."

The words were spoken in a friendly way, but Catalina's heart heard only *our guests* and *impatience*. She felt that Lorelei was subtly reminding her of her position in the house, and in Marc's life.

Catalina gulped back her acute embarrassment and straightened her shoulders. Lorelei was quite conscious that Catalina was frightened, and at that moment she was extremely annoyed with Marc. She had decided that Catalina was not the woman Marc had portrayed when he'd spoken to her after taking Catalina to her . . . his room.

"Really," Lorelei had said, "you are asking a great deal when you expect me to stoop to subterfuge. She's not the black-hearted woman you wrote about. Why, Marc, she's younger than I am."

"In years maybe."

"Oh," she had responded, her anger mounting at his teasing glance, "you, my dear brother, are as blind as a bat." Regaining control, she had smiled.

"Now what's that supposed to mean, that Cat is beautiful? I recognize that. But so is a panther." He had chuckled. "And she could be just as deadly."

"I hate your stubbornness."

"It's a family trait," he had declared pleasantly.

"I don't want to take part in hurting someone."

"Even someone who profited from all our problems," he'd said quietly. "Someone who laughed and danced and sang while Father was dying and we were scrabbling in the dirt?"

"Marc, you said her father was responsible. You took the boat he treasured, and you shamed his son. Why can't that be enough?"

It had been hard for him to believe that he could experience such a surge of guilt. He had had no answer for Lorelei because he had had none for himself, and he hadn't been aware that Lorelei had seen his uncertainty before he had turned away.

Now as Catalina and Lorelei walked down the long upstairs hall to the top of the steps, Lorelei prayed silently that she could stop Marc from driving toward his own destruction. Both women were surprised to find him below, waiting for them.

Catalina paused when she saw Marc and placed a hesitant and trembling hand on the banister. She was annoyed with herself because his cool, ice green gaze caused such a tumult in her.

Lorelei did not notice for she was concentrating on the warm appreciative way Marc gazed at Catalina. She had never seen him look at a woman like this.

Meanwhile Marc waited, laughing to himself. He could have been sharing a drink with two of his best friends, but he had foregone that pleasure because he'd wanted Catalina on his arm when he met them, wanted to see the looks in their eyes when they saw her.

He drew in his breath as his eyes feasted on Catalina, who stood immobile above him.

Their gazes met for a long moment; then, very slowly, she started down the stairs.

She had brushed her sable hair until it shone in the candlelight. That done, she had bound it atop of her head in a mass of soft curls.

The gown she wore was simple, yet it enhanced her beauty more than an elaborate one would have. Of a rich green color, it gracefully exposed her soft shoulders and the high curves of her breasts. Her skin seemed to glow in the golden candlelight.

When she reached his side, he looked again into golden brown eyes of unfathomable depth. They held unanswerable questions. He had a deep, almost uncontrollable urge to snatch her up in his arms and carry her to his bed, to make luxurious and unending love to her.

Catalina saw his heated gaze, and smiled as provocatively and invitingly as she could. She was as determined as he that one of the major battles of their silent but ever-present war would be fought here.

Catalina reached out and put her hand on his arm.

"You are outstandingly beautiful, Cat," Marc said softly. "It's a shame we have other plans. You look too inviting to share."

"Thank you. And I must say, you look quite handsome."

Again she saw the quizzical look in the depths of his eyes, but she allowed hers to widen into an innocent expression.

"I'm sorry." She laughed softly. "I sounded more like a wife than a mistress. I shall have to mind my tongue."

Before he could speak, Lorelei joined them, and he could only offer an arm to each lady and escort them to the waiting guests. The few people he had asked to dine were his closest friends, and he had that day arranged to have them refer to him as Marc Copeland or just Marc. He had also asked them to keep from mentioning his past as much as possible, or from saying that Lorelei was his sister. He had promised a fuller explanation later. They had all agreed, more from curiosity than for any other reason.

There were two couples and one lone man in the room when Marc, Catalina, and Lorelei entered. All five turned to look toward the doorway.

The first to speak was the unaccompanied man. He was attractive, of average height with wayward blond hair and deep penetrating brown eyes. He walked toward them as he spoke, his words directed to all, but his eyes on Catalina alone.

"My God, Marc old friend. You told me you had a surprise to share, but you didn't warn us to prepare for an exquisite creature such as this. My name is Randolph Hammond," he stated, and his eyes sparkled as Catalina extended her hand to him. "And I am enchanted."

"Thank you," Catalina murmured.

340

As Marc led her farther into the room, all present observed the flushed cheeks and sparkling eyes of this pair. Marc introduced Catalina to Rachel and William Maguire, and then to Patrica and Amos Dixon.

Catalina was surprised by their graciousness. There were no smirks or knowing looks. The women were warm and accepting, and the men, though their glances were appreciative, were neither suggestive in their behavior or remarks, nor amused.

As the evening began to flow Catalina was snatched from Marc's side by one of his friends, and although Marc accepted this with surface amusement he was again shaken by the realization of his need to keep Catalina near him.

His plan to flaunt their relationship seemed to go astray when the question of her background and her reason for being at Garrison Hall was broached.

"I can't understand how a lovely creature like you slipped past me," Randolph declared. "Obviously you didn't come from anywhere near Natchez or I would have known. Where are you from, Miss Carrington . . . or may I call you Catalina?"

"I would be pleased if you would call me Catalina."

Randolph's eyes glittered with humorous deviltry. "So you are a close friend of the Gar— ah . . . the Copeland family?"

Now it begins, she thought. But before she could answer, Marc replied.

"Cat's a friend of Lorelei's, I had the good fortune to bring her from New Orleans to Natchez so they could spend some time together."

No one was more surprised by his words than Marc or Catalina, or more amused than Lorelei.

Marc refused to meet his sister's eyes, and rose to get more wine. He was sure now that the evening was a total mistake, for the tables seemed to have been reversed. Catalina had reached out to capture all present, and had met with success.

From across the room he watched her laugh at something one of his friends had said, and despite himself he began to think of how she fit so easily into his home and among his friends. He remembered joking with Randolph, before Catalina had come down, about the world containing only three kinds of women: girls, women, and ladies. Watching Catalina he now realized she seemed to be all three. She was too complete, too perfect, for him to allow his thoughts to travel any further. If they did he would have to face what he had set as a goal—to force Catalina into a life of shame and disgrace.

He wished, at this moment, that the evening was over. Lorelei enjoyed his discomfort to the fullest, while Catalina seemed to be oblivious of it. She began to sparkle, to relax and talk, and she drew everyone toward her as a magnet draws pieces of metal. Meanwhile, Marc thrashed about in his own mental stress until the evening was finally at an end.

When the guests had gone, Lorelei and Marc and Catalina had a last glass of brandy before the fireplace. But after a few minutes Lorelei pleaded exhaustion, bade them a good night, and Marc and Catalina were left together in the candle-lit room, a heavy silence between them.

Marc rose to pour himself more brandy. After doing so, he turned to look at Catalina who was gazing meditatively into the low-burning fire. He watched the flames' pale glow reflect on her skin, and wondered what she was thinking. When he walked back to stand close to her, he realized she was caught up in some faraway thought. For a minute he was irritated, imagining that someone else occupied her mind.

Yet he was making no demands of a permanent

nature on her. It would not be long until she was gone from his life, until he had tasted his revenge. Amazed when that thought filled him with a vague kind of panic, he reached down and traced a finger lightly across the soft flesh of her shoulder. She looked up at him, and he frowned to see her eyes glistening suspiciously.

"What's wrong, Cat?" he said softly. "You were far away." He braced his hand on the chair arm and bent close to her. "Where were you?"

Unable to tell him that she had been facing a moment of fear, that she was adrift on a sea of uncertainty, she forced herself to smile. It was a tremulous smile, inviting and so utterly feminine that he was held silent.

"Wrong? Nothing. I was just thinking."

"Of what?"

She was feeling much too vulnerable to tell him her thoughts. Furthermore they had been about him and the life they could have together. Maybe, she thought, we would never have a place as magnificent as this, but if he would only meet me halfway, we could build something.

On the periphery of her mind she was aware that there was a part of Marc she did not know—a part of him she could never reach. It could tear them apart, for she knew a threat of some kind hovered just beyond her vision. And in this quiet sensitive moment she felt that threat more deeply than ever.

She stood and they were inches from each other, yet Catalina wondered if the distance between had not grown.

"It was nothing." She smiled. "Just old memories."

His eyes held hers, and he would have given anything in that moment to have been a part of her memories. Catalina's smile faded and her eyes widened as she realized how fragile the situation between them was.

He raised a hand to cup her chin gently and lift her mouth to his. The kiss was soft and so very gentle that she trembled.

When he released her lips, he realized he was more puzzled now than he had been at the moment he had met her. He had wanted her, and she had surrendered. He had reached for her, and she had filled his arms. Yet there was an elusive Catalina just beyond his reach, and of all the Catalinas he knew, he desired to touch that one.

Maybe one more night—one more taste of passionate magic that blossomed between them—would free him to do what he felt he must.

"You were utterly charming tonight, Cat. I'm afraid you've captured more hearts."

"Your friends were delightful," she countered. "For a while they almost made me forget just how . . . uncertain our situation is. I had to keep in mind that none of this can be any more than a passing pleasure, as all your pleasures are."

His eyes narrowed as he searched her words for a double meaning, at the same time trying his best to push from his mind the thoughts that had subtly insinuated themselves. Permanence was the last thing he wanted, but the pleasures she spoke of evoked vibrant memories when he looked into the deep pools of her eyes.

His arms went about her and he drew her close to him. "You are a pleasure no man in his right mind could resist. God, but you're beautiful, Cat," he whispered as he bent to kiss her again. His mouth smothered any words she would have uttered, and within moments any thoughts either harbored were melted by the heat that forged them together.

She moaned softly under his fierce fevered kisses, and clung to him as she gave herself wholly to her passion, becoming so enmeshed in its intensity that she found herself returning to that state of wild and free abandon that amazed her as well as him.

When their lips parted momentarily, they gazed at each other, astounded by the sensations that tore at them.

But this was not what Marc had planned for this night . . . not this night.

Catalina gave a startled gasp as he bent and lifted her up in his arms.

"Marc?"

"Shh . . . it's been a day to remember. Now we will share a night to remember . . . but not here."

Almost fearing this fabulous moment was a dream she closed her eyes and put her arms about his neck.

He strode to the stairway and carried her up it. Pushing the door to his room open, he stepped inside, then used his back to push the door shut.

Servants had lit candles and had turned down the bed after lighting a fire in the fireplace.

Gently he let her feet drop to the floor, but he held her close to him.

When she lifted her eyes to his, he molded her even more closely against him.

"I want you, Cat," he whispered as he pressed a searing kiss to her throat. "I have never wanted anyone as I have you. I will never understand you . . . but I want you."

"I am not so impossible to understand," she whispered. "You look too far away for answers."

Marc no longer cared, for she had lifted her mouth to his again in a yielding yet seductive kiss that sent a glorious sensation of rightness through him. He took her hand, and backing slowly toward the bed, he drew her with him. She offered no resistance, and when they reached the side of the bed, she moved into his arms willingly.

While their lips lingered, played and tasted and savored, their hands caressed and then moved to destroy the barrier of clothes that stood between them.

Catalina, he thought wildly, you make me forget all but your silken flesh.

He could feel her now, pressed to his heated skin. The entire length of her body melded perfectly with his.

He could not deny the almost unnatural physical desire he had for her, and he could not resist the magic web her lovemaking wove about him.

They dropped to the bed, their limbs too weak to control, and feverishly he caressed the slim length of her body, his hands drawing forth the streaks of passion that shot through her.

Mouths parted, hungering for the depths of delight. Tongues warred, while passions soared.

His hands slid down her waist to her belly, then sought a deeper warmth.

Here, in his bed, in the heart of his home, Marc sought to brand her as his.

Pushing her gently against the pillows he rose above her, to gaze for a moment at the graceful length of her body in the candle glow. He wanted to know every inch of her, and he let his fingers gently touch her shoulders. Their eyes met and held, and she remained quiet and motionless as his hand slid down to cup her breast.

He bent to lick lightly at one, then the other, hearing her soft sighing response. He caressed her soft mounds, feeling the velvet of her skin and the hardness of her peaked nipples. Then he captured one, sucking gently at first, then more urgently until her sighs turned to moans and she reached for him.

He savored her flesh, moving his mouth slowly, nibbling, tasting—sensing the heat within her. When he lifted his head for a moment, pleasure moved through him in a thick wave. Her eyes were closed, and he could feel her entire body tremble.

With an easy movement, he knelt between her legs. Her eyes opened, and she gazed at him, her eyes glazed with need. Running his hands down her hips and then up the inside of her thighs, gently he parted them. Then he bent to let his lips trace the same path, slowly, ever so slowly, until Catalina felt she would scream for her body pulsed with need and arched to seek release.

She cried out his name in blind and mindless surrender as his mouth touched, his tongue caressed, at first lightly in short strokes until she felt she could bear it no more. Then he penetrated deeply, seeking to drive her beyond reality. Only when her body quivered on the brink of release did he cease. Both were beyond anything but this blinding hot desire.

Suddenly, with a deep, almost violent thrust, he buried himself deep within her. Then he remained motionless until her eyes opened. Holding her gaze, he began to move in a tormentingly slow movement.

She reached to draw him to her, but he remained above her. She arched her hips, thrashing in her need, but still he moved slowly until she was beyond control.

"Marc . . . please . . . please."

The pace increased, the fire mounted until they were moving together in an almost wild and violent abandon.

When she cried out his name again at the pinnacle of release, he barely heard, for he was dissolving in a river of brilliant completion and could only groan her name softly in response.

Chapter 27

Travis had stood in the deep shadows on the lower deck and had watched Marc assist Catalina into the carriage. He knew quite well that Marc had deliberately not invited him to the evening meal, and had blatantly made a production of leaving with Catalina. But he had no idea that Marc was quite certain Travis was watching, and was enjoying himself.

Travis was so engrossed in jealous anger as he watched Marc and Catalina, he was not aware of Charlene's presence until she spoke.

"You're not going ashore in Natchez? It's a real exciting town."

"I'm afraid I do not intend to disembark here," he said. "In fact I've no plans for this evening at all."

"Then"—she moved closer to his side and tucked her hand under his arm—"maybe you'd like to come ashore with me. I'm meeting Nina, and we're going to have a party with some friends. It might be very interesting for you." Her voice was seductive and her eyes glimmered in open invitation.

Travis looked into her eyes for some time, realizing she was leaving words unsaid, words she hoped he would understand.

"I suppose it would be worth my while to come with you. I hear Nina and one of the crew were put ashore somewhat against their will. Does this have anything to do with our little . . . party?"

"It might." She laughed softly. "It just might at that. It seems Nina and her friend are a little upset with Marc. From what I've seen you're not too pleased either. Together we might all find some advantage."

"Just what do you have in mind?"

"Come ashore . . . and find out," she said teasingly. "I wouldn't be surprised if you enjoyed the evening. It might just remove a barrier or two from your path and give you what you're after."

"And just how do you know what I'm after?"

"Don't play games with me, Travis. I've known what you've been after since you had Willie pull that little trick with the door. I'd say the lady has a lot of money and you'd like to get her into a position where you could"—she shrugged—"share a little."

"Well, you might just be right. So"—he smiled—"why don't we just go and join your friends, and see what the evening has to offer?"

Charlene smiled again and Travis laughed as they walked toward the gangplank. Neither Travis or Charlene were aware of the piercing gaze of China, who had stood some distance away and had watched the two in conversation.

There was no doubt in her mind that whatever they were talking about, it boded no good for Marc.

She watched them walk down the gangplank and hire a carriage to take them into town. She motioned to a young darkie standing nearby and bent to whisper into his ear. Within minutes he flew down the gangplank and trotted nimbly in pursuit of the slow-moving carriage.

China returned to Marc's cabin and waited impatiently for the young boy's return. He was gone for an hour, but to China it felt like days before a timid knock on her cabin door told of his return.

"Well, Jasper?" she asked patiently.

"Dey be gwan to Miz Belle's house."

"Belle Towne?"

"Yessum, Miz China. Dat be whar dey go. Yo'all wants me to go watch to see iffen dey goes anywhere else?"

"No, Jasper." China smiled and slipped a gold coin into the boy's hand, watching his face light up. "You've done fine. Now go along and have some fun. Spend your money on some of those sweets you like so well."

"Yessum . . . Miz China, yo sho yo doan needs me. I be glad to stay."

"No, you go on, Jasper. But you can do one thing for me."

"Yessum . . . anything."

"While you're on your way to have some fun, tell one of the drivers to bring a carriage to the gangplank. I'll be going into Natchez in about a half-hour."

"Yessum, I'll get de bes and de fastus. He'll be dere when yo'all's ready."

"Thank you. Now go and enjoy yourself. We'll be leaving Natchez in a day or so I imagine."

"Yessum." Jasper flashed a broad white grin and then scampered away. China knew he would carefully choose one of the carriages for her use.

She closed the cabin door and saw that Shawna was in the condition she had expected. It was always so when Shawna was in close proximity to Natchez-under-the-hill. Drawn and pale, she was curled up on Marc's bed, obviously afraid.

China went to the bed and took one of Shawna's hands in hers. "You know you need have no more fears, Shawna," she said comfortingly. "Marc will never let anyone hurt you again. Natchez-under-the-hill can't reach you or touch you."

"I know, China. I . . . I don't have to go ashore. I don't have to go back there if I don't want to. Marc told me."

"Of course you don't. You are safe here, and we love you. But I must go ashore awhile to do an errand . . . something to help Marc."

"To help Marc," Shawna said timidly.

"Yes. You'll be all right for a while?"

"Yes . . . if you're going to help Marc."

"I am, child, but I shall return soon and we will have dinner together."

Shawna nodded, but China could still feel fear trembling through her. She wondered if the day would ever come when Shawna would be free of the ugliness of the past. It had taken China a long time to recover. And both women were very aware of the position Marc held in their lives, for he had been the one to walk between them and hell, and he was still the only wall between them and the blackness they knew existed here.

China rose to her feet and smiled reassuringly. "Why don't you just try to get some sleep? I'll be back soon and we'll have a quiet late-night dinner together."

Again Shawna nodded as she pulled the covers up to her chin. China patted her hand, then left, closing the door softly behind her. Shawna watched the closed door for a while as if she expected it to burst open, to see dark evil men race and snatch her from the bed. Finally she closed her eyes. And the dreams came again as they always did. . . .

She had been so young . . . so very young when they had caught her. She had lived with her mother on the very edge of Natchez-under-the-hill, and had been contented to follow her mother's orders to remain inside the house before dark. How could she have known of her mother's "after dark" profession? She did not understand when she had awakened one night to find her mother gone. Afraid to be alone, she had gone out to find her. . . .

Her dreams became terrifying. She was dragged to a brothel, and ravaged again and again. She could still feel the obscene hands tear at her, still feel the pain and the terror. She had never seen her mother again because she had been chained to the bed.

Night after night she had been sexually used and abused until she dropped into the inky blackness of forgetfulness.

Then Marc had come. He had seen her, and had gone mad with fury. He had killed one man and injured many. But he had dragged a fourteen-year-old child from the depths of degradation, and although her mind would never go beyond that age, her body had developed while Marc had kept her safe and protected.

Shawna clung to sanity only because of China and Marc. For them, she would give her life if it were necessary.

China sat in the carriage without looking to either side of the street as the carriage rolled along. She did not need to look; she, too, knew Natchez-under-the-hill well. She, too, had tasted its evil and its nightmares. And she was loyal to Marc, for almost the same reason as Shawna.

The carriage rolled to a stop in front of a house that seemed to be better cared for than most of the dwellings in the lower city, but it appeared to be deserted. China stepped down and sharply ordered the driver to wait. Then she walked to the door and knocked.

The door was opened by a small wizened old man

who smiled when he saw her.

"Ah, China . . . welcome, welcome. It is good to see your lovely face again."

China smiled. "Thank you. Is Emil at home?"

"Yes. He saw the boat arrive and he has been hoping you would call on him. Come in."

China stepped inside and the door was quickly closed.

Travis was welcomed to the group that sat around the table in the noisy barroom. Nina was there, with a man Travis had never seen before, and Willie Best. Willie seemed nervous.

"I'm glad to see you again," Nina said.

"I'm rather surprised to see you," Travis replied.

"Surprised . . . really?" Nina laughed.

"I told Nina I felt sure you would be interested in what she had to say." Charlene sat down and drew Travis down beside her.

"And just what do you have to say?" Travis asked coldly, his eyes never leaving Nina's face.

"I think," Nina declared softly, "you would like to rid yourself of Marc, and have your sweet-faced fancy lady back where you could handle her."

"Handle her?"

"Don't play with me, Travis," Nina said, half in anger. "We know what you had Willie here do. You want her in your bed and in your power, and you can damned well have her—as long as you promise to keep her away from Marc. We"—she shrugged and smiled—"would rather he didn't know what happened to her."

Travis folded his arms on the table and leaned toward Nina, a smile on his face. "And just what do you plan to do?"

"Whatever suits you."

"I want Catalina legally married to me. I want papers that prove it. After that you can dispose of her in any way you see fit."

"Oh," Nina said softly, "I can think of many ways here in Natchez-under-the-hill to dispose of a pretty thing like her."

"But I've got to be legally married to her before you . . . take care of her. And I will need a reliable witness so the marriage will stand up in a court of law."

"Don't worry, we'll get your witness. After that . . ."

"After that, we can solve your problem," Charlene put in. "Willie says he can make a lot of money on her pampered body. He can keep her in circulation for choice patrons for a long, long time."

"Sorry, Willie." Travis laughed. "I want the Carrington fortune. With her brother dead, I, as her legal husband, will be handsomely paid to . . . ah . . . keep the Carrington name clean. I plan to make a very great deal of money by holding Catalina and our marriage over their heads. They need never know where she is, but I must dangle before them the possibility that they might be able to see her . . . one day . . . sometime—if they pay well."

"Then we'll all get what we want. With that Carrington bitch out of the way, Marc will soon forget her. He'll belong to me again," Nina declared. "You'll have your money, and Willie will be able to find some . . . pleasure of his own."

Travis looked again at Willie, whose eyes glowed with the burning fire of a hungry rat. Travis shuddered to think of what his twisted mind might devise for Catalina.

"All right, Willie," he said softly. "We'll compensate you somehow for not being able to make money on Catalina's body."

Willie smiled and nodded his head.

"So," Travis added, "let's get our plans straight so there will be no slip-ups. If you want her, Willie, you had better make sure everything works smoothly."

"Don't worry." Nina spoke for Willie. "He knows. There won't be any mistakes."

"All right. Just what are we going to do?" Travis said quietly. The five bent close together to solidify their plans to separate Marc and Catalina forever and to send Catalina into a world of wickedness such as she had never dreamed of.

Travis and Charlene stepped down from the carriage alongside the *Belle* much later that night. They walked up the gangplank as if they had only gone on a pleasurable jaunt and had not plotted such evil things.

"Where is China?" Charlene asked of a roustabout that stood nearby.

"She's ashore, since this afternoon."

"And Marc?"

"He and the young lady haven't come back."

"Good," Charlene said softly. Then she smiled up at Travis. "Would you like to come to my cabin for a drink before you retire for the night?"

"I most certainly would." Travis drew her closer to him, knowing that the night promised more than the sharing of a drink, and that in the next few days they would be well rewarded.

Many hours later, after a large white moon had risen high in the night sky, China returned to the *Belle*.

Within minutes of her arrival, she knew that Travis and Charlene had returned and that they were both in Charlene's cabin. She frowned. Charlene and Travis were close. She did not care about that, but she realized they might be conspiring against Marc. Tomorrow she would ask more questions and try to learn where Travis had gone that day.

China went to Shawna's cabin and opened the door to slip quietly inside. A lamp, still lit, shed a pale glow across the room, revealing the figure that lay on the bed. China walked over and stood looking down at Shawna, who was curled up like a child.

The lamp remained lit because Shawna's fear of the dark bordered on hysteria when she woke and found herself surrounded by it. China could imagine the terrors that had been forced on Shawna under the cover of darkness, so she never questioned the young woman's need to keep a light burning at all times.

China, as always, felt a deep pang of sadness when she looked at Shawna. The evils of Natchez had destroyed her young life before it even had a chance to blossom. She knew of Shawna's intense fear of men. Marc was the only man who could come near her, and he was extremely careful when he approached Shawna. He rarely touched her, and if he did it was with the gentle touch of a loving father or brother. The protective love China felt for Marc was renewed every time she looked at Shawna.

As if she sensed another presence in the room, Shawna's eyes flew open and she sat up abruptly. China could see the terror in her wide childlike eyes before she recognized China and smiled a tremulous smile.

She stretched and yawned like a luxury-loving kitten.

"Go on back to sleep, Shawna," China soothed. "It's not morning yet."

"Where have you been?"

"Visiting some very old friends, and asking some questions."

"Questions? What kind of questions? There's nothing you don't know about Natchez."

"Not about Natchez . . . about Travis. I have a feeling he has some ulterior motives I should know about. And Marc should know them too." China walked across the room to prepare for bed.

Shawna shivered slightly. "I don't like him."

Aware that Shawna often saw people clearly through her child's eyes, China returned to the bed and sat on the edge.

"You don't like him, Shawna . . . why?"

"He has . . ." She shrugged. "He looks at me like . . . like those other terrible men used to. China . . . he . . . he makes me feel like I should take a bath. He looks at Catalina that way too. Catalina is such a nice sweet lady, but she doesn't see his eyes. His eyes are not like Marc's. Marc's eyes smile, Travis's . . . well, he . . . he looks like he is . . . hungry."

"Hungry," China mused. "You might be right, Shawna. I've had the same feeling about our Mr. Travis Sherman. By tomorrow I might have some answers."

"Anyway," Shawna said brightly, "Marc won't let Travis hurt Catalina."

"What makes you say that?"

"Marc likes Catalina a whole lot," Shawna said, a happy innocent smile on her face. "I can tell. He smiles from inside when he looks at her and when he's with her he's . . . he's happy. Yes, he's happy. I hope Catalina stays with Marc, and us, for a long time. We could treat her real nice China, and Marc would smile all the time."

"Marc smiles from inside." China laughed softly. "It's the first time I've heard falling in love described that way. But I do agree with you, Shawna. I just don't think Marc has any idea that he's in love with Catalina

357

yet. In fact"—she chuckled—"it might come as somewhat of a shock when he does realize it."

Shawna blinked, then frowned. "Don't laugh at Marc, China. He is very clever. There's nothing he doesn't know. Besides, he took Catalina home with him, so maybe he wants to keep her and not let her go away like all the other lady friends he's had. I think Marc would be sad if Catalina went away. You don't think she will, do you? Maybe you should tell her to stay."

"No, Shawna," China said slowly. She patted Shawna's hand. "And don't you say anything. If she wants to stay she will, and if she wants to go, she will. That's a decision she must make for herself, a decision only Marc can help her make. You understand me, don't you, Shawna?"

Shawna nodded, but her mind was caught up in a novel idea. Shawna rarely disobeyed China or Marc. But this time her mind had spun a web of happiness for her beloved Marc, and to make that a reality, she would even disobey China. Shawna decided that when Catalina came back on board the *Belle,* she was going to ask her to stay and make them all happier.

She sat cross-legged on the bed, and watched China prepare to retire. Her world could be complete, she thought. All she needed was her home on the *Belle,* China to be her friend, and Marc and Catalina to make up the family she had never known.

When China got into bed, the dimly lit room became quiet. All that could be heard was the gentle swish of water as the boat gently rocked the two women to sleep.

No one heard the soft moaning sounds of passion in Charlene's cabin or the rustling as bodies sated themselves. And no one heard the laughter and quiet conversation when passion was temporarily eased, and the evil pair took pleasure in the dark and wicked plans they had made.

The new day dawned, streaking the horizon, before the two conspirators slept, satisfied that the coming days would bring their plans to fruition.

Chapter 28

Seth and Charles stood side by side at the rail of the *Constitution*. Neither had been able to sleep so they smoked in companionable silence as the night waned. In fact there had been very little sleep for Seth since the journey had begun. Question after question tore at his mind, and he found himself torn between the desire to know Catalina was safe and well, and the aching need to return to his Aunt Charlotte to make sure Jake was also safe and well.

He laughed silently, wondering to himself if he would ever think of her as anything but Jake. He could not believe that he had actually dreamed of her when sleep had actually come. The little termagant was lodged in his thoughts and he found it hard to eject her. He was more than amused at himself when he realized if it wasn't necessary to make sure Cat was all right, he would dash back to Jake.

Charles spoke twice before he jolted Seth from his thoughts.

"What . . . what did you say, Charles?"

"I said we'll be reaching Natchez by this time tomorrow night."

"Thank God. The strain is making sleep nearly impossible. I'm sure Cat is all right."

"But you're a little worried about how your ward,

Jake, is doing?" Charles grinned.

"She's not exactly my ward." Seth laughed. "In fact she'd go off on one of her tangents if you labeled her as such. Of all the independent creatures I've ever known, Jake is the toughest. And she has one hell of a temper. You might get a taste of it if you refer to her as *my* anything."

"I'll try to remember not to do that, but I wonder if you will remember not to do it."

"What do you mean?"

"You've a connoisseur's eye, Seth, especially when it comes to women. You saw the sleeping beauty beneath the rough exterior. The most beautiful of diamonds is cut from the roughest stone."

"That's what makes me worry."

"About the metamorphosis you're going to be responsible for? I should think you'd feel quite proud of yourself. It's a very charitable act."

"I didn't do it to be charitable!"

"Well, then"—Charles turned to face Seth—"suppose you tell me . . . and yourself . . . just why you did do it."

Seth thought for a long silent moment, envisioning Jake . . . her rough men's clothes and her defensive temper. Slowly he replaced her clothes with others—a silk dress, even ribbons for her glorious hair. What Seth saw in his mind's eye disturbed him. He turned to look at Charles and his confusion was evident.

"I don't know what my motives are. I felt I was indebted to her and her grandfather."

"You could have bought them a new boat."

"Yes, I suppose I could." Again Seth was shaken. "Good God, Charles, you don't think I would take advantage of Jake, seek some kind of reward for what I'm doing?"

"Would you, Seth?" Charles questioned gently.

Seth searched his heart. His reputation had not always been untainted, and he couldn't blame Charles for having some doubts. But he suddenly felt secure in his answer. He also was pleased to have found a Seth he had never known existed.

"No, Charles. I want to see Jake happy. I don't think she's had much in her life. I don't want to hurt her—in any way. I think she and I can become friends . . . and that's all I demand from her."

"You know, Seth my boy, you have grown into quite a man. I know your aunt is going to be more than pleased, and so will Cat, when you meet again. I think it's the first time in our acquaintance that I can honestly say I'm proud to know you."

"Thank you," Seth replied. He felt good, and he realized he had a great deal more than saving his life to thank Jake for. He decided to buy her a nice present in Natchez.

The thought of Natchez turned his mind to Catalina and the problems she might be facing. Reevaluating his own life had led him to reevaluate his friends, and his opinions of some of them had changed. He now viewed Travis in a different light, and realized the man had goaded him toward his debauchery and had continually urged him into wilder excesses.

No wonder Cat disliked the man. Seth groaned silently. Because of him Cat had put herself in Travis's hands. He was terribly aware of his sister's love and of his own blind foolishness. He thought of Marc Copeland, a man of iron who might be much more of a threat to Cat than Travis.

But Seth knew that his own newly developed sense of honor would not allow him to let Cat pay any of his debts. If he had to call Marc out and fight a duel with him, he would, but he would no longer stand behind Cat's skirts. Grimly determined, Seth decided that if

Marc Copeland had harmed Cat in any way he would pay with his life. . . .

Jake laughed softly as she twirled the white-and-green ruffled parasol. She pretended to look flirtatiously from beneath the matching green-and-white bonnet as she studied herself in the full-length mirror.

The green silk dress she wore enhanced her extremely well proportioned figure. Its bodice and sleeves were snugly fitted, and its draped skirt was drawn back into a large ruffled bustle that magnified the slenderness of her waist. At the hem of her skirt the white lace of her petticoat was barely visible. With her hair pulled into a mass of burnished ringlets at the nape of her neck, Jake made an entrancing picture.

Sophie, having finished helping her dress, sat on the bed smiling admiringly at Jake. It was hard for her to believe that this was the rough and dirty urchin she had first seen a few weeks before.

"Miss Jake, you sure do look so pretty. You're going to take everybody at the party this afternoon by storm, especially all the young men. Miss Charlotte's having trouble now, but after today she's going to have to hire protectors to keep the young men in New Orleans from storming her house."

Jake's smile faded slightly as she regarded herself in the mirror. What she saw reflected there was a frightened girl hovering on the threshold of womanhood, and she was astounded by the change in her.

The doors Seth had opened were very wide.

She looked at herself critically. Was she pretty as Sophie said? Would Seth think her pretty? She was shaken by how important the answer to this question was.

Despite Charlotte's subtle warnings, Jake made

every move, bought every item of apparel with one thought in mind. Would Seth like this? She envisioned his quick smile or the disappointment in his eyes. This last possibility she could not bear.

She constantly reminded herself to abide by Charlotte's wishes, for she knew Charlotte's disapproval would ultimately lead to his.

"Am I really pretty, Sophie?"

"Oh, Miss Jake, you're one of the prettiest girls in New Orleans. I hear lots of people talking and they keep saying how pretty you are. All those invitations you get, do you think they just send 'em because of Miss Charlotte? No sir. Every eligible bachelor in New Orleans is frothing at the mouth to be first in line. In fact I've seen some of the married ones looking pretty funny too."

"Do you think," Jake asked hesitantly, "that Seth will like me?"

"He can't help but like you. Mister Seth has known a lot of pretty girls, but I'll bet he falls in love with you when he comes back and he just gets in line with all the other boys."

Jake's cheeks grew pink, for it seemed to her that Sophie had exposed her dream. And it was a dream, she knew; for men in Seth's position did not fall in love with girls from the docks, no matter how pretty they were. Still, it was a dream she could cling to until Seth returned.

Suddenly thinking of the changes in her life, she was reminded of the look in her grandfather's eyes when she and Charlotte had visited the boat.

Charlotte had given her a last critical look before they had left the house, and her smile of approval had made Jake feel much more secure. She had hoped to see the same look in her grandfather's eyes.

As they had ridden slowly toward the docks in an

open carriage, Jake had been made more aware of the changes in her by the realization that the docks on which she had been raised seemed to have changed. Had they always been this dirty and rowdy? Had they always been so filled with the dregs of humanity, with wandering souls that could not seem to find a permanent harbor?

When the carriage had at last stopped near the fishing boat on which she had been raised, she was even more shaken at seeing how small it suddenly seemed.

The driver aided Charlotte to descend from the carriage, then extended his hand to Jake, who stepped down with the regal bearing of a grand lady despite the fear that tore at her. Would her grandfather's feelings have changed—or would they change when he saw her?

With Charlotte behind her, she walked slowly up the gangplank. The deck of the boat was deserted, but she knew, even if the crew men were ashore, her grandfather would be in his cabin. Nervously, she walked toward it.

Charlotte watched her hesitant approach, aware that Jake was not lacking in courage. Dressed in an orchid silk gown with a matching bonnet and parasol, Jake seemed exceptionally delicate and very beautiful.

Benjamin sat at his desk, trying to sort out the figures in his record book. He did not hear Jake's approach until she spoke softly from the doorway.

"Grandpa?"

Benjamin immediately spun around, but for some moments he did not recognize the slim, beautiful, well-dressed young woman that stood in the doorway. When he saw tears glistening in her green eyes, his heart leapt in joy.

"Jake . . . baby," he cried, as he stood and extended his arms to her. Jake flew across the room and flung herself into her grandfather's warm embrace.

"Oh, Grandpa," she sobbed.

Benjamin took hold of Jake's shoulders and held her away from him while he looked her over closely.

"My God, you are such a beautiful young lady I can hardly recognize you."

"I'm still me, Grandpa; I didn't change. I've got some pretty clothes, but I'm still me."

Benjamin could hear the desperation in her words. She had not yet molded herself to her new life, and was afraid to break her ties to the old.

"Of course you are, child. You will always be my Jake. Do you know you look so much like your mother it's as if she's here too? And your pa would be so proud if he could see you now. Proud like I am."

"Are you, Grandpa? Are you pleased?"

"I couldn't be more pleased." He looked past Jake to Charlotte. "And I couldn't be more grateful for all you've done for my little girl," he said.

"I've done nothing but put pretty wrappings on the fine gift you created. What Jake is, you made, Benjamin Barde, and I won't take the credit for all the years you must have worked and sacrificed to raise her. May I come in?" Charlotte's smile was warm, and Ben was glad that she had crossed Jake's path.

He knew who Charlotte McNeil was, but she walked to him and held out a slender gloved hand.

"I'm Seth's aunt, Charlotte McNeil, and I am most pleased to make your acquaintace, Mr. Barde. Jake has spoken of you quite often, and I have been looking forward to meeting you from the moment Seth brought Jake home."

"Meeting me?" Ben asked with a smile. "Just why would you want to meet me?"

"As I told Jake, I wanted to meet the man who took the time to make her into the sweet girl she is."

Ben smiled.

"Come and sit down," he invited, brushing off a chair for Charlotte. She did so, then watched as Benjamin again turned to Jake. "And where is young Seth? Didn't he come with you?"

"He's not in New Orleans, Grandpa," Jake began. She began to relate all that had happened since she and Seth had left the boat.

"Travis Sherman," Ben mused. "Seems to me I've heard a few stories about him."

"You know Travis Sherman?" Charlotte questioned.

"Well, not exactly," Ben confessed. "But I've heard a lot about him, and I know some gentlemen who've . . . ah . . . done business with him."

"That doesn't sound so favorable," Charlotte said, her gaze holding Ben's.

"Is Mr. Sherman a friend of yours?"

"Hardly," Charlotte responded dryly.

"Then the truth is, it's not too favorable. The man's a sly fox I wouldn't trust."

"I see."

"Miss McNeil, I'm right pleased you came to pay me a visit and that you brought my girl," Ben declared.

"Seems to me, Mr. Barde"—Charlotte smiled—"that no family should be separated. We look forward to your coming to visit us also. Jake has missed you, I'm sure, so you must come as often as you can."

"I don't think that would be very wise," Ben said gently.

"Grandpa! Don't you want to come and see me?"

Jake went to his side and knelt beside him, and Ben reached out to place a hand on her cheek. His smile was patient.

"Jake girl," he said quietly, "this is your chance to be something special. People will look at you and smile and say what a lovely lady Charlotte McNeil's ward is. You can go so far, be so much. But"—he paused as if searching for words—"what are people going to say if they see this old fisherman hanging around? They're going to say, well maybe that girl's not a lady at all. No, Jake. Your old grandpa's not going to spoil things for you by being a weight around your neck. No. You go and be what you need to be, and I'll stay here where I belong."

Jake gazed at her grandfather for several moments. Then she stood and turned to face Charlotte.

"Aunt Charlotte," she said softly, "you can go back home alone. I won't be returning with you. Tell Seth when he comes back that he can find me here if he wants to talk to me."

"Now just a darn minute, girl!" Ben rose abruptly to his feet. "You can't do that. This is the chance of your life. You can't throw it aside!"

"Grandpa," Jake said softly, "you're my family. You've given me all the love I've ever known. Do you want me to be the kind of person who would give up those who had loved and cared for her just to have pretty clothes and sweet-smelling perfume? Well, I won't. I love you, Grandpa, and if you won't be a part of my life up there, then I won't be there. There is no choice when it comes to you or being a lady."

Ben's eyes glowed and they were suspiciously moist. He reached out and drew Jake into his arms.

"All right, girl," he choked out. "If you want to invite me again . . . well I guess I'll come."

"Come soon, Grandpa, please, I want to show you so much. I can read, Grandpa . . . well almost. I get stuck on some big words, but I'm pretty good. And I'm learning to ride a horse! Oh, come soon, Grandpa!"

"I will, child. I will."

"I extend an invitation to come and see us at any time you choose, Mr. Barde." Charlotte smiled.

"The name is Ben, Miss McNeil." He chuckled. "I

guess if I'm going to be around some, you might just call me by my name."

Charlotte rose from her chair, a warm smile lighting her eyes. "Then you must also call me Charlotte, for I do believe we are going to be good friends."

"I wouldn't doubt it. Seems my girl wouldn't have it any other way."

They all laughed, and then they spent the balance of the afternoon talking of both the past and the future.

The words Charlotte had spoken when they had left resounded in Jake's ears as she dressed for the afternoon party to which Ben had been invited.

My dear Jake, there is nothing more in this world that I or anyone else can teach you. What you did today has proven to me that Seth was right about you from the beginning. You are a lady, and at this moment I couldn't be prouder of you if you were my own child. Come, Jake, let's go home.

Now Jake gazed at herself in the mirror and then drew herself erect, feeling a pride she had never known before.

"Seth," she whispered softly. He was the only person she wanted to look at her. It was his approval she needed to make her world complete. To Jake, Seth was a knight in armor who had rescued her and taken her to his castle to live like the princesses in the fairy tales Charlotte had let her read.

Jake knew nothing of love. She just wanted Seth to know he had chosen well and had not made a mistake.

Chapter 29

Catalina stirred and wakened very early. The sun had not risen so the room was filled with dark shadows and vague light. But the birds had begun to sing an early medley, and a soft breeze rustled the curtains at the window, bringing a fresh scent into the room.

She lay very still as she savored the sense of security she felt at being encircled by Marc's strong arm. Her head lay against his shoulder, and she could hear the steady solid beat of his heart.

She wanted to hold back time, to keep the day from coming. She wanted to enjoy this contented peace for just a while longer. Her arm crept around him and she drew closer to his warmth.

She would give everything just to hear him tell her that he loved her, to know that he wanted to change their situation from its temporary status to a permanent one. But she feared that would not be. She had agreed to be his mistress, and she now wondered if it would not end there. He might return the *Belle* to her and walk away . . . but if he did he would take more of her with him than he would ever know.

The game would begin again when he awoke, but for now she could dream and hope that the night they had just shared had proved to him that they shared something that was bigger than all their battles.

Catalina had no way of knowing that Marc had wakened long before she had, and was fighting a battle of which she was completely unaware. Nothing seemed to be following the pattern of his well-set plans.

He searched for an explanation for the guilt he felt. He had meant to bring Catalina Carrington to her knees, to make her feel the shame he had known when people had enjoyed the Garrisons' fall from the heights.

Now was the time. He could take Catalina to a place in Natchez-under-the-hill and leave her, knowing she would experience destruction beyond belief. Why was he reluctant to even move, to break the feeling that pervaded him as her sensuous body lay curled close to his.

He could still taste the sweetness of her lips as they'd sought his with an urgency that had, at first, startled him. But her giving passion had overwhelmed and captured him. He was not yet ready to let go of the delightful pleasures she offered, he decided, totally denying that he would never be ready to let her go.

But she wanted only her precious boat—the *Belle* was the only hold he had on her. He gave no thought to the hold she had on him, telling himself that she was cold and devious like all the Carringtons. He had reached out to hurt them—through the *Belle* and the Carrington wealth.

Nonetheless, he knew the trip from Natchez to Memphis would be a delight, for she would still be his. But at the end of it, he would have to decide to fulfill his plan for her . . . or to give her back the *Belle* and let her go. He found both alternatives too difficult to think about, so he postponed making the decision. After all, the brothels in Memphis were as ugly and dirty as the ones in Natchez-under-the-hill.

Since he was caught in thought, it was some time

before Marc sensed that Catalina was awake. When he did, he brushed his cheek lightly against Catalina's tousled hair and drew her closer to him, searching again for resistance he could shatter. But he found none as slim arms encircled him and soft lips brushed the flesh of his throat.

"Good morning," he murmured, and Catalina raised her eyes to his. Her soft mouth was curved in a half-smile, and her eyes were warm and inviting.

He bent his head to kiss her moist parted lips, leisurely and gently. The sheer pleasure of the night before seemed to blossom again at this heated renewal of contact, and again he was amazed that no matter how many times he possessed her, he still wanted her. Of course, he assured himself, by the time they reached Memphis he would have tired of her. The sensual intoxication of her passion would have dissipated and he would be capable of leaving her . . . of forgetting her. . . . But that was Memphis. Now she was here, warm and responsive.

"Marc?"

"Umm," he murmured, as his lips traced a pattern of feather-light kisses along her throat and shoulders.

"Do . . . do we leave for the *Belle* this morning?" Her eyes were half-closed as the warmth of his body and the touch of his hands roused her senses.

"We won't leave until late tonight. We have a lot of time," he whispered, his hands becoming intent on seeking sensitive places. He stimulated her until the blood raced in her veins and all thought was pushed from her mind.

She wanted so desperately to speak of her love, to tell him that she would go with him anywhere, live whatever kind of life he chose. But she knew the danger of doing this.

He would laugh, would tell her in so many ways that

she was only another conquest, that he had defeated her. No, she could not say the words, nor could she expect to hear them. But she could enjoy the amazing brilliance of their passion, hold the memory of it when he returned the *Belle* to her and walked out of her life.

Although logic told her the futility of her love for Marc, her body answered the call of his, and she was soon possessed by a wild and overpowering need that chained her to him with fetters of pleasure.

He kissed her until her senses swirled. His hands were caressing, gentle. Then he sought to arouse in her a heated need that matched his.

"Marc," she gasped, "it's . . . it's morning."

"Making love in the daylight can be exciting." Marc chuckled. "Besides, I like to look into your eyes when you lose control. Do you know your eyes change color?" he teased, enjoying the flush that tinged her cheeks. "You're an exciting woman, Cat, and our time is too short to waste," he added. Then he silenced her resistance with a searing kiss. He heard her moan softly as he drew her beneath him and entered her, moving with sure hard strokes meant to drive them both beyond thoughts of tomorrow.

Lorelei had requested that breakfast be served on the terrace, for it offered bright sunshine and a breath-taking view of the river.

She sat there now, sipping tea and waiting patiently for Marc and Catalina to appear. Her mood was cheerful, for Lorelei was completely convinced that whether he knew it or not Marc was captivated by Catalina. That pleased Marc's sister immensely. She had always been against what Marc intended; she liked Catalina and couldn't place any of the responsibility for their past problems at her door.

She was almost ready to go ahead and eat, when the sound of voices made her turn to look back at the house just in time to see Marc and Catalina approaching.

How perfect they look together, Lorelei thought. She wondered if either of them realized how they looked when their eyes met, knew that they laughed as lovers do. She imagined both would vehemently deny such behavior.

"Good morning," she called.

"Good morning," Catalina responded. "What a lovely place to have breakfast. Why, you can see for miles, and what a lovely view."

"Isn't it though?" Marc responded. "I've always enjoyed it."

Lorelei noted that Catalina's smile became strained as she turned to Marc. "You've been here often?" she questioned, trying to keep her voice conversational.

Lorelei enjoyed Marc's discomfort. He deserved to be caught in his web of lies. "Well, not often enough, but I've been here a time or two."

Marc was deliberately allowing Catalina to imagine what he might have done in this house, with Lorelei . . . or other women.

If Lorelei hadn't been certain that Catalina was in love with Marc before, she was now, and her annoyance grew. It didn't take Marc long to realize it.

"Right after breakfast I'm going to take Catalina on a tour of . . . your property and the rest of the town," he said quickly. "We'll have to leave right after dinner tonight."

"So soon, Marc?" Lorelei taunted, watching the flicker of anger in his eyes.

"I'm afraid so, Lorelei."

"That's a shame," Lorelei said with deceptive regret. "I had so many things to talk about with

Catalina. Maybe you'll come back on your trip downriver."

"I doubt it," Marc said stiffly, wishing he could throttle Lorelei.

"Oh, Catalina"—Lorelei fluttered and Marc glowered—"convince him to stop on the way back. Why"—she looked at Marc innocently—"I have a feeling we could be such friends . . . almost sisters." She smiled pleasantly.

Catalina looked from Lorelei to Marc, sensing something between the pair. Whatever it was it didn't please Marc too well, and he ate very little for breakfast, then hustled her to a carriage.

They rode slowly through upper Natchez. This part of town was obviously occupied by the rich and elegant. Its mansions were impressive. Catalina was taken by the graceful beauty of Belle Grove, a beautiful Greek revival mansion and a prime example of plantation living on a grand scale. It was framed by graceful trees, and its great green porticoes were hung with thousands of lights which shone far out over the river. Catalina listened while Marc told stories of the wondrous parties and feasts held there.

As they passed plantation after plantation—Belair Plantation followed Belle Grove—Catalina became more and more intrigued by Marc's voice. It had warm affection in it, as if he felt a great love for this area, as if he knew it as he knew no other.

Questions arose in Catalina's mind, but she knew Marc would never answer them. He kept his past shrouded in darkness. He had no intention of letting her penetrate it, and she knew that.

As they passed a particularly beautiful mansion, Cat asked about it.

"It belongs to Simon Gere," Marc said, offering no

other explanation.

"Simon Geŕe? Do you know him well?"

"He is somewhat of a shady character. Most inhabitants of Natchez attend his parties, but no one questions his dealings. He gives elaborate affairs. Married a girl from New Orleans, and they have three sons. One is my age and the others are a little younger."

"Are they friendly with Lorelei?"

"Hardly," Marc retorted shortly. He had no intention of elaborating on the mansion of Simon Geŕe.

It occurred to Catalina that Marc's background must be interesting, for he seemed to have touched on all walks of life, from the depths of Natchez-under-the-hill to the heights of society in upper Natchez.

She sighed. Marc did not want her in his present or his future, and most assuredly he did not want her in his past; yet she felt it contained a puzzle she should understand. But the solid wall of his resistance forbade her entrance. How could she ever reach Marc's heart when he held it in the secret caverns of his mind, refusing to share anything with her.

She knew the key to his behavior lay somewhere in his past. That key would let her open the door between them. But Marc was careful to keep it from her.

Catalina turned to the rare beauty of upper Natchez, and they made an extensive tour of it before returning to Lorelei's home for a quiet dinner.

It was late afternoon when China received a message and immediately made ready to go back into town, cautioning Shawna to remain in her cabin until she or Marc returned. Her departure was watched by a smugly smiling Travis and Charlene, who expected Marc and Catalina to return soon. They were quite pleased that China would not be present to disrupt their plans. Indeed, they had been searching for a way to temporarily rid themselves of her, but she was doing it for them.

"So, Charlene"—Travis smiled—"we can put our plan in motion as soon as Marc and Catalina appear. We're supposed to sail in about two hours, so I expect they'll come aboard at any moment."

"Marc will be on time, and I'm sure Nina will be too," Charlene replied. "She can't wait to pay back both of them."

"Well, she should have everything her way."

"And you should have things your way, too. You'll have the girl and her money, and you'll be rid of Marc."

"And Marc will be left with some bad memories of the deceptiveness of women."

They laughed again as they watched China's carriage disappear into Natchez-under-the-hill. Neither of them gave much consideration to the message she had received or to where she was going. They were too glad to have her out of the way.

Travis watched the dock from a spot in which those arriving in carriages would not see him. Timing was of the utmost importance now, and he knew that Marc was clever enough to sense something if given a moment to react.

A carriage drew to a halt, and Marc stepped down, then turned to help Catalina. Just as Catalina stood beside him a young boy came toward them.

"Mr. Copeland?"

"Yes," Marc replied, as he turned to look down at the boy.

"I have a message from a lady."

Marc was surprised, and Catalina pressed her lips together and turned away so Marc could not see the hurt in her eyes. She could not allow him to know that his affairs with other women touched her in any way.

"Lady? What lady?"

"A Miss China, suh, she asked me to run and find you."

"Is she in trouble?" Marc was alarmed.

"No, suh. She ain't in trouble. She just said for you to come right away. She has something real important for you to see. She says hurry. It's real important."

Marc knew China would never send for him in this way unless the matter was urgent.

"Cat, go aboard. I'll go see what China wants. Will you be all right? I'll be back in an hour."

"I'll be fine."

"Good."

As Catalina left him and walked up the gangplank, Marc stood for a moment, watching her and again experiencing the strange feeling of loss he always felt when she was no longer beside him. Then he turned and got back into the carriage, motioning the boy to join him. Within moments, the carriage had disappeared.

Catalina went directly to the cabin she shared with Marc. She moved slowly, as if she were weighted down by the thoughts that plagued her.

She felt that Marc would walk away from her as easily for another woman as for China. Closing the door behind her, she stood in the center of the cabin. Its emptiness gave her a leaden feeling.

She had tried, she had wanted him to love her, to put away their battles and share a life together. But now her dreadful thoughts made her see the truth. Marc did not love her, nor would he. She had played the game . . . and she had lost. She had to face an uncertain future without him, and she would never be the same once he had left her.

Could she spend the days and nights with him for the balance of the trip to Memphis in return for the *Belle?* She would have to, for the *Belle* was all she would have—the *Belle* and memories of what might have been.

Marc's carriage stopped before a house he knew well. He was puzzled, for it was not a house China would frequent. But he walked up the steps and knocked.

The door was opened by a woman who, at one time, must have been pretty. Now she was slatternly and disheveled. Her painted lips widened in a smile, and her eyes raked him appreciatively.

"Well," she said suggestively, "she said ya was a handsome one. She sure was right."

"Is China here? What's the problem, where is she?" Marc replied, ignoring her rapacious gaze.

"She was here. She said she had to do somethin' and she would be right back. You wuz to wait for her. It's real important that ya do. She said she could tell ya somethin' you have to know."

The last thing Marc wanted to do was spend time with this creature, but if China felt it essential, he would wait. He walked into a hovel.

Catalina waited patiently, but as time ticked slowly by she couldn't stop thinking that Marc had put her from his mind to attend to things he considered more important . . . perhaps even to see another woman. At that thought she became depressed. Perhaps it would be better to admit defeat and go home without the *Belle*. Travis would escort her. Perhaps Seth had returned since Marc had continually protested that he didn't know where Seth was. After all Seth had never been the most predictable of persons.

She sighed deeply, and tried to imagine a future

without Marc in it. How had she come so far from her goals? How had she let herself be brought to the point where she would sacrifice her pride and a promising life for a man who cared nothing for her, a man who would discard her as he had many other women. Hadn't she seen an example of that when Nina had been set aside?

But Catalina answered her questions as fast as they formed. She had fallen in love with Marc, and as a result she had put herself in this position.

Catalina Carrington, who had never vied for the favors of any man, now trembled at the thought that the one man she wanted didn't want her. Could she still win him? Before they reached Memphis, could she convince him that they could have a world of love together?

She pictured the way Marc's green eyes grew warm, yet faintly puzzled when he looked at her, the way they crinkled at the corners when he laughed. She could feel the touch of his hard mouth against hers, sense the masculine scent of him pervading the cabin.

My God, she thought wildly, will I ever be able to forget him? To wipe the taste of him from my lips or the feel of him from my body? At this moment these were thoughts she could hardly entertain.

She stood again and began to pace the floor, seeking some way to ease her anxiety. Finally she decided that when he returned, she would tell him the truth, would declare how she felt and then face staying on his terms or finding her way back to New Orleans alone to face whatever the future offered her . . . without Marc.

She shivered with expectancy. When she told him she was in love with him, would he laugh and deride her for being so foolishly easy? Would he force her to complete their bargain, give her more enchanting nights, then destroy her world by leaving? But she had no other choice. For her own peace of mind, she must tell him.

She walked over to the bed and sat upon it. The night had deepened so she lit the oil lantern, flooding the cabin with mellow gold light.

But the cabin felt emptier than it had before. If only Marc would return . . . If only they could face the truth so she would not have to live with uncertainty any longer.

Someone came down the passageway, and Catalina leapt to her feet. The person approaching stopped before her door.

"Marc," she breathed softly.

But when the door swung open, Nina walked in, a defiant and victorious smile on her face.

"I'm afraid I have some news for you."

"Where's Marc?"

"He's chosen to stay ashore until you vacate his cabin. You see . . . he's asked me to move back in. It seems he's tired of you and he finds it time to make changes. He'd like you to leave with your friend. Mr. Sherman is waiting for you in his cabin. I'm sure if you ask him nicely he'll be pleased to take you back to his bed—at least until you get back home."

"I don't believe you," Catalina gasped.

Nina shrugged. "Go ask Travis yourself. My baggage is being brought here, so I'll just have to toss yours into the passage." Nina laughed. "Like a stray cat, you'll just have to find a nook somewhere."

Catalina was stunned momentarily, but at the sound of Nina's soft laughter her pride returned and she walked from the room. Nina slammed the door, very solidly and very finally, behind her.

Chapter 30

Travis stood just within his stateroom listening for Catalina's approach, sure that in her defeat she would come to him. But it had been over a half-hour since Nina had gone to Catalina's cabin to break the news as brutally as she could.

All had been arranged, and he was certain that Catalina would be so devastated, he would be able to persuade her that to save her family's reputation and hers they should immediately marry. That way they could tell everyone at home that they had eloped.

Now his uncertainty was growing. Cat had had more than enough time. He opened the door and looked down the passageway, but no one was in sight. Going rapidly to Catalina's cabin, he listened for some confrontation between Nina and Cat . . . but the cabin was silent.

Finally he opened the door to find in the cabin only a very pleased Nina.

"Where did Catalina go?" he asked.

"Go? I thought she'd come to you. I told her exactly what we'd planned."

"Well she didn't. Are some of our men on the docks?"

"Yes."

"Go down and tell them to grab her if she leaves the

boat. We'll take her to Belle's."

"What are you going to do?"

"I'll look around. She can't be too far away. One way or the other we'll find her and finish what we started."

Nina and Travis left the cabin both intent on seeing through their plan.

Cat had stood in frozen disbelief, Nina's words flooding her mind with excruciating pain. Her logic told her that Nina could only be telling the truth, but her heart, her senses, and her very disobedient body told her the woman lied. But if so, where was Marc?

She fought a battle in the quiet hallway. She could deny all things except the fact that she loved Marc and was not going to let him push her away without explanation. If he didn't want to face her, that was because he felt guilty. She would have to make him look into her eyes and tell her why he had so suddenly denied a bargain she had lived up to.

China! China would give her honest answers, she thought, and China would know where Marc had gone. It did not even occur to her to go to Travis. She made her way quickly to China's cabin and knocked. There was no response so she knocked again.

Inside the cabin, Shawna stirred and came up from dream-filled slumber. At first she did not pay attention to the persistent knock on the door. China had a key, and no one else would come to her cabin. But finally, struggling against her fear, she climbed from the bed.

Opening the door slightly, Shawna saw Catalina, smiled, and opened it wide.

"Catalina, how nice to see you. Come in."

Catalina quickly stepped inside, expecting to see China within. She was momentarily silenced by her absence.

"Shawna, where's China?" she said at last.

"China? Oh, China is in town."

"In town! I thought women didn't run around Natchez-under-the-hill without escorts."

"They don't, but nobody would hurt China. They know Marc would hurt them back . . . he'd hurt them real bad."

"Shawna, Marc has gone into Natchez-under-the-hill and I've got to find him." Catalina was desperate.

"Find Marc? Why? He'll come back."

"Shawna"—Catalina tried to calm herself—"I can't explain, but I've got to find Marc and to do that I've got to find China first. So please, Shawna, tell me where I can find China."

Shawna's eyes widened. "But you can't go into Natchez-under-the-hill alone! Marc would be ever so mad—you can't."

"I have to. I can't stay here."

"But"—Shawna was near tears—"you'll be hurt. There're so many bad people there. You don't know how bad they are. You just can't go alone."

"This is important, Shawna. If I don't find China and Marc, then I have to stay here when the *Belle* leaves."

"Stay here," Shawna cried. She, of all people, knew the terrors that could befall Catalina in Natchez-under-the-hill. No woman could remain there alone and survive.

Shawna trembled with fear, but her profound ability to love began to battle that fear. She knew where China might be. She blinked tears from her wide gray eyes.

"I'll go with you," she whispered raggedly. "I can find China. I can take you to her."

Catalina was aware of the sacrifice Shawna was making, but she knew she could not find China alone.

"We'll take a closed carriage, Shawna. Nobody will

384

know us. We'll keep hoods over our faces so no one can tell."

"You don't know the people of this town," Shawna said solemnly. "They make it a point to know everything."

"We need a man—some kind of a guard," Catalina mused. Then her face brightened. "Jacob! Jacob is big enough to protect the entire boat. Come on, let's go below and ask Jacob to go with us."

Now Shawna brightened again. She could control some of her fear if she had someone like Jacob along. She nodded. They took two dark cloaks with hoods from a cupboard and left the cabin to go down and talk to Jacob.

Jacob, stripped to the waist, his huge body glistening with sweat, was working diligently in the hold of the boat.

His eyes widened with surprise when he saw the two women, and they widened even more when he heard the words they spoke.

"Wha fo' yo wants ta go inta a city lik dat one be. Yo kin gets yoself awful hurt in dere. Miz Cat, yo'all jus' can't do dat," he protested.

Catalina sensed the big man's vulnerability, and she hated to use it against him. She promised herself she'd give him a profound apology and a nice gift at a later time. Now she needed him.

"Jacob, if you won't go along," she said gently but very firmly, "Shawna and I will go alone."

Jacob looked both confused and pained. He couldn't let them be hurt or Marc would be angry, yet he couldn't stop them for they could easily slip away. No, he couldn't let them go into a city like Natchez-under-the-hill alone.

"All right, Miz Cat . . . Miz Shawna. I goes wit yo, but yo'all are askin' for trouble. Yassuh, yo'all is askin' for trouble and Mister Marc is goin' to be powerful mad."

"Don't worry, Jacob. I intend for Marc to know it was all my idea and you only agreed to go to protect us."

"Yessum," Jacob agreed glumly, for he doubted that Marc was going to listen to explanations.

Jacob dried off his sweaty skin, then put on his shirt and a ragged jacket before the three of them walked onto the deck. The night was dark, the only lights being the few on the boat, and the dock was still as they descended the gangplank as quietly as possible.

On the dock, Jacob turned to both heavily cloaked women. "Yo'all stands right here 'til I gets a carriage. It'll only take me a minute or two. Don't move, and if anybody cums yo doan knows, yo'all runs up de gangplank. Yo hears me?"

"Yes, Jacob," Catalina said quickly. "We understand." She would have said anything to pacify him, but she had no intention of reboarding the boat until China led her to Marc and she heard the truth from him. If what Nina said was true, she would never board the *Belle* again.

Jacob was only gone for a few minutes, but they seemed like hours to the two women.

Neither of them knew that Nina stood beside Travis on the shadowy deck above them, both smiling. Very soon they would be rid of Catalina, and it bothered them not at all that the innocent Shawna and Jacob would be hurt as well.

The carriage appeared phantomlike from the mist-filled darkness. It stopped before them and the door swung open. The women couldn't see into the interior, but neither of them expected anyone but Jacob.

Catalina pushed Shawna before her and paid little

attention to the inarticulate sound she made. Then, as Catalina gripped the side of the carriage to enter, a hand reached out, gripped her arm, and jerked her forcefully into the equipage. She landed on a man's lap, and he held her in a grip of iron. Catalina got out a half-scream before a hand closed over her mouth to stifle all sound. Then the carriage moved forward with a jolt, and was soon rattling through the streets.

In the dim light within, Catalina could make out Shawna huddled in wide-eyed terror next to a completely unconscious Jacob. From the look of Jacob, Catalina knew he had been beaten severely before he'd been tossed into the carriage. She could imagine the force it had taken to overcome him.

As the carriage moved on through the night, Catalina cried soundlessly because of the rough man who held her. Her misery was enhanced by her awareness of Shawna's utter terror and Jacob's unconsciousness, for she blamed herself for their situation.

Marc did not like waiting, and his dissatisfaction was enhanced by the brazen creature who sat before him, her legs stretched out before her and a drink in her hand. She wore a thin wrap that revealed an overused and dissipated body.

She had offered him a drink at first. He had refused it, and he had ignored her other blatant offers.

He could not help but compare her faded looks with the unique charms of Catalina, nor could he help but realize that this was what he had intended to do to Cat. This was the kind of future he had planned for her. That violent and ugly truth came to him, and another bitter truth followed. He never could have done it. He knew that now. He loved her. The realization exploded

387

brilliantly within him. He loved her and he didn't want to lose her.

He sat in remote silence, unaware of the close scrutiny of the woman. Her job was to hold him here as long as she could. She found the idea pleasant. A tussle on the sheets with this handsome buck would be a pleasure, and besides, she was being well paid.

Marc's attention was drawn to her as she rose, hand on hip, a smile on her face. She walked closer.

"What did China say to you? Where has she gone and why does she want me to wait here?" he demanded.

"I dunno," she replied. "She only said fer ya ta stay until she cum. That it wuz important to both of ya."

"Just how long did she have in mind for me to sit and wait? I've a boat set to leave for Memphis in less than half an hour."

"What's yer rush?" She laughed softly. "I could make the time go easier for ya."

The more flirtatious she became, the more Marc realized what he had nearly condemned Catalina to. Feeling stifled, he decided he could stand to wait no longer. He would return to the boat and tell Cat the truth. Then he would ask her to stay with him. He prayed that the truth would set him free and give him Cat.

"I can't wait here any longer," he said, abruptly pushing past her. "Tell China that she'll find me with Catalina on the *Belle*. Whatever she has to say, she can tell me there."

"But wait! I . . ."

He took several gold coins from his pocket and placed them on the table. Then he turned and left.

China returned to the boat moments after Catalina and Shawna had gone. She had never thought they

388

would do such a thing. The idea that Shawna would leave the boat was so remote she hadn't even considered it. When she found Shawna's cabin empty, she decided the young woman was with Catalina.

China needed to rest and to reassemble the information she had accumulated, and since the *Belle* would be leaving soon, she lay down on her bed and fell into a restless sleep.

The door to the carriage swung open and Marc's feet touched the ground before it came to a halt. He tossed the driver a coin and ran up the gangplank.

Making his way to China's cabin, he entered it and found it dark. He made out her form on the bed and smiled. If she was asleep he would explain to her tomorrow. He was more than sure his change of plan would make her happy.

He would go and find Cat. He wanted to feel her in his arms again, wanted to clear up the things that stood between them. In his urgent need to get to her, he threw aside caution. His every thought was of Catalina—beautiful, loving Catalina.

He didn't bother to knock. Smiling to himself, he hoped to find her in a warm bed for he fully intended to join her there.

He swung the door open, his smile fading rapidly when he came face to face with Nina. For a moment he was surprised into speechlessness. Then he crossed the room in a few quick strides and gripped her arm in a fierce hold.

"What the hell are you doing here, and where's Cat?"

"Your precious Cat left you."

"What are you talking about?" he demanded, his heart pounding fiercely.

"She's gone . . . but she left a message for you."

"With you?" he asked doubtfully.

"Why not?" Nina laughed. "She said she thought you might need another bed partner since she was tired of you and that you can do whatever you like now. She intends to marry Mr. Travis Sherman. In fact, by this time I'm sure those two are having a very warm rendezvous."

"Where?" Marc said through gritted teeth.

"Now how would I know what those lovers planned or where they're . . . enjoying themselves. Marc"—her voice softened—"I only came because I thought you might want a friend to—"

Marc shook her violently, and she cried out.

"I said where did they go?"

"I don't know. Marc, you're hurting me."

Marc thrust her from him and stood immobile. It couldn't be. She was not the kind . . . but was she? Was she really the deceitful creature he had first thought her to be? Had he set a trap for her only to fall into its velvet teeth himself? He spun about and walked out, leaving the door open.

Nina remained in the cabin, certain that Marc would return when he had finally exhausted all efforts to find his love. She need only wait.

Marc strode purposefully down the passageway, his mind spinning. He pushed open the door of China's cabin and entered, the noise he made abruptly waking China.

"Marc!"

"Get up," he half snarled. He had never used this tone with her before.

She swung her feet to the floor and moved quickly to his side.

"What is it, Marc? What happened?"

"Cat's gone and Nina's in her cabin." He proceeded to explain all that had happened, ending with "And Nina would have me believe that Cat, to save her reputation, has gone off to marry Travis Sherman."

"I don't believe it," China said quietly.

"Why?"

"I went ashore today to see if I could find out whether Charlene, Nina, and Willie had joined forces against you. I learned they had met and been together most of the day. I'm sure they had something to do with this."

"And Travis?"

"I don't know."

"Would she go to him?" Marc's voice was thick with pain.

China wanted to know his true feelings. She had hoped for this too long not to see it be true.

"What does it really matter, Marc? You have put her where you always wanted her to be. Now she will pay. Let her go. You know Travis is what she deserves. He probably won't marry her and she will drop to the bottom as you planned."

He turned to her, his eyes filled with pain and anger. "I can't, China." He groaned. "I can't let her go."

"Why?" she prodded. "You're finished with her, aren't you? You've used her . . . now throw her away."

"Throw her away." He half laughed, half groaned. "I think," he added quietly, "I could throw away my life more easily." He went to China who stood without speaking. "I love her. I'm caught in my own trap, and there's no way out. I love her and I can't let her go."

China's eyes filled with tears as she reached out to place both her hands on his arm. "I'm glad, Marc. I've wanted so long for you to see how futile and destructive this terrible vendetta has been. I watched, and I hoped you were falling in love with her."

"And so I did," he said bitterly, "only to have her turn the tables on me and walk out of my life as if I meant nothing."

"What are you going to do?"

"Find her," he declared firmly.

"You know in Natchez-under-the-hill that is well near impossible."

"This time, China, it's important that we do the impossible. You see I can't let her be lost in that quagmire out there. I brought her here to hurt her, but I couldn't have lived with myself if I'd condemned her to that. I love her . . . and I have to find her. I may have to tear this town apart, but I'll damned well accomplish two things. I'll find Cat . . . and I'll kill Travis Sherman."

Chapter 31

Catalina was grateful when the carriage came to a halt. The three men that held them prisoner and Shawna's shivering terror were stretching her nerves to the breaking point. Her fear that Marc had, indeed, deserted her and so would not even look for her began to stir in her the same terror she saw in Shawna.

When the carriage halted, one man stayed behind to guard her and Shawna while the other two carried Jacob into a dark building that looked, from what Catalina could see, like a warehouse. She had no idea where she might be, only that she was somewhere in Natchez-under-the-hill.

Stories Marc had told her sent shivers of anxiety through her. There was only one reason why anyone would want to kidnap her, but why had they taken Jacob? Wouldn't they have left him behind, unless they felt Marc might follow and a living Jacob would join forces with him?

Another thought filled her with hope. If Marc would not search for her surely he would look for Shawna and Jacob. No matter what she might mean to him, Shawna and Jacob meant a great deal. He would search . . . but her heart darkened at the thought that he might not have done so had she been the only one taken.

When the two men returned, Shawna and Catalina were pulled roughly from the carriage and half dragged within the confines of the nearly dark warehouse. Thrust into a small room, they were left together. Jacob lay on the floor, his hands bound behind him and his ankles bound together. He was still unconscious.

Catalina ran to him at once and knelt beside him, her cold trembling fingers working at his bonds, but Shawna cowered silently in a corner. Catalina was afraid she had lost all contact with the world about her.

The three men returned before Jacob had been freed.

"Get up from there, girl, and let him be. We ain't goin' to untie him."

Reluctantly Catalina complied. Only then did she see the ropes the men carried in their hands.

The men dragged her to Shawna and tied them both securely. Then they left and the silence magnified the dark emptiness about them. Catalina closed her eyes, telling herself that Marc would be searching, if not for her, at least for the wide-eyed Shawna who sat beside her against the clammy wall.

To Catalina it seemed hours had passed before Jacob stirred and began to regain his consciousness. Shawna had remained totally silent and Catalina feared that she was escaping into a void from which she might never return.

Jacob groaned, tried to lift his hands to his aching head, and found them securely bound. At first he was disoriented; then the memory of what had happened rushed back to him and with a mumbled curse he pulled himself to a sitting position. He looked about him wildly, finally saw Catalina and Shawna tied and sitting against the wall across the room from him.

He groaned. Then, with a gathering of strength, and despite the pounding in his head, he worked his way across the floor until he sat, panting from the effort, near Catalina and Shawna.

"Miz Cat, yo all right?"

"I'm not hurt, Jacob, but I'm scared." She tried to laugh and failed.

"Miz Shawna," Jacob whispered, somewhat awed by Shawna's condition, "she gwan ta be all right?"

"I don't know," Catalina replied honestly.

"Wha' fo' dez men do such a thing? Mistah Marc, he gwan be fightin' mad. He sho' sets store in you and Miz Shawna. He gonna cum and gib dez gentlemens some trouble."

"I hope you're right, Jacob, but I've no idea how he'll ever find us . . . or how he'll get us out."

"Iffen I could get dez darn ropes off I'd beat their heads in fo' cauzin' Miz Shawna so much hurtin'. De po' girl done hab enough to handle already."

Their hands were bound behind them and Catalina wasn't sure she could do much to help, but she knew if Jacob were released, they might all have a better chance.

Before she could make any suggestions, however, the door opened and the three men returned. This time a shocked gasp escaped Cat as she looked up into the face of Travis Sherman.

Her fear fled in the face of the blazing rage that inflamed her.

"You!" she spat out. "I should have known. What is it you want, Travis?"

"You, my dear Cat." Travis laughed softly. "You and the very large fortune you have."

"You don't stand a chance. I would die before I would surrender myself or anything I have to you. When Marc finds you he's going to kill you."

"Over you?" Travis laughed aloud. "My dear Cat, Marc has no care for what happens to you. I've found out a lot about him since we came here. Do you have the remotest idea that this is what he planned for you right from the beginning?"

"I don't believe you! You're lying!"

"Am I? Well, let me tell you a little story about your beloved Marc. It seems Copeland isn't even his name, and he has a deep hatred for the Carringtons. All of this was just a little part of his vengeance. He planned to leave you here to warm a bed for the scum of Natchez-under-the-hill, in the vilest brothel he could find."

Cat wanted to lash out at him, to scream, to cry; but some inner sense told her he was only telling the truth. She did not know he would embroider it to suit his purposes.

"Let me explain something so you will have no doubts, my love," Travis said quietly. He knelt beside her and their eyes held. "He took your brother's boat on purpose. He enticed you on purpose . . . and he intends to destroy every Carrington. It seems, from what my friend Stanton told me, that your father and his had business dealings, and because your father forced him into bankruptcy, Marc's father committed suicide. So my dear, if you expect help from him, be assured that it will never come. In fact, he would take great pleasure in knowing you are suffering. It will be due to me that you don't, and one day we can repay his treachery."

Tears burned Catalina's cheeks as something within her crumbled. Could Marc have hated her and made love to her as he did . . . just to see her destroyed? Her mind was torn between disbelief of Marc's monumental treachery and vibrant distrust of Travis and all he said.

She clenched her jaw firmly. She would cry no more, nor would she beg Travis.

"Whatever it is you want from me, Travis, you will

never get it."

"Will I not?" He smiled. "My dear sweet Cat, you are soon to be my very happy bride and I shall see that we spend a long and happy life together."

"You are insane! I would never agree to marry you!"

"No? I'm going to leave you alone to reconsider while I go to upper Natchez and arrange for the wedding to be held at the plantation of some friends. I want all of society to see that wedding so you cannot deny it. After that, I shall keep a very close watch on you."

"Never. I'll die first!"

"Maybe you would." He grasped Shawna's hair and shook her so violently she cried out, as did Catalina. "But would you let her and your very large friend suffer? I won't have them killed. But for every moment you resist Shawna will pay with her body in the worst way you can imagine."

"You are a foul beast!"

"Now, Cat my love, is that any way to talk to the man who will soon be your warm and loving husband?" He lowered his voice suggestively, and his words were heavy with barely controlled passion. "I have waited a long time to possess you, sweet Cat, and make sure of one thing: I will consummate the marriage soon and very often. Decide. I'll be back soon."

He rose and walked away, and again they were left in the semidarkness. Cat was aware only of Shawna's muffled tears and uncontrolled shaking. With a sinking heart she realized she could not make Shawna suffer the unspeakable things Travis had threatened. If it was true that Marc had wanted this vengeance, then he would not help them.

She was suddenly aware that Jacob had been silent for a long time.

"Jacob?" she questioned.

"Ah's all right. Now I 'members whar I saw dat man befo'. He been cumin' ta Natchez a long time. He be good friends wif de Geŕe's. Dat man and Simon Geŕe, dey sho be sumpthin' bad. Yassah, Mistah Marc he sure gwan to kill that man one day . . . he sho is."

"I'm not so sure, Jacob," Catalina said bitterly.

Jacob turned to look closely at her. "Don' yo start believin' dat scum," he said. "Mistah Marc, he ain't like dat man say. He be comin' fo' yo and Miz Shawna. Dat man, he loves ya Miz Cat and doan yo go believin' nothin' else lessen ya asks Mistah Marc fo' de truth. Yo see, pretty quick he cum lookin'. He be gonna kill dat man. Lessen," Jacob added softly, "ah gets free. Iffen I does dat man sho bettah say his prayers to de lawd fo' ah'm shore gonna rip off his head fo' scarin' Miz Shawna like dat. Po' chile," he looked at Shawna who, tear stained and disheveled, was shaking like a leaf in a storm. Both Jacob and Catalina knew she was on the brink of insanity.

If Marc did come for them it would have to be soon, for Shawna could not suffer much longer. Catalina knew if she submitted to Travis, she could never again reach out to Marc. Yet, in the back of her mind, she feared Travis's words had been true.

When Travis left Catalina he took a carriage to upper Natchez and stopped it in front of one of the most luxurious mansions there—the home of Simon Geŕe and of his sons: Stanton, James, and Holland.

He rapped on the door and was admitted by a butler who took his hat and gloves. There was no need for the man to guide Travis to the library; he had been a guest here often.

When Stanton Geŕe and his father Simon rose to greet Travis, his satisfied smile told them of the success

398

of the plan they had laid together so many years before.

"So I take it you have the girl safely tucked away?" Stanton sneered.

"I do, in a place Marc Garrison will never find, at least until it's time to bring her here. By then it won't really matter what Garrison finds out. It will be too late."

"Well"—Simon chuckled evilly—"I think we must prepare for a wedding."

"Yes, and make sure only the right witnesses are invited. I don't want word to get to the Garrisons until it's over. I'll have a boat ready, and by the time Marc learns of this, Cat and I will be gone."

"Where do you intend to take her?"

"To Europe, of course. I have friends there who will keep her under control until I milk her family dry."

"Friends?" Simon leered. "Friends who might want a taste or two of your bride."

"They can have her. By then I'll be tired of her anyway. It's her wealth that's important to me. Her family will pay for a very long time."

"Marc Garrison is still not aware of how he's been duped into believing the Carringtons are responsible for his father's demise? I cannot believe he got back on his feet as he did, but there are still ways to destroy him and the rest of that family," Simon grated out, his voice thickened by his abiding hatred.

Travis knew Simon had hated Marc's father. That hatred had fit into his plans so he had nurtured it until it could be used.

"Marc knows nothing except that Cat chose to leave him here in Natchez. He will, of course, hate the Carringtons even more now. Who knows?" Travis laughed. "I may send her back to him one day—when I've finished with her."

"That should prove interesting," Stanton observed.

"Marc has walked to our music all this time. I expect at the final blow, when she is discarded a few years from now, he will see the truth."

"Oh, he may blame Catalina for what will ultimately happen to his friends."

"You plan to get rid of them?" Simon questioned.

"I don't see what other choice I have. They're a nuisance, and I only need them until Catalina is safely married and we're on our way."

"Marc Garrison," Simon said softly, his gaze introverted, as if he were seeing beyond that time and place to another. "I have finally evened the debt, finally seen them fall as I swore I would. Once we have finished him"—his voice became a malevolent whisper—"I will have his sister at my mercy. The Garrisons will be no more—no more."

The pall of oppressive hatred was so thick in the air that for a moment everyone was silent.

The entire plot that had enmeshed Catalina and Marc had been the product of the mental deterioration of Simon Gere. Because of old hatreds he was purposely destroying the lives of many.

Even Travis, degenerate that he had become, was speechless before the black power of Simon. For one heartbeat, one fragile moment, even he felt the touch of fear. This man had a blacker soul than any other he had known.

Travis had done many things in his life that needed to be hidden, like arranging for the murder of Seth Carrington, but he himself did not have the stomach or the courage to do them. Simon Gere did, and there was no limit to his evil. Travis suddenly was glad that he was going to take Catalina and be gone. He shuddered to think of what would happen to Marc and his friends.

* * *

Marc was frantic. As the night slowly eased into pale gray dawn, he returned to China's cabin only to find her in very nearly the same state. China, always his calming conscience, was in tears. That startled Marc out of his own hell for a minute.

He had spent the night turning Natchez-under-the-hill upside down, but at dawn there was no sign of Catalina. So he had returned, weary and spent, and for the first time in his life afraid.

Fear pierced him now as he looked into China's tear-stained face.

"Someone's found her," he said in an expressionless voice. "She's dead." He felt life draining from him like sand from an hourglass.

"No, Marc. I've heard nothing of Catalina. But after you rushed out I remembered something."

"What?"

"I thought she was supposed to be with Shawna. When I remembered . . . well I became frightened. I looked for Shawna. I've searched the boat from top to bottom—Shawna is gone and so is Jacob."

"Shawna would never leave the boat of her own free will!"

"I know," China said softly.

"And Jacob would not abandon his duties without telling me."

"I know that, too."

They looked at each other, horror dawning in them.

"They might have left here together, but only for one reason," he whispered raggedly.

"Catalina." China answered his fears. "They would both go to help her. If she was taken by someone instead of leaving on her own—"

"My God, it will kill Shawna."

"But she would have gone if she thought she had to."

"Yes, she would."

"And so would Jacob."

"I've got to find them," he said desperately, "but . . . I don't know where else to look. In Natchez-under-the-hill I get blank stares and negative answers."

Marc started toward the door.

"Where are you going?"

He turned, his face revealing both doubt and grim determination.

"If I have to rip this town to shreds, if I have to pound a few heads and pay a fortune in bribes—no matter what it takes—I'll find them. And whoever's got them had better move fast, because if one of them is hurt there won't be a place far enough from me."

"Marc."

He had turned away from her, but she could see the knuckles of his hands grow white as he clenched his hands in an attempt to regain control of himself.

"I've got to find her, China." His voice was soft. "I never told her . . ." He stopped and sucked in his breath. "I have to find her."

"I know, Marc, I know."

He turned to face her, his obvious grief making her shiver.

"Do you know, China," he said quietly, "if it hadn't been for me and my need for revenge, she wouldn't be where she is. She'd be safe in her own home. If something happens to her it might just as well happen to me. I think I can stand a whole lot of things . . . but not losing her, not losing her while she still doesn't know that I loved her—that what we shared was more important than anything else."

"But you've got help—me and your friends. You can't do it alone."

"There's so much I don't understand. Why would Shawna and Jacob go with her if she was running from me? She's never been in Natchez before, she told me so

402

herself. Where would she expect to run to? There's just too much that doesn't make sense. And I found no sign of Travis either. Just what kind of a hole did that snake find to crawl in? It's damn well hidden, and it's in Natchez-under-the-hill."

"Let us take a moment to think. We must plan what we will do, think of those who will help. You and I both know some well-placed money might just bring us some answers. Someone might have seen them." She went to him. "Marc, if it turns out that no one has seen any of them in Natchez-under-the-hill, then maybe you're looking in the wrong place. Maybe she's somewhere else."

Marc turned to look at her again, his eyes glittering green crystals as new hope brightened them.

Chapter 32

Jacob kept his eyes on Shawna who was lost in an intense nightmare. She tossed her head back and forth, as soft moans escaped lips drawn back in a grimace of pain. He did not know where her mind was, and her state terrified him. It also stirred his fury and his desire to take Shawna from this evil place. But he believed that Marc was the only one who could reach into the depths of hell to rescue her.

He looked at Cat, whose eyes were on Shawna. With a sinking heart, he saw the pity and fear in them. He knew that Cat would sacrifice her life for him and for Shawna, and he felt an overpowering need to help her. He gritted his teeth in frustration; he had never felt so helpless in his life. He strained against the bonds that held him, to no avail. So he decided to contain his fury and wait . . . wait for one slip, one mistake.

Cat sighed and tried again to move so she could keep her blood circulating. Cramped and sore, she closed her eyes and sought to hold on to her courage which had begun to fail. Tears came to her eyes, but she refused to surrender to them for she knew there was no way back if she did.

"Jacob?" she called softly.

"Yassum?"

"When . . . when Travis comes back I will tell him—"

"No! No, Miz Cat! Doan yo do dat! Doan yo let dat man hab his way. Yo gots ta hold on. Mistah Marc, he come."

"Jacob"—she sobbed—"I can't let her be hurt anymore; or you. I can't let them kill you. I've got to do something."

"Yo jus' hang on. Ah ain't afeered fo' me. I kin take whatever dey wants ta do. Doan do nuthin'.'"

"I can't, Jacob! I can't. Look at her. Don't you see she can't take much more of this?"

"Miz Cat, Miz Cat"—he groaned—"what's Mistah Marc gwine ta say iffen he comes an yo gone. He gonna skin me fo' sho' fo' lettin' yo'all get into dis mess."

She almost wept at his words. His hope in Marc had not waned. He still believed Marc would come.

She was about to assure him that Marc would not come for her, but before she could speak the door was flung open and Travis entered, accompanied by two other men.

Catalina watched him stride forward and kneel beside her, calmly ignoring both Jacob and Shawna.

"Well, Cat, I've given you adequate time to think my proposition over. You need only say the word, and once the wedding is over and we're on our way to sea, they'll be set free."

"How can I believe you?" she cried. "You lie. You'll kill them anyway."

"I'll let you write a letter and you can make sure it's delivered before we leave. That way your friends will be found."

She gazed into his eyes, her every sense screaming out a denial. But she had only to look at Jacob and Shawna to know she was defeated.

Travis knew the moment her decision was made, before she put it into words.

"All right," she whispered. "I'll do what you want."

"Very smart, Cat." He rose and turned to his men. "Make sure you're not seen. Get those two up to Gere's. Don't worry about her; I have my own carriage. I'll take her with me."

"No!" Catalina cried. "How do I know you're not going to kill them?"

"They'll be where you are. You'll see them before and after the ceremony."

Catalina protested no more. She watched as Jacob was hauled out. Then one of the men came back and pulled Shawna into his arms.

"Don't hurt her!" Catalina cried out.

Travis motioned to the man, who smiled and carried Shawna's inert form out. Then, turning to Cat, he knelt and cut the bonds on her ankles.

"I'm going to release you. Just remember who pays if you do anything foolish. I won't hesitate to kill Shawna and the black. Is that clear?"

She nodded, unable to put into words her intense anger. Travis smiled, then cut the ropes about her wrists.

For a moment she wanted to cry out from the pain as blood circulated anew in her hands and arms.

Travis put an arm about her waist and drew her against him.

"Ah, Cat, it's time you learned to whom you will belong. You made a very foolish mistake in believing Marc really wanted you. But I'll forgive you. You'll see. I intend to be a very devoted husband, and you'll soon forget him in my bed."

He bent his head and took her mouth in a kiss meant to subdue, ravaging her lips until he was satisfied she would resist no more. Then he looked at her, and she held his gaze.

"Take me wherever we're going. I want to see that Shawna is all right."

"Still the tigress, still fighting." He laughed. "But don't worry, soon . . . very soon, my sweet, you will lose your defiance."

He pulled her along beside him, out the door and into a carriage. Then they rode in silence for some time.

When the carriage door was opened and Travis urged Catalina out, she was shocked. She knew she was in upper Natchez, and she recognized the house Marc had pointed out to her. What was the name he had mentioned? Gere! Simon Gere. Why would a man of such great wealth be involved in such a thing as this? Surely not for money. What did he have to gain? She must see if she could find the answer . . . or some means to get help.

Travis took her through a side entrance and up a long flight of steps. When they came to a closed door, Catalina turned to him.

"Where are Jacob and Shawna? I want to see them."

"You'll see them within the hour. Now get inside before I lose my patience."

He pushed her into a remarkably beautiful room, then pulled the door shut. She heard a soft click and did not have to try the handle to know the door was locked.

She walked to the window and found it impossible to open. Then she returned to the bed and sat down to wait. Unless she saw Jacob and Shawna with her own eyes, she would not go along with Travis's devious plan.

She tried to figure out his ultimate goal, but she couldn't so she waited . . . and waited . . . and waited.

It was midafternoon and Catalina stood by the

window looking out. She wondered if Marc was searching for her. No matter how she fought it, the hope that he was refused to be extinguished. She closed her eyes and pressed her head against the glass. Vivid memories of love, of gentleness, of passion came to her. They were all she had.

She brushed away her tears and concentrated on the dreams she had once had, dreams now lost. But as the hours ticked by, Catalina's nerves became so taut that she began to pace the floor.

She spun about when she heard the key in the lock, in time to see Travis and an older man she did not know enter the room.

When the door was closed, Catalina stood in defiant silence, waiting for them to speak first. The older man watched her for a while, then laughed softly.

His laugh made Catalina's skin crawl, but she remained silent.

"My dear Miss Carrington, you are quite a lovely creature. I can see why Travis wants you so badly."

She remained silent, and again he uttered the same crackling laugh. "Still the proud lady. Well, I will be delighted to give you away at your wedding in the morning. Some people of reknown have been invited, but not the friends of your . . . ah . . . former love. I'm afraid he wouldn't enjoy the ceremony so we will just exclude him. In the meantime, please make yourself comfortable. Food will be brought to you and you need only ask if there is something you desire."

"I want to see Jacob and Shawna," she demanded.

"Ah yes . . . your two friends. They are just across the hall. Come, I'll let you spend a little time with them."

He motioned to her to precede him, and she tentatively moved past him. Then they crossed the hall and entered the room. Jacob was firmly bound to a chair, and Shawna lay on the bed, unbound, but extremely still.

Catalina's eyes darted to the old man, who smiled. "I gave her a light sedative. She will sleep until the wedding. Then, when you have sent your message, she and the black will be set free. We have no quarrel with them."

"And what quarrel do you have with me?" Catalina snapped, and was answered with a rumbling chuckle.

"Don't ask so many questions, Cat," Travis said. "Their safety is your only concern. Otherwise, do what we tell you and by tomorrow afternoon they will be free."

Catalina looked into Jacob's eyes and she saw his denial. When he shook his head, she only smiled encouragingly at him. "It's all right, Jacob," she said gently. "We have to get Shawna back to the *Belle,* you know that. She can't exist in the world. She's worth it, Jacob. She deserves that chance."

Travis and Simon exchanged satisfied looks; then Travis gripped Catalina's arm and forced her across the hall. Once more she was alone as the lock clicked softly behind her.

Jacob could not take his eyes from Shawna. She had been too still for too long. Even the mental battles she'd fought were better than this quietness.

As the late afternoon sun warmed the room, he again strained against the ropes that bound him, but they held despite his strength.

He was becoming desperate. He feared that Marc would never dream that they were being held in upper Natchez, and he knew that once Catalina was married to Travis and the pair was gone, the merciless old man with the reptilian eyes would not hesitate to dispose of them.

He sighed and struggled against the ropes, but they

refused to give. Again he turned his eyes on Shawna. He held his gaze steady, concentrating on her, willing her to waken.

Shawna swam in an inky darkness. She was safe there, safe from the evil laughter and tearing claws of the shadowy forms that brought pain.

But why was a force drawing her back? Back from warmth to coldness, back from peace to pain. She didn't want to go back, and resisted, but she could still feel the relentless pull.

Shawna's hands had been freed after she had been forced to drink the sleep-inducing drug. But even that was not enough to keep her unconscious. She stirred, then opened heavy lids.

The room had been left unlit, but the hazy white glow of moonlight now pervaded it.

At first she was completely disoriented. Then bits and pieces of what had occurred to her slowly returned.

Listlessly, she turned her head, and her sleepy eyes met Jacob's. He had gazed on her so long, concentrating his will on drawing her to wakefulness, that he didn't even notice her slight movement. It came as a shock to him that his intense regard had actually gotten through to Shawna.

She looked at him for long moments before his name came to her.

"Jacob?" she said softly.

Jacob's body jerked with tension. He was afraid, afraid she was too lost and fragile to obey him.

"Miz Shawna," he said gently, "how be yo feelin', chile?"

"I . . . I'm so tired, Jacob. I want to go to sleep."

"Miz Shawna, please," Jacob pleaded. "Yo gots to help me."

"Help you?" she said sluggishly. "Help you do what? . . . Where's Marc?"

"Marc said fo' me to wait here and yo'd help me, Miz Shawna. Now yo gots to do what I tell you, or Mistah Marc, he ain't gwan ta be pleased."

He hated to deceive her, but he had no choice. She might just go back to sleep, and if she did he was lost. He waited breathlessly to see what she would do.

Very slowly, she rose from the bed and walked to his side, then knelt by his chair.

"Why are your hands tied, Jacob?"

"Somebody's been playin' games wif me, girl." He tried to smile. "But I's gwan ta fool 'em. All yo have to do is untie my hands."

"Oh . . . a game." She smiled, a vacant smile, and reached toward the ropes that bound him.

He wanted to growl at her to hurry, but he knew that might destroy any chance he had for freedom—for himself, Shawna, and maybe Cat, if he could get to her.

Slowly, so slowly, she fumbled with the ropes, while Jacob gritted his teeth to keep his frazzled nerves under control. Just as slowly the ropes loosened.

Freeing his hands, Jacob quickly bent to untie his legs. Then he stood, waiting until circulation returned to his limbs.

"Miz Shawna, go back ta de bed whilst Ah checks ta see if dere's anyone in de hall."

Like a silent wraith, Shawna obediently crossed the dark room and sat on the bed.

Then Jacob went to the door. Quietly, he pressed his ear against it to see if anyone was on guard in the hall. He could hear nothing, but he knew he couldn't afford to make a mistake. He knelt to press his eye to the keyhole and was more than pleased that he had done so.

The hallway was guarded. Two men sat on low

411

chairs braced against the wall. They were both half-asleep, but Jacob knew he could not risk searching for Cat. He didn't even know how he could get away with Shawna.

He rose and went to the window. It had been sealed shut.

He examined the room, but not a glimmer of an idea came to him. He could think of no way to escape with Shawna, and he knew he would not leave without her.

He turned to her. She looked so utterly helpless, but she was the club held over Catalina's head. If he could manage to get Shawna away, Catalina would soon learn that they were no longer prisoners. Given her strength and courage, Jacob knew she could then resist until he could bring help.

He looked about him in desperation, while Shawna smiled the innocent smile of a child who doesn't understand a silly game.

Within her room, Cat sat, racking her brain to think of some way to assure herself that Shawna and Jacob would actually be set free. Not for a minute did she trust Travis or any of the others. Their word meant nothing to her, nor did the idea of sending a message. Any messenger could be bought.

Only one way was certain. She had to witness their release. Slowly, she devised a plan to do that. Lorelei Thatcher was her only hope. She would demand that Lorelei be present at the wedding, and that, when the ceremony was over, Jacob and Shawna be allowed to leave with her. That would assure their safety.

She knew someone would be appearing soon, so she might be assured that Jacob and Shawna were still alive . . . at least for tonight. In the morning, she would see them again. Then it would all be over, and Marc would have both Jacob and Shawna back.

She wanted to lie down on the bed and cry, but she could not afford the luxury of doing so. There was no doubt in her mind that her parents would pay well for her continued safety and for her release. But as far as the world would know, she would be Travis's legal wife, and she would only be freed by the sacrifice of the Carrington fortune.

Thoughts of her parents and of her beloved Aunt Charlotte brought fresh tears, and she could not bear her pain. With silent determination, she forced those thoughts from her mind, turning to her only source of comfort, memories of Marc. She welcomed them because they were helping her to survive. Even though she knew Marc had never loved her, still the memory of his gentle warmth was a shield against Travis.

Marc had not been untruthful. He had never said that he loved her. He had professed that she was his mistress, and a mistress was all he had wanted.

When Catalina heard the door being unlocked, she turned from the window.

Travis stood in the open doorway. "You wanted to check on your friends to see if they were all right."

"Yes."

"Then come with me."

He watched wary disbelief dance in her eyes. Then he chuckled softly. It was good to keep her off balance, uncertain. That way she would not be making foolish plans to escape.

She moved past him, aware of the scrutiny of the two guards in the hall. Even if she could get out of her room, she could not escape them.

Travis unlocked the door and permitted Catalina to stand on the threshold. He would not let her enter the room.

Jacob was tied securely to a chair and Shawna lay on

the bed deep in sleep.

"Satisfied?" Travis drew her from the doorway and again locked the door, slipping the key into his pocket. Then he pushed Catalina across the hall to her room. This time he entered and closed the door behind him. Cat turned to look at him, and the smile that touched his lips turned her heart cold.

Inside the room, Jacob breathed a ragged sigh of relief. "Dat wuz a close one," he muttered. When he had heard the movement in the hall, he had whispered to Shawna to return to the bed and pretend that she slept. It was, he had said patiently, all part of Marc's game.

Shawna had obeyed—after all, it was what Marc wanted—and Jacob had quickly wrapped the ropes about his ankles, and had put his hands behind him. If the guards were checking, he would look tied. If someone else was coming, he would be free to act, though he had no idea of what he could do against the force that must be in this house.

When Travis and Catalina stood in the doorway, rage shook Jacob. Travis looked so pleased, Catalina so despairing. When Travis closed and locked the door, Jacob knew that if Marc didn't kill Travis, he would.

Chapter 33

Travis stood just inside the door, his back braced against it and his arms folded across his chest. Catalina returned his gaze with as much control as she could manage. She had to catch her lip between her teeth to keep from expressing aloud her disgust and anger, but since the lives of Jacob and Shawna were in his hands, she could not afford to push him into doing them any harm.

Still, she would not let him crush her courage . . . or take advantage of her before the bargain was complete.

"You've no business here, Travis," she said stonily.

"Always the fighter, Cat. But you can be tamed, and I intend to make sure you are."

"Not now you won't. Because if you touch me, you can be certain there will be no wedding. You will have lost your chance at all that money." She smiled, showing much more courage than she felt. Inside she was quivering with fear.

"Oh, there will be a wedding." He laughed. "I know you too well. After all it was your soft heart that sent you dashing off after that stupid weak brother of yours, wasn't it? Too bad you were unsuccessful." He shrugged. "But of course you were following the wrong trail. All this time you played right into our hands. You truly thought Marc knew where your brother was.

How neatly you fell into my lap."

"Seth," Catalina breathed softly, certain now that it was Travis, not Marc, who had the answer—an answer she was afraid to hear, yet afraid not to. "Marc never did see Seth after that game, did he?"

"I'm afraid not, my love. I was forced to . . . ah . . . rid myself of a nuisance."

"Rid yourself . . . Where is Seth? He's . . . he's dead, isn't he?"

"Unless he had the strength of ten men and the power of God, he's resting quite silently on the bottom of the Mississippi or his body has washed ashore miles and miles away."

Catalina gasped at this blatant confession of murder. Seth was gone! Dead! Only the fact that Marc was not responsible permitted her to keep her control. At least he had been truthful to her once in their topsy-turvy relationship. He hadn't known where Seth had gone.

Travis watched pure hatred glow to life in the depths of Catalina's golden brown eyes. For a moment he was shaken, and sensed that one day he would have to rid himself of her, for if he gave her an opportunity, turned his back on her once, she would strike.

Catalina fought back the anguish that tore at her. Someday, somehow she would escape Travis's clutches. Then she would see justice done. He would pay for the death of her brother. She wanted to cry, but she would not give Travis the satisfaction of seeing her weaken. She glared back at him.

Travis's smile faded before the animal-like snarl that drew back Catalina's lips. Yet he knew it was only a matter of time before he forced her to his will.

As soon as the wedding was over, he would make certain that Catalina's parents met with a fatal "accident," an accident that would leave Catalina's husband in possession of their fortune.

As far as he was concerned, he had only to wait to have everything he wanted. Cat could fight him, but she would be his when he decided to take her.

"Get a good night's sleep, love," he said coolly. "Tomorrow night we will leave Natchez as husband and wife, and I guarantee you, you will not sleep for many nights. You have put me off for too long. This time you will see who is the master. You will bend to my will. Sleep, Cat . . . if you can."

He turned and left the room, and Catalina gazed at the closed door, knowing she would die before she would bend to his will.

Catalina could not lie down, nor could she seek sleep. Her fear for herself was still secondary to her concern for Jacob and Shawna. Sure that they would be killed when the wedding was over, she furiously tried to think of some way to save their lives.

Midnight had passed, but Catalina had lost track of the time. She stood by the window and watched the moon rise higher and higher in the night sky.

Then the lock clicked and the door opened and closed before Catalina realized there was another person in the room with her. She turned and a soft sound involuntarily escaped her when she met the hot gaze of Simon Gere.

As soon as Catalina and Travis had left and the lock had been turned again, Jacob tossed the ropes aside and rose silently from his chair. Shawna sat up, a pleased smile on her face for she had played the game well. Marc would like that, and in her very tiny world that was all that mattered. She watched Jacob move silently to the door and listen, then waited patiently for him to tell her what she must do next.

But Jacob did not know how to escape. Catalina had come and gone. He was sure the visit had been arranged to convince her that they were still alive, but he had no way of knowing where Catalina was being held.

His chances of escaping with Shawna were slim, but if he had to search this huge house, they were nonexistent. Even if he did manage to get out, it would take some time to dodge his pursuers and get to Marc. Still, he was worried about what these men might do with Catalina before he could get back with help.

Jacob was sure of one thing, however. The darkest hour was just before dawn, and that was also the time the guards would be sleepiest. Their alertness would be at its lowest. He decided to wait a few hours before making his attempt.

"Sit down, Miss Carrington. You needn't worry about my touching you. I would kill a Carrington or a Garrison, but never find pleasure with one."

"Garrison?"

"Did Travis not tell you that is your lover's real name? Marc Copeland Garrison."

"No he . . ." Suddenly the name Garrison brought another swift memory. Marc had referred to Lorelei as Lorelei Garrison; then he had said her married name was Thatcher. Lorelei Garrison! She was amazed at the pleasure this gave her. The lovely woman whose house they had shared was related to Marc—she was not his mistress.

And the masculine room in which they had slept, could it have belonged to Marc? Could that be his home as well? Then, with all his secrets and plans for vengeance, why had he made a special point of taking her to his own home?

Simon stood watching her. He had to admit that Travis and Marc had excellent taste in women. She was a beauty.

Catalina's attention was again drawn to Simon when he crossed the room.

"I have been thinking that it would be appropriate to tell you why you have been a partner, albeit an unwilling partner, in my plans."

"I have never met you," she declared. "Why should I have played a part in your plans?"

"Because you were a means to an end, an end I had in mind long before you were born. Since my plans are almost concluded, and since neither you nor I can sleep, I felt you might want to be told a . . . ah . . . bedtime story." He laughed softly.

"You hate Marc?"

"I hate all the Garrisons—and the Carringtons since they chose to stand together against me."

"But why, why? As far as I know my father never mentioned your name . . . or the Garrisons'. We've no connection to you. What do you hope to gain from all of this, and why have you joined forces with a man like Travis Sherman?"

"Travis Sherman is a tool, a very useful tool," Simon answered. "Sit down," he commanded.

Wanting to know why she was being forced to marry Travis when he had just been labeled a tool in a far larger plan, Catalina obediently sat.

Simon walked to the window and looked out. For some time he was silent and deep in thought.

"We were young together—Pierce, Joseph, and I," he began. "They were brilliant, as I was. If we had remained together, we could have ruled the world."

Catalina remained silent, for it seemed to her that Simon Gere was in another time and place.

"We used our wealth well in those days. We bought whatever we desired . . . and whoever we desired. But they were weak, and each let a woman come into his life. I tried to warn them that women could be bought and paid for and discarded. But they chose to marry—both of them. The women sapped their strength, their brilliance, and they became weaker and weaker. They refused one profitable deal after another until I was forced to the wall. I needed them to join with me so I could extend my power. There would have been no limit to it. I could have—" He stopped suddenly and turned to look at her. "Do you have any idea what money and power can do? You can control lives, worlds. I could have had all that, but they refused to back me. They said I was mad for power. They let me fail, and I almost lost everything. But I remembered . . . I remembered. I fought back and regained some wealth, but always I remembered. By then they had children, and my vengeance would be richer because I could hurt them more.

"I learned of a business deal they were both involved in. It cost me a lot to insure its failure, but I made it look as though Joseph was responsible for that. And eventually we made the death of Marc's father look like suicide, made it look as though Joseph had ruined him.

"That turned Marc against your family, just as I'd planned. The Garrisons would destroy the Carringtons, and I would eliminate the survivor. Travis was a convenient tool, he was the catalyst I needed to push Marc along in case he became weak like his father. I dangled your money before Travis, and he rose to the bait." Simon's smile was like that of a death's head. "It seems I shall have to give you to him for a while to satisfy his . . . needs. But rest assured, one day the Carrington money—the Garrison money—will all be mine, and so will the power that goes with it."

420

"And after you have all that, you'll reach out and destroy Travis?"

"Loose ends must be eliminated or they come back to haunt one. Never leave an enemy at your back. He will kill you. Travis Sherman is a conceited fool—and he's expendable now that I have the last of these two families in my power."

"Marc . . . what will you do to him?"

"Ah. Young Mr. Garrison. I'm afraid, now that he's served his purpose, he is expendable. Despite what Travis believes, he will eventually come for his friends . . . and for you. It seems he's cursed with the same weakness as his father."

"Weakness? Love, loyalty, friendship. You consider them weaknesses?"

"They are unnecessary burdens that some feel they must carry. With them holding one back, nothing truly important is ever achieved."

"Wealth and power."

"They are one and the same." He chuckled.

"But you didn't answer me. What do you plan to do to Marc?"

"Why, my dear," he said softly, "the very same thing that Travis did to your brother. It will all be over in a very short while."

"Marc will not be that easy to kill," she said with as much conviction as possible. "And I will never be used by Travis Sherman. I'll find a way to escape him. You will not destroy your enemies so easily, but you don't understand that. You're so eaten up by the diseases of greed and hatred that you're hollow inside. Maybe you were always hollow. Maybe that's what my father and Marc's father saw in you. Maybe that's why they avoided you. But they've gifted us with something special, neither of us will surrender easily. You can kill—but you can't destroy that. So you see . . . you've really failed."

For a moment she thought he was going to strike her. She saw him as he was and she had told him so, as two friends had many years ago.

Seeing what hatred had created, she suddenly wanted to face Marc just one more time, to be able to say she loved him, to let that love wipe away the hatred and vengeance that had been in him. At that moment, she would have given her soul to have held Marc in her arms.

"I bid you good night, Miss Carrington. It is useless to talk to you. You are like your father, filled with stupid ideals. You and your lover will pay for them."

"Thank you," Catalina said softly.

He turned away, and after he was gone Catalina found that she was weak and trembling and her body was slicked with sweat. She had never before been in the presence of such complete wickedness.

She felt tired, and for the first time knew a smothering fear. As she lay upon the bed, despite the sweating she shivered. She drew a blanket about her, closed her eyes, and fought to hold onto the dream of Marc. With it in mind, she fell into a restless sleep.

Jacob remained silent as he watched the moon rise higher and higher. Shawna was in a dreamlike state.

For hours he had heard no sound, and he prayed that the alertness of their guards was sapped by weariness. He walked to the door and knelt to look through the keyhole. The two guards were still there, but both were still. He couldn't tell if they were asleep or not, but now was the time. . . .

He walked back to the bed and stood near Shawna; then he reached out to touch her lightly.

"Miz Shawna," he whispered.

Shawna opened her eyes and sat up. She was about

to speak when Jacob touched her lips with his fingers.

"Yo talks quiet, Miz Shawna. Ah doan wants de people out in de hall to know we's awake."

"What are you doing up so late, Jacob?"

"Miz Shawna, yo gots ta do sumthin' impotant fo' me. We's got ta get out of here. Mistah Marc, he be waitin' fo' us."

"All right. What do you want me to do?"

"Can you gets up real quiet like?"

She swung her legs over the side of the bed and sat up, her wide eyes on Jacob as if she were a child following the careful instructions of a teacher. There was no worry in Shawna's mind, no sense of danger. She would do whatever Jacob said because he was her only connection to Marc, and Marc was her only connection to the world.

With a gentle hand, Jacob guided her away from the bed until she stood a few feet from the door, where the light would fall if the door was opened. He prayed Shawna would understand and not be startled by his request.

"Miz Shawna," he said in a low whisper, "yo gots ta take off yo dress."

He waited in breathless suspense to see what her reaction might be. If he had terrified her, she might be of no use to him. Worse yet, she might draw the attention of the guards.

"Why?"

"Because I needs fo' ya ta just stan' dere an' look real pretty so dose men kin see yo belongs to Mistah Marc. When dey does dey gwan to let us go, and I'll takes ya back to de boat."

This explanation was quite acceptable to her, and without question she removed her dress and Jacob placed it on the bed. She would need it soon if his plan went well. If it didn't, she might never need it again.

He looked at her and saw what the two guards would

see if they opened the door—a rare beauty with the innocent look of the untouched. Her wide eyes and delicate body would draw the undivided attention of any man.

"Now yo jus stan' dere Miz Shawna and fo' gawd's sake doan look at me. You jus' look at de door. Do yo unnerstan' me, Miz Shawna . . . jus' look at de door."

"All right, Jacob. Is this another game?"

"Yessum . . . yessum, it be jus' a game."

"Okay," she replied. She stood where he told her, and fixed her attention on the door.

Jacob moved so that he would be behind the door when it opened. He sucked in his breath and held it, then reached down, jiggled the knob, knocked very lightly on the door, and waited.

The two guards were in a state of suspension, almost overcome by sleep but struggling to remain awake. Still, they didn't really believe they had to be alert. After all, the doors were locked.

When they heard the gentle rustling of the door and the light knock, they couldn't quite believe their ears. They exchanged glances. The soft rapping came again, and yet again.

"You suppose one of them got loose?"

"I don't see how. What about the girl that was drugged? Do you suppose she's wandering around."

"She was a little . . . strange. She might get into some trouble in there."

"Maybe we'd better go and check. The old man will have us shot if we let anything happen to them."

They rose and moved stealthily toward the door. One reached into his pocket and removed a key which he slipped into the lock.

Within the room, Jacob heard the key turn and he knew this would be his only chance for freedom. If he failed, there would be no other. He reached out and gently rapped on the door again.

The knob turned and the door was pushed slowly open. The two guards stood, in open-mouthed awe, mesmerized by the eerie vision that met their gaze.

Shawna stood in the path of the light from the hall. She wore a smile, but it was not that or her beauty that drew the men into the room; it was her state of undress. The guards took the few steps Jacob needed.

His strength was more than a match for the two of them, and the element of surprise was an advantage. He reached out two immense hands, caught the side of each man's head, and knocked their noggins together with a solid thud. Then he caught each man by the back of the collar before he had a chance to hit the floor.

Silently Jacob let the unconscious men slip to the floor. Then he stepped over to Shawna whose eyes had widened with fear. She looked as if she were about to scream.

"Miz Shawna, please," he begged softly, "doan yo cry or scream please. Ah'm gwine to take yo to Mistah Marc. Yo wants to go see him doan yo?" Jacob had never been quite so scared in his life. Between the danger in this house and his uncertainty of Shawna's behavior, he was thoroughly shaken.

"Cum on, Miz Shawna . . . please," he begged.

Very slowly Shawna extended a hand to him, and he grasped her delicate fingers.

"Now yo cum with me, li'l miss. Ah'm gwine ta take yo where dey can' hurt yo any mo'. Yo'all cum wit' me. We can't save no one but us right now, and I'm still not sho' we's gwine ta do dat yet. So yo cum wid me, li'l miss. Ah'll tak' yo home."

"Home," Shawna whispered. Then she smiled, a confident child's smile. "All right, Jacob. Let's go home. I want to see Marc."

Chapter 34

Jacob knew he should make some effort to find Catalina, but the house was so large that he had no idea how to go about it. Besides, he was scared, and he had the helpless Shawna to see to. If he escaped, he would bring the help Catalina needed. If he failed, it would no longer matter.

Jacob knew the two guards wouldn't come around for a long time, but he didn't know how many more men were posted throughout the house. The hallway was very dimly lit, and he made his way down it slowly, leading Shawna by hand. At the top of the steps, he pressed himself against the wall, then peeked down, and his heart lurched. There were two more guards at the bottom of the steps, and they seemed much more alert. He would have no chance to get to them.

He turned back down the hallway, intending to try the back stairs. There he met the same barrier. At the bottom two men were lethargically playing cards. Jacob felt real despair. He would have gone down fighting if it hadn't been for Shawna and Catalina, but he wouldn't stop trying. He knew he'd never be able to answer to Marc if he escaped and left the two women behind.

There were eight doors in the hallway, and he decided to try one. If it was empty he might find an unbarred window, a way out.

He took a deep breath and put his hand on a knob. It turned easily. The door was unlocked. Opening it very slowly, he stepped inside and drew Shawna with him, cautioning her to silence. Then he closed the door and stood very still until his eyes became accustomed to the dark. He breathed a sigh of relief when he realized the room was empty.

As he started across it, a cry came from the hallway, and the sound of running feet told him that their escape had been discovered. He quickly dragged Shawna to the window. Again he felt that his prayers had been answered. The window led to a small veranda, and he looked down into a garden.

As the voices drew nearer and the door was slammed open, Jacob snatched Shawna up in his arms and climbed onto the balcony. There was a shot. Jacob's body jerked violently, and Shawna screamed. Then Jacob leaped.

Marc had not slept in forty-eight hours. His eyes burned and his hair was tousled. A dark stubble of beard made him look almost piratical. He had not changed his clothes, and those about him thought that the usually immaculate Marc Garrison had gone mad.

Though he had continued the search, each report brought to him was negative. During this time he had not eaten but had drunk brandy. He showed no sign of being drunk, but his mood was a violent one.

Rage simmered within him, ready to explode at any time. He walked a razor edge, and those about him tread easily lest he find them responsible for the loss of the three people he held dear.

He had sent men to the house he had been lured to by the fake message from China, and they had found it empty as he had suspected it would be. Then he had set them to searching for the elusive woman who had been there.

It was nearly three o'clock in the morning. Marc had returned to the *Belle* and had just gulped down a liberal glass of brandy to ease his sense of failure over not finding a lead to Catalina.

"Marc," China asid sympathetically, "you must eat something before you go out again. You can't keep drinking like that."

"Let me alone," he growled.

"I'm afraid too. But you can't destroy yourself," she declared softly.

"What more do I deserve for what I've done. I can't believe that there's no trace of her, China. I've been thinking about what you said, about her being someplace where we wouldn't think to look." He turned to face China. "The only place we haven't gone to is upper Natchez. But who up there would be involved in a thing like this?"

"I don't know . . . but—"

"And another thing how do I go about searching the houses up there? Just burst in and tell them I'm looking for a girl who's been kidnapped. I don't think I'd get far before the authorities put a stop to my search. Damn it, China, there's some element here we just don't understand. Do you know if Travis has any friends up there?"

"I don't. He said he hadn't been in Natchez before, but he's lied about so many things we can't believe that."

Marc was about to answer when there was a loud noise outside the cabin. It was followed by muffled voices, the sound of a scuffle, and then a woman's angry voice. Finally the door burst open and two of Marc's men entered, dragging with them the woman who had delayed Marc while Catalina was being taken.

There was no doubt that she was terrified, and Marc did nothing to lessen her fear. Deciding to take advantage of it, he moved very close to her and watched her shrink in terror as she strained against the two men holding her arms. She watched Marc with wide eyes.

"So," he said, in a voice so soft that her terror grew. This man was a raging storm about to explode, and she was now his target. "We meet again. Maybe you still feel . . . conversational? I'm afraid the last time we met I did not. Now, my dear, what is your name?"

"Lil," she muttered.

"Well, Lil, it's time you and I had a long and very informative talk."

"I don't know anything." She moaned. "I only gave you a message."

"You know who sent it!" he growled.

"No! No, I never saw him before!"

"Just what were your orders?"

"I was just supposed to keep you away from your boat for as long as I could. I swear I don't know anything more . . . I don't."

"You were paid well, Lil?" Marc asked mildly.

"Y-yes," she replied.

"And you do have a name for me?"

"A name?"

"They had to find you somehow, Lil. They had to know you'd take pay for a thing like this. I want a name, any name."

"I can't do that," she cried. "He'll kill me for bringing you down on him!"

"I want to tell you something." Marc's voice was dangerously soft. "Cat was loved by those aboard this boat. Now give me a name . . . or you will find the

Mississippi deep and very cold."

"You wouldn't—"

"If I don't have a name in five minutes, I will have you taken to the deepest part of the river . . . and I'll make sure you don't come back. Are you a good swimmer, Lil? The current is awfully strong."

The two men who held Lil had never seen Marc in this condition, nor had they ever heard him give such a brutal order, but they remained impassive. Even China, who knew Marc would never really hurt Lil, kept her silence.

Lil looked from one to the other, seeking some support, some pity; but she saw none. Her courage failed, and she sagged in the grasp of her captors.

"All right . . . It was McNally who came to me with the money. McNally—he runs the Three Stars tavern."

Excited about getting the name, Marc reached into his pocket and offered several gold coins to Lil.

"Take this and get on the first boat leaving Natchez," he said quickly. "Leave town as fast as you can if you don't want to be caught in the backwash."

Lil blinked in surprise. She'd been certain McNally would get her once he learned she'd named him. Now the man she had deceived was helping her to escape. She found this hard to believe and hesitated, suspecting treachery, which was all she had ever known in her lifetime.

Marc nodded to the two men who held her. When they released her, he took her hand and put the money into it.

"You don't have much time, Lil. All hell is going to break loose when I get my hands on McNally. You'd better be gone."

Lil backed away, still stunned. Then she suddenly turned and ran from the room. Marc turned to his two men.

"McNally," he said crisply. "Do either of you know him?"

"Yes, sir," one replied. "He runs the place down on the lower end. It's pretty bad."

"You two come with me. We're going to pay Mr. McNally a visit." Marc turned to China. "Nina still locked in the cabin?"

"Yes," she replied. "She's screamed and cried herself out, but she won't tell me a thing."

"Keep after her, she must know more than she's saying."

Marc walked to his desk, took a pistol from the drawer, and tucked it into his belt. "Go and arm yourselves. Be on deck in five minutes," he ordered, and the men swiftly left.

"Marc, please be careful. This man McNally sounds very dangerous."

"He doesn't know what danger is yet, but if he doesn't answer my questions, he's sure as hell going to find out."

"Just watch yourself. You won't be of any use to Cat if you wind up dead in an alley. This lot is treacherous."

"I'll be careful, China, but I'll get my answers," he said quietly. "You can count on that."

He strode to the door, and when his quick footsteps faded, China went to the cabin where a now-silent Nina waited.

Marc and his two men stopped before the disintegrating tavern. When they walked inside, it took only moments to see the type of riffraff that frequented the place. The dregs of river travelers washed up here, and Marc was sure thieves and murderers were regular patrons.

They walked through dark mists of smoke and

crowded tables to the bar, where they faced a man who had most obviously weathered some brutal days.

His face was as furrowed as a well-traveled highway. If he immediately realized that Marc was not the type to be a habitual customer, he kept it to himself. He had learned long ago that it paid to stay out of people's affairs. He scowled darkly across the bar.

"What'll ya have, gents?"

"Whiskey," Marc said shortly, "and conversation."

The man eyed Marc thoughtfully as he poured three drinks.

"Conversation ain't cheap, friend," he stated suggestively.

Marc smiled and drew two coins from his pocket. The man's eyes narrowed as he looked from the coins Marc had placed on the bar to Marc's face.

"What's your name, friend?" he inquired.

"I'll ask the questions . . . I'm paying," Marc replied. "What's your name?"

"Henry."

"Well, Henry, I'm looking for a man named McNally."

"Ned McNally. He owns this place here."

"I know. Where can I find him?"

"He's in the back room."

"Alone?"

"Mister, you can't go back there."

Without speaking, Marc took three more coins from his pocket and placed them atop the other two. For a few minutes Henry looked at them. Then his eyes returned to Marc, and he half smiled as he reached out to take them.

"I don't want you to even consider warning him," Marc said coldly as he drew the pistol from his pocket. "I'm a dead shot, and any sound from you will most definitely be your last."

The man smiled and shrugged, then moved down to the other end of the bar.

Marc strode to the door at the back of the place, pistol in hand, his men close behind.

He broke into the room so abruptly that the large man seated at the table had little chance to move before Marc was beside him, the pistol nearly touching his forehead.

Ned McNally, never having been blessed with an overabundance of courage, broke into a sweat when he looked into the muzzle of the pistol and then up into cold green eyes that had not one touch of mercy in them. Attempting to exhibit some bravado, he snarled, "What you gents doin' bustin' in on a man in his private office?"

"We should have made an appointment I guess." Marc smiled coldly. "But we were afraid you might be too busy to see us. You aren't too busy to talk to me now are you, Ned?"

"What do you want with me? How do you know my name?"

"That's irrelevant. I want a name from you."

"Name . . . what are you talkin' about?"

"A few hours ago a lady and two friends were kidnapped near my boat. A little bird has informed me that you just might have some answers to who kidnapped them, who was behind it, and where they were taken. I want some answers, Ned"—he cocked the pistol—"and I want them before I get very nervous and blow your brains all over this room."

Ned had been sweating before, but now he began to tremble, for he knew that Marc meant business.

"What do you want?" he gasped, as the muzzle of the pistol nudged his brow.

"You had me kept busy while you arranged the kidnapping. I want to know who set you to it."

"Willie . . . Willie Best was part of it. Him and those other three."

"Three? You know their names?"

"Sure. I knowed Nina Brent and Charlene Gilbert and Willie a long time. The other gent . . . well I seen him around Natchez some."

"Gent," Marc repeated, realizing, with a new surge of rage, that Catalina was most likely in Travis's hands.

"I don't know his name."

"Don't worry . . . I do. I want to know where these three were taken."

Ned licked his lips and his body trembled even more. "Mister, I can't tell you that. My life wouldn't be worth a plug nickel if I named any names."

"Your life isn't worth much more right now." Marc tapped the pistol lightly against Ned's forehead.

"That man's too big, mister. You can shoot me if you want, but I can't throw his name out."

Marc was puzzled for a minute. He knew Ned was afraid of him and of the pistol, but he was obviously more afraid of the unnamed man who was at the source of the problem. Whoever he was, this man must be very rich and very powerful. Power and wealth could not be found in Natchez-under-the-hill . . . he had to come from upper Natchez.

"He's not from down here, is he?"

Ned's response was a negative shake of the head. Marc realized that something or someone much bigger than Travis was behind all this, like some pervading dark shadow.

Travis did not have the means to achieve so much control or to get so much help from Natchez-under-the-hill. This man could strike fear into men of Ned's caliber. Marc had to think.

He watched Ned's face closely as he began slowly and methodically to name those families in upper

Natchez wealthy enough to accomplish what had been done. He meant to find a motive after he learned the identity of the person behind this deed.

Name after name was spoken, but there was no reaction from Ned, who now refused to meet Marc's eyes.

"Simon Gere," Marc said. Then he stopped, and the prolonged silence made Ned squirm. "Simon Gere," Marc repeated gently.

He had seen Ned go pale when he'd spoken this name, had seen him hold his breath as he tried to look as though he were not reacting.

Marc uncocked the pistol and stepped back from Ned.

"It was Simon Gere, wasn't it?"

Ned licked lips that had suddenly gone very dry.

"I didn't say that," he protested.

"You didn't have to. The name scared you to death. What does he have to do with all this?"

"Mister," Ned said weakly, "you just go ahead and shoot. I ain't sayin' a word to make a man like that think I been tossin' his name around."

"I'm not going to shoot you, Ned. You've told me all I need to know. But I'd advise you to get out of Natchez-under-the-hill"—Marc's voice was heavy with murderous anger—"because I intend to tell Gere that you told me all I wanted to hear—that you chattered like a baby."

"He'll kill me! You can't do that!"

"I can and I will. You'd better run very fast, and very far."

Marc returned his pistol to his belt. Intending to leave a terrified Ned McNally behind, he crossed the room and was at the door when it swung open and he faced a pistol held by one of the two cold-faced men who seemed intent on killing him.

435

Chapter 35

Seth and Charles were both impatient to round the next bend of the river. When they did it would finally bring them in sight of Natchez.

"There it is, boy," Charles said. "Natchez-under-the-hill, one of the nastiest little places on earth, at least under the hill. Up there"—he pointed to the mansions above—"close to heaven."

"Some combination, isn't it?" Seth responded thoughtfully. "And where is my sister, I wonder?"

"We have to believe she's safe, Seth. We have to. We'll move heaven and hell to get news. Surely they stopped here, and they can't be that far ahead of us. Someone must have seen them, and will at least tell us if she's well."

"I hope you're right."

The lights of Natchez-under-the-hill greeted them as did raucous music and sounds of vibrant activity.

As they drew nearer and were about ready to dock, Seth cried out, "Charles, look!"

He pointed, and Charles could read intense excitement on his face. He followed Seth's trembling finger, his eyes widening in surprise.

"Why . . . I believe . . ."

"It's the *Belle!* The *Belle.*"

"By God, it is. We've caught up to them, boy. We've

caught up to them."

"I hope I've really caught them," Seth said through clenched teeth. "I have a score to settle with Marc Garrison and Travis Sherman."

"First we had better find Cat, and make sure she's all right. Then we can do whatever else needs to be done. We can't just assume that she's been harmed. What will you do if you find no problem aboard the *Belle?*"

"I've had my mind set on catching up for so long, I hadn't thought about that. But you're right, Charles. Let's find Cat first. Everything depends on that."

"What do you want to do about the loss of the *Belle* if Cat is all right?"

"There is not much I can do, except stay with my original plan. I'll face my father with the truth and tell him I want to start again, if he'll let me. As long as Cat isn't hurt, I don't mind starting over."

"I'm glad to hear you talk like that, as I'm sure your father will be. All he's ever wanted is for you to straighten up your life and stand beside him in the business."

"You think he'll accept me now, since I've lost the *Belle?*"

"I think he'd be damned proud to."

"Thanks, Charles." Seth returned his gaze to the docks as the *Constitution* came to a halt and the gangplank was lowered.

Charles and Seth were the first to descend, and they made their way as rapidly as possible to the *Belle,* which they boarded quickly, well aware that it seemed to be deserted.

"Where is everybody?" Seth said. "In a town like this, surely they post some kind of guard."

"Unless the owner is well known and respected here."

"In this town? I can't imagine what kind of man would get the respect of this town. He'd have to be

437

a . . ." Seth stopped and looked at Charles; then he said softly, "Just what kind of a man is Marc Garrison?"

"Suppose we go down and face him and find out for sure."

They went to the cabin in which they expected to find Marc. It was empty, but Seth knew the *Belle,* so he moved swiftly from stateroom to stateroom, with Charles following, until he opened a door and faced a very surprised China.

It only took China seconds to put a name to Seth's face, and Seth recognized her immediately. He had only seen her the night of the game, and they had not really spoken. But they knew each other.

"Seth Carrington."

"Yes," he answered stiffly. "And you are Marc Garrison's friend, China. Just where is he, and where is my sister?"

"You have arrived at a very uncomfortable time, Mr. Carrington."

"I said where is my sister?"

"At this moment . . . I don't know."

"Where is your boss?" Seth demanded.

"If you're speaking of Marc, he isn't here either," China replied.

"And"—Seth laughed angrily—"I suppose you don't know where he is either?"

"Truthfully I don't."

"Truthfully? I don't think you or Marc know what the truth is."

"If you calm down and give me a chance to explain, I may be able to help you."

"I'm as calm as I intend to get," Seth declared, "so tell me whatever it is you want to say."

"Please, Mr. Carrington," China said quietly, "I know you will not believe this, but I am pleased that you are here."

438

"I find that hard to believe. The last time I crossed the path of Marc Garrison, two of his men tossed me in the river, after they knocked me senseless. Now you tell me you're pleased I'm here."

China knew why Seth was angry, but she was beginning to be annoyed.

"Mr. Carrington, Travis Sherman was responsible for the attempt on your life. Now, if you will be so kind as to allow me to explain, I can answer many of your questions. Time is of the essence if you're going to find Marc and Catalina."

"All right," Seth finally agreed, and Charles smiled at China's sudden exhibition of authority.

When Seth and Charles sat, China began to speak rapidly and precisely. She watched Seth's face pale, saw his jaw twitch and his fury grow.

"So you see I speak the truth when I say I don't know where either of them are."

Seth wanted to believe her, but he had run into too much deception. He had to find Marc Garrison. He stood up.

"What are you going to do?" China asked.

"I'm going to be hot on Marc's trail. I'm going to see McNally too. I'll catch both of them sooner or later."

He had started for the door, Charles behind him, when China spoke again.

"Seth?"

"What?" Impatiently, Seth turned to look at her.

"I can understand how you must feel, but . . ."

"But?"

"Give Marc a chance to explain, to tell you the truth, and at least try to understand. He doesn't want Catalina hurt." Her voice was gentle, and Seth gazed at her, his eyes narrowed and his brows drawn together in a frown. For a minute their eyes remained locked.

"China, what is between my sister and Marc?"

"Marc is in love with her," China replied honestly.

"And Cat?"

"I firmly believe she loves him, too."

"I suppose this is a long story?"

"And complicated."

"I think I'd like to hear this story from Marc himself. I'll have to find Cat and ask her, too."

"I know. I just want to make sure you don't shoot first and ask questions later."

"I'm not a blood-hungry fool. I just want Catalina out of this mess, and I want her to know I'm all right. After all, I am the one responsible for all this."

China just nodded, hoping she could believe Seth, for she had read more in his eyes than he had voiced.

Seth and Charles left and quickly made their way toward the tavern owned by Ned McNally.

Upon entering it, both men were appalled by the atmosphere. Each silently hoped Cat had not been brought to a place like this.

They went over to the bar, and Henry approached to serve them.

"What'll you gents be havin'?"

"Some information."

"What?"

"We're looking for a man. He must have been here not long ago. Marc Garrison. He was looking for McNally."

"Yeah, there was a man here lookin' for Ned."

"Well, where is he? Did he talk to McNally? Where did he go?"

"Them's expensive questions, friend." Henry chuckled humorlessly.

Seth was about to argue that point with his pistol, but Charles placed a restraining hand on his arm. When Seth turned to him, Charles was looking at Henry.

"I believe these will cover our expenses," he said quietly, as he placed a few gold coins on the bar.

"Yeah, it just might," Henry replied. He reached out deftly, and the coins disappeared into his pocket. "The man you're lookin' for is still in the back room with Ned. He got here just before you."

Seth nodded and strode to the back. Outside the door, they paused to listen and heard the last of Marc's cold and angry exchange with Ned.

Seth burst into the room, gun in hand, just as Marc reached the door. Seth was the last person Marc had expected to see, and it took him a moment to regain his equilibrium. He looked at the pistol directed at him as if he were annoyed. "I don't have time for this. If you plan to shoot you'd best do it quickly because I'm leaving."

Seth stared at Marc blankly for a minute, astounded by his small regard for the pistol . . . and by the way he looked.

"I could kill you for what you've done," Seth finally grated out. "Where's Cat?"

"You'd better make your choice quickly," Marc responded. "I don't have time to explain everything that's happened. I've got a good lead on where Cat is, and I'm going after her. If you want to try to stop me, you'd best do it now."

"I'm going with you," Seth replied, still not able to believe everything Marc had said. "If you're pulling a fast one this time, you won't get away with it."

Marc snorted in angry disgust. His nerves and his temper were entirely too frayed to allow him to be tolerant. With total disregard for the danger to himself, he reached out, wrenched the pistol from Seth's grip, and tossed it aside.

"Come along if you want to, but don't get in my way. Cat's life depends on me, and I'm in no mood to play games with you."

Marc pushed past Seth and Charles. Then Seth quickly picked up his pistol and he and Charles headed after Marc. They were both shocked by Marc's behavior, but Charles knew that both of them couldn't stop him.

Outside the tavern, Marc gave orders to his two men in a crisp commanding voice.

"I'm going to Lorelei's first. Go back to the boat and get more men—at least a dozen—and take them there as fast as you can. And you might as well bring China because she'll come anyway. We're going to give Simon Gere and Travis Sherman the surprise of their lives."

The men left with dispatch. Then Marc motioned to Seth and Charles to follow him as he sought a carriage to take them to upper Natchez. It would be daybreak before his men could get to Lorelei's. If Travis and Catalina were in the Gere mansion, he must try to control his murderous intent, for there would be plenty of men protecting it. Later he would strike swiftly— and with all the strength he had.

He sighed and closed his eyes, but Seth's voice broke into his thoughts.

"Now that you've got everything planned, would you mind telling me what the hell has been going on since I was tossed into the river. And where the hell is Cat?"

Marc smiled. Seth's patience was at an end, and he could understand it.

"Sit back and relax, Seth. I've a long, long story to tell you."

Jacob leapt from the balcony, with Shawna in his arms. He took the shock of the fall, but Shawna was knocked from his arms as they landed.

She rose shakily to her feet, and Jacob tried to do the

same. But as he pressed his hand on the ground for support, pain struck and he realized that his shoulder and arm were wet with blood.

He got up, using his good arm, and staggered to Shawna. Grabbing her hand, he began to run. He could already hear the shouts and running feet, and he knew pursuit was not far behind.

When Shawna whimpered, Jacob knew he would not move very fast that way so he snatched her up in his arms and put all his strength into running toward the trees. Once in their cover, he slowed to listen. Between each mansion was a dark area with bushes and bare spots. As Jacob looked around he figured that if he could just lose his pursuers he would have a chance to escape.

But where could he escape to?

"Jacob," Shawna cried softly, "I want to go home. I don't like this game anymore. I want to go home. Where's Marc, Jacob? You said you'd take me to Marc."

"Shh now, Miz Shawna, please," Jacob begged softly. "They ain't no mo' games, Miz Shawna. Yo jus come long wif me. Ah'm sho' gwine ta do what ah said ah'd do. Yo just be good fo' a li'l while longer and ah'll tak' yo home."

But he knew Shawna had neither the emotional nor the physical strength to reach the boat. It was a long way off even by carriage. And the way he was bleeding from what he had discovered was a shoulder wound, he wasn't too certain he could make it either. If he didn't, Shawna certainly wouldn't.

Then Jacob expelled a ragged sigh as a thought broke through his fear. Lorelei! Lorelei! Marc's sister. What safer place would there be to take Shawna than to Marc's home. That was far from them too, but not nearly as far as the boat.

Not hearing anyone follow, he was reasonably sure they had tried to second-guess him and had gone on ahead to prevent him from getting to the *Belle*. Maybe they had gone to Marc's home to prevent him from getting there as well. But he had to try, if not for his own sake, at least for Shawna's, for she was an innocent creature caught in something she had no way of understanding.

Jacob moved as fast as he could, but he couldn't lie to himself, he was weakening. He felt as though his feet were becoming heavier and heavier, and his breathing was becoming labored. Still he moved on and on and on, very deliberately taking one step after another. One more, his mind urged, one more.

He lost all sense of what surrounded him and struggled only with two thoughts, he must reach Lorelei and he must stay out of sight.

By the time Jacob struggled up the drive to Marc's house he was beyond total awareness. He simply saw the lights of the house and moved toward them.

Lorelei had not been able to sleep. She was too worried about her brother. She did not know everything about his situation, but she had faith in Marc.

It is true, she assured herself. I saw love in his eyes when he looked at Catalina.

She hoped that the terrible dark thing in Marc would be killed by Catalina's love, that he would be able to let go of his need for revenge and would reach for something that would give him peace.

Lorelei, too, had suspected that her father's death was not due to suicide. Although it couldn't be proven, neither she nor Marc believed he had killed himself. They had known their father too well to believe it.

It was nearing dawn. The first faint light of day

already bordered the horizon as Lorelei walked out onto the patio and stood looking down at Natchez-under-the-hill and at the boats docked along the riverfront. The *Belle* was there . . . Marc was there . . . and Catalina was there.

She wanted to believe that they were returning, putting aside all lies to find happiness with each other. It would be wonderful to see her brother happy again.

She sighed and walked back into the house, intending to go upstairs and bathe to get ready for the new day. She had placed a foot on the first step when she heard a sound near the front of the house.

Within a moment someone was pounding on the door. Running to it and throwing it open, Lorelei let out a soft cry of dismay when Jacob half stumbled, half fell inside. Both Jacob and Shawna were near exhaustion, but Jacob had not lost his fear of those who might be following. He staggered back to the door and closed it quickly.

Shawna rested on her knees just inside the house, and Lorelei went to kneel beside her and soothe her. As she rocked Shawna against her, she looked up at Jacob.

"Jacob, what in God's name is going on? Shawna is exhausted. What have you two been doing?"

"Runnin' fo' our lives, Miz Lorelei. We have ta gets a message to Mistah Marc."

"Marc," Shawna sobbed. "I want to go home."

"In heaven's name, Jacob, please tell me what's been happening. Look at you, you're bleeding."

"Miz Lorelei, doan pay dat no mind right now. It's mo' impo'tant yo'all gets a message ta de boat right away. Miz Cat, she been took and we'uns know where dey gots her. Yo'all send a message please, Miz Lorelei."

"Of course. I'll send a message right away. Then I'll

445

care for that shoulder."

Jacob knelt beside Shawna and gently took her arm.

"Now yo cum along, Miz Shawna," he said softly. "Yo gots ta wash and dress so's Mistah Marc he won't be thinking bad o' yo. C'mon, now, Miz Shawna."

As he helped Shawna to her feet, Lorelei went to her side. Then, suddenly, the door opened and all three spun around, terrified.

But Jacob's face broke into a smile. "Mistah Marc! I sho' is powerful glad ta see yo."

"Jacob, Shawna." Marc's surprise was total as he strode to Jacob's side. "Were you with Cat when she was taken?"

"Yassuh, yassuh we both was. But we ain't seen her since dey took her sumplace else. Mistah Marc, ah's powerful sorry ah couldn't get ta Miz Cat. Ah'd a brung her ah swear ah would," Jacob said worriedly.

"Don't worry, Jacob," Marc said coldly. "We are about to get Cat back . . . and to take care of the men who took her."

Chapter 36

Lorelei looked at Marc, shock on her face. She had never seen her brother in such a condition, not even during their worst times.

Marc walked across to Shawna and lifted her in his arms as easily as he would have lifted a child.

"I'll take her upstairs so she can rest. Lorelei, see to Jacob's shoulder and get him something to eat and drink, preferably brandy."

Lorelei didn't hesitate. Marc's voice was filled with too much cold anger for her to question him.

She washed Jacob's shoulder and by the time she had begun to bandage it, Marc returned. She had not questioned the two men who had arrived with Marc, fearing the answers she would get. Had Marc not asked where Cat was? Jacob was shot. The picture was becoming painfully clear. Again, someone had taken from Marc someone he loved.

Lorelei finished binding Jacob's shoulder. "The wound is clean and I've done the best I can. I think it will be fine, Jacob, if you just don't move it any more than you have to."

"Thank ya, Miz Lorelei," Jacob said firmly. "But iffen Mistah Marc goes after Miz Cat ah'm gwine wif him. Dose men, dey's real bad, and we gots ta gets Miz Cat outta dere."

Lorelei watched as Seth went to Jacob's side. She did not know who he was, but he seemed familiar.

"I take it your name is Jacob?" Seth smiled to calm Jacob's wariness.

"Yassuh."

"You were with Catalina and Shawna when they were taken; what do these men want with them? Is it money?"

"Ah doan know, suh. When dey took us to dat house, dey done put Miz Cat somewhere's else. Ah ain't seen her since we wuz took."

"Then you have no idea whether she is still in that house?"

"No, suh, ah doan. But dey was an awful lot of guards jus' to be guardin' me and Miz Shawna. No suh, dey was dere to make shore nobody got to Miz Cat."

"Then she must still be there. Marc was right." Seth spoke half to himself.

"Sir," Lorelei said, "I'm Marc's sister—Lorelei. I'm afraid my brother quite forgot to introduce us."

"I'm Seth Carrington, Catalina's brother, and this is a very dear friend of my family, Charles Dante. We have been on Catalina's trail for quite some time."

"I'm sorry to meet you under such circumstances, Mr. Carrington, Mr. Dante. I'm afraid my brother is not himself. It seems he is quite fond of your sister."

Lorelei tried to smile, but barely succeeded in the face of what had happened.

"Yes. Marc explained a great deal to us on the way up here. I just hope we free Catalina before she is hurt."

"Don't worry, Mr. Carrington," Lorelei responded softly, "I have only seen my brother like this once before. Trust me when I tell you that whoever has done this will pay."

*   *   *

As Marc placed Shawna on the bed gently he noted the innocent and warm love in her eyes. Again he damned the men who had put her through this. To him, they had brutalized and beaten a child. That was another score he meant to settle.

He had to force his mind away from what they might have done to Cat because he could barely control his murderous rage.

"Marc," Shawna whimpered softly, "I want to go home. I'm afraid . . . I want to go home."

"Don't worry, little one. I'll take you home as soon as you rest for a while. You're safe here. This bed was mine when I was a little boy. You just sleep now and I'll take you home later," Marc said comfortingly.

Her love for Marc and her confidence in him eased Shawna's fear, and she nodded and closed her eyes like an obedient child.

Marc covered her and left the room. Then he went to the drawing room, entering it in time to hear Lorelei's last words.

"You're right, Lorelei my dear. I still don't know the reason behind this but the Geres are mixed up in it."

"Simon Gere," Lorelei repeated, shivering slightly.

"What I don't understand is why? What does he want? There's no message, no word."

"What are you going to do? Jacob says the house is well guarded. There are only three of you."

"Temporarily," Marc replied. "I've sent for the men from the *Belle*. They should be here pretty soon." He turned to Jacob. "Cat didn't say anything . . . anything special before you were separated that might give us some explanation for this?"

Jacob furrowed his brow as he tried to recall the words Travis had spoken when Cat was bound in the warehouse.

"Dat man, dat mistah Travis, he done cum and said

449

sum bad things to Miz Cat. He made her cry."

"Bad things? Like what?"

"Well, he done tol' her yo was Marc Garrison. Den he say yo plan all dis and yo wuz gwine to leave her in a place like Belle Towne's cuz yo doan want her fo' true. He say yo's gettin' even wit' her fo' . . . fo' sumpthin'. He say yo took de *Belle* apurpose ta hurt Mistah Seth too. Den he say mo', but ah doan members. Ah only members Miz Cat she feel real po'."

"Christ," Marc muttered as the pain of guilt filled him. Lorelei could have wept to see the misery in her brother's eyes.

"Ah members, he say Miz Cat she gonna marry wif him, den he has all her money and her folks gwine ta pay a long time. He say he take her someplace . . . ah doan rightly know. Someplace far away."

"Marry," Marc said through clenched teeth. "That's what that bastard has been aiming for since we left New Orleans. Now I see why he arranged that door business with Willie."

"Door business?" Seth frowned.

"Something to be explained later," Marc quickly replied. "For now, we have to make some plans. Jacob, do you think you can tell me how the house is laid out—where the rooms are and where you were held?"

"Yassuh, ah kin try."

"Good. Lorelei go and get some paper." Marc turned to Seth and Charles. "We must make a plan because I want to catch them unprepared. This time," he added softly, "Travis Sherman is going to pay and pay dearly. At least," he added, "we'll not be expected. Right now, surprise is our only hope. If we don't succeed, Cat . . ." He couldn't go on.

But in Simon's house Marc's hopes were being

450

dashed. Gere glared at his men while Travis stood beside him.

"What do you mean they got away? He'll find his way straight to Marc Garrison. Can't you damn fools do anything right!"

"There was blood on the ledge," one man protested. "I winged him, maybe even worse. He's probably—"

"Probably," Simon snarled. "Do you think I built what I have on probablys!"

"What now, Simon?" Travis asked. "He'll come here you can count on it."

"I know that." Simon sat silently for a minute; then he smiled. "Let him. I have nothing to hide. I've no idea who he's looking for or why."

"I don't understand," Travis said.

"I'm sure you don't," Simon retorted dryly. "I have a boat *The Royal* at the docks. Take the girl there, get steam up, and run *The Royal* to Memphis. I'll give you a contact. Once you're there, see to the wedding. I'll take care of Mr. Garrison when he gets here. In fact, it will give me a great deal of pleasure to see his face when there's no sign of her."

Travis smiled and nodded. Then Simon took paper from his desk and jotted two notes—one to the captain of *The Royal* and the other to his friend in Memphis. He handed both to Travis.

"Get going. Send me word as soon as you get there."

Travis left the room, ascended the stairs two at a time, then ran down the hall to the room in which Catalina was being held. He'd been given a key so he unlocked the door and stepped inside.

Catalina paced the floor anxiously. Unable to leave the room, she could only listen. She had heard more movement throughout the house in the past few hours

451

than she had since she had been imprisoned here. Then shots had been fired and a long deathly silence had followed. After that the time had passed with unbelievable slowness, yet she had found it impossible to sit down.

Now, as she turned from the sunlit window, she heard footsteps stop before her door and heard a key turn in the lock.

Within moments, she was again face to face with Travis Sherman.

"We're leaving," he stated firmly.

"Tell me where we are going," she demanded.

"No point in asking questions, Cat. Come along."

"I'm not going anywhere until I see Shawna and Jacob. What has been happening? I've heard the activity and the gun shots. If you've harmed either of them, I'll never do what you want."

"They're both alive and well."

"And I'm supposed to believe you," she snapped. "That's hard to do. I'm not going anywhere until you show me Shawna and Jacob."

Travis was so afraid that Marc would catch up with them, his courage disintegrated. Compared to his strength, Catalina's was negligible, so he gripped her and proceeded to shake her until she cried out.

Her hair came unbound at this rough handling, and she was too stunned to speak. But Travis slammed her against the door, then held her there as he snarled in her ear.

"Don't push me into doing what I don't want to do. Now come along without a battle or I'll be forced to donate your friend Shawna's charms to the men in this house. They won't be gentle with her, I promise."

Catalina could hear the frustration and anger in his voice. It was clear to her that he was totally unstable and that he would do exactly what he had promised.

"All right," she panted. "I'll go, but there will be no wedding unless I know that Shawna and Jacob are all right."

"You're in no position to make demands," Travis snarled. He reached into his pocket and took from it a short piece of rope. Drawing her hands behind her, he bound them securely. Then he went to a cupboard and withdrew a dark cloak, which he put about her shoulders.

He pushed her ahead of him, down the hall to the back steps, then down them and through a door. A carriage waited, and within moments, they were driving away from the house. Catalina's fear increased. She had no idea where they were going, but she knew that now no one could follow her. Even if Marc came to rescue her, Jacob and Shawna would be able to tell him nothing.

When the carriage came to a halt, she was roughly dragged out and she found herself on the docks, beside a boat she had never seen before. When she saw the *Belle* farther down, a soft inarticulate sound of despair escaped her. Then Travis pushed her up the gangplank.

As soon as they were safely in a cabin Travis seemed to relax. Catalina stood across the room from him, her hands tied, as he smiled and walked toward her.

When Marc's men arrived, he quickly explained what he planned. Then he told China she must wait for him with Lorelei. This was hardly agreeable to her, but she could see that Marc was in no mood for an argument. As the men prepared to leave, Jacob joined them.

"You've been through too much already," Marc said to him. "You'd best go upstairs and get some rest."

"Mistah Marc," Jacob declared solemnly, "ah's

gwine wif yo ta gets Miz Cat. Ah done promised yo ah'd tak' care of her, an' ah done promised Miz Shawna she'd be all right. Ah just cain't go to sleep. Ah axes you Mistah Marc, doan tell me ta do dat. Sides ah gots a score ta settle wit some of doz men."

Seeing the determination in Jacob's eyes and his need to salve his manly pride, Marc could only nod his head. Jacob's smile was broad as they left the house and started toward the mansion of Simon Geŕe.

It was not a long way from Marc's house to Simon's, but en route there was total silence among the men, who were reflecting the serious moods of Marc, Seth, Charles, and Jacob.

Marc was deeply involved with thoughts of Cat, and he was reexperiencing his vivid sense of loss. Terrified that he might be too late to halt the enactment of the ugly things he had once planned, he was lost in a morass of guilt. Catalina was paying the price for his need for vengeance, and he was tasting bitter regret. The possibility that he would never see her again, never be able to ask her to forgive him or to tell her of his love, ate into him like a destructive parasite.

Seth, Charles, and Jacob read him well, and they knew no words could ease his pain.

When they stopped in front of the Geŕe mansion it, too, was disturbingly silent and frighteningly unguarded.

"There isn't a soul around," Seth declared.

"Yes," Marc said softly, "and that's enough to scare you, isn't it? This man is like a spider . . . . and I think he wants us to walk into his web. I have a feeling he expects us."

"How could he?" Charles asked. "And what are we going to do?"

"We"—Marc smiled again—"are going to walk into his web . . . because Catalina is in there. We're going in—and we're not coming out without her."

Marc descended from the carriage, and the others followed. He did not bother to knock, but, with a well-placed foot, slammed the door open and charged in, expecting resistance and finding none. He and his men then stood in the entrance hall and looked about. There was no sign of anyone.

A moment later a door opened—it led to a library—and Simon Gere appeared, a look of mild shock on his face.

"My, my," he said softly, "wouldn't it have been much easier to knock? This is a surprise visit, but I would have most certainly invited you in."

Marc's face was a study in controlled rage as he walked slowly toward the man, but Simon's innocent smile remained intact.

"Where is she?"

"She? Who?"

"Don't play games with me, Simon." Marc waved his hand toward Jacob. "One of your prisoners escaped and made his way back to me. Now tell me where she is or I'll take extreme pleasure in blowing your head off."

"Prisoner? Good heavens, what a delightful imagination." Simon laughed, a rough cackling sound. "I suppose a court of law would be amused. In fact, my dear Marc Garrison, you would be laughed at. My word against that of a black and an imbecile girl. Truly your charges are amusing."

Marc's cold smile made Simon's fade momentarily.

"I said nothing about a girl, Simon. Why do you mention her if she wasn't here?"

"You are quite free to search my house if you care to. I have nothing to hide."

Marc stared at him, an icy feeling climbing his spine. Then he turned to his men. "One of you stay with him. If he so much as bats an eye shoot him. I'll answer for it later."

Simon chuckled again, but the malevolent look in

his eyes could have burnt Marc to a cinder.

With Seth and Charles close behind, Marc raced up the stairs, and the three of them checked the rooms above while some of his men went through the downstairs.

When Marc entered the room in which Cat had been held, he surveyed it and was about to make a quick inspection of the closet when he suddenly stopped. He had sensed it first; then the subtle touch of her perfume had touched him. He moved closer to the bed and sat on its edge, his hand reaching out to trace the slight indentation in the pillow.

He picked the pillow up and lifted it to his face. The scent of the perfume he remembered so well assailed his senses, leaving him weak with the knowledge that Cat had lain here, lain here knowing that he was responsible for all she faced. A new anger filled him, and he rose, tossed the pillow aside, and then left the room.

He returned to the library, where the others had congregated, bringing with him the few men and servants they had found in the house.

"Where is she, Simon?" Marc said coldly. "I know what room she was in, I can still smell her perfume. Now, where have you taken her?"

"I have taken her nowhere," Simon proclaimed, his eyes denying his innocence and revealing his horrible amusement.

Marc gritted his teeth. If he could not trace Catalina from here she might be irretrievably lost. He surveyed all present, then his eyes stopped on a man whose dark eyes glittered with fear and whose face was wet with sweat. The man licked his lips as Marc looked at him. It was then that Marc smiled.

"Take him to the other room," he said coldly as he pointed to the trembling man. "We will see how much he can take before he decides to reveal the truth."

Simon glared his hatred as Marc left the room.

Chapter 37

The man was pushed roughly into a chair. The grim air and the silence of his captors heightened his terror.

Marc had chosen two of his men to help with the questioning. The others had stayed with Simon in case some of his men attempted to rescue him. Marc didn't know that Simon's men were not held by loyalty to the man, but by greed. He had told them to leave, and so they did not even think of returning.

Simon had not counted on a weak link in his chain. He had often used fear to get what he wanted. He had not thought the same tactic would be used against him.

Marc stood in stony silence while the man, who could not seem to take his eyes from him, was tied firmly to the chair. Then, as if he were going to indulge in casual conversation, Marc dragged a chair toward the prisoner and straddled it. He folded his arms comfortably across the back, and remained silent for so long the man began to shake.

Marc's green eyes were now filled with the fanatic's glow, and in them the prisoner could not see one bit of mercy.

"My friend," Marc said in a deceptively soft voice. "You have some information I happen to want very badly. I want—"

"I don't know nothing," the man squeaked. "I ain't

important around here. They don't tell me nothing!"

"Ah now." Marc's smile was colder than his eyes. "I have a feeling you aren't being quite truthful with me. That upsets me. In fact it upsets me so much I feel I must insist on the truth. I do not have much time, my friend, and I warn you, if they get away from me you are going to be a dead man. Let me tell you how you will die. First I will take you to my boat—I wouldn't want any interference from your friends—and when I get you there I'm going to tie you to the paddle wheel. Then I'm going to leave Natchez and head for Memphis. Tell me, just how long do you think you can manage to stay alive?"

The man gulped and his eyes grew wide. This cold-faced Garrison meant to do what he threatened.

To hasten his decision, Marc sighed and rose. "Bring him along, boys," he said as if believing in the man's reluctance. "I'm afraid he needs a little proof."

"No! Wait!" the man cried as they reached for his bonds. "She's gone to *The Royal* with Travis Sherman. They're leaving for Memphis!"

"Untie him!" Marc commanded.

"You're not gonna kill me? I told you what you wanted to know."

"I wouldn't waste the energy," Marc snapped. "Take him and the others to the authorities. Tell them we'll send Charles Dante down to confirm the charges. We ought to be able to put this bunch away for a long time."

When Marc finished instructing his men, he ran back to the library. "Seth, come with me. I'll explain on the way. Right now we've got to hurry. Charles, will you see to the charges? I'll be back as soon as I can."

"You needn't hurry." Simon smiled. "The authorities here will do nothing to me. Some of my men might be inconvenienced temporarily, but we'll survive. Remember that I'll still be here."

Marc knew Simon's power, and he feared the man was right. But he could not waste anymore time in the race to get Catalina.

"You are something I should dispose of by stepping on, but now I'm going for Cat. Remember something, though—I have no intention of forgetting you . . . not for a minute."

As Seth and Marc left, Simon chuckled softly and then settled into a comfortable chair. Charles watched him intently, a smile on his own face.

"You find something amusing?" Simon asked.

"You are, as Marc said, a malignancy that ought to be exorcised. I have a feeling, if I use the power the combined Carrington and Garrison wealth will provide I might just begin to dig up your past, Simon old boy. I might just dig until I find out all about you. Somewhere along the line you've made a mistake or two, and believe me," Charles said softly, "I'll find them."

Simon glared at him . . . but somewhere in the depths of his soul he was shaken.

Marc cracked the whip over the rumps of the racing horses, while a pale-faced Seth clung to the side of the carriage.

"Where are we going?" Seth shouted over the racing wind.

"Back to the docks!"

"What for?" Seth heroically held on despite his somewhat shaky stomach, as they took a bend so sharply the carriage nearly overturned.

Marc was standing now, holding the reins in one hand while he cracked the whip with the other. He looked like a maniacal giant, strong and broad shouldered, braced against the wind. Seth was convinced he wouldn't want to be in Marc Garrison's way this night.

They drew to a sudden halt near the *Belle,* and Seth heard Marc laugh as he leapt from the carriage and ran down the dock, searching for the boat he wanted. Following after, Seth nearly collided with Marc when he stopped without warning.

"Damn!" Seth cursed. Then he looked at Marc's face and saw utter dismay written there. He followed Marc's gaze to the receding lights of a boat.

"Cat," Marc whispered softly. Seth could hear his anguish.

"Come on," Marc said.

"Now where?"

"To a race." Marc ran past him, and Seth could do little but follow. He soon realized they were on their way back to the *Belle.* Obviously Marc intended to race after *The Royal.* Catalina's life hung in the balance.

Marc was already shouting orders while he ran up the gangplank. As his men scurried about, Seth decided they had been well trained. He realized Marc was a better master of the *Belle* than he would ever be.

Steam was built up and soon the *Belle* was moving away from the lights of Natchez.

Now all Marc and Seth could do was wait for the *Belle*'s speed to increase.

"Will we catch them, Marc?" Seth asked quietly.

"We'll catch them," Marc responded grimly. "We'll catch them." He turned to look at Seth, his eyes cold, his brutal intent evident. "We're going to do two things. We're going to get Cat back . . . and we're going to make sure Travis Sherman causes no more problems."

*   *   *

Catalina watched Travis walk toward her, feeling helpless because her hands were bound behind her. At the instant Travis drew close to her, she felt the boat lift and realized steam was building and they were beginning to move.

She looked at Travis, mustering all the defiance she could, though she wanted to scream out the disgust she felt for him.

He smiled and stopped within inches of her. Then he reached out and removed the cloak from her shoulders, tossing it onto the bed. After which, to her surprise, he took hold of her shoulders and turned her around so he could untie her.

She faced him and rubbed her wrists, but didn't take her eyes from him. What little trust she had ever had in him was long dead.

"You're a fool, Travis," she stated coolly. "We'll be followed."

"By whom, Cat?" He laughed. "Who will tell your friends where you have gone? You seem to find it very difficult to understand that the game is over."

"I repeat, you're a fool. You don't really believe Simon Gere intends for you to get your hands on my money, do you?"

"Don't try that with me. Playing one of us against the other won't work. We planned this well, and you just can't get away with it."

"He planned it well, Travis, not you," she threw back at him. "Do you want to know how I know?"

"How?" he asked, trying to appear disinterested.

"He told me."

"I don't believe you," Travis declared. "You have no idea just how much Simon Gere hates women do you? He would as soon kill you as explain his motives to you."

"Say what you like, Travis. He came to my room just

461

before dawn. He was gloating over how well he had used you and how soon everything would be his."

"Stop it, Cat. It won't work."

"Travis, if you let me go, I'll forget all this ever happened."

"Of course, just as your friends will. I'm not fool enough to let a fortune slip through my fingers. I've worked too hard to get hold of it . . . and you, sweet Cat, and you."

"That will never be," she replied as she backed away from him. "For heaven's sake, listen to me. Simon Gere is an expert at deception. He has duped everybody, but especially you. There's no reward in this for anyone but Simon Gere. When you reach Memphis his men will finish what you started. Can't you see? He doesn't need you anymore. You're a liability. He thinks I can be forced to lie with any man, any man of his choosing!"

Travis reached out and gripped her shoulders, pulling her against him.

"Well, it won't happen that way, Cat," he said softly. "I have no intention of stopping in Memphis. Do you really believe I'm such a fool? We'll go beyond Memphis . . . and we will be married. I have friends to help me with that. I'm going to have you—and the money."

"There won't be any money. My parents will never pay you."

"Again you underestimate me. Do you think I didn't check on all the trusts that had been set up for you? With your own little hands, Cat my love, you can reach out and pluck over three-quarters of a million dollars. That will be fine for a start. But I don't doubt that your parents will pay well to have you safely returned to them. So don't play with me. Besides"—he smiled—"I have other plan for our travels."

He kissed her with a subdued violence, and he

462

seemed to have forgotten the first time he had thought he had Catalina trapped. The feel of her in his arms, the taste of her mouth, sent a surge of passion through Travis. He had wanted her for too long, and he was not about to deny himself any longer. That she was unable to escape him excited him, for he enjoyed his women helpless and frightened.

But Catalina was beyond fright. She had been through too much. Now she was determined and angry.

She lashed out with her doubled fists and caught Travis on the temple. When he staggered back from her in surprise, she kicked out, catching him on the thigh and provoking a cry of pain and a curse.

He lunged for her again, catching the sleeve of her dress and ripping it from her, but she spun away from him, leaving the piece of material in his hands. He threw it aside as he charged for her.

The cabin was not really big enough for her to escape him for long and they both knew it. She saw a satisfied glow in his eyes as he drew near.

She backed away again, desperately seeking some weapon of defense. Her hands reached wildly about, and as she backed against a wall, they found a square wooden box.

She gripped it firmly and flung it, catching Travis on the cheekbone. As he dropped to his knees, she dashed past him to the door.

Flinging it open, she ran down the passageway to the steps that led to the next deck. Once there, she ran for the steps to the upper deck. There she might have a moment to think. When she reached the upper deck, she looked over the rail at the rapid flowing river beneath her.

The current was amazingly swift, and fear gripped her. If she jumped, she stood very little chance of surviving the leap or the swift dark river.

Tears of desperation came to her eyes. She thought of Marc and of their lost chance for happiness. At this moment she wanted him more than her own life.

The *Belle* raced up the river. The boat ahead of them, like an elusive wisp, staying just beyond his reach.

Marc cursed, paced, and glared at *The Royal* as if he could will it to slow down.

Between his mumbled words, which Seth felt he really didn't want to hear and the way Marc occasionally struck the rail with a clenched fist, Seth felt he'd best keep his observations to himself, though he feared they wouldn't catch up with the boat ahead.

But the *Belle* was a magnificent performer, built to master the swift current of the Mississippi. She was expertly shaped, and Marc seemed to be aware of that. He had placed his hopes on the *Belle*'s ability to outrace any other boat that had a head start.

Seth remained silent, and after a while he began to realize that they actually were lessening the distance.

Slowly, ever so slowly, they began to close the gap, until after another hour of traveling they were only half as far from *The Royal* as they had been at the start.

Closer . . . closer they came, until there was no more than a hundred feet between the *Belle* and *The Royal*.

"Marc," Seth said quietly, "we're going to catch her! We're actually going to catch her!"

"You should have had more faith in her, Seth," Marc replied. "She's a lady that knows when she's needed and she responds like the marvelous thing she is."

"I guess you've developed quite a feel for her."

"I've grown fond of her," Marc admitted.

"You've grown fond of Cat, too," Seth declared. "God, I'm sorry for all this."

"You're not to blame for it. Old Simon would have arranged it some other way if you hadn't fallen in with his plan."

"Well, at least I'm grateful for one thing that came out of this."

"Grateful?"

"You and Cat. It's because of me you met in the first place. I hope she's as grateful when we catch up with her and is able to forget that I got her into this mess."

"We'll worry about Cat's gratitude shortly because I think we're about to catch up with her."

The boat before them seemed to have reached her maximum speed. She was fast . . . but not quite fast enough to beat the *Belle*.

Nearer and nearer they drew, until all the details of *The Royal* could be clearly seen.

It was then that they noticed the figure that appeared on the second deck. Catalina. Marc knew it at once, just as he knew she was being pursued. He clenched his teeth and gripped the rail as he peered at *The Royal*.

Catalina ran from the second deck, up the stairs to the top deck. It was an act of desperation and he was afraid she might decide to jump.

He watched her leave the front rail and head toward the back. Marc knew the instant she saw him. It happened in the same moment Travis appeared on the top deck and Catalina turned to face him.

At that same moment the *Belle* came abreast of *The Royal*, and Marc ran to the rail and climbed upon it, his body precariously balanced when he did so.

Seth watched in total awe as Marc stood as though transfixed while he carefully judged the distance between the two boats.

He knew that if Marc failed to make it to *The Royal* all would be lost for him and for Cat.

After a heart-stopping moment, Marc leaped.

Chapter 38

While Marc was poised on the rail, Catalina watched in utter fascination, unaware that Travis was on the upper deck now and moving rapidly toward the rail. Her heart leaped when she turned and saw him withdraw a pistol from beneath his coat, then aim it at the unarmed and totally helpless Marc. Catalina moved swiftly, sure that Travis was concentrating on Marc and had temporarily forgotten her.

She was right. Certain that Marc was vulnerable, Travis did, for a few seconds, concentrate all his attention on aiming at him. It was his fatal mistake.

At the moment when Travis pulled the trigger, Catalina shoved his arm with all her might. The bullet sang by Marc, only inches away, and he landed on the deck of *The Royal,* then raced for the steps to the upper deck.

Travis pushed Catalina aside and prepared to meet Marc with his pistol. But she ran to him and again gripped his arm. This time he spun from her and jerked his arm free.

Swinging his hand, he caught Catalina on the cheek and sent her stumbling back just as Marc reached the deck and flung himself onto Travis. Both men tumbled to the deck.

Travis fought with desperation, but Marc's fury was

momentous. His rage had built until there was no room in him for anything else.

Travis was in his hands, and the past hurts to him and his family were magnified by what Travis had meant to do to Cat . . . and the painful guilt that he carried.

They rolled across the deck, each man searching for a hold. Catalina stood near the rail as she watched them struggle.

They were nearly matched in size and weight, Marc being slightly larger. But Travis was less driven than Marc. Travis wanted to survive; Marc wanted to kill.

As they struggled like two Goliaths, Catalina soon became aware that Marc intended to kill Travis. Desperate, she sought some way to end the battle. She had run from Travis, but she now knew he could hurt her no more. She and Marc would be free . . . but not if Marc killed Travis.

Then she saw the pistol that had been torn from Travis's grasp when the two men had come together, and had fallen to the deck. She started to make her way toward it, skirting the thrashing figures.

Meanwhile Marc and Travis struggled to their feet, and Travis pushed Marc away from him. What happened next was like a *danse macabre*. Her eyes on the pistol, Catalina was not concentrating on Travis or Marc. She dashed just too close to Travis who had caught on to her plan. He leaped toward her and the pistol, taking Marc by surprise for he had expected an attack. Travis came up with one arm about Catalina and the other holding the pistol, a look of triumph on his face.

They all stood frozen for a minute; then Travis let out a soft, very pleased laugh.

"Too bad, Garrison," he said. "It seems your heroics are for nothing. Would you like to say a word to your lady—or should I say my lady—before I shoot you?"

"You're a damned lying coward, Travis." Marc sneered. "Come out from behind her and fight me."

"Now why would I be fool enough to do that when I can just shoot you and then do exactly what I planned?"

"I'll tell you something," Marc said calmly, his eyes holding Cat's, "I'm coming to get you. So you'd better shoot very straight. You see with the boat moving like it is, I don't think you stand a snowball's chance in hell of hitting me dead center. And"—his voice was deadly—"if you don't, I sure as hell am going to kill you when I get my hands on you."

Marc seemed like a devil from the deepest pits of hell. His hair was disheveled by the wind and his face was bearded. His green eyes glowed.

Travis's smile faded, for he realized Marc meant exactly what he said. Catalina could already visualize Marc being shot.

None of the three had taken Seth into account. During the whole confrontation, he had racked his brain in desperation, trying to think of a way to help Marc. He decided it would help if Travis lost his footing . . . a bump. . . .

Seth smiled and ran for the wheelhouse of the *Belle*. This would be a fine opportunity to prove to Marc that he was a good river man, too.

Seth edged slowly toward *The Royal,* maneuvering the *Belle* closer and closer until there were only inches between the boats. Then he turned the wheel and braced himself for the solid bump he knew was coming.

The shock reverberated through *The Royal,* knocking all on board from their feet. Marc had been knocked to his knees, and Catalina had been torn from Travis's grasp and thrown to the deck. But Travis had been knocked backward with such force that he had broken through the rail and had tumbled into the rapidly flowing river. Due to the speed the boats were making and the swift current flowing away from their sterns, Travis was immediately lost from sight.

Marc leapt to his feet and ran to Cat, who was staring in shock at the broken rail.

He reached down and pulled her up, and when her eyes lifted to his, he heard his name softly spoken. Then she was in his arms and he was crushing her to him, his mouth taking hers in a kiss that melted their souls.

He could hardly stand to release her, but there were a lot of things he had to say. He wanted to tell her the reasons for what he had done. Though doing so might end their chance of future happiness, he could no longer live with the guilt.

"Oh, Marc." Catalina laughed and cried in this breathless moment. "I thought I would never see you again!"

"Don't ever believe that, Cat. I will never let you go. I happen to be very much in love with you."

Catalina's laugh was almost triumphant. "Those are words I never expected to hear from you."

"Cat," he said seriously, "there are a lot of things you must hear—and you must hear them from me."

"Nothing can be as important as what you have just said. It's enough to make everything else—"

"No, we'll talk, but first, there's something on the *Belle* you should see. It will be a happy surprise and might make everything else a little easier."

"What?"

"Come on, let's slow this boat down and go over to the *Belle*." He drew her into his arms to kiss her again, hunger for her building inside him again. He hoped she would be able to forgive him and to forget that he had nearly destroyed her life.

Catalina suddenly tightened her arms about his neck

and pressed her body to his as if she wanted to mold them into one. Her lips were warm and searching as she returned his kiss with a passion he'd remembered and often longed for.

Seth slowed the *Belle* to match the speed of *The Royal,* and soon the bows of the two boats neared the shore and, as it is with steamboats, touched the land without going aground.

The captain of *The Royal,* knowing it was futile to search for Travis in the powerful Mississippi, listened to Marc's explanation. Then he decided to just put the pair ashore and keep as much distance between himself and Simon Gere as was possible.

Taking Catalina by the hand, Marc started toward the *Belle.*

"Marc, what is so exciting?" Catalina laughed as he dragged her along behind him.

"I've no intention of telling you"—he chuckled—"because you might not believe me, and besides I want to see your eyes when you come face to face with my surprise."

Ignoring her questions, he led Catalina up the gangplank of the *Belle,* and then she looked questioningly at him. She had prepared herself for almost anything except the sudden appearance of a grinning Seth.

At first she could not believe her eyes. Her jaw dropped in open-mouthed shock. She had been told that he had died. Then joy suddenly filled her as Seth laughed and stretched out his arms to her. With a cry, she ran to him and he caught her to him in a fierce hug. They were both laughing and crying at the same time.

"Seth! Seth! My God, I thought you were dead. Oh, Seth my dear."

"Cat, the Carringtons are hard to kill, but my story is a long and complicated one. I think we'd better get the *Belle* back to Natchez, then pick up Charles and get home before Aunt Charlotte thinks we're all lost."

"You must tell me what happened that night when you didn't come home."

"I will, I will." Seth laughed. "You have not changed one bit. You're still the bossy sister."

Catalina gazed up at Seth, suddenly aware of the changes in him.

"But I've a feeling you're not about to be bossed anymore," she said thoughtfully.

"Well, maybe a little now and then. I've grown so used to it I think I'd miss it." He looked quickly at Marc, then back to Cat. "I think you and Marc have a lot to discuss. I'm going to get the *Belle* turned around. Later tonight we can talk."

Catalina nodded, and when Seth had headed toward the wheelhouse, she went to Marc, put her arms around him, and stood on tiptoe to kiss him. When his response wasn't what she expected, she looked up questioningly.

"I think it's time we went to my . . . your cabin and talked," Marc said seriously.

Catalina didn't realize that his seeming coldness was due to fear that he could not control himself in her presence. He wanted her in his arms so badly, his need for her was like pain, but the truth had to be spoken first.

"I love you, Marc," Catalina said softly, hoping her words would ease the barrier between them.

She watched his green eyes warm. "And I love you, Cat," he replied. "I love you so much that it scares me."

"Scares you? To love me?"

"No, to think of losing you."

"After all we've faced, how can you think we would

lose each other?"

"Cat, don't make this any harder than it is. Come below with me . . . where we can talk."

"On one condition," Catalina said firmly. She smiled at his very serious, inquisitive look. "I'll listen to whatever you have to say, but you have to promise that afterward you'll listen to me."

"All right. I promise."

Catalina walked ahead of Marc to the cabin in which they had met . . . and had first made love. Once there, she turned to Marc. It was the first time, in her relief at having found him again, that she had really looked at him. Now, in this poignant silence, she realized how truly troubled he was.

"What is it?" she asked.

Damn, he thought, has she ever looked more beautiful, more desirable than she does now? Why can't I just tell her I love her and let everything else go? He knew the answer, and slowly he began to tell Catalina everything. She made no effort to stop him as he explained his anger and grief, all his misunderstandings from the moment of his father's death. When he had finished he waited for condemnation, for a look in her eyes that would end everything.

All the pieces were now in place in Catalina's mind. In fact, she knew answers even Marc didn't know.

"If you have finished," she said quietly, "it's my turn."

He was momentarily surprised by her lack of emotion. But his surprise grew by leaps and bounds as she began to talk.

Catalina described Simon Gere's visit to her and the terrible things he had said. "But what he had made clear, Marc, was that you were not guilty. You, me, and all the others in his plan were only actors playing parts he had written."

"I intended to hurt you in a way you can't even imagine," Marc declared.

Then Catalina went to him. She put her arms about him and smiled up into his eyes.

"Shall I tell you about intentions, Marc?" she asked softly. "Did you ever wonder why I didn't go, why I chose to be your mistress? Did you think the *Belle* was what held me? No, my love, I wanted much more than that. I wanted you."

"Cat—"

"No, you will listen. You promised."

"Go on."

"I love you, Marc. I love you so deeply that it's hard to believe I existed before I knew you. I wanted to capture your heart. I came to you on your terms because I thought I could change them to mine. I wanted you . . . and I still do. I want only to hear you say I love you. Don't you see, Marc, you are all I ever wanted? Money, the *Belle,* anything I had I would have sacrificed if you had said you loved me."

Marc gazed at her for a moment in silence. He found his good fortune hard to believe, but the love in her eyes and the feel of her in his arms slowly made him realize the truth of her words. He smiled, and his arms tightened about her.

"And just when did you decide our future?"

"Oh," she replied mischievously, "about the first time you kissed me. I have you trapped, my dear," she added softly, "so why don't you surrender and ask me to marry you? Or must I do the proposing?"

"Don't worry, Cat"—he laughed—"I know when I don't stand a chance. A good gambler never draws to an inside straight—especially when the lady he's looking for is the queen of hearts. Catalina Carrington . . . will you be my wife?"

"It's about time," she whispered as she drew his head

down to hers and their lips met in a kiss of promise.

He bent to lift her in his arms and carry her to the bed upon which they had begun their passionate journey. Then, slowly and gently, he undressed her, savoring each moment, each touch. Meanwhile, her restless hands could not resist reaching for him to remove the last barrier that stood between them.

For a while they lay close to each other, tasting the brilliant newness of their declared love. Marc caressed the silk of her hair, catching it in his hands and burying his face in it to inhale the sweet scent of it. He savored the heated giving of her parted lips.

With agonizing slowness he denied himself the pleasure of possessing her quickly and fiercely. He had dreamed of this moment too long, fantasized about having her in his arms too often to let the wonder of these moments slip away.

They laughed softly together, and whispered words of passion as if the world of love had just been opened to them.

He traced the lines of her slim body with sensitive fingertips, heard her whisper his name, felt her warm breath against his throat. His lips worked magic as they followed the tingling trail of his fingers.

They explored, tasted, and knew joy in each other as they melded to find, at last, the total possession only a boundless love can give.

Seth stood on the deck of the *Belle* and felt an overwhelming satisfaction. He knew, when they reached Natchez, their problems would be over. They would retrieve Charles and head back to New Orleans.

He thought of his father, and again sensed a new satisfaction. Maybe now he was the man his father had wanted him to be.

He sighed and chuckled softly. He was going home . . . home.

Thoughts of home brought him suddenly to thoughts of Jake. He wondered if Aunt Charlotte had been in any way successful in rubbing off some of her rough edges.

He promised himself he would spend a great deal of time with her. It hadn't been fair to drop her off like that.

He would explain, and perhaps she would understand. He wanted Cat to meet Jake and to show her the fun a young girl could have.

The longer he thought about the future, the more impatient he became. He knew Cat and Marc were rebuilding the broken bridges between them, and in a few days—a few days—they would be home.

Chapter 39

The morning sky was bright blue and was filled with white clouds that drifted lazily by on the languid breeze. A carriage stood on the dock and its driver was aware of the fascinated glances men cast at the woman who stood nearby.

She was startlingly attractive. Her red-gold hair, blown by the breeze, caught the glow of the sun. And her deep violet gown enhanced her almost fragile beauty.

Jake gazed up the river, as she had every morning for the past two weeks. Annoyance, mixed with another emotion that resembled fear, moved across her face.

"Oh, Seth," she muttered angrily, "why don't you come back?"

The driver climbed down from his seat and walked to her side.

"Miss Barde, Miss Charlotte will be impatient if we're gone any longer."

"I know, George." Jake smiled as she turned to face the driver. "I was just so sure he'd be back today."

George could not help but return her smile. Of course, he thought, not many in New Orleans can resist the charm of Jacqueline Barde. He did not understand why a young man like Seth Carrington stayed away so long when a lady like Jacqueline was waiting so impatiently for him.

"Miss Jacqueline, if the *Belle* does get back today, someone will bring us word right away."

Jake sighed. "All right, George. I suppose we had best get back." She stood for a long moment, then headed toward the carriage. The driver returned to his seat and urged the horses into motion.

As the carriage turned away from the docks and started toward the McNeil home, neither Jacqueline nor George were aware that the boat they sought had just rounded a curve in the river and had come into view.

Inside the carriage, Jake sat in silence. She knew she would come back to the docks the next morning—and every morning until Seth returned. She thought of his parents, who had arrived the morning before. Charlotte had tried to explain all that had happened since they had been gone, but her explanation had only made them more worried.

Charlotte had tried to make clear to Joseph Carrington the changes in Seth. Although he half believed them, he still had some doubts. Yet, he had had to admire what Seth had tried to do for Jake. Jake smiled to herself. After she had gotten over their initial surprise at her presence, Jake had gotten on very well with the Carringtons. In fact, she had grown quite fond of them. Even her grandfather was friendly with them.

Jake had everything she had ever wished for, but it was the look in Seth's eyes that she wanted—no, had—to see.

When the carriage stopped before the house, George helped her alight. Then she walked up to the front door and knocked.

The butler let her in, smiling warmly. It was obvious that Jake had found a place in the affections of everyone in the household.

"Good morning, Miss Jacqueline. I see the boat has not returned yet."

"No, I'm afraid not. Is Miss Charlotte in the drawing room?"

"Yes, miss. She's just having her last cup of morning tea. Mr. and Mrs. Carrington are with her. I guess everyone is impatient for the *Belle* to return."

Jake entered the drawing room. As she was removing her gloves, Joseph Carrington rose.

"You've been down to the docks again, Jake?" Charlotte asked.

"Yes, Aunt Charlotte, but there's no sign of the *Belle*."

"Sit down and have a cup of tea, dear. It doesn't do any good to go down there every day."

"I know," Jake said resignedly. "It's just that they've been gone for so long."

"Don't worry so. Charles will make sure that Seth comes to no harm." Charlotte's eyes glowed with a teasing humor. "And I'm sure Seth will bring Catalina back safely."

Jake's cheeks flushed slightly, but she did not deny that worry haunted her. After all, she thought, there are a lot of pretty girls between New Orleans and Memphis.

"This Marc Garrison," Jessie Carrington said quietly, "what do you know of him?"

"Very little, Jess," Charlotte answered honestly. "Charles and Seth were in such a hurry to catch up with Catalina that he had very little time to elaborate. I'm sure Charles and Seth will provide all the answers we need when they get back."

"I'm worried about my daughter. From all you tell me, Charlotte, both of these men are of doubtful character."

Charlotte replied quietly, "Cat has enough character

for both of them. She will disgrace you in no way." Charlotte spoke firmly, but her thoughts were also on Cat. She had prayed every night that Seth and Charles would find Cat safe, and that they would bring her back soon.

The *Belle* pulled into the dock, and the gangplank was lowered. Almost immediately Catalina, Seth, Marc, and Charles descended to stand in an impatient group while arrangements were made for a carriage.

Marc and Catalina were caught up in each other, Charles was preparing himself for Charlotte's questioning, and Seth was a model of silent self-control.

He feared Jake might have had a change of heart, and returned to her grandfather. His eyes scanned the length of the dock, but he could see no sign of Ben's fishing boat. If it was gone, Jake might very well be on it. Then she might just be gone out of his life. He was saddened by this thought.

He sat back in the carriage and counted the moments until it finally came to a stop before the house.

Inside Jake had just finished her tea and had set her cup aside.

"I believe I shall change and go for a ride. That will help me to keep my patience."

When Charlotte nodded her agreement, Jake rose and walked to the door. Then she paused for a moment, upon hearing voices, laughter, and a great deal of activity in the hall.

Jake was less than three feet from the door when it was thrown open. Gasps of shock and surprise came from everyone in the room as the four they had worried about for so long stood before them.

Seth, unprepared for the changes in Jake, did not recognize her. His attention went to his parents and to his aunt Charlotte.

Thinking Jake a visitor, he muttered a quick "excuse me miss," as he moved past her to greet his mother, whom he kissed fondly, before enveloping Charlotte in a huge hug.

Soon the room was full of laughter and tears as Catalina and Charles were also welcomed.

Marc stood just within the door, and he was the only one who noticed the pretty young girl with tears on her cheeks run from the room and up the steps.

When the confusion had died down, Seth asked, "Where's Jake? I didn't see her grandfather's boat at the dock when we arrived."

"Jake?" Charlotte suddenly remembered. She looked past Seth to scan the room. "Why, she was here just a minute ago. In fact she had just come back from the docks. She has been going every morning to see if the *Belle* has arrived. She must have just missed you."

"Are you by any chance talking about that lovely little creature who just ran past me in tears?" Marc queried.

Seth's mouth dropped open as he suddenly realized that beautiful girl he had passed so abruptly had been Jake. He was struck by the thought that she must have felt he had pushed her aside, as if she were unimportant. What a crude and ugly thing he had done.

"Oh, God," he groaned. "I didn't recognize her."

"I doubt that you could have," Charlotte said, amusement in her voice. "But if you'd care to know, her room is the third one on the left."

Seth laughed, and was halfway out the door before Charlotte finished speaking.

"Really, Charlotte!" Jessie said, her shock evident. "It's unseeming for Seth to go to a young lady's bedroom. It's . . . it's somewhat scandalous."

"Oh, fudge, Jess." Charlotte chuckled happily. "I have a feeling he'll be quite welcome there."

"Charlotte!"

"Don't be so prudish," Charlotte responded briskly. "The boy isn't going to attack her, and they need to talk. I have a feeling this confrontation is going to be as much of a shock to Seth as it is to Jake. Yes, yes." Charlotte looked like a designing matchmaker. "I have a feeling this little confrontation just might prove to be very interesting. Now"—Charlotte's eagle eyes rested on Marc's amused face—"young man, suppose you come over here and tell me just what deviltry you've been up to. I have a feeling this is going to be another interesting little story."

Marc grinned, certain now that his first estimation of Charlotte had been accurate and that he was going to become extremely fond of this lady.

He walked to Catalina's side and put an arm about her waist. Charlotte did not miss the look in Catalina's eyes when she looked up at him, nor did she fail to note Marc's gaze of near adoration. The two were completely and thoroughly in love, and this, despite what others might think, satisfied Charlotte very much.

Charles and Marc recounted what had happened to them from the moment they had left New Orleans.

Of course, Charlotte had millions of questions, and all three did their best to explain the shadowy past that had reached out to touch them. "You mean you now believe your father's death was not suicide, but a well-planned murder?"

"When Simon held Cat in his home, he was so sure of himself that he boasted about it," Marc replied. "I'm sure we can find some proof. I know it might seem inconsequential to everyone else, but Lorelei and I need to do that so people will know our father did not

481

die in disgrace." Marc spoke quietly, but he was determined.

"I can understand that." Charlotte smiled. "You see, at one time I knew your father quite well, and I never really believed he had killed himself. He had too much courage and pride to do that."

"You knew my father! How?"

"I will tell you that later." She placed a hand on Marc's arm. "Maybe," she added softly, "just you and Cat." Marc nodded. Another secret from the past would soon be unfolded.

Charlotte turned to Charles, who smiled and immediately answered the question he knew she was about to ask.

"In the morning I'm going to instigate a full investigation into Simon Gere's financial activities and his connection to Marc's father," he declared firmly.

"As you told us, Joseph, Simon Gere is a scoundrel. I can see why you never mentioned doing business with him."

"Charlotte, to tell the truth, I put Simon out of my life so long ago that I had completely forgotten him."

"Do you think you will find evidence of what he has done at this late date, Charles?" Charlotte questioned.

"I'm sure I will."

"We'll help in every way we can," Marc promised, "by going over my father's affairs again and again until we find a trace of the time Father and Simon crossed paths."

"In the meantime"—Charlotte smiled—"I do believe we had best begin to plan a wedding, unless we want this young gallant to abduct our Cat again. From the way he looks at her, the thought is not far from his mind."

Marc laughed, and his green eyes sparkled mischievously. "That thought has crossed my mind once or twice in the last few hours," he admitted. "I hope nobody is planning on a long engagement."

"I'm not," Catalina offered, as she joined her laughter to Marc's. "I've had to chase this man up the entire length of the Mississippi, and I wouldn't want to have to do it again."

"Who's running?" Marc replied quickly. "In fact, I'm waiting not too patiently. I don't intend to let you slip through my fingers, love." Suddenly he became serious. "I almost let that happen once, and I don't think I could handle that twice."

Their love was evident to everyone, but Charles was the only person aware of the depth of Charlotte's emotions. As she watched Marc and Catalina, they flitted across her face quick as the whisper of memories—happiness, loneliness, and a touch of sorrow. But, with her usual control, Charlotte overcame them, and her look became warmed by sincere pleasure.

"We will have a grand time with your wedding, Cat," she said enthusiastically, "what with a new trousseau to buy and a gown and all the invitations."

"Aunt Charlotte," Catalina interrupted, "Marc and I have decided on a relatively small wedding with just family and a very few friends. It would take too long to plan something so large. I don't want to hurt you, but a large affair isn't as important to us as being together as soon as we can. Please try to understand."

"My dear girl," Charlotte said gently, "of course I understand. It will be exactly as you want it. I want you always to be as happy as you are now, and I'm sure this handsome young devil has the same thought. So we will plan a very small, and"—she smiled at Marc—"a very quick wedding."

His eyes sparkled as he bent to kiss Charlotte's cheek. "Aunt Charlotte," he declared, "I have a feeling you and I are going to get along very, very well. We have a lot in common."

Charlotte laughed. She was sure of two things now. Marc and Catalina were going to be happy . . . and she would have another wedding to plan; for she was sure that at this very minute Seth was getting one of the biggest surprises in his life.

Chapter 40

Jake had run to the sanctuary of her room, unable to control her tears. Seth had thought so little of her that he hadn't even remembered her presence. He had pushed past her as if she were invisible, with no sign of recognition. Obviously Jake was just something in his past, easily forgotten.

She wanted to die. She wanted to curl up in a ball and cry away her disappointment. She tried to ease her hurt with logic. Seth owed her nothing, had promised her nothing of himself. It didn't work. She had dreamed about Seth for weeks.

Then the old Jake began to surface, and anger grew in her. He owed her nothing, but she owed him nothing either.

Seth took the steps two and three at a time. When he stopped before Jake's door, he realized he was shaking. He raised his hand and knocked.

"Go away!" was the muffled reply. He could hear the tears being choked under control.

"Jake, open the door. I'm sorry I was so rude. I just didn't recognize you. You must admit you do look a lot different from the last time I saw you. Come on, let me in. I have to talk to you."

Jake stood in the center of the room, trying to deny that she was suddenly afraid to face Seth. What if he was disappointed in her?

Jake had never been lacking in courage. This uncertainty irritated her. What should she care whether he liked her this way or not? Her belligerence was a self-protective cloak that she held about her as she walked across the room, unlocked the door, and jerked it open.

Her green eyes were two defiant emeralds, and her chin was tipped up in stubborn pride, as she and Seth looked at each other for long quiet moments.

He was stunned. He had expected a change in her, but the beauty that stood before him exceeded his imaginings.

"I can't believe how you've changed, Jake. It's almost . . . like a miracle."

"Then you're not disappointed?" she said.

"Disappointed?"

"I mean"—she hesitated—"you're . . . pleased."

"Are you pleased? Are you happy here?"

"Oh yes, Seth, I am. Your aunt is truly a kind lady. She's made everything so wonderful, not only for me but for Grandpa as well. I never realized living could be so much fun."

"Then it was all worth the struggle, Jake. You've certainly done well."

"I've tried hard to learn so many things. Sometimes my mind gets all jumbled up. Then I think about you and . . ." Her enthusiasm suddenly seemed blocked, and Jake flushed. Seth, too, suddenly seemed unable to find words.

They stood gazing at each other until the humor of the situation rescued them. Jake caught her lower lip between her teeth to keep back the soft giggle that teased her throat. Caught in the same dilemma, Seth felt if he laughed Jake might become offended.

But despite their efforts both lost control, and began

to laugh. It was good medicine and relieved the tension between them.

"Come downstairs, Jake," Seth said gently. "I'd love to introduce you to my sister and her future husband, Marc Garrison. I'm sure you and Catalina will become friends."

"All right," Jake answered, her confidence restored.

As they walked down the hallway, Seth questioned Jake regarding her grandfather's whereabouts.

"I didn't see the boat anywhere."

"Grandpa has sold it."

"Sold it? Whatever for?"

"Your Aunt Charlotte convinced him that she wanted to make an investment, so she and Grandpa are buying a new boat."

Seth chuckled. "Leave it to Aunt Charlotte to do such a thing. She'll most likely expect a profit, too."

"I wouldn't be surprised."

"Jake . . . ah . . . it's going to be awfully hard to call you by a boy's name." He smiled. "I'd rather call you Jacqueline. You're much too pretty and too much a lady to be called Jake anymore."

Jake paused and looked up into Seth's eyes. Suddenly they were both caught up in something vital that neither could name.

"I suppose you should," Jake said softly.

"Yes," he murmured. Again, as they stood close, something swift and uncertain wrapped them in its embrace.

"We should hurry," Seth said, but suddenly that was the last thing he wanted to do. In fact, he was startled by his thoughts, and he knew they would shock Jake if he gathered enough courage to voice them.

"I'm just a little nervous," she proclaimed.

"Nervous?"

"I'm anxious about meeting your sister."

"Cat?" Seth laughed. "Don't be nervous about meeting her. She's so happy right now, she loves everyone. She'll greet you like a sister. Watch and see."

"Does she love Marc Garrison that much?"

"She certainly does. Come. Look in their eyes and see for yourself." Seth took Jake's elbow as they descended the stairs.

The others were talking animatedly when Jake and Seth entered the room, but the gentlemen rose as they approached. Then Seth introduced Jake to Catalina and Marc.

Before long Catalina and Jake were discussing Cat's wedding, and Jake was as caught up in the planning as everyone else was. She was profoundly affected when Catalina asked her to take part in the ceremony.

"Since I have no sisters, and you and Seth are such good friends, would you consider being my maid of honor? I know it's a great deal to ask, since we've only met, but I—"

"Oh please, don't say that. It's so thoughtful of you to ask me. I've never participated in a wedding."

Seeing her excitement, Seth realized how little pleasure Jake had had in her life, and he decided to fill her days with it.

In fact Seth was beginning to feel quite noble about the whole affair. Hadn't he rescued Jake from a terrible fate? Hadn't he been the one to open up her life? Why, if it hadn't been for him, she would still be scrubbing the deck of her grandfather's boat, and dressing like a ragged boy. Seth's self-esteem expanded like an air-filled balloon as he decided to make the weeks before Catalina's wedding exciting for Jake.

As Charlotte watched Seth and Jake, her eyes sparkled with amusement. Maybe it was time for Jake to let Seth know just what he had helped to create. She was certain she was going to enjoy the next few weeks, for far more reasons than Catalina's and Marc's wedding.

The next morning, when Seth came down for breakfast, he found only Charlotte at the table.

"Where's everyone?" he questioned.

"Cat and Marc have gone, as Marc says, 'to buy the most beautiful ring New Orleans can offer.'"

"And where's Jake—I mean Jacqueline?"

"Oh, Jacqueline's gone riding."

"Riding?"

"In the park, of course."

"Alone!"

"Good heavens, Seth, she's not alone."

"She's not? Who is she with? I didn't know she had any women friends here."

"She doesn't. She's riding with young William Drake."

"William Drake," Seth replied blankly.

"Why, Seth, Jacqueline has a great many admirers. The child has hardly been unescorted, almost from the time she arrived. I guess she's just making up for lost time." Charlotte retained her innocent look with some effort. She knew that Seth had received only his first jolt.

A flurry of shopping and parties followed, and it seemed to Seth that he saw Jake only when she was coming from or going to another engagement. That wasn't bad enough, but she seemed to be prettier and more exciting each time he saw her. He wanted to enjoy her beauty. He felt he deserved that pleasure. His over-inflated ego began to suffer, and it soon dissolved into disbelieving anger and a liberal dose of self-pity.

There was to be a grand ball two nights before the wedding, and Seth was amazed to find that he did not even consider asking one of the young women he knew. He was in a less than jovial mood when he appeared at Catalina's door as she was preparing to dine with Marc.

She was in the midst of getting ready when Seth knocked, but she invited him in.

"Seth, what brings you here?" Catalina said as she went to the mirror to check her appearance. "And you do look glum. What's the matter?"

"Nothing. Ah . . . did you see Jake today?"

"Yes. She went visiting with David McNight. He's a charming young man. You should be so proud of what you've done for Jacqueline. I know I am."

"I guess she's really enjoying herself. I haven't been able to pin her down and talk since we came home."

"Well, you do want her to enjoy herself."

"Of course."

"Then why are you upset?"

"I would think she'd show some sign of gratitude!" he declared defensively. "She can't spare a minute for me, but she has time for every other man in New Orleans!"

"Why, Seth," Catalina said softly, and rose to pick up her cloak and gloves. "You sound jealous."

"Don't be ridiculous, Cat," he scoffed. "I'm not jealous. It's just that . . . well . . . I feel she's a little ungrateful."

Catalina went to her brother and patted his cheek as she smiled up into his eyes. "She's a sweet charming woman—very much a woman. Maybe you should give that a thought." Before he could reply, Catalina turned and left the room.

Seth slowly sat down on the edge of Catalina's bed and did as Catalina had suggested. He gave Jacqueline Barde a great deal of thought.

*   *   *

It was well after midnight when the carriage rolled to a halt before Charlotte's home. David McNight stepped down and helped Jacqueline alight. Then they walked to the door.

"David, I do want to thank you for a very lovely evening."

"I most certainly enjoyed it, Jacqueline, and I'd like to see you again. There is a party at the Grayfields' tomorrow evening. I would be most pleased if you would accompany me."

"Oh, David, I'm afraid I must decline. I have a family commitment, then the wedding party and the wedding."

"In that case, may I call on you next week?"

"Of course."

He lifted her hand and kissed it; then Jacqueline went inside. She closed the door softly and leaned against it. The house was almost dark except for a candle or two. They emitted a soft glow, which lit her way to the stairs.

She sighed deeply and stood immobile, thinking of how much she had come to love this house, to love Charlotte, and to love . . . She could not allow that thought, it hurt too much.

She slowly crossed the hall and put her foot on the first step. "Jake." Her name was spoken so softly she thought she had imagined it. When she started up the stairs again, it was repeated a little more firmly. "Jake, I've got to talk to you."

She spun around to see Seth standing at the entrance to the library.

"Seth?"

"Come into the library . . . please," he said softly.

She was astounded by his use of her old name, and by his quiet and serious attitude.

"Of course," she replied. She walked to him, and he stepped aside to let her enter. When she heard the door click shut, she turned to face him.

In the pale candle glow, Seth was transfixed for a moment by the ethereal beauty of this girl who had suddenly turned into a graceful and delicate woman.

"Seth, what is it? Is something wrong? Nothing has happened to Aunt Charlotte, has it?" Jake was suddenly frightened.

"No . . . no, nothing's wrong. I just want to talk to you."

"All right." She smiled. "What can be important enough to keep you up so late? You could have talked to me at breakfast."

"Not very well. You're always scooting off with some fellow or the other. Don't you ever stay home once in a while? Don't you have any time for me?"

"Seth!" she was shocked. She took a step toward him. "I . . . I thought this was what you wanted. I never meant to make you angry."

Seth regretted what he had said and the way he had said it, but he had reached the end of his endurance. He went to Jacqueline and gripped her shoulders, gave her a rough little shake and glared at her.

"I'll tell you why, damn your beautiful soul, because I'm in love with you and I can't stand the thought of your being with any other man. Because I don't want you flitting from one conquest to another. Because you're driving me crazy and I don't know what to do about it."

He stopped talking, and the silence was so profound that the ticking of the clock on the mantel seemed thunderous.

"Now you know. I guess I've wanted to tell you that, and how beautiful you are since I came home. I just haven't been able to catch up with you." He released her slowly, alarmed by her silence. He knew he had shaken and frightened her because her wide eyes were fixed on him. "I'm not going to say I'm sorry, so you might just as well tell me how you feel. Then we can fight it out right here. I'm not going to let you go easily. You're in for one hell of a fight. What do you have to say, Jake?"

Jacqueline's eyes filled with tears and Seth only had time for a startled exclamation before he found his arms filled with a soft, sweet-scented woman.

"I always said, bilge rat, that you did too much talking. Why don't you just show me instead of yellin' so loud?"

"Jake?"

"There you go again, bilge rat. Maybe another dunk in the river could loosen your tongue."

Seth laughed softly, then swept her up into his arms and claimed her mouth in a deep and most satisfying kiss. She was breathless when he finally set her down.

"I don't want another dunking," he said softly, "but I do need a new captain for my boat. What do you say, Jake Barde, do you want the job? Of course it would mean changing your name. What do you say to Jake Carrington?"

"I'd say wonderful . . . only I think I'd better start to convince you I'm as much a Jacqueline as a Jake."

"I love them both." He grinned. "But if you want to show me the difference, suppose you start now," he whispered.

She nodded and her eyes closed as his lips met hers, offering a promise of love.

"Umm," Seth murmured. "There's definitely a difference."

He continued to kiss her until she clung dizzily to him, struggling to control an emotion that was so new, it confused and startled her. Seth realized this. In fact, his own control was shaky.

He held her away from him and smiled down into her

warm green eyes. "I want you to marry me, Jake," he said softly, "and just as soon as possible."

"Aunt Charlotte will be surprised." She laughed.

"Somehow I doubt that." Seth grinned. "I wouldn't put it past the old girl to be making plans already. She's crafty, and very wise."

"Seth?"

"What?"

"I don't want you to believe I don't want to marry you; I do, with all my heart. But I don't think it would be fair to Cat to have a hasty wedding. Her ceremony is being planned, and I wouldn't want to spoil it." Her eyes pleaded for him to understand.

"You've become quite a lady," he said softly.

"Then you do understand."

"Of course I do."

"We can tell Aunt Charlotte now."

"We'll tell her tomorrow. Tonight," he murmured, "I'd like to discuss the difference between Jake and Jacqueline."

"I'll always be Jake, too," she replied. "But both of us love you very much."

"You know, I think I fell in love with you the minute I saw you on your grandfather's boat."

"And I was scared of what you made me feel. I had never felt such . . . wonderful things."

"Well, fate tossed me into your arms, and I, for one, am more than grateful. It was an experience I would never have wanted to miss . . . I love you, Jake."

"And I love you," she whispered. His arms tightened about her and their lips met in a warm sensual giving that filled both with the sense of oneness. In this stolen moment, the world was excluded, and they greeted the promise of the future with open arms.

Epilogue

The night was warm, but a breeze rustled in the trees along the river. The soft singing of the men who worked the *Belle* floated on the night air. It soothed the pair who lay together in the main cabin.

Sated, they had relaxed in each other's arms, their silence filled with contentment.

"Did I tell you that you made the most beautiful bride in existence?" Marc murmured against her hair.

"You're prejudiced." Catalina laughed softly.

"I'm not. I merely made the observation, and every person present agreed with me."

"Marc, you are impossible," Catalina teased, but she was pleased by her new husband's pleasure in her.

Again they were silent for a short time; then Marc chuckled.

"What's so funny?"

"Did you by any chance watch your brother's face at the wedding?"

"No. I was too busy watching you," she replied.

He kissed her leisurely and deeply.

"He's head over heels in love with Jacqueline, and I wouldn't be surprised to see another wedding in the making by the time we get back."

"I couldn't be happier about that. Jacqueline is lovely, and she and I have become good friends. She did make an exceptionally lovely bridesmaid. Didn't you notice?"

"No." Marc laughed. "With you there, it's hard enough for me to control my baser needs, much less notice any other woman. Besides, not one is lovelier than you."

Catalina turned in his arms to mold her body more tightly to his, then drew his head down for a kiss that disintegrated whatever control he had.

He caught her in his arms and smiled into her warm eyes. "I love you, my dear wife. And this honeymoon is going to last a lifetime."

"Yes . . . a lifetime," she breathed softly, as their passion again began to blossom into the flame of love that would warm them throughout their lives.